Praise for Maggi

'Alderson … controls her material cleverly. She has a nifty ability to leave each vignette or chapter with a cliffhanger, and then keep you waiting as she proceeds to another character's personal drama'
Sydney Morning Herald

'Brimming with wit and wisdom. A delightful read' *Courier-Mail*

'Alderson's books have heart' *Melbourne Weekly*

'An engrossing story that will make you laugh and cry'
Australian Women's Weekly

'Great fun. If you don't finish it ready to revamp your house and your wardrobe then there's something wrong with you!'
Sunday Mail (Brisbane)

'A funny, lighthearted read' *Glamour*

'A supreme commentator on the vagaries of fashion' *Sunday Age*

'A wicked read – funny, sexy and stylish' *Best* magazine

'A witty modern romance … much more than a *Bridget Jones's Diary*' *Vogue*

'a deft and flawless authorial voice … Alderson has a sly sense of humour when she pricks the consciences of her characters, and there are some lovely laugh-out-loud moments'
Newtown Review of Books

'It is Alderson's real-life drama style that is so enjoyable – in so many cases you see a little bit of yourself in her characters'
Chronicle

'Reading a Maggie Alderson book, I swear, is like slipping into a bubble bath after a long day of bleurgh' Hannah Louey, Goodreads

'wonderfully complex and interwoven' Daisy, Goodreads

'An enjoyable, smart, insightful yet easy read. Love Maggie!'
Josanne, Goodreads

Maggie Alderson

The Scent of You

A NOVEL IN PERFUMES

HarperCollins*Publishers*

HarperCollins*Publishers*

First published in Australia in 2017
This edition published in 2019
by HarperCollins*Publishers* Australia Pty Limited
ABN 36 009 913 517
harpercollins.com.au

HarperCollins*Publishers*
Unit D1, 63 Apollo Drive, Rosedale, Auckland 0632, New Zealand
Level 13, 201 Elizabeth Street, Sydney NSW 2000, Australia
A 53, Sector 57, Noida, UP, India
1 London Bridge Street, London, SE1 9GF, United Kingdom
Bay Adelaide Centre, East Tower, 22 Adelaide Street West, 41st floor, Toronto,
Ontario M5H 4E3, Canada
195 Broadway, New York NY 10007, USA

National Library of Australia Cataloguing-in-Publication data:

Alderson, Maggie, author.
The scent of you / Maggie Alderson.
978 1 4607 5798 7 (pbk.)
978 1 4607 0583 4 (ebook)
Families – fiction.
Women – fiction.

Cover design by Lisa White, HarperCollins Design Studio
Perfume bottle by shutterstock.com
Author photograph by Adrian Peacock
Typeset in Sabon LT Std by Kirby Jones

For Mark Connolly
(Musc Ravageur by Frédéric Malle)
and
Josephine Fairley
(Mitsouko by Guerlain)

I want to see you

Know your voice

Recognise you when you
first come 'round the corner.

Sense your scent when I come
into a room you've just left.

Know the lift of your heel,
the glide of your foot.

Become familiar with the way
you purse your lips
then let them part,
just the slightest bit
when I lean in to your space
and kiss you.

I want to know the joy
of how you whisper
'more'

Rumi (1207–1273)

FragrantCloud.net

I think in perfume

I experience the world through smell – I always have. Smell isn't a subsidiary sense to me, it's always been up front, equal with seeing, hearing, feeling and tasting.

While I can't remember a time when I wasn't sniffing things – everything! – I discovered the miracle of perfume as a very young child through the fragrant delights on my mum's dressing table. It was the pretty bottles which attracted me initially, but once I got a whiff of what was inside, my world changed forever.

My mother is the model Daphne Masterson, known for the iconic pictures taken of her by Cecil Beaton, Norman Parkinson and others for *Vogue* in the 1950s (although she still hasn't retired at the age of eighty-five!), and she had a pretty amazing collection of perfumes, many of them given to her by the couturiers themselves, Christian Dior, Hubert Givenchy and Pierre Balmain, to name a few.

She was away a lot working when I was little, and as a lonely only child I'd go and take the caps off those tempting flacons and sniff them to find the ones that most reminded me of her. Sometimes I'd even take a bottle to bed with me for comfort.

So, without understanding what I was doing, I honed my appreciation of fragrance by comparing all the different perfumes she had and forming associations with each one.

Balmain's Jolie Madame was 'shopping', Fracas was 'parties', Calèche was 'Mummy going away', Diorissimo was 'Easter', Joy was 'Mummy going out for dinner', and so on.

I had an exercise book that I kept by my bed and every night I would write about what I'd smelled that day and found interesting. Not just perfumes – although I tried as many of those as possible – but also things like butter heating up in a frying pan, a new school jumper, my cat's head, the plastic feet of my Barbie dolls: how they all smelled and how they made me feel.

I still think of perfumes and smells in this way. It's the emotional associations which really interest me. There are lots of amazing perfume bloggers who write brilliantly about scent from historical, fashion, business, sociological, scientific, gastronomical, business and new-release perspectives. I love all that and will write about those elements too when I can, but my passionate interest is in that powerful emotional connection a smell can trigger.

When I list in my posts the particular scents that represent an occasion, an idea, a person or a group of people, it's not necessarily an exact ingredient match, or what a particular person would actually wear, but simply what feels right to me. I go for the gut inspiration, the first associations that spring into my head from my heart and my olfactory bulb.

Some of the perfumes I refer to you will know; others are obscure, produced by small niche brands; and there are some that are no longer made, but that I've been lucky enough to sample in various people's collections, including my mum's.

Sometimes I hope you'll agree with me, other times I'm sure you won't – so please tell me what you think and what your own scent associations are. I'd love to hear from you.

Thanks for looking – and keep on smelling.

Polly

PS As well as sniffing my mum's precious bottles, I loved squirting the perfume onto myself, so from a very young age I walked around in a rather overpowering haze of scent. My father started calling me Fragrant Cloud, after his favourite rose – hence the name of this blog.

COMMENTS

JayneAgain: I love this! I used to try all my mum's perfumes, too, when I was a little girl. She died last year and every time I want to feel close to her I spray on some of her Calèche. I really look forward to reading more of your posts.

FragrantCloud: Thanks Jayne – I'm so sorry you lost your mum. I'm so glad you liked my blog and thanks for signing up. Polly x

AgathaF: This is very interesting. I love perfumes too. I live in Germany.

FragrantCloud: Hi Agatha. Thanks for reading my blog. Let me know what's happening with the perfume scene in Germany. I'd love to know. Polly x

EastLondonNostrils: How about posting a pic of your mum's perfume collection? ELN

FragrantCloud: That's a great idea ELN, I will! Thanks, Polly x (and thanks for signing up to the blog too)

Thursday, 31 December

TWO YEARS LATER

When you've been happily married for twenty-four years, you don't expect to find yourself lying in bed alone just before midnight on New Year's Eve.

Polly didn't even know where her husband was. She hadn't seen him for over a week. It had been so strange having Christmas without him, and now this.

She pulled the duvet up over her head and then straight back down again. It was no good, she couldn't sleep through it.

Growing up, she'd celebrated every New Year at her grandparents' house in the Scottish Highlands with all the traditional celebrations, and she'd always loved it. Her body was biologically programmed to stay awake on 31 December.

She'd thought spending the whole day cleaning the house – one of her granny's New Year rituals – would have tired her out, but it seemed not. Even a couple of drams of her dad's favourite single malt hadn't done the trick; in fact, it seemed to have had the opposite effect, making her feel hyped up and ready for action rather than sleep.

She picked up her phone, looking for a distraction. But Facebook was full of people boasting that they were going to bed because they loathed the occasion, and Instagram was all drunken-party pictures.

Her daughter Clemmie beamed out of a photo with her boyfriend, taken in Cambridge, where she was studying Medicine and lived full-time. Polly's son Lucas, home from his first term at uni for the Christmas holidays, was out somewhere in London with friends, and had posted several snaps of pub tables covered in empty beer and shot glasses. He'd be a mess in the morning.

Polly checked the time. Five to twelve. She turned the radio on and got out of bed, heading over to the window with her whisky tumbler.

Opening the curtains, she peered out at the clear black night, the stars shining brightly. A splendid near-full moon hanging right in the middle of the view just made her solitude more painful.

How lovely it would be to look up at that glowing disc with strong arms around you, wondering what the year ahead would bring. For the two of you. You and your husband.

As the chimes of Big Ben rang out, she raised her glass.

'Happy New Year, David,' she said, 'wherever you are.'

She took a sip then raised the glass again.

'Happy Hogmanay, Daddy,' she followed up, picturing the beautiful strand of beach in Sunderland where they'd scattered his ashes three years before.

She swirled the Scotch in the glass and lifted it to her nose, closing her eyes as she breathed in the peaty aroma, feeling transported back to her grandparents' house. Pine trees, wood smoke, damp dead bracken and the metallic sweetness of frost in your nostrils. Her granny's heather perfume, the dusty warm wool smell of a kilt, the lanolin of itchy jumpers, wet dogs and furniture polish.

She took a sip then, just as she was raising the glass again to her toast her children, the land line rang. She ran to grab it, thinking it would be one of them wishing her a happy New Year, but it was her mother's voice she heard.

'When are you coming to lunch?' her mother snapped.

'Monday, Mummy,' said Polly, as brightly and calmly as she could, walking back to the bed, sinking down onto it and closing her eyes. 'In four days.'

'Are you sure?' said her mother, in a suspicious voice.

'That's what we arranged,' said Polly, 'but I can come sooner if you'd like me to—'

'Hmmph,' said her mother dismissively, then hung up without another word.

'Happy New Year, Mummy,' Polly whispered to the dial tone, then fell back onto the softness of the duvet, tears stinging her eyes. Mostly her mother was fine, but these odd moments of disconnectedness were becoming more frequent, and Polly found them very difficult to deal with. On top of everything else that was going on, it was just too much.

A moment later, she sat up and reached for her mobile to see if Clemmie or Lucas had messaged her. Nothing. Then, seeing the Instagram icon, she tapped it and there was Clemmie's smiling face, holding up a sign saying 'Happy Hogmanay, Mum!'

Polly kissed the screen. That was her Clemmie. Such a loving, thoughtful girl; she'd never forget her mum and how important this night was to her. Polly had told her kids she was going out with friends herself, so they wouldn't worry about her, but her darling daughter had still made the effort.

Then the phone pinged announcing a text. Lucas. Her boy.

A long string of emojis: a smiley face with heart eyes, hearts in every colour, fireworks, flowers, cocktail glasses, champagne bottles, high heels, lipsticks, shooting stars, a full moon and some random cute animals.

Polly laughed. It was so like him. No words, just pictures, but she knew exactly what he meant. She replied with six glasses of beer followed by a piano keyboard, a drum kit and several guitars, and ended with a line of pink hearts.

She started another emjoi message but deleted it. She knew she had to leave him to it – and since she'd told him and Clemmie that porky about going out herself, she had to keep up the act. There wouldn't be much time for texting if you were out having a good time.

And at least she would see him at some point tomorrow. Lucas still considered the family house his home and slept in his childhood bedroom, the walls plastered with Tottenham Hotspur regalia.

Clemmie's old bedroom was now a stark spare room, with all her things taken to her Cambridge flat or stashed in the attic, the pink pussy-cat wallpaper she'd chosen when she was nine painted over in tasteful grey. In weak moments Polly still found herself drifting in there, half-expecting the ranks of Sylvanian Families and teenagers' posters still to be in place. It never stopped being painful that they weren't.

She checked her texts again. Nothing from David. She wondered if she should send one to him, but had no idea what time it was in Nepal. If he was even still there. She'd established that that was where he'd gone first – something to do with Gurkhas, for a book he was writing – but he hadn't said how long for.

Then she remembered he'd changed his phone number too. And not given her the new one. It was all part of 'needing some space', he'd told her, before setting off on a six-month research sabbatical with no notice. Just an email. And by the time she got it, he'd already packed up and left.

She practically knew it off by heart, but kept a printout next to the bed so she could remind herself she wasn't imagining it whenever she needed to, which was quite often. This was one of those times.

Dear Polly,

I know this will be hard for you to understand, and I barely understand it myself, but I need some time completely alone.

The university has agreed to a six-month research sabbatical and I'll be travelling for all of that time. It will be easier for me if we have no contact while I'm away, so I won't be using my current phone or email address.

Please try to understand that this has nothing to do with you, or anything you've done. It's all about me. It's not that I need time away from you specifically, but that I need time completely alone. I have no choice.

When I come back I will be able to explain it to you better.

Please don't press me for more explanations before I go, as I have nothing more to tell you than this and I want to minimise friction between us. And please don't try to make inquiries after I've gone, or discuss it with anyone else. No one knows any more than I've told you here.

As far as everyone – especially the university – is concerned, I'm away on a research trip and it's vitally important that we keep the exact nature of my absence between us. It could create profound difficulties for us if you don't.

I'm more sorry than I can say to put you in this situation. You don't deserve it, but I have no choice, and it will be far worse for us both – and the children – if I don't do it.

D x

P.S. I've written separately to the kids, to say I'm going away for work and will be out of touch with you all for a while. That's all they need to know and it will be better if you don't discuss it with them in any more detail than that.

Polly sighed deeply. Thinking about him and all that weirdness made her feel so mixed up. She felt physically tired, but her mind was racing. Trying to get comfortable, she pulled the duvet up, then threw it off again, lay on her front and on her back, but nothing was any good. Then she had an idea, got out of bed and ran downstairs into the kitchen.

Digger – David's dog, who he'd wanted and chosen from the shelter and had now left her to look after – was asleep in his bed by the radiator. He woke up when he heard her come in and wagged his tail weakly in what seemed like a demonstration of canine good manners, like standing up when a lady came into the room.

'Come on,' said Polly, lifting him and burying her nose in his furry neck. 'You can come up and sleep on the bed tonight. If I've got to look after you, I might as well get something out of the deal.'

She carried him up the stairs, because David had trained him never to go further than paws on the first step. As they ascended, Digger turned his head from side to side, taking in the unfamiliar territory, then sniffed the covers as she put him down on the bed and climbed in on the other side. Digger immediately stood up, clearly nervous in the unknown – and forbidden – surroundings.

'It's OK, Diggie,' said Polly, stroking and patting him until he lay down on the bed and put his head on one paw, looking up at her with anxious eyes. 'It's just for one night and no one will know. I need a bit of company and you're all I've got tonight.'

The dog yawned and seemed to settle, and Polly let her eyes close – only to have them snap open as a terrible smell drifted over to her. One of Digger's industrial-strength farts.

'Oh no,' she said, pulling the covers up to her nose. 'I do wish you wouldn't do that, Digger.'

She used the duvet to fan the air, then turned to look at the rank of perfumes on her bedside table, all in their original boxes.

What would be good to drown out extreme canine flatulence? A heavyweight oud for strength? It would do the job but would be too heady to sleep with.

Perhaps a tuberose, she thought. Very pervasive, but not headachy. Her fingers lingered for a moment over her bottle of Fracas. She adored the classic punchy floral, but it was one of her mother's favourites, so not conducive to a good night's sleep either. Not after that phone call earlier.

Maybe something woody? The black tea, leather and tobacco in Atelier Cologne's Oolang Infini would be deep enough to drown out Digger's pungent expulsion, yet subtle enough to sleep on. But no, the guaiac wood in it reminded her too much of old-fashioned coal-tar soap, which was David's smell.

It had been one of the first things she'd noticed about him when they'd met at a cocktail party for postgraduate students. She'd just been starting her PhD at King's College London, where he was already a lecturer.

Since he'd gone away, even the faintest hint of a tarry smell sent her into a confused spin. She made a mental note to put the Oolang Infini back in her perfume cupboard.

Then the solution to fumigate Digger's unwelcome miasma became obvious. Chanel's Jersey had a strong note of sleep-friendly lavender, which would then melt deliciously into the musk, vanilla, rose, jasmine and other slinky elements, all very soothing.

She reached over for the classic chunky bottle and squirted the perfume generously into the air and onto each wrist, one then the other – none of that rubbing together, which she'd learned bruised the fragrance, the friction heating it too fast on the skin – then she closed her eyes and let the heavenly aroma settle around her. There was still a whiff of Eau de Digger in the air, but using her finely honed olfactory skills, Polly was able to tune it out in favour of the glorious perfume.

That was better.

She turned over to look at the dog, who had his head up, sniffing.

'Good boy,' she said, rubbing the scruffy black mutt behind the ears. 'Are you getting the second notes of grass and tonka bean? Your sense of smell is ten million times more sensitive than mine, so you could probably teach me a thing or two, eh?'

Digger responded by releasing another of his scud missiles.

'Oh, boy,' muttered Polly, grabbing the Jersey bottle again for some more lavish spraying. 'Now I see why David doesn't let you up here. It's a good job the Chanel PR gives me this stuff for nothing. Really, Digger, you have the manners of a guttersnipe, but I'm grateful for your company tonight. You're a dear thing, in your way. Now, go to sleep, and—'

She realised she had been about to say 'Happy New Year' to a dog and stopped herself. She might be in the midst of some kind of mid-life crisis, but she wasn't ready to lose it yet.

It was a bank holiday in the morning, a day lost to hangovers for most people – usually for her too – but this year she had a lot to do. She had a yoga class to teach, with five of her most loyal regulars coming to the house at 9 a.m., and after that she had two perfume events to prepare for.

In the two years since she'd launched her blog, FragrantCloud had turned into something like a full-time job, and one of the events was a big deal: the first she'd been asked to do by a big department store, interviewing one of the world's leading noses. The other was at her mother's retirement village, and almost more terrifying.

So with all that on, a disappeared husband, a potty mother and an empty nest, she did feel fully justified in going loopy – just not quite yet.

Friday, 1 January

The doorbell rang at five past eight, way before Polly had expected anyone to arrive for the nine o'clock yoga class. Even the keen ones rarely came more than fifteen minutes early. She was still in bed, lying on her back, staring at the ceiling, thinking about David.

Swearing under her breath, she grabbed her wrap and ran to answer the door.

'Happy New Year, honey!' yelled Shirlee, one of her most stalwart regulars, putting the emphasis on 'New' in her broad New York accent.

'How great is it waking up on Jan 1 with a clear head and two hours of yoga to look forward to?' continued Shirlee, without pausing for breath. 'You'll never celebrate New Year's again, right? Now, where shall I put all this?'

She held up two bulging canvas shopping bags.

'All the girls are bringing something,' she said to Polly's surprised face. 'We're laying on a New Year brunch for you. Fun, huh? All you have to provide is the kettle and the mugs. Louise is bringing her NutriBullet.'

'Gosh,' said Polly, stepping back against the wall as Shirlee bustled past, nearly filling the narrow hall with her down jacket and own considerable heft. 'How kind of you. Happy New Year.'

Not the greatest start, though, she thought. According to Scottish tradition it was supposed to be a dark-haired man who was first over the threshold on New Year's Day.

She followed Shirlee into the kitchen to find her already busily unloading her bags and stuffing things into the fridge.

'Right,' Shirlee was saying, opening random cupboards and drawers and banging them shut again. 'I'll lay the table. Is this your breakfast flatware?'

Shirlee had clearly noticed Polly's puzzled expression. 'Morning cutlery,' she explained, lifting the spoon up and down to her mouth like an oversized, superannuated Goldilocks with a mass of grey corkscrew curls.

'That's my only "flatware",' said Polly. 'How many sets do you have?'

'Three,' said Shirlee, as though Polly were weird. 'Mind you, my mom had two kitchens – one for meat, one for milk. The full kosher deal.'

She carried on ransacking the place. 'Where are your cereal bowls? We'll need them for Annie's oat-milk bircher.'

Polly went over to the dresser. 'How many for?' she asked, hoping it wouldn't be more than the five regulars she was expecting.

'With you, there'll be ten of us,' said Shirlee.

Polly was glad she had her back to Shirlee. Nine pupils. That would be a tight squeeze in her so-called studio, which was just the former dining room of her Edwardian house. It wasn't what she'd had in mind for a serene New Year's Day class.

'Do you have a toast rack?' asked Shirlee, pulling open more cupboard doors. 'I've brought one of my quinoa loaves and it's soooo good toasted.'

Polly shook her head.

'We don't really go in for that sort of stuff,' she said, an image of David's face coming into her head, with the expression it would be wearing at the very notion of breakfast flatware and toast racks.

Unimpressed didn't go near it. David thought material objects, apart from what was needed for basic survival, were 'the devil's chattels': an expression she remembered had impressed her deeply when she was twenty-two and made the mistake of expressing her admiration for an Alessi lemon squeezer.

But she didn't want to think about David now. It wasn't an allotted moment for David-thinking, past, present or future.

'Will you be OK for a minute, while I go and get dressed?' she said. 'Rummage around to find what you need – if we've got it – and make yourself some tea, or maybe just hot water and lemon would be better, before class ...'

'Sure,' said Shirlee, practically throwing plates at the table, like they were Frisbees.

Polly ran up the stairs, working out she just had time to shower and dress, then ten minutes to stretch and meditate herself into a place of stillness before the rest of the group started arriving—

Not. The doorbell rang just as she was stepping into the shower.

Grabbing a towel, she ran to the top of the stairs and called down. 'Shirlee! Would you mind getting that? I'll be down as soon as I can.'

'Not a problem,' replied Shirlee, opening the door to what must have been a group of them, judging by the volume of shrieked greetings.

'Happy New Year!' she could hear Shirlee practically yodel.

A chorus of felicitations came back in kind and Polly could hear the hubbub as they trampled along the bare floorboards to the kitchen, with stray words such as 'spelt muffins' and 'cocoa nibs' floating up to her.

Despite the hectic start, the cramped conditions and the fact that Polly didn't know all of the people there, the class went well. She could tell they were all truly zoned out during the meditation at the end. They were much slower to move than usual when she rang her little temple cymbals.

'Whoa,' said Shirlee, getting up from her mat. 'I was out. Did I snore?'

The whole class laughed.

'No,' said Annie, another of Polly's most regular attendees, 'but you rolled over and told me you loved me.'

'You weren't asleep,' said Polly.

'How can you tell?' said Shirlee, rolling up her mat and bending from the hip with a perfectly straight back. Despite her ample mid-section she was one of Polly's most able pupils.

'The quality of the breathing. The brainwaves are different when you meditate.'

'Theta waves,' said a small, wiry woman with short-cropped hair and deep wrinkles on her brown face. She was one of the four in the class who Polly hadn't met before. 'Maxine,' she added, holding out her hand.

Polly shook it, smiling back. Maxine looked like a pretty little monkey and Polly decided she liked her immediately.

'I wonder if anyone's called their child Theta yet,' said Shirlee, laughing heartily at her own joke as she headed out of the door. '"Hey, Theta, bring me my smokes."'

'I hope you don't mind my showing up unannounced like this,' said Maxine, handing Polly two folded bank notes. 'Twenty – is that right?'

'Yes, thank you,' said Polly, taking the cash, 'and you're very welcome. Normally I would've asked you about injuries and all that before the class, but it was a bit hectic this morning and you were clearly fine.'

'I've done yoga on and off for years,' said Maxine. 'You're a very good teacher. I can see why Shirlee is so devoted to your sessions. I hope you'll be able to fit me into some of your regular classes.'

'Definitely,' said Polly. 'Just text me to book a place. Do you live nearby?

'Belsize Park,' said Maxine, 'so pretty handy.'

'Oh, that's great,' said Polly.

She walked into the kitchen to find people bustling about and the table laden with food. Another woman Shirlee had brought along was taking pictures of it all with her phone. Polly would have introduced herself but conversation was impossible over the ear-splitting volume of a machine into which one of her regulars, Louise, was feeding large quantities of dark green leaves.

'Can you turn that goddamn thing off a minute?' yelled Shirlee, who was making mugs of tea and passing them over to the table at her usual high speed.

'OK,' she was saying, 'here's another two matcha teas. Agave syrup is on the table. What do you want to drink, Polly?'

'Oh, I'll have builder's,' she said. 'It's in that red canister by the kettle there.'

The room went quiet.

'Builder's?' said Shirlee, as though Polly had asked for a cup of bleach.

'Yes,' said Polly, laughing. 'That's what I like in the morning after yoga. With milk. From cows. Full fat.'

'You can make that yourself,' said Shirlee.

'Good,' said Polly, walking over to grab the kettle and bumping Shirlee with her hip as she passed. 'No one else makes it right.'

'Am I good to go?' asked Louise, finger poised on her machine.

'Hit it,' said Shirlee, 'and can you put extra ginger in mine? Some like it hot.' She tossed her curls like a diva and everyone laughed.

Relishing her first mouthful of life-giving English breakfast, Polly sat down at the table between Shirlee and Annie and considered the spread before her.

Her stomach rumbled and her heart sank. Most of it was beige.

There were plates of various unidentifiable brown nurdles and a stack of small round discs, which looked like Plasticine when all the colours have been mixed together by dirty little fingers. There were jam jars holding some kind of grey gloop, and a couple of loaves of very dense bread-like substance, one of which Polly reckoned must be Shirlee's quinoa loaf. A bowl of yoghurt and another of blueberries were the only instantly recognisable foodstuffs.

'Are these organic?' asked Annie, pointing at the berries.

'Yes,' said Maxine. 'I bought them in Whole Foods.'

'What would you like?' Shirlee asked Polly, her face bright with anticipation as she piled her own plate high with – whatever it was. 'Can I pass you something?'

A bacon sandwich? thought Polly.

'Gosh, what do you suggest?' she said out loud. 'There's, er, so much ...'

'Well,' said Shirlee, 'Louise's amazing mix is in that jug – what's in it, Lou?'

'Kale, courgette, sprout tops, celery and ginger,' said Louise proudly, pouring some into a glass and passing it to Polly.

She took a sniff. Dirty pond, with a sweet top note of compost heap and a tiny hint of ginger. She pretended to take a sip and gave Louise a thumbs-up.

'Isn't it great?' said Shirlee, taking an enthusiastic pull on her own glass. 'It's not like juice – you get all the fibre too. But you might want to stay near a bathroom. It can have an explosive effect.'

'Thanks for the tip,' said Polly. 'So what are all these other lovely things?'

'Annie's brought her chia-seed porridge,' said Shirlee, 'which is super-delish. And those are date-and-acai muesli bars. That's coconut yoghurt in the bowl, obvs, and that's my quinoa loaf – I toast it and then spread it with almond butter and sugar-free goji-berry jam, it's so good ...'

'What's the other loaf?' asked Polly, pointing at a particularly sinister-looking object.

'Oh, that's Chiara's new banana bread. She wants us to test it for her site. She's a blogger like you, Poll – well, maybe not quite at your level, but Chiara's clean-food blog is great. That's how we met, isn't it, Chia? I stalked her in the comments.'

Chiara was the woman who'd been taking pictures. She was smiling shyly, but with a keen look in her eye.

'That's so sweet of you, Shirlee,' she said. 'It would be really great if you could all give me some feedback – you know, post some comments on the blog?'

'What's it called?' asked Polly.

'CleanChia-ra,' she said, proudly. 'I hyphenate my name, Chia-ra. Chia seed – get it?'

'Great,' said Polly, 'I'll have a look.' She was all geared up to start a blogger conversation – what platform do you use? How often do you post? Do you take your own pictures? The usual stuff – but Chiara spoke first.

'Are you a clean eater, Polly?' she inquired, picking up one of the jam jars of sludge and licking the tiniest bit off the end of a teaspoon, while looking at Polly intently. 'As part of your yoga practice?'

'Um ...' began Polly, bemused. She certainly avoided processed food and bought organic whenever it was possible without having to spend silly money, but to claim she was a 'clean eater' seemed a bit of a stretch. What did it even mean?

'Well, I don't eat Greggs sausage rolls, much as I love them, ha ha, and I try to avoid sugar, except when strictly medically necessary, of course ...'

Chiara didn't look very impressed and Polly noticed some of the other women giving her rather disappointed looks. She couldn't help feeling as though she was letting them down in some way.

'I don't eat much meat,' she added, hoping to make it up to them. 'My daughter has been vegetarian since she was fourteen and it was often easier just to feed the whole family the same thing.'

And cook a couple of chops for my son as a side dish.

Chiara was nodding enthusiastically now. 'That's great about not eating meat,' she said. 'It's so toxic. How can dead tissue nourish a living being? I've been eating clean for a year now and it's really transformed my energy.'

Polly didn't think she looked very energetic. She was slim and lithe-looking, certainly, and only in her early thirties Polly reckoned, but she'd struggled to get her leg up into bow pose. And she had a large spot on her chin.

'So who's going to try the banana bread?' asked Shirlee, clearly keen to get going on it herself. She'd already polished off several slices of her own loaf and a couple of the pancakes, which she'd told Polly were made from sweet potato and rice flour.

'I'll have some,' said Polly. 'I love banana bread.'

'Put some almond butter on it,' said Chiara, beaming, 'and the goji jam, like Shirlee said.'

Polly could feel Chiara's eyes following her every move as she cut the loaf – she had to saw at it with the bread knife – and layered the suggested spreads on it. They did, in fact, make it look quite appealing. Polly lifted it to her mouth with enthusiasm, but after two chews, she had to struggle to control her facial expression.

Had her repulsion been obvious? She hoped not, and carried on chewing. How the hell was she going to swallow it? She felt like she was doing a bushtucker trial.

Dry, lumpy, gritty, with an overwhelming amount of cinnamon, which was burning the roof of her mouth. That gave her an idea for a get-out.

She put her hand in front of her mouth and looked at Chiara, who was staring at her with slightly wild eyes, her spoon still in mid-air.

'Has this got cinnamon in it?' asked Polly, as best she could with a full mouth.

'Yes,' said Chiara, smiling broadly. 'It boosts the metabolism.'

'Sorry!' said Polly, standing up and running to the bin, where she spat the repulsive clod out of her mouth. 'I can't eat cinnamon. I'm allergic to it.'

She wasn't, but thought anyone probably would be, if they ate it in that volume.

'Oh, I'm so sorry!' said Chiara. 'I should have warned you. I didn't know you had allergies.'

'Well, just that one, really,' said Polly, rinsing her mouth out with water. As of now. 'I'm sure it's delicious, if you can tolerate cinnamon. There is quite a lot in there ... You must really love it.'

'I'm not that keen, actually,' said Chiara. 'In fact, I don't like it at all. I put it in for the metabolic boost, not the taste.'

Polly was really puzzled now.

'If you don't like cinnamon, isn't it hard for you to gauge how much to use in the recipe? It can't be much fun testing your own creations if they have stuff in them you don't like.'

'Oh, I don't taste them,' said Chiara, finally licking the tiny smudge of porridge, or frog spawn, or whatever it was, off the teaspoon. 'That's what the comments are for, on the blog.'

'OK,' said Polly, nodding and looking round the table to see if anyone else thought this was a little unusual. None of them seemed to have reacted. Shirlee was cutting herself another slice of her quinoa bread.

'So will you write a comment for me?' said Chiara, dipping the point of the spoon in the jam jar again. 'You could say you loved it, but you made it with cumin and ... turmeric ... instead of cinnamon, because of your allergies.'

'I'll have to try that,' said Polly, thinking it would almost be worth it, to see how bad something could really taste. 'What flour did you use?'

'Buckwheat,' said Chiara with pride. 'The recipe's up on the site. You can tell your daughter about my blog. She'd love it.'

'Sure,' said Polly, thinking that Clemmie was a much better cook than Chiara seemed to be and actually ate what she made.

'Well,' said Chiara, putting the teaspoon down, unlicked, 'that was great. Thanks so much for organising it, Shirlee, and thanks for having us, Polly. I'm going home to do a post about how great it is to start the New Year with yoga and a clean-food pot-luck brunch. I'll just do a quick group shot of you all at the table, and then I'd like a picture with you, Polly – it will be great promotion for your yoga classes – and I can say how much you loved the banana bread.'

'Do you have a lot of followers, then?' asked Polly.

'About ninety thousand on Instagram,' said Chiara casually. She looked down and checked her phone. 'Ninety-two thousand, three hundred and twelve, it says here.'

Again, Polly hoped she had contained her facial expression.

'Wow,' she said. 'I think in that case, I'd like to leave the picture this time ...'

She didn't want to be associated with that banana bread in any context. There was way too much 'wellness' neurosis in the yoga scene. She did her best to stay apart from it.

'I haven't washed my hair,' she added, 'and with you having such a big following, I don't want to look bad in the shot ... it wouldn't be good for my, er, professional profile.'

Chiara looked crestfallen.

'Perhaps you'd like to come to another class, as my guest, and we could do it then,' added Polly. 'When I've got time to make myself look more like the exponent of health and vitality I'm supposed to be.'

'I think you look amazing,' said Chiara quietly.

'Oh, you're too kind,' said Polly, feeling guilty. The younger woman really did seem disappointed. 'Go on, then, a quick shot can't hurt.'

'Great!' said Chiara, her face lighting up. 'I can get the post up today.'

She pounced on her handbag and pulled out a selfie stick, which she quickly attached to her phone. Polly stood next to her and put her arm round Chiara's waist – only to find herself being pushed round to the other side and nearly nutted as Chiara gazed at herself in the small screen, tilting her head from side to side.

Polly turned to look at her and saw she had her mouth open, her lips pouting out, her eyes half-closed, like a 1950s starlet. It went on like this for quite a while.

'Are we done yet?' asked Polly eventually.

'Pack it in, Chiara,' said Shirlee testily. 'Polly probably has to get her family lunch or something. We all need to get going.'

Polly was very grateful for the lifeline.

'Yes, I do have quite a lot to do,' she said quickly, but Chiara didn't seem to hear. She'd taken her phone off the selfie stick and was studying the pictures intently, tapping the screen with busy fingers.

'Right, everyone,' said Shirlee, 'off you go. I'll stay to clear up, and Maxine can stay too, because she's driving me, but the rest of you need to shift it. Who wants to take their food home?'

'Oh no,' said Annie, 'I'm going to leave mine for Polly and her family. You won't have to cook then.'

'Really, it's fine,' said Polly. 'Only my son's here at the moment – he's home from uni – and he's more of a steak and chips kind of guy ...'

'No, do keep it,' persisted Annie, and the others agreed. 'You can have it for breakfast tomorrow. Just keep the jars for me and I'll grab them next time I come to class.'

'Well, that's very kind,' said Polly, thinking it was interesting they weren't longing to take their breakfast treats home with them. Maybe the birds would like them. She was sure Digger wouldn't be interested.

Polly was really pleased that Shirlee and Maxine stayed on after the others left. Even though she did have plenty of work to be getting on with, suddenly the thought of being on her own again was appalling.

She made fresh mugs of tea – more builder's for her, fresh ginger for Shirlee and rooibos for Maxine – and sat down at the table.

'Thanks for organising that,' she said to Shirlee. 'It was a bright way to start the New Year.'

Much better than it was at midnight, she thought.

'I'm glad you enjoyed it,' said Shirlee. 'I just thought as none of us were partying last night, we should at least do something festive this morning.'

'Yes,' said Polly. 'I must admit it was really weird staying in on New Year's Eve on my own. It was a first for me ...'

She went on and told them about the Scottish traditions of her childhood, possibly in too much detail, but once she'd started she couldn't stop herself. It felt good to talk about it.

'That sounds so great,' said Shirlee. 'I've heard about those Hogmanay hoo-hahs ... So how come you were all on your lonesome this year? Where was your family?'

Polly cursed herself mentally for laying herself open to this question.

'Well, my daughter Clemmie is studying Medicine at Cambridge, so she has a crazy workload and she went straight back after Christmas. Lucas – that's my son – is here and he went out with old school friends. He'll roll in sooner or later.'

'What about your husband?' asked Shirlee, breaking a piece off yet another slice of her loaf and popping it into her mouth.

Polly froze. She still didn't have her stock answer off pat. What was she supposed to say? *He seems to be having some kind of mid-life freak-out, which means he can't stand the sight of me, or even the sound of my voice on the telephone?*

'He's away on quite a, er, long research project. He's an academic.'

'What's his subject?' asked Maxine.

'History,' said Polly, relieved she had a straightforward answer to that one. 'First World War ... specifically the role of the British colonies. That's why he has to travel to do his research – we even lived in Sydney for a couple of years while he was doing a big paper about the ANZACs.'

'But he didn't come back for Christmas and New Year?' asked Shirlee, never one to tread delicately. 'Where is he? Mars?'

'Er, Nepal,' said Polly, hoping Shirlee wouldn't pursue the subject. She was relieved when there was a loud knock on the door.

She ran to answer it and was delighted to see Lucas standing there.

'Hey, Mum,' he said, giving her a big sloppy hug in the doorway. 'Happy New Year.'

'Happy New Year, darling!' said Polly, wrapping her arms round him and kissing his cheek, which she had to reach up to do. He was even taller than David now ... She batted the thought out of her head as quickly as it had come in.

'Have you lost your keys, sweetheart?' she asked him.

'Couldn't get them out,' said Lucas, tripping over the step. 'Too hard ...'

'Not feeling so good, eh?'

He shook his head, reminding her very strongly of the tousle-haired little boy he had once been.

She gave him another hug. 'I'm sure it was worth it, though, eh?' she said.

'Yeah,' said Lucas. 'Good times.'

'Have you eaten anything?'

He shook his head, kicking off his boots and dropping his coat on the floor. Polly picked it up, saying nothing. It wasn't the moment to start nagging him.

'Have you got any painkillers?' he asked. 'Industrial strength.'

'I've got some paracetamol,' said Polly, 'but you'll have to eat something first. I've got some friends over, they're in the kitchen. Come and say hi to them and I'll fix something for you.'

Polly felt proud to introduce her son, happy that – despite the state he was in – Lucas shook hands with both of them, looking them in the eye. Then, as usual on arrival in the kitchen, he headed straight for the stereo system in the corner, which David had installed years before to stream music throughout the house. It was one of David's little quirks, to have it playing all the time, from the moment he got up. Polly really missed it.

'Got to have some sounds on, Mum,' Lucas said. 'It's weird in here without them.'

'What about your headache?' said Polly.

'Music never hurts my head,' he said as the distinctive opening chords of 'Chelsea Morning' played out.

'Good choice,' said Shirlee, holding up a hand to high-five Lucas, as he headed past. 'Loving me some Joni M.'

Lucas smiled back at her, but as he sat down and took in what was on the table his eyes widened.

'What's all this, Mum?' he asked. 'Is this breakfast?'

He picked up one of the sweet-potato pancakes, sniffed it cautiously and put it down again quickly. Polly couldn't help laughing.

'I taught a yoga class this morning and my lovely students brought this brunch for me.'

'You did yoga on New Year's Day?' he said, pushing Chiara's barely touched jar of chia porridge away from him with a grimace. 'In the morning?'

'Sure,' said Shirlee. 'No better time. When your mom said she was staying in last night, I suggested we all did a class.'

'You stayed in?' asked Lucas, looking at Polly. 'Who with?'

'Um, on my own,' she said.

'What?' said Lucas, incredulous. 'But you always celebrate New Year. You told me you were going to a party ...'

'Well, I changed my mind,' said Polly, 'and when Shirlee suggested doing a class today, I thought it was a great idea, and then she made it even better by organising this lovely surprise brunch for me.'

'It's because of Dad, isn't it?' said Lucas, looking upset.

'No,' said Polly, alarmed at the turn of the conversation. 'I just felt like having a quiet one for a change. Now, would you like some bacon and eggs?'

He looked up at her and she widened her eyes at him, indicating Shirlee and Maxine by inclining her head slightly.

He seemed to get the message. Not the time to talk about his father.

'I'd love some, please, Mum,' he said. 'And can I have a hot chocolate?'

'Of course you can!' said Polly, ruffling his hair. 'You know what? I think I'm going to have some bacon and eggs too. Would anyone else like some?'

'I'd love some,' said Maxine, 'if you're sure you've got enough.'

'I stocked up,' said Polly, laughing. 'I knew what Lucas would need today. How about you, Shirlee?'

'I don't eat eggs,' she said, 'or bacon. I'm good.'

'You can have some of Chiara's cinnamon banana bread, then,' said Polly, on her way to the fridge. 'Go on, try it.'

Shirlee picked up the bread knife and started sawing.

'Jeez, it's a bit tough, isn't it?' she said.

'Wait till you try chewing it,' said Polly.

Shirlee broke a piece off and put it in her mouth.

'Holy shit!' she said, pulling a face. 'That is disgusting.'

Polly passed her a piece of kitchen roll to spit it out into, laughing. 'See why I developed a sudden cinnamon allergy?' she said.

'Oh, that's bad,' said Shirlee, taking a sip of the thick green juice that was still in a glass next to her, then looking down at it ruefully. 'And you know what? That's not so great either ...'

'Shall I make you some coffee, Shirlee?' said Polly.

'That'd be nice,' she said.

'I'll make it,' said Maxine, standing up. 'I could do with one too.'

Lucas was sniffing the banana bread.

'That is seriously rank,' he said, then looked up at Shirlee and Maxine, alarmed. 'Neither of you made it, right?'

'No, it wasn't us,' said Shirlee, 'although I do admit to bringing that other loaf there, which isn't all that great either. I can only eat it if I pile that jam stuff on it, and that's pretty awful, if you really want to know.'

'Why do you do this to yourself, Shirlee?' asked Polly, from the stove.

'Supposed to be good for you,' said Shirlee. She put her hand to her mouth and belched. 'Excuse me. I thought you'd be into all that stuff too, being a yoga teacher and beautiful and everything. I thought if I ate that shit I might start looking like you.'

She laughed loudly.

'There's nothing wrong with the way you look, Shirlee,' said Polly. 'And you're the best in any of my classes. Best balance, best symmetry, all of it.'

'Aw shucks, Poll,' said Shirlee. 'You're too kind. Don't stop.'

'Do you eat "clean", Maxine?' asked Polly.

'No,' she said. 'I try to eat normally. Not rubbish – but not wallpaper paste and sawdust, like this. And I have to confess that the blueberries I brought were actually from Aldi ... but I did wash them!'

Polly laughed.

'So who did make this so-called banana bread?' asked Lucas.

Polly told him about Chiara's blog and huge Instagram following and Lucas picked up his phone to investigate.

'Hey, look, Mum!' he said. 'She's posted a picture of you. Are you sure you're not hung over? You look terrible in this shot.'

He passed the phone across the table to Shirlee, who had a look, hooted with laughter and passed it to Polly.

She glanced at the picture, then brought it closer to be sure it was as bad as it seemed. It was. She looked like a half-dead zombie, desiccated and haggard, next to Chiara, who had her head back, laughing, as though lit from within.

'With my wonderful yoga teacher Polly Masterson-Mackay', said the caption. 'At her New Year's clean-food brunch. Polly adores my new banana bread – check it out at cleanchia-ra.com'

Polly was staring at the screen in a mix of disbelief and horror that someone might cook that terrible recipe and blame her for it – which was likely, considering Chiara had all those followers – when she noticed Shirlee getting up from the table.

Polly looked round to see her opening the crockery cupboard and taking out a plate.

She sat down again and smiled sheepishly back at Polly.

'I'm gonna have some of that bacon,' she said. 'Don't tell my rabbi.'

FragrantCloud.net

The scent of ... yoga

I've been doing yoga since I was a teenager in Cambridge, where my dad was a Professor of History. I went along to a class with a friend out of curiosity and was immediately hooked. I loved the way it seemed to have mental benefits as well as the physical workout. Friends rave about the endorphin hit they get from running, but that slow, quiet yoga buzz really works for me.

I learned the discipline of daily solo practice when I went to university in a small town in Scotland, where there were no yoga classes at all. When I moved to London to do a PhD, I trained as a yoga teacher as a handy way to make some cash while studying, but then quite unexpectedly it became my career. It fitted in brilliantly with being a mum, and I used to do classes at my kids' primary school, which were hilarious.

I've taught in all kinds of places, from cold and draughty church halls to health clubs so swishy the parquet floors in the yoga studio probably cost more than my whole house, and one of the things I've loved about it is meeting so many different kinds of people. As well as the seriously yummy-mummy set, I've worked with pensioners and young offenders, which I found really rewarding.

These days I'm very happy teaching just five morning classes a week in what was the dining room at home. I have a lovely group of regulars, with drops-ins welcome, and sometimes we have brunch together after the class, which is really nice for me, now both my kids are away at uni.

But I must confess they're not the kind of 'clean eating' events you might expect from a yoga teacher. I do love porridge – my

Scottish blood - but I'm also a bacon-and-eggs girl and I do like a morning hit of fatty protein. It keeps me full for hours.

So chia seeds and goji berries are not for me and I was very glad to find some friends who feel the same.

The smells I associate with yoga are contradictory. Freshly showered bodies and sweat. Sandalwood from a scented candle mixed with hot feet on rubber mats.

Head-clearing pure air, ozonic freshness - and deep oriental mystery. Stillness and invigorating renewal. Feminine grace and masculine strength. Anima and animus.

My scents of yoga are:

Madagascan Jasmine by Grandiflora
Lime Basil and Mandarin Cologne by Jo Malone London
Exhale by B Never Too Busy To Be Beautiful
Pour Monsieur by Chanel
Oud by Maison Francis Kurkdjian
New West for Her by Aramis
Black Lapsang by Bodhidharma
Santal by Diptyque (my favourite candle for the yoga studio)

COMMENTS

AgathaF: In Germany we always eat protein for breakfast. It is good nutrition. Today I had Black Forest Ham.

FragrantCloud: Hi, Agatha - sounds delish! Polly x

LuxuryGal: Next time I'm in London, I'd love to come to one of your classes. Can anyone come?

FragrantCloud: Of course. Just email me via the address on the main menu. It would be great to meet you.

PerfumedWorld: I'm so happy to see you reference New West for Her! That was the first perfume I ever bought for myself. I still love it and it's so sad that you can't get the original any more. I can still remember the first time I smelled that amazing ozonic top note. It was so new and exciting.

FragrantCloud: I loved New West too.

WhirlyShirlee: Chia berries are for the birds! As sure as eggs is eggs!

FragrantCloud: Ha ha, see you on the mat in the morning. I've got the eggs in! x

CleanChia-ra: I thought you didn't eat meat? Maybe that's what's made you write this negative post. Eating decay can't feed your soul. Eat clean and free your heart. Love and light Chia-ra cleanchia-ra.com

FragrantCloud: Just being honest, Chiara!

EastLondonNostrils: Clean eating is a great foulness. It always makes me think of antibacterial wipes and mothers who give their kids baths in Dettol. Keep on bringing home the bacon. ELN

Monday, 4 January

Polly and Digger had been waiting in her mother's sitting room for over half an hour, and it was hard to say which of them was more restless. Despite Polly's constant entreaties to him to settle, the dog kept walking over to the floor-length window, pressing his nose against it and coming back.

'Oh, for flipping heck's sake, Digger, can you not sit still for one minute?' she hissed at him.

She immediately felt guilty for snapping at him. It wasn't Digger's fault David had let the poor animal bond to him like superglue and then gaily disappeared off on some bogus research trip, leaving Polly to look after a bereft canine with digestive tract issues.

Digger looked at her balefully and headed for the window again.

Polly glanced at her phone. There was still plenty of time before she was due to start her talk before the residents of Rockham Park, the upmarket retirement village where her mother now lived. Instead of sitting here impatiently, she'd much rather have been sipping a quiet cup of tea down in the residents' lounge, getting used to the space and checking that her laptop was set up for the slide show.

She wasn't nervous about what she was going to say – she'd

done this talk so many times now she knew it by heart – but she didn't want to make a rushed late arrival into a room full of impatient oldsters. It was much better to be there smiling as they came in. However, she knew her mother preferred the grand-entrance option.

Polly checked the time again. She'd been sitting here now for close to forty-five minutes, staring at the framed black-and-white photographs of her mother that crowded the walls and at the magazines fanned out on the coffee table featuring Daphne's more recent shoots, while Daphne finished her elaborate toilette.

Several times Polly had gone into the bedroom to see how she was doing, only to be briskly reprimanded and told to stop hurrying her. Daphne had even insisted on pressing her dress and polishing her bloody handbag herself. Polly had only been allowed to get the ironing board out.

It had taken all her self-control not to ask her mother why she hadn't done her preparations the night before. Daphne had been awake for most of it, judging by the number of times she'd rung Polly to ask her what time she was coming. Two in the morning, three-fifteen and then again at five.

Along with serious memory lapses, these nocturnal phone calls were one of the distressing new developments in her mother's behaviour, and Polly had been concerned what state she might find Daphne in when she got there. But she seemed absolutely fine, engaged in her favourite activity of maintaining her ridiculously high standard of appearance, which had been such a theme of Polly's life.

Polly felt sorry for the other residents, who had to hear constantly about 'dear Cecil – Beaton,' at lunch, and what he'd said about Daphne's neck in 1956, while she threw back her head and laughed, all the better to show it off.

Polly knew every one of those stories off by heart, and years of listening to them were the main reason she'd never taken up modelling seriously herself, despite her mother's encouragement. She'd done a bit, to earn some extra cash when she'd moved to London, but she'd known from a young age that she didn't want to spend her life as an admired decorative object, which was exactly how her mother had always seemed so happy to define herself.

Polly had initially chosen instead to follow in her father's academic footsteps – he was a historian like David – and after finishing her MA at St Andrews had enrolled to do a PhD on the impact of the women's suffrage movement in provincial Britain. But she'd quickly got discouraged and never completed it, finding she got much more satisfaction from working as a yoga teacher than she did from studying or modelling.

She did sometimes wonder if her looks, while not being anything like her mother's standard – 'once in a generation', as Daphne had been described in *Vogue* – had held her back in the academic world, which had its own complex standards and snobberies. No matter how she tried to play her looks down, Polly had always felt she wasn't quite taken seriously at the university. But she'd never regretted starting the doctorate because that was how she'd met David, which had made it worthwhile.

Or that was what she'd always thought. She didn't know anything any more, where he was concerned.

'OK, that's it,' she said out loud, as those unwelcome thoughts started to crowd into her head. They were the last thing she needed on her mind before show time.

She stood up and walked purposefully through to her mother's bedroom.

Daphne was sitting at her dressing table, the same one she'd had for as long as Polly could remember. She was fully dressed and immaculately made up, her hair perfectly set, then artfully messed up a little, as was her signature trick.

Her chin was raised and she was patting herself with light fingertip taps in upwards movements from her décolletage to her jawline. She was so engrossed in this activity that she didn't notice Polly come in. It was only Digger's more hectic entrance that finally distracted her from gazing at her own image.

'Oh, that wretched dog!' she said, returning to her neck-patting. 'Can't you put it in a kennel or something until David comes back?'

Polly decided to ignore that remark – not that she hadn't considered it. Looking after Digger was like having a toddler again. She couldn't go anywhere for longer than a few hours without either taking him along or getting someone to look after him. Fortunately she had a very kind near-ish neighbour who was happy to have him for 'doggy play dates' with her pets, but even then Polly had to deliver him, pick him up and make canine conversation before she could politely leave.

She gently shooed Digger out of the bedroom and closed the door.

'You look simply wonderful, Mummy,' she said, hoping flattery would work its usual magic. Ideally it would have come from a man, but Daphne was happy to accept a compliment from any source. She visibly purred when she received one.

'Will I do, darling?' she asked, her eyes never leaving the mirror, as she turned her head from side to side, touching her earrings delicately with her fingertips.

Finally she pulled her eyes away from her own reflection to look at Polly, who had come into view behind her.

'Are you going to put some lipstick on?' she said, a slightly critical tone creeping into her voice. Most people wouldn't have noticed it, but it rang crystal-clear to Polly, after decades of listening to her mother nag her to wear more make-up.

'Of course,' Polly replied, thinking about the nice tinted lip balm in her handbag.

Most of the time she didn't wear anything. She knew it was a reaction to her mother's cosmetics over-obsession, but she felt more comfortable that way, and it was one of the things David had always said he liked about her. He hated her wearing lipstick.

'And are you going to do your hair?' continued Daphne, her eyes narrowing as she took in her daughter's quite long, mostly blonde, centre-parted, un-blowdried hair. The bits that weren't blonde were grey, and a bit wiry. Polly's plan for today's hairdo had been to pull her polo neck off and then back on again, leaving all the hair tucked inside. She thought of it as the No Scissors Bob.

'Of course,' said Polly again, trying to keep an edge out of her voice. 'May I borrow your brush? I didn't have time before I came over.'

'You really should have it cut shorter, Polly,' said Daphne, handing Polly her Mason Pearson over her shoulder, and shifting her attention straight back to her own reflection. 'You're much too old to have long hair. It's really not becoming at your age. Would you like me to put it up into a nice chignon for you? That would be better than having it all hanging down like that.'

Polly glanced at the little porcelain clock on the dressing table. There was probably just time, and if it would stop her mother criticising her it would be worth looking like a 1950s air hostess for the afternoon.

'Oh, that would be amazing, Mummy,' said Polly, with as much fake enthusiasm as she could muster. 'Would you mind? You're so good with hair …'

'Well, of course, we always had to do our hair and make-up ourselves in my day,' started Daphne, leaning heavily on the glass top of the dressing table to push herself to her feet.

'We didn't have your Sam McKnights to do it for us, we had to be able to do whatever style the photographer wanted – although Mr McKnight has done my hair a few times and I must say he's a charming fellow. He says I'm a hair icon …'

Polly sat on the stool and let her mother go on with her monologue about herself and what other people had said about her over the past sixty-five years. It was a subject Daphne simply never tired of – and one about which she could still be relied upon to stay lucid. Other areas – such as where she'd put her hearing aids or the hundred pounds Polly had got out of the bank for her a few days before, and whether she'd eaten anything other than a few dry crispbreads and cups of very weak China tea in the last few days – she was less reliable on.

Polly sat and listened, watching as her mother whipped her tatty hair into a remarkably sleek French pleat, with fingers that were still deft, despite the arthritis beginning to swell the knuckles, pausing only in her mono-themed soliloquy to apply what seemed like several ozone layers' worth of hair spray.

'There,' said Daphne, putting her hands on her daughter's shoulders. She leaned in towards the mirror to see better, smoothing a strand of stray hair back behind Polly's ear.

'See how much more elegant you look, darling?' she said. 'At your age, you don't have the luxury of going *au naturel*. You're not the ingenue any more. Why don't you let me pop a little colour on your face too?'

Polly was so discombobulated by the helmet-headed stranger looking back at her in the mirror she couldn't think of a reason to object.

'That would be wonderful,' she said weakly.

Daphne set to with enthusiasm – creaming, powdering, lining, brushing and buffing. Polly just sat there opening and closing eyes and mouth as instructed, letting go as she had learned to in yoga.

It wasn't like she was going to see anyone she knew, so she might as well let her mother be proud of her for once, rather than apologising for her scruffy appearance, as she usually did. None of the other residents would know it wasn't her normal style; they would probably think it was very 'becoming'. And Daphne would have the added pleasure of being able to brag that it was she who had created the transformation from clapped-out duckling to soignée swan.

'There!' exclaimed Daphne, just as Polly was starting to nod off. 'Super. Have a look.'

Polly opened her eyes and immediately sat up very straight. What did she look like? She peered more closely. A drag queen? She had to admit not. An old lady? No. She looked grown-up. Like the sophisticated women she met in the perfume world who went in for all the accessorising and grooming her mother was so keen on but Polly never bothered with. The look was maybe a little overdone for the twenty-first century, and the coral lipstick was heinous, but the overall effect was glamorous, she had to admit. Better than she usually looked. Much.

'Gosh,' she said, smiling up at her mother. 'Thanks, Mummy. I hardly recognise myself.'

'Well, this is how you should look all the time, darling. As I'm always telling you, at a certain age, every woman needs more help. Men are very unforgiving about all that. They're allowed to go grey and whiskery, but they expect their wives to stay beautiful or else they go and find younger meat. If you want to keep David interested, you'll simply have to make more effort.'

Polly flinched at another mention of her absent husband. She was certain he'd be appalled to see her all done up like a dog's dinner, as he'd call it, but her mother's remark still cut her.

Was that why he'd insisted on going away without her? Was he off somewhere pursuing 'younger meat'? Ugh, what a horrible phrase, and an even more horrible thought.

Determined not to get upset before she had to perform, she put it out of her mind. Again.

Her mother was now busy putting the finishing touches to her own look. Standing in front of the glass doors of her extensive wardrobe, she was shrugging on the neatly fitted jacket that matched her navy-blue crêpe dress and adjusting her pearls to sit perfectly on her chest. Then she went to her dressing table and, after a moment's thought, picked up her bottle of Fracas and sprayed herself liberally. Finally, she slipped her feet into patent-leather pumps with heels, much too vain to wear flats or use the stick she really needed.

Polly took advantage of Daphne's full absorption in her own reflection and nipped into the bathroom, grabbing the lip balm out of her handbag on the way. Wiping off the hideous coral lipstick, she slicked the balm on, instantly feeling more like herself. Then she lightly rubbed her hands over the sides of the hairdo, as she'd seen her mother do so many times, softening it just a little. It really did make it look better.

She nodded at her reflection, then headed out into the hall to find her mother waiting outside, handbag over one arm with the hand turned out and upwards, the other hand low on her hip, feet in ballet fourth position, looking for all the world as if she were waiting for 'dear Cecil' to adjust his focus.

When she saw Polly, she threw up her chin and tinkled with laughter.

'You've done my hair trick,' she said, 'just as I hoped you would. Doesn't it look better with Daphne Masterson's Magic Mess-up?'

Polly had to agree that it did, and after calling for Digger to come with them she put out her elbow for her mother to take, and arm in arm they set off for the coffee lounge.

FragrantCloud.net

The scent of ... the elders

Yesterday I did a talk for the residents at the retirement village where my mother lives.

It's not a sad old people's home of the kind we all dread ending up in, with high-backed plastic chairs in rows along the walls, but a very sophisticated purpose-built development where they have their own apartments, with post and milk delivered to their own front doors, so they feel independent. They all have kitchens, but most of them have their meals in the dining room, where they can consume an excellent three-course lunch or dinner served by waiters in white gloves, or in the more casual café.

There's even a bar, a hairdresser and a spa ... so really, it has more the atmosphere of a luxury liner than of 'God's waiting room' – and it certainly doesn't have the dreaded smell of wee and boiled fish that we tend to associate with old people's homes. The public areas are subtly scented with bowls of pot pourri and infuser sticks, not those terrible plug-in things, which give me an instant migraine.

I chose 'A Short History of Perfume – The First Ten Thousand Years' as my theme, because I thought my audience would enjoy hearing about perfumes they might remember their own parents wearing in the 1920s and '30s, and the ones they wore themselves in their own mid-century heydays.

They were such an interesting crowd. There was a bit of nodding off, but they pepped up whenever I passed blotters around for them to smell.

They shared the loveliest stories about their own early experiences of scent – they all called it 'scent' – how precious it was and how hard it was to get during the war. There were twinkles in the eyes of a couple of ladies who told us about handsome GIs who'd given them bottles of perfume as well as the usual nylons.

It was very special to hear all their stories and I felt privileged that they shared them with me.

As well as all that, one very interesting thing happened. After I'd passed around the second lot of blotters, one lady said rather sadly that she was afraid it was all wasted on her because her sense of smell had become much duller as she'd aged.

Several others agreed, so I broke off from my talk and asked them to try some of the techniques I've learned to improve your sense of smell.

I got the kitchen to give me an onion, a lemon, a piece of ginger and some ground coffee, and I passed them around, asking the residents to sniff each one and think about what memories it brought back. I also told them trick of smelling the skin on their inner elbows to freshen the nose between sniffs.

They seemed to really enjoy it and became more animated, with a lot of giggling about the arm-sniffing. After we'd done that, we went back and revisited some of the blotters I'd sent round first, to make a comparison.

One of the few men there positively lit up when he smelled Mitsouko.

'My mother,' he said very quietly, and looked up at me with tears in his eyes. It was so touching that it was all I could do not to hug him.

At the end he came over to me and asked if he could respray the blotter. I tried to give him the whole bottle, but he wouldn't take it, saying he couldn't possibly, and joking that the cleaners might be a bit surprised if they saw a lady's scent in his bathroom.

He was such a dear, a proper old-school gentleman, immaculately turned out in a cravat, with a yellow waistcoat under his jacket, of the kind I remember my dad wearing. That was very special.

As well as talking about times past, I thought it was also important to bring my presentation into the present, so I asked the residents what perfumes they wear now. I could smell Youth Dew the moment I walked into the room and one of the ladies said she'd been wearing it non-stop since the 1950s.

Yardley Lavender, one of my own favourites for its beautiful simplicity, also had some fans. More unusually, one lady told us she's worn Dior's Poison since it came out 1985, which made me feel rather sorry for whoever has to sit next to her at lunch.

That thought prompted me to ask how often they wear scent, and most of them said only for special occasions – that old chestnut.

'What are you saving it for?' I asked cheekily, and luckily they got the joke. So that's a reminder to us all: don't save your favourite perfumes for 'best'; wear them whenever you feel like it.

So the smells I associate with the Elders are freshly cut garden flower arrangements – roses, lilac and endless sweet peas and the fougère hints of random greenery lavishly added to the vases, in the Constance Spry style.

Also, modest shop-bought flowers, particularly daffodils, tulips and freesias, which are such an economical way to brighten a room for that thrifty generation.

My scents for the elders are:

Lavender by Yardley
Blue Grass by Elizabeth Arden
Rose in Wonderland by Atkinsons
Femme by Rochas
Ostara by Penhaligon's
Tweed by Lenthéric (A mention of this elicited a big response at the event; it seemed all the women had worn it at some time and had happy associations with it. I do wish they would re-release it in the original tweed fabric-effect box.)

The men in this age group are the last of the true British gentlemen, so especially for them:

Old Spice
St Johns Bay Rum by St Johns Fragrance Company
Royal Mayfair by Creed

COMMENTS

LuxuryGal: This is so great! I'm going to do an event like this at my mom's retirement home. She's worn Youth Dew since the 1950s too! I keep buying her new perfumes, but she'll only wear that one. I wear a different one every day, just like you.

FragrantCloud: Perhaps I'll get to come to LA sometime and I can do it for you! Polly x

TheSpritzer: I'd love to hear more about Mr Mitsouko. Imagine if he still had a bottle of his mother's original brew ...

It's changed so much since then with all the restrictions on perfume ingredients. I would love to have smelled it in the 1930s as he did.

FragrantCloud: I know! I thought the same thing ...

LeichhardtLori: Give Daphne our love! What did she wear for this event?

FragrantCloud: Hi Lolster! I will. Fracas ... She did my hair and make-up. You would have cracked up. I looked like Lady Penelope, but better than I normally look LOL. Skype soon? xxxxx

EastLondonNostrils: Love the picture of your mum's perfumes. Please will you do an event in London with her?

FragrantCloud: She'd love that!

Tuesday, 5 January

Polly was passing her time waiting for Clemmie at the lunch venue her daughter had chosen, a concrete-walled space right on Shoreditch High Street, memorising the ridiculous items on the menu. The combinations on offer were almost as bonkers as the clean-eating brunch, but at least Clemmie's vegetarian diet was inspired by wanting to cut back on CO_2 emissions, rather than calories.

Leaning down to give Digger a pat, she reminded herself not to let it slip that she'd driven there. Clemmie would not approve, but Polly still wasn't used to taking public transport with the dog. Another major inconvenience of having to look after him. She was terrified he was going to jump down the gap between the Tube train and the platform, or let off on a bus with one of his signature fragrances.

And it was handy this restaurant actually allowed dogs in – she'd rung ahead to check, because it was amazing how many places didn't and she couldn't leave him at home. David used to take Digger to work with him every day and the poor hound wasn't used to spending much time alone. The one time Polly had tried leaving him there since David had gone away, she'd come back to a furious neighbour, complaining Digger had howled all day.

She was glad he was behaving now, lying under the table, his head resting on one of her feet. At least that felt nice and cosy on a freezing January day. She'd just reached down to scratch his neck when she saw Clemmie walk through the restaurant door in a fluster of coat, scarve, gloves and bobble hat, her cheeks bright pink.

'Sorry I'm late, Mummy, the train was crap,' she said, rushing over to the table and giving Polly a hug and a warm kiss, before she started the long process of taking off her layers.

'I take it the Siberian winds are blowing into Cambridge, then,' said Polly, remembering the uniquely bitter winter air in her childhood town.

'Straight from Omsk without stopping,' said Clemmie, squeezing into what was left of her seat after she'd draped it with clothing. 'I'm going to knit myself a full-face balaclava. Cycling to lectures from the flat is a major endurance event with that wind blowing in your face. It's enough to make me want to get a car. Nearly.'

Polly smiled at her. Definitely keep quiet about driving there.

'What's the vegan spesh today?' asked Clemmie. 'Have you looked?'

'A braised aubergine and quinoa tacu-tacu pancake, with an avocado and amaranth superfood stack,' said Polly.

'Mmmm,' said Clemmie, 'that sounds great.'

'What is tacu tacu?' asked Polly, thinking it would be easier to order the same thing than have a long discussion about methane gases and deforestation.

'It's this yummy Peruvian thing, where they mix up leftover rice and beans and fry it into a sort of patty,' said Clemmie.

'Peruvian bubble and squeak, then?' said Polly, and Clemmie had the good nature to laugh.

'When do lectures start again?' asked Polly, immediately hoping it didn't come over too obviously as a suggestion that Clemmie come and spend some time at home before the term officially began. Which was exactly what it was.

Two nights over Christmas, with everyone trying to pretend it wasn't extremely bizarre that David wasn't there, hadn't been nearly enough Clemmie time for Polly. Especially as she'd brought her boyfriend Bruno with her. Not that Polly had a problem with Bruno, he seemed a very nice young man – and as Lucas had said, teasing his big sister about her hunky new chap, 'What was it about the rich Italian Cambridge rowing Blue which attracted you to Bruno?'

It was just that particular year, after Daphne had gone home, Polly couldn't help wanting to spend some time just with her children. Coming so soon after David's surprising departure, Christmas had felt like a time for hunkering down together, rather than welcoming people in. She still had all David's presents, which had been wrapped up, ready, before he went. She'd stuffed them in a cupboard on Christmas morning, suddenly realising how weird it would have been to have them still sitting under the tree when all the other packages had been opened.

'Oh, there's no official classes for another couple of weeks,' said Clemmie, 'but we go straight into some really heavy tests, so I've got to study like crazy. It's hard work, this doctor-becoming business.'

'But it will be so worth it in the end,' said Polly, pride in her clever daughter's academic commitment going some way towards soothing her disappointment. Clemmie had decided she was going to be a doctor even before she became a vegetarian, at the age of twelve, and once she made her mind up about something there were no halts and no reversals. She was like her father in that way.

Lucas's university choice of music production had been a lot more vague – he played bass guitar and had thought the course sounded 'quite cool' – but he'd make his own way, even if it was the long way round: a bit like her becoming a yoga teacher and now a perfume blogger.

She and Clemmie placed their orders – two vegan specials and two tap waters, not exactly living it large – and Polly asked the usual interested-parent questions about Bruno and other friends of Clemmie's, until she hardly knew what was coming out of her mouth for the clamour in her head of wanting to talk to Clemmie about David.

She was finding it hard to eat, her mouth dry with anxiety from trying to stop herself mentioning him.

It wasn't that she felt she had to stick to his ridiculous request for her not to talk to the kids about him – she didn't think she owed him that courtesy in the circs – but for fear of upsetting Clemmie. What would it be like for Clemmie to know her father actively wanted no contact with any of them for six months?

Eventually Polly found that the cutlery had dropped from her hands and she was close to tears.

'I've got to talk to you about your dad,' she said. 'I managed to hold it together over Christmas for everyone's sake, but I can't keep it up any more. I'm going mad. I've been married to him for over twenty years and I don't know where he is, let alone why he's left ...'

Clemmie's face immediately looked stricken. She leaned across the table and took her mother's hand, then lifted up her napkin and wiped away the tear that had rolled down Polly's cheek.

'Oh, Mum,' said Clemmie, 'I thought you were being strong, and I didn't want to bring it up because I felt I had to take the lead from you. I'm not surprised you're confused, it's so unfair on you.'

Polly wondered how much Clemmie knew. Was she aware that David wanted no contact with any of them? He had been so dramatic about the dire consequences of discussing the situation with anyone – but how could that apply to their own children?

'I don't even know what he's told you,' Polly said. 'He asked me not to discuss it with you and Lucas, which is why I spent Christmas with an invisible gag on, but are we really supposed to stop talking to each other for his convenience? It's simply not fair.'

Clemmie looked thoughtful for a moment before she answered.

'Nothing about this is fair,' said Clemmie. 'It's terrible for you – and for me and Lucas. The only thing we can hang on to is that he must have been really desperate to do this to us.'

'Desperate about what? And how could he not trust us?' asked Polly, brushing away another tear and trying to pull herself together. 'Whatever it is, anything would be better than this. It's the not knowing that I can't bear.'

Clemmie had tears in her eyes now.

'I just don't know, Mummy,' she said, shaking her head. 'I don't know what to say and I don't know what to think. How's Lucas coping with it?'

'Badly,' said Polly. 'You know what he's like. He keeps it all bottled up and then it comes bubbling out and he has a freak-out. I thought it was amusing when he got roaring drunk on New Year's Eve and came rolling home the next day, but now he seems to be doing that every night, which isn't funny at all. It really hasn't been a great end to his first term at uni. Did

David even think about that? Apparently not. Lucas is only nineteen and he's young for his age. You've always been so mature, Clemmie. It's like you got all the common sense and your brother got none. So I'm worried about him, on top of everything else.'

'I'll ring him,' said Clemmie.

There was something about the way she said it that suddenly irritated Polly. Like that would sort it out. One phone call from Big Sister. What Clemmie actually needed to do was to come home with Polly and sit down with her and Lucas to talk about this. Make a plan. It wasn't a quick-fix-phone-call kind of situation. And the way her daughter was staring down at her food, stirring it around with her fork, rather than looking Polly in the eye made her suddenly suspicious.

'Do you know where your father is, Clemmie?' she said firmly.

Clemmie immediately screwed up her eyes, then nodded, very quickly.

'Where?' asked Polly, trying not to let her raging anger with David come into her voice and unfairly hurt her daughter.

'He's in London,' said Clemmie, very quietly, looking down at her hands and then up again, sighing deeply.

'London?' said Polly slowly. 'Has he been here all the time?'

'No,' said Clemmie. 'He's been in Turkey.'

'Turkey?' said Polly. 'I thought he was supposed to be in Nepal.'

'He told me it was Turkey,' said Clemmie. 'Anyway, he came back to London on New Year's Eve.'

When I was all alone, looking up at the moon, wishing I was in his arms, thought Polly.

'Well, where's he staying in London? Why hasn't he come home?' she pressed.

'I don't know about any of that, I just know he's here and he's going away again tomorrow, he just had to come back quickly for some reason, to get some stuff he needs ...'

'Some stuff?' said Polly. 'From the house?'

Clemmie nodded, looking quite sick.

'Well, when's he going to come round?' asked Polly. 'I'll make a cake.'

Clemmie looked even more uneasy and Polly felt slightly ashamed for being sarcastic to her daughter, but she didn't feel quite in charge of herself.

Clemmie swallowed before answering.

'He's there now,' she said.

Polly just looked at her daughter for a moment as her stomach seemed to drop away.

'Are you serious?' she said quietly.

Clemmie nodded again, a tear now running down her cheek.

'Is this a set-up?' asked Polly.

'Not exactly,' said Clemmie, looking wretched.

'But he asked you if you knew when I might be out of the house?'

Clemmie nodded silently again.

The nodding was really beginning to irritate Polly, which she knew was irrational and a distraction from the real issue. She sat in silence, finding it very hard to take it all in and not really wanting to; it was so very hurtful.

'So David is making you collude with him to avoid me?' she said eventually.

'Oh, Mum, don't take it like that,' said Clemmie.

'What other way is there to take it?' said Polly. 'Does Lucas know he's there? Are they there together, right now, having some quality father-and-son time?'

'No,' said Clemmie, looking even more ashamed. 'I knew Lucas was going to be out today too.'

Polly felt a flash of rage go through her. It was a bit like an electric shock and made her feel almost afraid of what she might say, in public, to her daughter.

She fished hastily in her bag, pulled two twenty-pound notes out of her wallet, threw them on the table and stood up.

'As, unlike me, it seems you are allowed to talk to him, will you please give your father a message, Clemmie?' she said, trying to keep her voice low and level. 'Will you tell him he's a total arsehole? And while you're doing it, have a think yourself about which parent you might like to be loyal to. The one who's been abandoned with no explanation, or the one who's just fucked off to do his own thing for no good reason? And you might like to give your brother a moment's thought too. He's a lot more sensitive than you are.'

She picked up her coat and bag, and had just started heading towards the door when she remembered Digger. She turned back to see he'd stood up and was looking at her expectantly.

She bent down and picked up the end of his lead and handed it to Clemmie.

'And you can give him his dog to look after too. Goodbye.'

'Mum, wait!' cried Clemmie and Polly heard her chair crash to the floor as she stood up, weighed down as it was by all her coats and scarves.

Polly kept walking as fast as she could without actually breaking into a trot. To her great relief, just as she got to the restaurant door, a bus pulled up at the stop right outside.

She jumped on it without looking at the number. She could go back for the car later.

She heard Clemmie call out to her again as the bus doors closed, but she didn't look round. Then she heard a yap and her head turned despite itself. Clemmie was looking distraught, chasing Digger, who was running after the bus.

She felt a pang of guilt for putting her daughter in that situation – and another for Digger – then dismissed them both. She was sure the dog had enough sense of self-preservation not to run into the traffic, and as for Clemmie, what she'd done was just plain wrong.

She'd colluded with her father to help him avoid seeing Polly, and Polly just couldn't let that go. Of course, she would over time. She wasn't going to lose her daughter as well as her husband – and she did understand how torn Clemmie must be between her parents in this bizarre situation. But Clemmie was an adult now; she had to get used to being treated like one.

Polly's phone rang. She knew it was her daughter without even looking. She dropped the call and sent her a text.

Not now, Clemmie. I'll call you later when I'm ready to talk about this. You must understand how much this has hurt me on top of everything else. Mum

No kisses. It was harsh, but this was an exceptional situation. Exceptionally hurtful.

~

As the bus turned into Commercial Street, Polly gazed unseeingly out of the window, until her attention was grabbed by a man walking by with an adorable little girl of about four holding his hand and skipping by his side. She looked as though she was singing.

The poignancy of the moment was like a fist to Polly's gut, a sharp reminder that Clemmie had grown up with a strong case of my-heart-belongs-to-Daddy – which Polly really couldn't blame her for, because she'd been exactly the same herself.

Daphne had been so self-obsessed and preoccupied with her career that Polly's steady, thoughtful father had been a much safer haven during her own childhood. And unlike many academics, who shut themselves away to work, he hadn't minded being interrupted.

In fact, Polly had very fond memories of sitting on his knee while he typed, or being given what felt like the very important job of collecting particular books from the sofa, floor, windowsill or wherever they were perched, and opening them for him at the marked pages.

He'd put her name in the acknowledgments in several of his books – 'A special thank you to Polly, my delightful personal elf' was one she particularly remembered – and now those dusty volumes were probably her most treasured possessions.

But while Polly understood Clemmie's special relationship with her dad – and also had to acknowledge that she harboured a special kind of tenderness for Lucas, not more love than she had for Clemmie, just differently flavoured – she still felt this was a terrible betrayal.

Maybe the Digger thing had been a bit childish, but it had seemed important to make a statement that would force Clemmie and her father to confront the practical consequences of his irresponsible behaviour, seeing as he seemed immune to the emotional ones.

As the bus turned left at the big junction at the bottom of Commerical Street, Polly decided she was well beyond the point where Clemmie could catch up with her and got off at the next stop.

She stood outside the Whitechapel Gallery and wondered what the hell she should do now. Cross the road and get a bus back to the car? Then what? Go home and risk running into David – or go home and not run into him? She didn't know which would be worse.

Then, getting her bearings, she realised she was at the bottom of Brick Lane, so she could walk back to the car along there and through Spitalfields. That made her think of her father again. His academic speciality had been the Age of Enlightenment – the period in the middle of the eighteenth century when Europe burst into intellectual bloom – and when Polly was a child he'd brought her here to show her the magical old streets from that period. He said they made him feel as though Sir Isaac Newton and Adam Smith might come walking around the corner at any moment.

As she turned into the narrow start of Brick Lane, bustling with cool-looking young people, she wondered what he'd think of the area now. The houses that had been virtual slums when she was a kid were now perfectly restored, prime real estate, but the waves of immigrants who'd lived in them – Huguenot silk-weavers, European Jews, Bangladeshis – had all added to its richness.

Feeling pleasantly distracted by all the history, she resolved to stop thinking about David and Clemmie and the whole sorry situation until she got home, and give herself some respite from the anxiety that seemed to have become her default setting at the moment. Being able to partition her thoughts in this way was a useful technique that years of yoga meditation had given her. Acknowledge the unpleasant ones and then just bat them away.

First, though, she stopped to text Lucas. After the horrible scene with Clemmie, she would need the reassurance of her other child's company when she got home, even though she had no intention of telling him what had gone on. Knowing

David had been in London – and in the bloody house! – and deliberately not seen them would hurt Lucas even more than it had her.

R u home for dinner? 😸😸😸

Lucas's reply came back immediately:

Polly grinned down at it. Lucas always cheered her up. And now she knew exactly what to make for dinner. With the prospect of a cosy night in with him she felt much stronger, and free to immerse herself in the fascinating sights – and smells – of Brick Lane.

The remaining Bangladeshi restaurants planted little nose-tickling bursts of spice aromas along the street, which mixed exotically with the staler smells of garbage, soot, diesel fumes and dank puddles, with added interest from the slightly fungal, damp wafts coming out of the many vintage clothing shops.

Polly wrote her next blog post in her head as she walked along, stopping in a doorway to make some notes in her phone, so she wouldn't forget the smell and perfume associations jumping into her mind.

When she got to the corner of Cheshire Street, she caught a whiff of something very different, a rich smell – spices, but not the food kind. It was so interesting she turned off Brick Lane away from her destination and followed her nose like a beagle. The fragrant wafts got stronger the further she went, with the depth of exotic oud, along with with patchouli, sandalwood and musk.

Eventually she came to a stop outside a shop with the words the 'Great Eastern Fragrance Company' in gold-painted letters on its shiny black frontage, the original eighteenth-century shutters still in place.

Closing her eyes and getting distinct whiffs of frankincense and cedarwood along with the oud, Polly thought it was an excellent name for a brand that was clearly specialising in perfumes in the oriental style – based in London's East End.

When she opened the shop door, which made an old-fashioned bell jingle, the combined odours were almost overpowering, causing her to stop and close her eyes. She felt quite dizzy for a moment.

When she regained her equilibrium and opened them again, blinking in the low light, she heard someone laugh and, as her eyes adjusted, she saw a man walking towards her, his right hand held out in front of him.

'I should have known a nose as sensitive as yours would find my overblown oud conceit a bit much,' he was saying.

He stopped with the hand still extended towards her and Polly realised she was supposed to take it.

'Guy Webber,' he said, returning her handshake with an almost finger-crushing grip. 'So good to finally meet you, Polly.'

'Hi, er, Guy,' she said, nearly thrown off balance again by the heady aromas and the surprise of this complete stranger knowing her name. Although as she blinked back at him, there was something – very black hair, short at the sides, long on top and slicked back like a matinée idol, liquid dark-brown eyes, heavy brows – that seemed vaguely familiar.

He had the Shoreditch beard, as black as his hair and neatly groomed. But, clichéd face-rug aside, he wasn't sporting the usual East End hipster look. He was just the age to be one – early thirties, Polly reckoned – but there wasn't a trace of tweed, selvedge denim or corduroy. Not even an artisanal apron. Instead, he wore a black polo neck and an immaculately cut suit, charcoal-grey with a slight mohair sheen.

'I'm a great fan of your blog,' he said. 'Would you like to sit down? You looked a bit shaky there for a moment.'

Polly was very happy to sink onto the elegant black velvet sofa at the back of the shop, beyond the shelves of sparkling perfume bottles topped with rose-gold caps.

Guy propped himself on a high stool next to her, his left arm on the counter as though it were a bar top. With one velvet slipper propped on the bottom rung of the stool, the other long leg stretched out, he reminded Polly of one of the men who had sometimes featured in 1950s fashion shoots with her mother.

'I've seen you around at various perfume events,' he said. 'I've been to a couple of yours.'

'Oh,' said Polly, 'that explains it. I thought you looked familiar.'

'A very junior member of the perfume pack,' he said. 'Not nearly as well known as you. Yet.'

He laughed again and Polly smiled back at him. Like many people she met in the very particular world of fragrance, which was densely populated with eccentrics, Guy Webber was clearly his own man.

'And I might not have had a beard then,' he added, stroking it luxuriantly. 'It's a new addition, to fit into the neighbourhood.'

Although she felt awkward having to look up at him from the low vantage of the sofa, Polly found she was smiling again.

'So, how did you hear about the shop?' he asked, looking at her keenly, his dark eyes narrowed. He had very long eyelashes, Polly noticed. 'I've done no publicity, no PR.'

'I smelled it,' said Polly. 'From on Brick Lane and followed my nose to find out what the source of powerful oud was.'

Guy looked at her for a moment, and then roared with laughter.

'You actually sniffed me out,' he said. 'How brilliant. Oh, you really do deserve your reputation as London's leading perfume blogger. You found me all on your own – by nose. I've only been open a week. So you could be the first to write about my perfume. If you like it, of course.'

Still feeling slightly wobbly, Polly wasn't entirely sure she did like it. She respected the heavyweight oriental perfumes – they were particularly hard to get right – but she rarely wore them herself. The bad ones made her want to unscrew her own arm if she was ever foolish enough to actually spray them onto her skin.

'So why didn't you have a launch campaign, or an opening?' she asked.

'To be different,' said Guy. 'I imagine you get invited to several launches a week, don't you? Or even a day.'

Polly nodded. With over fifteen hundred perfumes coming out a year – and that number was rising – it was hard to keep track of all the press releases and invitations that flooded her inbox and letterbox.

'So,' said Guy, 'I thought I'd be deliberately obscure and build myself up as an insider-secret type of brand. Would you like some tea?'

'I'd love some,' said Polly, realising she was thirsty and hungry after leaving the restaurant without having any lunch, which was probably why the overpowering scent had made her feel faint when she came into the shop.

'You don't have a biscuit or anything, do you, Guy?' she

said. 'I hope you don't mind my asking, but I missed lunch and I'm feeling a bit light-headed.'

'Of course,' said Guy. 'And there I was thinking you'd been overcome by my ravishing aromas. Won't be a tick.'

He disappeared through a curtain of dark-red glass beads behind the counter, which made a pretty jangling noise as he passed, and Polly stood up to have a better look at the shop.

She could see at a casual glance that the fittings were very high-spec. The interior was panelled in polished dark wood, the perfume bottles sitting on glass shelves in mirror-backed cabinets.

She picked up a bottle and its weight suggested it was made of crystal. Her eyebrows went up. You didn't expect to find that in a smutty little street off Brick Lane; crystal bottles were more of a Knightsbridge–Mayfair scenario. She glanced up at the chandelier in the middle of the room, and there it was: one little red crystal drop among all the clear ones, which showed it was genuine Baccarat. How surprising.

Pulling the pretty rose-gold cap from the top of the bottle in her hand, she found that also had a pleasing heft to it. This was quality stuff.

She raised the cap to her nose to smell, which she preferred to do before spraying onto a blotter. It gave a more accurate idea of the essence of the fragrance without needing to wait for the alcohol to evaporate.

She pulled the cap away from her nose in surprise, then smelled again. Yes, she'd been right the first time. A pretty extraordinary fragrance. It was based on a foundation of amber, shifting into incense and pure patchouli, with a touch of leather, but with a sharp green accord that pulled it back from the overbearing sickliness that put her off heavy orientals. Still way too strong for her, but interesting.

She smelled another cap. Woodier, with an interesting hint of sweet vanilla, balanced with the smart white note of jasmine, much closer to the kind of perfume she liked to wear.

Looking over the shelves, she saw there were six fragrances in total, but she didn't want to smell them all in one go. She was weak with hunger and the slump after the adrenalin rush of her scene with Clemmie, and this wasn't the time. These fragrances deserved more respect than that. She knew she'd be coming back to the Great Eastern Fragrance Company and would try the others then.

After a moment's thought she picked up the second bottle and sprayed the perfume decisively on both wrists, just as Guy came back through the door.

'Straight to the skin?' he said, looking very pleased as he put a silver tray down on the counter top. 'That's a bold move.'

'I really like it,' said Polly, 'and I want to see how it develops on me. I'll come back and look at the others another time. I'd like to do a piece about your range and the shop – and you – but I don't have enough time today. Perhaps we can fix a date before I go.'

She brought her wrist up to her nose again. Mmm, it was getting even more interesting. That vanilla note, then something sharper. But it wasn't jasmine, as she'd first thought; it was more lemony, but not obvious kitchen-cleaner lemon ... a kind of warm, smoky citrus. Burned lemon peel, that was it. Like the flavour of the dish she was making for Lucas tonight: chicken thighs baked in the oven with lemon wedges, which went black and sticky and were delicious to eat.

'Which one is that?' asked Guy, pouring tea from a tall silver pot with a long curved spout.

Polly looked at the label.

'Half Past Eight,' she said.

'Interesting,' said Guy. 'What are you getting?'

'Well,' said Polly, putting the scent bottle down, then taking the gold-rimmed lilac teacup and saucer that Guy was holding out for her and going back to the small sofa. 'On top of the more obvious sandalwood and vanilla: roasted lemon peel.'

Guy's face broke into a beam.

'Spot on,' he said. 'It was inspired by dinner at my grandmother's house – hence the name. She used to serve a wonderful dish that featured preserved lemon wedges roasted with partridges, with lots of garlic and apricots.'

'She sounds like an amazing cook,' said Polly, sniffing her wrist again and wondering if there wasn't a hint of apricot in there too.

'Oh, she didn't make it,' said Guy. 'She served it – well, had it served. Would you like one of these?'

He held out a plate that matched the teacups, piled up with different kinds of baklava.

'I'm half-Persian,' said Guy. 'Half-Iranian, to be more accurate. Hence the overwhelming smell of the kasbah and the Edgeware Road snacks. We can smoke a hubba bubba if you like ...'

He had that expression on his face again – camp, but ironic – that made it hard for Polly to know how serious he was being. She had assumed he was joking about the hookah pipe, but he reached behind the counter and pulled one out. It looked, to her inexpert eye, to be rather beautifully made.

'My grandfather's,' he said. 'I inhale pure fragrance through it, not tobacco, not even the scented versions. That's why there was a bit of an overwhelming miasma when you arrived. I'd been having a suck on that. Next time you come, you can try it. It's a very intense way to experience aromas.'

'Gosh,' said Polly, 'that sounds almost illegal.'

'It is,' said Guy, laughing, and once again she didn't know whether he was joking or not.

The sugar and caffeine hit of the baklava and the tea, which Guy served black, with no offer of milk, was making Polly feel much better. After some more general chat about the perfume world, they fixed a date for her to go back to interview him for the blog, and she made her departure.

She was nearly back at the junction with Brick Lane when she heard footsteps behind her. Turning quickly in case her bag was about to be snatched, she saw it was Guy, grinning and waving something in the air.

'Glad I caught you,' he said, puffing. 'I want you to have this.'

He put one of his heavy crystal perfume bottles into her hand. A big one with an old-fashioned silk puffer spray. She looked at the label and saw it wasn't the one she'd sprayed on her wrist, but the first cap she'd smelled and hadn't liked so much. It was called The Darkest Hour.

'I know you like Half Past Eight more,' said Guy. 'You think you're not a spicy-orientals girl, with your Celtic blood and your dry skin; I read your blog, I know about your fetish for chypre fragrances. It's the oakmoss and patchouli combo alongside the burned lemon you're responding to in Half Past Eight.'

Polly had to laugh.

'Bang to rights,' she said. 'Halfway to chypre paradise ...'

'But I want you to try this,' he said, 'and live with it for a bit before you come to do the interview.'

'OK,' said Polly, hoping she wouldn't be spending a day with both arms extended as far away from her nose as possible.

Guy leaned in towards her. Assuming he was about to give her a social kiss – and used to such over-familiarity in the perfume world – Polly turned her left cheek to receive the first 'mwah' and was surprised when instead she felt his warm breath up against her ear.

'Spray it on late at night,' he said, 'when you're in bed.'

And before she could answer, he'd turned and started jogging back up the street, one arm raised over his head in a farewell salute.

Polly stood outside her own front door, nervous even to put her key in the lock. What if David was still in there? What if he wasn't? She didn't know which would be worse.

Telling herself to get a grip, she opened it quickly, stepped inside and closed it noisily behind her. If he was there, she wanted him to know she was back.

She leaned against the back of the door, cocking her ears to listen. Nothing.

'Hello?' she called out, her heart pounding with anxiety. 'David?'

There was no reply. The house felt empty, completely still, but she couldn't relax. Walking slowly, feeling as though she were in the kind of film where an axe murderer could jump out at any moment, she went through to the kitchen, looking into the sitting and dining rooms on the way. He wasn't there.

Then she checked every part of the house – even the broom cupboard and under the stairs – until she was certain he wasn't inside, but she still felt uneasy. A sense of intrusion, that was what it was, she realised. Something like the violation people feel when they've been burgled.

It was so horrible and so bizarre to feel like that about her own husband that Polly found herself face down on the bed, heaving with painful, wracking sobs. How had they got to this place? Could they ever return to normal when he came back? If he came back ...

Once she'd recovered enough to stand up and wash her face – terrified Lucas would come back and find her in that state and she'd have to explain it – she looked right through the house again for clues to what David might have come back for, but couldn't find anything changed.

The only thing was the smell, which was subtly different from when she'd left that morning. Even beyond all the scented candles and diffusers – and her huge collection of perfumes, which added a light hum of fragrance to the place – the house had its own smell, and Polly was very attuned to it.

It had been there the first time they'd looked round the house twenty years before, and it grew stronger again any time they went away. The first thing she'd notice when she opened the door after coming back from holiday was how the very particular Edwardian odour – stale gas, dead flowers, old soap – had settled in again.

This new smell was something different, though. She followed her nose and it took her into the sitting room and over to the wood burner. She lit it every night at this time of year to add some cheer to the place, so it shouldn't be surprising that there was a smell of cold wood cinders. But this time there was something else.

Opening the stove door, she saw very clearly that there was a layer of new ashes on top of what she would normally rake over in the evening to set a new fire. They were blacker and flatter than the log ash and quite smooth, more flakes than crumbs. She picked some up in her fingers and they disintegrated straight to dust, but lifting them to her nose Polly knew immediately what they were. Paper. Burned paper.

So David had come back to the house and burned paper. Why?

Polly sat back on her heels feeling almost dizzy. It was so weird. What on earth would he have burned? Couldn't he have shredded it, or at least taken it away with him? Whatever could it be?

She leaned down and put her head almost inside the stove to see if she could read any of the remains, but they were stubbornly black. Standing up, she rubbed her hands to dust the ashes from them, feeling quite nauseous with the strangeness of this new development. Then, fired by curiosity, she ran up the stairs to the top floor where David's office was.

She'd been through all his things a couple of times already, rifling his filing cabinet, taking down his books and shaking the pages to see if anything was folded between them, deriving some pleasure from messing it all up a bit. David was organised to the point of obsession. Over the years she'd forced him to lighten up a bit in the kitchen, but in his office his ridiculous standards ruled, all books filed alphabetically within categories, a row of identical yellow pencils in a line beside an A4 pad of paper on his otherwise empty desk.

When they'd first met, the contrast between David's work room and her father's study, with books, papers and empty mugs on every surface, had amused her. Now his office just seemed cold and detached.

She stood in front of the closed door and felt uneasy again. Hadn't she left it open after throwing some post on his desk that morning? Polly didn't like closed doors.

Turning the handle she found it was locked, with no key in it. A chill ran down her back. Was he in there?

'David?' she called out.

Nothing. Was he in there dead? She crouched down and peered through the keyhole, but she could hardly see anything and felt ridiculous doing it – but this was a ridiculous situation, she told herself. Not able to get into a room in her own house.

Standing up, she rattled the door handle and shouted through it.

'Open up, if you're in there, you coward!'

There was no reply, and she felt instinctively now that he wasn't in there – dead or alive. But she wasn't prepared to leave it at that. The locked door stared back at her like another gross insult.

Polly stood glaring at it, trying to summon all her yoga-centredness to come to terms with this new challenge – the sort of thing she was always telling other people to do – but all her years of meditation were not enough to deal with this. Her shock and curiosity had turned into a cold fury. She kicked the door as hard as she could, but it didn't do much more than hurt her foot.

So it turned out it wasn't as easy to kick in a door as it looked on cop shows, but she was too sick of David's weird secrecy to give up. She ran down to the utility room, to grab a claw hammer and a chisel out of his tool box.

A few jabs from the chisel splintered the wood, then jamming the curved end of the hammer into the gash and pulling it back towards her, she was able to prise part of the panel right off. Then she knocked the rest of it out with the chisel and suddenly she could see into the room.

Her heart thumping, she leaned down and looked through the gap.

Nothing. No one there. But it was back to its normal sterile tidy state.

All the books she'd dropped on the floor and the filing cabinet drawers she'd left hanging open had been returned to their former order. The post she'd thrown on the desk – catalogues and academic journals – was gone. She was glad he knew she'd been through his office, but felt irrationally furious that during his clandestine visit to the house he'd taken the time to tidy it all again.

Fuck him, she thought, standing up and kicking the hammer out of the way in her anger. Tomorrow she was getting a bloody locksmith. If David wanted to go off for six months, he didn't get to dictate which rooms Polly was allowed to go into in her own house.

~

By 9.30 p.m. Polly was starting to feel a bit disappointed in Lucas, but hadn't entirely given up on him. She'd eaten her chicken legs and left his on the kitchen counter covered in tin foil.

He'd said he be home for dinner by eight and hadn't answered the text she'd sent him at eight forty-five. She'd tried calling his phone, but it went straight to his voicemail. She didn't leave a message. She couldn't trust herself not to get hysterical, and the last thing she wanted was to dump her unhappiness about the insane situation with his father – and now his sister – on him.

Separation, she reminded herself. Lucas's non-appearance and David's desertion, or whatever it even was, were two separate issues and she mustn't bundle them up into one big toxic ball.

While she'd been calling Lucas, Clemmie had left another emotional message and a text begging Polly to call her back. Taking her glass of red wine into the small room on the ground floor, which she used as a study now it was no longer required as a playroom, Polly wrote Clemmie an email instead.

> Darling Clemms,
>
> Please don't fret. I still love you, nothing can change that, you are my golden girl always.
>
> We'll speak soon, but I just need some time to digest all this. I'm cross with your dad for putting you in this situation – not with you, but I just need some time to process it.
>
> It will all be fine. I'll call you tomorrow, sweet pea.
>
> All my love always
>
> Mum xxx
>
> P.S. And I'll take Digger back!

She hadn't realised until she typed the last sentence that she was actually missing the smelly old hound. The house was so deadly still and quiet without him. The skitter of his nails as he trotted across the wooden floorboards had become a welcome distraction. The deadly silence of the house was one of the worst things about this cruelly imposed purdah she was in, not having David's beloved music playing all the time.

He said he needed it to make his brain work properly and Polly loved it. He had wonderfully eclectic taste and she never knew what she'd wake up to – David Bowie, Debussy, dubstep ... She'd tried putting it on herself, but whatever track she played reminded her of him and happy family times so much she'd had to turn it straight off again.

And it felt even stranger in the house on her own tonight, knowing that David had been there earlier. The lingering sense of intrusion made the isolation more acute. With all that, on top of the horrible scene with Clemmie, Polly sat in front of her computer's glowing screen, feeling at her lowest ebb since David had left.

Her beloved home, where her children's heights were recorded on the kitchen wall, where they'd had so many lovely birthday parties and Christmases, felt more like a theme-park fright ride than a sheltered haven.

'Solitary – the silent prison of secrets,' thought Polly. 'Dare you spend a night in it?'

She didn't want to, but neither did she feel like going out on her own at nine-thirty on a Tuesday night. There wasn't even anyone she could call for a casual chat.

It wasn't that she didn't have any friends. She had her yoga gang and lots of fun new acquaintances from the perfume world, but they weren't the kind of pals you rang up. They were more a case of who was there in the moment, or chatting on Facebook.

With her old friends it was tricky for a different reason. She and David were a popular couple, with a busy social life – or they had been. It was true they didn't go out nearly as much as they used to, but she'd just put that down to getting a bit older. That wasn't the issue now, though. The truth was she was avoiding people, because it meant making up some nonsense to explain where David was.

Apart from David's – outrageous – instructions that she mustn't tell anyone, she didn't want to. It made her feel oddly ashamed. Like she was some kind of failure for being in this situation. It had been fine at Christmas parties because she'd really thought he was on a research trip to Nepal then, but if she saw anyone now, she'd have to lie about it. Yet another humiliation his selfishness had imposed on her.

What made it even more insufferable was his expecting her to honour his plea not to tell anyone about his absence –

without giving her a reason for it. How could she keep a secret if she didn't even know what it was?

She just couldn't get past why, after twenty-five years together, he didn't think she would support him in whatever he was going through. She could understand why he might not want the university to know he was having a meltdown, but why couldn't he trust *her* enough?

She'd spent hours wondering what the hell it could be to demand such strictures. The first thing she'd thought of was that he was coming to terms with being gay – but she really didn't think that was it. Their sex life, while not exactly chandelier-swinging, wasn't that tragic for a couple who'd been together for twenty-five years.

Polly sipped her wine and ran through the scenarios again. Was he on the run from some kind of crime? Or debt?

Was he a secret gambler who'd mortgaged the house without telling her? She didn't think it was that, because he'd left all their financial affairs in typically ultra efficient order. His salary was being paid into their joint account to cover the bills, plus he'd parked quite a large sum in Polly's private account in case of emergency.

Had he defrauded the university in some way? Cheated on expenses? Fabricated research? Plagiarised?

Was he a functioning heroin addict who'd decided it was time to go into secret rehab?

They'd known people for whom all those things had been realities, but she was sure he would have told her if it had been any of them.

Perhaps he was a spy and murderous Russians were pursuing him with radioactive cups of tea ...

Enough, thought Polly, closing her eyes, as something like panic started to rise in her chest. Enough thinking about things

I can't change. Exist only in the moment. Breathe. She sat still for a while, slowing her breathing and concentrating only on that. In. Out. Hold. In. Out. Hold.

When she opened her eyes again, she felt much better and opened Facebook for a distraction. She was sick of this anxiety; she needed some cute baby animal photos.

Scrolling down the usual mixture of funny videos, outrageous deeds by American politicians, adorable hedgehogs, Buzzfeed quizzes and other people's dinners, she came across a post that made her smile. It was a photograph of her very best friend, Lori, holding two ice-cream cones up to her head like Viking horns.

#summer #beach #livingthedream #Sydney #sosueme, read the caption.

Darling Lori. The one person Polly felt she could tell about her situation, without expecting that she would be judged as some kind of hideous old loser whose husband just couldn't stand to be around her. Or a gullible idiot, who couldn't see that he was off having a wild affair with someone.

Polly glanced at the clock. Ten-fifteen at night in London; it would be nine-fifteen in the morning in Sydney. Summer, January holidays. No wonder she was at the beach.

Polly picked up her phone and hit FaceTime.

Lori answered immediately.

'Poll Star!' she exclaimed. 'How are you, darls? We're on the beach, look ...'

She did a three-sixty and Polly took in the white sand, the slightly choppy waves, the trees coming right down to the edge of the beach.

'Watson's Bay?' she asked.

'You're not wrong,' said Lori. 'Got here at eight, to get a park.'

It was comforting to Polly just to see her friend's smiling face and to be reminded of all the times they'd taken their kids to that very beach together when they were little. So many shared memories.

'So, all good with you, then?' asked Lori, settling herself down on her towel. 'Clems and Luca-loo well?'

'Yes, we're all good,' said Polly, lightly. If she was going to tell Lori what was going on with David, she couldn't just launch into it. She had to choose the right moment to bring the subject up. 'Your crew?'

'We're all fine. The kids came home for Chrissie, which was nice. Can't wait for them to go now – only joshing. Nearly!'

'How's Rich?' asked Polly, not wanting to be taken off guard by having Lori ask her about David first.

'His usual moody old self,' said Lori, laughing. 'But he's not bad. He says David's off on some big research trip, is that right?'

'Yes,' said Polly, slightly too quickly. 'He's gone to Nepal. Initially. He's got a six-month sabbatical.'

'Nepal? Weren't you tempted to go with him?' asked Lori. 'You could have done a yoga thing there.'

Polly took a deep breath, thinking this was the moment to start telling Lori why she hadn't gone with David, but before she could begin, Lori started speaking again.

'Mind you,' she said. 'People think it's great, gallivanting around the world with your history-professor husband, but mostly they just go to really boring shitholes. I remember spending two weeks in France once with Rich, all on bloody battlefields. Christ, it was boring. Why couldn't he be a historian of Paris shoe shops?'

Polly laughed, but she felt winded. She hadn't missed Lori's passing reference to Rich's new academic status. He was a professor now. David still wasn't. And Polly realised, with a lurch of her stomach, that her adored best friend – the one person she thought she could open up to about David's disturbing behaviour – was very much the one person she couldn't tell. Because although Rich and David were good friends, they were also close rivals in a narrow historical field. Rich's speciality was the ANZAC–British war effort, while David looked at all the colonial forces, but it was a big enough cross-over to be tricky at times.

And David had told her ages ago that as soon as the big job came up at King's College, Rich would be on a plane back to London to try and grab it. He'd said it was inevitable that one day they'd either be fighting for the same gig – or Rich would be his boss.

Either way, Polly could see that telling Rich's wife that David was either on the run from Interpol or having some kind of severe mid-life crisis would not be politic.

Feeling almost sick with disappointment that she couldn't even be real with her best friend, Polly got the conversation back onto more general chat, asking about mutual friends, but now she was finding it hard to concentrate, constantly policing her thoughts before she turned them into words. It was exhausting.

After they said goodbye and made a promise to Skype each other soon for a longer chat, Polly felt she'd never been more alone. She took her now-empty wine glass back to the kitchen and refilled it, then settled down to write the post about Brick Lane for the blog. Anything to stop herself thinking about her situation.

By the time she finished it, her eyes were closing as she sat at the desk. Bed and oblivion seemed like a welcome prospect, so, after putting Lucas's chicken legs in the fridge and writing him a note, she went upstairs.

She'd just closed her eyes when she remembered something.

Turning on the light, she fished The Darkest Hour out of her bedside cabinet and sprayed herself with it liberally.

Wednesday, 6 January

Polly was woken from what felt like a bottomless sleep by a loud crashing sound. She sat straight up in bed, her heart pounding with fear.

What the hell had it been? Should she go down to see or lock the door and stay in the room with her phone in her hand, ready to dial the police?

She bitterly regretted leaving Digger with Clemmie. His loud bark would have been a very welcome comfort in this situation.

Even as she was wondering what to do, she was almost overwhelmed by the smell that filled the room, more like a fog than a fragrance. Oh yes, The Darkest Hour. She glanced at the clock. Four ten in the morning. It really was the darkest bloody hour, and waking suddenly in an unlit room seemed to make the heady mix of tuberose and patchouli even more powerful. It was too much.

There was another noise. Not loud like the first one, but definitely inside the house.

She froze. Then, almost petrified with fear, she crept over and carefully opened the bedroom door – to distinctly hear the word 'Muuuum ...'

She ran down the stairs to find Lucas sprawled face down on the hall floor, the console table tipped on its side, the big crystal vase of flowers smashed, water and lilies all over the tiled floor, the ceramic bowl they kept keys in broken into pieces, keys scattered.

'Oh, Lucas,' she said, crossly taking in the state of him. He smelled terrible – of roll-up cigarettes and stale beer and something else she couldn't quite identify, sickly and metallic.

He turned his head towards her and she could see he was cross-eyed drunk. Then he lifted one hand and she saw that blood was flowing from it.

That was the other smell. Her stomach churned.

'Cut m'self,' he stammered out, then she saw his back spasm, and he retched.

'Shit!' said Polly, wondering how the hell she was going to get him up on her own, with razor-sharp bits of glass on the floor all around him. At least he was lying on his front, so if he did vomit, he was less likely to choke on it.

'Stay there,' she said stupidly. 'I'm going to get some shoes on.'

She ran back upstairs, put on some heavy boots and opened the drawer where David kept his thickest leather gloves.

They weren't there and she felt a stab of pain. Not now. She wasn't going to think about him now. She had enough on her plate.

After grabbing a pair of sheepskin mittens of her own, she rushed back down to Lucas.

He'd managed to crawl forward a foot or so, and as she put the hall light on, she saw it flash off a large shard of glass, right in front of his face, dangerously close to his left eye.

'Don't move!' she yelled, and jumped down the last step, glass crunching beneath the boots. Crouching down, she carefully picked up all the pieces of glass that were closest to his head – not easy in the bulky mittens; it felt like some kind of sinister party game. She put them in a pile next to the wall behind her, working back and outwards, until she couldn't see any more.

Lucas groaned again.

'Fing killing me ...' he managed to croak out. 'Issa playing fing ...'

She looked back at his left hand and saw it was the pad of his middle finger that was cut. Not good for a bassist.

'Hang on,' she said. She ran into the kitchen grabbed a roll of kitchen paper, then wound a piece tightly round the cut.

Using what felt like superhuman strength, she somehow managed to get him onto his feet and half-dragged him into the sitting room, where he fell back onto the sofa. She glanced at the scrap of paper towel round his finger and was alarmed to see it was already soaked with blood.

Taking it off very carefully, she flinched when she saw how deep the cut was. It definitely needed stitches. She'd have to take him to Emergency. Oh, joy. But how the hell was she going to get him there? Should she ring an ambulance, or was that overdramatic?

It was a bad cut and he was losing blood, but it wasn't an artery and the Whittington Hospital was so close it would be much quicker to drive him.

She shook his shoulder to rouse him but he just groaned.

'Lukie,' she said, crouching down next to the sofa and stroking his dear head. 'Lukie, my darling, you have to wake up, I've got to get you to hospital. You need stitches in that finger.'

He just mumbled and turned his head away, then gasped with pain when he tried to roll on his side and knocked his cut finger.

Looking down at the bulk of her son, over six foot of him, Polly knew she couldn't do it on her own. He would need practically carrying to the car. She urgently needed help, but who the hell could she ask? Not her nearest neighbours, that was for sure. They were very grumpy people. If only Lori still lived around the corner ...

For a moment she felt something like blind panic. Should she ring Clemmie to get a calm, sensible opinion – with some medical knowledge thrown in? But what use was she in Cambridge?

Then she had an idea. Shirlee. She lived pretty close, and Polly had a gut feeling she'd be good in a crisis. It was a big ask to ring anyone at that time of night – morning – let alone someone she hardly knew, but there was something about Shirlee. She just felt she could.

Polly brushed Lucas's hair away from his face, out of some kind of weird maternal instinct – what good was that going to do him? – then went and grabbed her phone from the bedroom. She tapped Shirlee's number and crossed her fingers.

'What the fuck?' said a very groggy-sounding Shirlee. 'What's up? Who is this?'

'Shirlee,' said Polly, feeling a bit sick, 'it's Polly. I'm so sorry to wake you up like this, but it's an emergency. I need your help.

There was a rustling noise.

'What's happened?' asked Shirlee, all dopiness gone. 'Keep talking, I'm getting my Ugg boots on. I'm coming right over. Do you need me to call the police?'

'No, it's just I have to get my son to the hospital. He's passed out drunk and cut himself badly and I can't get him into the car on my own.'

Somehow she could say it straight to her. She knew Shirlee wouldn't judge her.

'I'm already walking out the door,' said Shirlee, and hung up.

Five minutes later – the whole of which time Polly moved restlessly back and forth between Lucas and the sitting-room window – Shirlee's car pulled up. Polly rushed to open the front door.

'Thank you so much,' she said breathlessly. 'It's so good of you to do this.'

'Don't sweat it,' said Shirlee, putting her arm round Polly's shoulder. 'Show me where he is.'

Polly led her through to the sitting room and was horrified to see that the blood from Lucas's finger had seeped out of the kitchen-roll bandage to make a large, bright-red stain on his shirt.

'Holy shitola,' said Shirlee. 'We gotta get this kid to the hospital. OK, here's what we'll do.'

Shirlee managed to get Lucas into a slumped sitting position, then, issuing instructions firmly but calmly, showed Polly how they could haul him up off the sofa onto to his feet. With his arms over their shoulders, they managed to drag him out through the hall and onto the street.

'Do you think he's unconscious?' asked Polly, when Lucas didn't seem to stir, even as the tops of his shoes dragged along the pavement to Shirlee's car, which she'd left with the back door wide open.

'I think he might be,' said Shirlee, 'but more likely from the booze than the blood loss.'

With some effort, they managed to get him onto the back seat. Polly tried not to cry as she had flashbacks to all the times she'd strapped him safely into a car seat as an adorable little boy.

She ran back to the house to grab her keys and close the front door, then jumped into the car, which Shirlee already had revved up, ready to go.

'OK,' said Shirlee, handing Polly her phone before releasing the hand brake and shooting off at an alarming speed. 'Just hit the number that's up on the screen and you'll get through to the Whittington. Ask for Emergency and tell them we're bringing in an unconscious adult male and we need assistance on arrival. Five minutes max. Lucky it's so early, I can shoot a few lights.'

Polly did as she was told, while Shirlee drove rather terrifyingly, but got them safely to the doors of the Emergency Department, where two porters were waiting with a wheelchair.

'Hey!' called Shirlee, and they came straight over – getting Lucas out of the car, into the chair and through the doors of the hospital at what seemed like lightning speed to Polly, who was starting to feel a bit light-headed.

'OK, kiddo,' said Shirlee, linking her arm through Polly's and patting her hand. 'I'm gonna look after you now. Let's do the name-and-address stuff and then I'm gonna get us some coffee.'

The routine felt all too familiar to Polly as she sat in an uncomfortable plastic chair in the waiting room, while Lucas was being assessed.

She looked round, remembering the brutal lighting of the place, like something from Stasi-era East Berlin – and the smell. Gallons of disinfectant waging a losing battle against the sheer press of humanity coming through the place in all manner of ugly messes. The almost unbearable staleness of a densely occupied area with no windows, where the smallest breath of outside air only came in when the automatic doors opened.

You could come in there in perfect good health, she thought, and get ill just from sitting in the fug. She pulled the front of her jumper forward to release a welcome waft of The Darkest Hour. Pungent fragrances had their advantages.

On top of the general unpleasantness of the surroundings, she was reminded all too vividly of the times she and David had brought the kids here after falls in playgrounds and bangs to the head, and one memorable time when Lucas had plunged his tiny hand into a saucepan of boiling spaghetti. One time it had been David who'd slipped on an icy pavement right outside the house and broken his wrist.

Well, fuck him. Not only had he left her alone to cope with this crisis, in her opinion he'd also caused it. She was convinced the crazy drinking was Lucas acting out his distress about his father's unexplained absence.

There'd been the usual teenage gallivanting before, with Lucas learning through painful experience why people generally don't drink cider, beer, wine and cherry brandy in the same glass – and not just because of the awful taste. But she'd never known him to get so drunk so often.

Had one term at uni made him into a serial binger? You heard about student excess, but this seemed beyond that. There was a sense of commitment to it.

Then, remembering those childhood visits to that waiting room, she started to stand up. Shouldn't she be with him? Hadn't they always stayed with the kids while the doctors assessed them and did any necessary stitching or bandaging?

'Where are you going?' asked Shirlee coming round the corner carrying a cardboard tray holding two paper coffee cups, with various other things precariously balanced on it. 'Sit down and drink this. You'll need to have your brain in gear when they tell us what's up.'

Shirlee sat down and passed Polly one of the coffees, followed by a Kit Kat.

'Eat it,' she commanded. 'You've had a shock. You need some sugar, or you'll faint on me, and I'm not up to hauling another unconscious body around tonight.'

She snapped a finger off her own Kit Kat and chewed it up with the speed of a rodent.

'I just spoke to the sister and they're still checking him over,' she continued. 'They've done the stitches but they just want to make sure he didn't bang his head, or something like that, when he fell. Ah, sugar, don't you just love it? The white lady.'

'Yes,' said Polly, breaking off another piece of her Kit Kat. 'Nothing like it. And caffeine – cheers!'

She raised her coffee cup to Shirlee, who tapped hers against it, grinning broadly.

'I don't feel like a NutriBullet barf drink and a quinoa muffin right now, do you?' she said, her chest shaking with laughter.

'No,' said Polly, 'or any of that appalling banana bread.'

'Christ, that stuff!' said Shirlee, 'I needed dental after one bite. How did we ever kid ourselves?'

'Mass hysteria,' said Polly, then she put out her hand and squeezed Shirlee's. Her tone became more serious. 'Thanks so much. You really saved my life tonight – well, Lucas's. I don't know what I would have done if I hadn't had you here. I somehow knew I could call on you and you were really there for me. It means a lot.'

'Ach,' said Shirlee, 'it was nothing. I'm happy to be useful. Glad all that training was worth it.'

'Training?' asked Polly. 'I could see you knew what you were doing, but I didn't realise you were actually trained. Are you a doctor? A nurse?'

'Neither,' said Shirlee. 'When I was living in Israel, I did National Service and learned army first aid: hauling half-dead people around.'

'Did you ever have to do it for real?'

'Yeah,' said Shirlee, 'and not always half-dead. There were a couple who were fully dead.'

'Blimey,' said Polly. 'I had no idea. That must have been very difficult.'

'Well, it grew me up pretty fast,' said Shirlee. 'I didn't have to do much of that kind of thing back in Queens. It's why I moved here.'

Polly raised her eyebrows, waiting for Shirlee to say more. It didn't feel like the moment to come rushing in with a reply.

'You see, I went home after being in Israel and there were all the same people – the ones I'd been to high school with, the children of my parents' friends, my cousins, my goddamn sister – but I just didn't feel I could slot back into that life.

'Don't get me wrong, they're good people, I love them. But after doing the dead-body thing and the bomb thing in Israel, I was a different person and I couldn't go back to my old life. So I came over here to stay with my aunt – she and my mom were British, well, they came here with the Kindertransport from Austria – and it felt like I could start again as the new person I'd become and I stayed. Best decision I ever made.'

'Wow,' said Polly, 'I wondered why a native New Yorker was living in North London. When did you come?'

'In 1981,' said Shirlee, her face splitting into one of her Fozzie Bear grins. 'Thirty-five years and I still sound like Harvey Keitel's little sister, eh?'

Polly smiled back at her and was about to ask her how often she went home when a nurse came over to them.

'Mrs Masterson-Mackay?' she said to Polly. 'Would you come through, please? The doctor would like to talk to you.'

Polly looked up at the nurse and then over to Shirlee, who was already getting to her feet.

'Can she come too?' asked Polly.

'I'm family,' said Shirlee, heading for the door into the consulting area without waiting for an answer.

Polly heard Digger whimpering with impatience before Clemmie had even got her key in the front door and ran down to the hall to greet them.

'Oh, my baby!' she said, throwing the door open and enveloping Clemmie in her arms, wondering how she could ever have been so angry with her. 'I'm so happy to see you, and it will really cheer Lucas up to have you here.'

Lucas and me, she thought, as Clemmie gave her mum's shoulder a squeeze, then ran up the stairs to see her brother.

Polly felt Digger's wet nose pushing insistently against her hand.

'Hey, you,' she said, dropping to her knees, then sitting back on her feet so she could look him in the eye and make a fuss of him. 'How did you enjoy your Cambridge mini-break? Did you meet any brainy lady dogs? Did you discuss the great issues of the day with them? Oh, I bet you did. Sausages, treats, biscuits ...'

Digger seemed to be literally jumping for joy, licking her face and prancing back and forth over her knees, his tail whipping against her in his excitement. Polly got him in a clinch and hugged him, kissing the top of his doggy head.

'Well, who knew?' she said. 'Who knew how much I would miss a stinky mutt like you? Come and get a treat and then you can give your toys a good savaging.'

Soon Polly was sitting at the kitchen table with a mug of tea, absentmindedly watching Digger monstering his favourite rubber pheasant and wondering if it was wrong to feel so happy to have both her kids home when it had taken such a trauma to make it happen.

Clemmie returned from upstairs.

'He's going to have another sleep,' she said. 'Best thing he could do. He's had a hell of a shock.'

'And he's got a hell of a hangover,' said Polly. 'Would you like some tea?'

Clemmie nodded and Polly filled the kettle, grabbing another extra-strong English Breakfast teabag for herself. She found she was yawning uncontrollably.

'I'm so sorry,' she said. 'Can't help it. I've been up since 4 a.m., when this all kicked off, and I think I'll have to have a nap soon, but I want to talk to you first.'

'There's no rush,' said Clemmie. 'I'm going to stay here for a while, Mum, to help you look after Lucas.'

'That would be sooo lovely,' said Polly, ready to squeal with delight. 'I know how conscientious you are, my love, with your studying – you're just like your grandfather ...'

And your father, she thought, but decided not to say it.

'It was thoughtless of me to dash off like that after Christmas,' said Clemmie, looking so guilty that Polly's heart clenched. 'I can do my revision here perfectly well. In all honesty, I think I was running away from the whole Dad situation. It's easier not to think about it when I'm away from home. But you need me and Lucas at the moment. We need each other.'

The kettle boiled and Polly was glad of an excuse to turn away, not wanting Clemmie to see the tears in her eyes.

'Thanks, Clem,' she said, sitting back down at the table and pushing the mug towards her daughter. 'It's true, I do need you. I'm feeling pretty messed up, but I'm still sorry I overreacted like that in the restaurant. It just freaked me out so much, the thought that your father would sneak into the house when I was out.'

'It's fine, Mum,' said Clemmie. 'You had every right to freak out. It was outrageous of him. I should never have told him when you were going out, but I felt ... I feel ... so torn.'

She put her face in her hands and shook her head. Polly reached over and stroked her hair, as she'd done when Clemmie was a little girl.

'Hey, honeybun,' she said, 'it's all right. We'll get through it, but I'm furious with him for doing this to you. And to Lucas. He was blind drunk, Clemmie, practically unconscious. That's how he cut himself. He fell over the hall table, smashed the vase and the key bowl, and then fell on top of it all. It could have been much worse, though. There was a huge shard of glass right next to his eye.'

Clemmie winced.

'So you think he's drinking because of Dad,' she said.

Polly nodded.

'I'm sure he is. You know what Lucas is like. He'll rant and rave about some stupid little thing, but when he's really upset about something, he doesn't say a word, he just goes quiet. I can remember when he was little he'd refuse to eat his dinner, then disappear to his bedroom and scoff down a whole packet of biscuits and be sick, and I'd only find out later – sometimes not for days – that it was because some kid at school had called him a thicko, because of his dyslexia. Once he ate most of the ingredients for a Christmas cake.'

Clemmie laughed.

'I remember that,' she said. 'His stomach swelled up like he was pregnant.'

She looked thoughtful for a moment and then spoke again.

'So when it was something that really bothered him,' Clemmie continued, 'Lucas wouldn't talk about it, he'd just clam up and act weirdly?'

Polly nodded, taking a sip of her tea.

'Who does that remind you of?' asked Clemmie.

It took a moment for Polly to understand what she meant, but then it struck her and she felt her eyebrows shoot up.

'Omigod,' she said, 'you're so right. He's exactly like his father. Why didn't I make that connection?'

'You didn't make the connection because you're living in the middle of all this weirdness,' said Clemmie. 'And it must be very hard to think clearly about anything.'

Polly realised she now had her hands over her face – exactly as her daughter had a few moments earlier.

'Look at me,' she said, sitting up and putting her hands in the air. 'I'm doing exactly what you just did. Like mother, like daughter – like father, like son. You're studious like your father, but you act out your emotions like me. Lucas is a bit drifty and vague, like me, but when he's upset, he clams up like Dad. It's all written in our DNA, this behaviour. But even knowing that doesn't make this any easier to take, does it, Clemmie? I don't know where to put myself these days.'

'I'm not going to collude with him again, Mum. I'm so sorry I did, but … I just didn't know how to say no.'

'Was he in a state?'

'No, not at all. That was what made it so hard to argue with him. He called me out of the blue – with the number he was ringing from carefully blocked, of course – completely calm, and made it sound like coming to the house when you were out was a perfectly reasonable thing to want to do. It wasn't until you quizzed me about it that I realised how awful it actually was.'

They both sat in silence for a moment and Polly was relieved when Digger brought his pheasant over to show her.

'Oh, have you killed it good and proper, Diggs?' she said, scratching him behind his ears. 'What a clever dog. Now, go and do it again.'

She threw the pheasant to the other end of the kitchen and Digger ran to catch it, pinning it on the floor with his front paws and pulling at it. They both watched the show, glad of the distraction, until Polly could stand it no more.

She turned to look at her daughter, seeing the tension in Clemmie's lovely young face. A little crease between the eyebrows that hadn't been there before.

How could David have done that to his daughter?

'What do you think it is, Clemmie?' Polly asked her quietly. 'I've driven myself nearly crazy trying to work it out. Have you got any idea?'

Clemmie sighed.

'I just don't know,' she said, 'but last term we did a module on mental health, and from what I learned then I reckon Dad's behaviour is well along the neurotic spectrum, getting towards psychosis. It's his ability to stay so calm while he does something completely crazy – like he did with me, talking about coming here – that freaks me out. Psychotics think they're the normal ones and we're all mad for thinking their behaviour is unusual.'

'He wasn't like this before,' said Polly. 'Was he? I mean, he's always been a bit eccentric, with his tidiness and all that, but nothing you wouldn't expect from a massive brainbox – they're usually a bit quirky, it goes with the territory and all that. But this is a whole new level.'

Clemmie sighed again.

'What he's doing now,' she said, 'is just not reasonable behaviour, and what's so hard for us – especially you – is that it's not possible to process his irrational logic with our rational thought. They're completely incompatible, like trying to play a violin with a banana.'

Polly nodded, smiling.

'That makes sense,' she said, enjoying a moment's light relief. 'I must try that some time.'

'It would somehow be easier to handle if he was ranting and raving like a madman,' Clemmie continued. 'We'd know he was nuts then. But he's so calm and cool about it all, it's scarier.'

Polly felt a strong surge of love for her daughter.

'Thanks for coming home,' she said. 'I feel so much better when I can talk freely about it all – and you're the only person on earth I can do that with.

Clemmie got up and sat on the edge of the kitchen table, facing Polly, and held her mother's hands in her own.

'You can talk to me about it whenever you like,' she said. 'And you know, Mum ... I've come to the conclusion that the best way for you to survive this is to be as selfish as he is. You're always looking after other people – him, me and Lucas, your yoga students, and now you've got Digger too. Do what you damn well like for once. Come and stay with me, if it's too weird being here on your own, or go away somewhere. I can have Digger. Dad told me he'd left you a stash of money in case of emergencies. I think this is an emergency – so spend it.'

FragrantCloud.net

The scent of ... a daughter

Sugar and spice and all things nice is supposed to be the recipe for little girls, but it never fitted my daughter. She was always more likely to be covered in mud from wading into a pond looking for tadpoles.

For her sixth birthday present, when all her friends seemed to want horrible Bratz dolls, Clemmie asked for a telescope.

A science-minded eco-warrior vegetarian, she's a very studious girl. She got straight As in all her exams and is now at Cambridge uni training to be a doctor. So I make no apology for being a superproud mum!

But while she might be ultra serious about her studies, Clemmie has a very loving nature. She's always been very close to her dad – she would go off to the science museum with him on Sunday afternoons as a kid, while her brother would curl up with me on the sofa and watch DVDs of old musicals – but as she's grown up (she's twenty-three) she's started taking more interest in the things I love. Like yoga – and perfume ...

She was never particularly interested in my perfume life before – growing up, it must have just been something boring that Mum did – but it turns out some of her friends at Cambridge follow this blog (hello, if any of you are reading this!) and she's decided there must be something to it after all, which is lovely for me.

She's been to a few launches with me, helped out at a couple of my events and has started poking around in my perfume cupboard, looking for things to steal – always a good sign of a new perfumista in the making.

So I find that something I once saw embroidered on a cushion is turning out to be true: 'A daughter is a little girl who grows up to be a friend'.

As for the smells I associate with her, I was a bit of a swot too, so I love all the stationery aromas: the woody/metallic aroma of pencil shavings, the flat winey smell of ink, the sticky sweetness of a leaking biro and – my favourite – the almost talcum-powder softness of a new exercise book.

For her veggie diet there is the powerful grassiness of leafy vegetables, the caramel of sweet potatoes, carrots and beetroots roasting, and the sulphurous note of brassicas. The nutty starchiness of brown rice and other whole grains. The green tang of fresh herbs, warm ginger. The bite of garlic and the spiciness of coriander seeds, cardamom, turmeric and chili. White flowers for her youthful freshness and lemon for her mental sharpness.

So my scents for a daughter are:

Gold Heart v.4 by Map of the Heart
Botanical Essence No.20 Rose by Liz Earle (it has a carrot seed note in it!)
Wild Green by Bronnley
White Musk by The Body Shop
Neroli by Annick Goutal
Cristalle by Chanel

COMMENTS

JustRos: This is lovely. It brought a tear to my eye!
FragrantCloud: Thanks, Ros x

PerspiringDreams: I'm at Cambridge with Clemmie! She's so lucky to have a mother who blogs – mine still calls it the Interweb and the thing she smells most of is compost heaps because she's always gardening. I love your blog.

FragrantCloud: That's so lovely of you. Will Clemmie know who you are from that name?

PerspiringDreams: Yes! I'm always asking her questions about you! It's driving her mad ha ha. My name is Talitha.

NoseFirst: I love this. I do a perfume blog, perhaps you'd like to have a look?

FragrantCloud: I will – and thanks for subscribing.

LeichhardtLori: Darling Clems. Give her my love. xxx

FragrantCloud: Back at you xxx

Monday, 11 January

Lucas was singing along to the car radio, opening the window to share his performance with pedestrians at a crossing in Finchley, and conducting himself for a moment with his bandaged left hand.

'Ouch,' he said, putting it back on his lap and resuming with the other one.

Polly was delighted he was so cheerful, although the dog joining in on the chorus was making her head throb.

'Pack it in, Digger,' she said over her shoulder.

'Let him sing, Mum,' said Lucas. 'He's an essential part of my soundscape. Now I've knackered my finger, I might have to give up bass and become a vocalist, and I'll need all the help I can get. Come on, Digs, from the top.'

Polly smiled as Lucas howled along with the dog. She felt happier than she had for weeks, so relieved after that conversation with Clemmie. And here she was, as a result of it, on her way to spend some of David's 'emergency' money, taking Lucas and her mother away for a few days to a gorgeous country house hotel near the Suffolk coast, which was famous for its spa. It might not be running away to Zanzibar in rebellion, but it was what she wanted to do.

Lucas was reading about the hotel on his phone. Having chosen what he was going to have for dinner, late-night snacks, later-night snacks and breakfast, he was now looking at the spa section.

'I can have a manicure,' he was saying, 'of my nine good fingers. Would you like a manicure, Digger? It doesn't give a price for paws. Do you think I'll be able to go in the pool, Mum? It'll be so annoying if I can't, I've brought my trunks. But ooh, look, there's a big hot tub – actually there are two, one inside and one outside – so we can sit in hot water with total strangers, sharing toe jam in a hot soup of organic detritus, under the stars. I could go in that with my left hand up in the air.'

His good humour was very infectious. Getting away from home for a bit was exactly what Polly needed – and getting Lucas away from his friends was exactly what he needed.

A crowd of them had come to visit him the day after his accident, arriving with a bag containing a bottle of bourbon and several cans of Coke. Polly had confiscated it in the hall, telling them she wasn't risking another booze-related accident before he was even over this one.

She'd been concerned Lucas might be angry with her for interfering with his social life, but he'd seemed relieved to sink back into mother-and-child mode, with Polly taking his meals up to him on a tray for the first couple of days. He'd even asked for porridge with golden syrup and a copy of *The Beano*, which had been their ritual during childhood illness.

Polly had been happy to indulge him, and she'd been delighted at his enthusiasm over her suggestion of a little holiday with Granny.

She knew Daphne would love it. Lucas was the one person in the world she seemed able to put before herself. She doted on him.

Daphne was waiting for them in the reception area when they arrived. She was sitting on the edge of a sofa, swathed in a black mohair coat, one of her long shins hooked behind the other, her feet off to one side in their shiny black pumps, long manicured fingers holding the coat shut at her neck, as though she were sitting in howling gale. Daphne was always ready for her close-up.

'Granny hardly needs to go to a five-star hotel,' said Lucas, as they waited for the receptionist to press the button to open the sliding glass doors for them. 'She already lives in one.'

Polly laughed. Rockham Park was pretty glam, which was exactly why her mother had chosen it, of course. There had been several perfectly nice developments of a similar kind much nearer Polly's house, but the on-site hairdresser and beauty salon at Rockham had prevailed over anyone else's needs, so Polly was stuck with a fifty-minute drive each way.

'Lucas, my darling!' cried Daphne, standing up and opening her arms for him to run into.

'Hello, Granny,' said Lucas, hugging her and lifting her off her feet, which she loved.

'Oh, put me down, you naughty boy,' she said with her best tinkly laugh.

While everything Daphne did was for show and attention, Polly knew the happiness in her voice this time was genuine and it was touching to witness.

'Let me look at you,' she was saying, cupping his face in her hands and pushing his long shaggy hair back from his forehead. 'I do wish you wouldn't hide your lovely face behind this mop. You have such good bones.'

Polly could read her implication as clearly as if it were subtitled: 'You've got *my* bones.'

'Hello, Mummy,' she said, kissing her mother's cheek and hoping Lucas's presence would distract Daphne's attention from her hair. She'd absentmindedly plaited it that morning, as she often did for yoga, forgetting it was the style that provoked the most criticism about age inappropriateness from her mother. She dropped the offending braid quickly behind her coat collar before Daphne could notice it.

'Hello, Polly, darling,' said Daphne, offering a sculpted cheek. 'Now, come along, or we'll be late for lunch.'

She looked pointedly at Lucas – with her heels on, she was nearly as tall as him – and he got the hint and put out his arm so she could link her own through it.

They didn't so much walk through to the restaurant as process, with Polly and Digger bringing up the rear. Polly felt as though she should be carrying Daphne's train, as her mother graciously nodded and waved to the people they passed.

On arrival at the dining room, the maître d' – as Daphne insisted on referring to him, although Polly had also seen him doing shifts on the front desk and in the ironing room – almost bowed to Daphne.

'Miss Masterson,' he said, in a strong but oddly unidentifiable accent, using Daphne's professional name. No doubt she'd asked him to. 'How radiant you look, madame. I have your special table ready. Please come with me.'

'Isn't he a dear?' said Daphne, after he'd pulled out her chair, helped her sit down and gently pushed it in again, before bustling off to get menus. 'He used to work at the Crillon.'

Polly strongly doubted that he had, but kept that thought to herself. She glanced around the room, waving at a couple of very nice women who'd been at her talk and taking in the usual mix of a few couples, many tables of all women and the odd family group, like their own.

She was pleased to see the man she now thought of as 'Mr Mitsouko' on the far side of the room and raised a hand in greeting to him. She had a present for him in her bag and was glad she'd be able to give it to him directly, rather than having to try to find out who he was at the front desk.

He was sitting with someone Polly thought must be his son. The man had his back to the room, but she could tell by his hair and straight back that he was younger. Mr Mitsouko was laughing heartily at something he was saying, which made Polly smile.

Several of Daphne's friends came over to say hello to them and to be introduced to Lucas, who did his grandmother proud, standing up each time a lady came to their table, shaking hands and being utterly charming.

Lunch was the usual three-course torture, served by waiters in white gloves. Polly normally had an apple and some cheese for her midday meal and it took a big effort to hide her frustration at having to sit through this one, delaying their departure to the hotel, where they would be having another three courses for dinner.

She'd suggested they get a light snack in the café before setting off, but Daphne had been appalled at the idea. Polly had immediately backed down, understanding that her mother wanted to show Lucas off. She was now glad she had, watching him happily chomping his way through his own food then finishing Daphne's after she barely took a mouthful from her plate, chatting away while he fondly teased her.

She'd been a bit concerned when Lucas had ordered a glass of wine to go with his lunch and had tried to talk him out of it – only to have Daphne tell her she was being a spoilsport, they were going on holiday, and had ordered one for herself too.

Then Polly had to rally all her patience anew when Daphne insisted Lucas must be allowed to have cheese after apple crumble and custard. It would now be another fifteen minutes at least before they could set off, even longer with the inevitable loo stop and lipstick reapplication.

She looked around the room to distract herself and noticed that Mr Mitsouko had put his napkin down on the table next to his empty plate and appeared to be feeling around for his stick. The son, or whoever he was, had already left.

She didn't want to miss the opportunity to give him the bottle of Mitsouko she'd brought for him, and thinking it would also be a good idea to check on Digger – who she'd left with his lead looped under a chair leg in the coffee lounge – Polly told Daphne and Lucas she'd be back in a minute and nipped across the room.

'Hello,' she said, just as Mr Mitsouko was getting to his feet. 'I'm Polly, we met at my perfume talk.'

'Of course, my dear,' he said, smiling then taking her hand and patting it. 'How could I have forgotten? It was such an interesting afternoon. Have you come to visit your mother?'

'Yes,' said Polly. 'We're going away for a few days, with my son. That's him at the table with her.'

'Very nice,' said Mr Mitsouko. 'I've been having lunch with my stepson. He's just popped off to check on his dog.'

'Ah,' said Polly, smiling. 'I'm just off to do that as well. I left mine in the coffee lounge.'

'So did Edward,' said the man. 'I wonder if they've made each other's acquaintance.'

Polly laughed.

'I rather hope not,' she said. 'Digger's not the best behaved animal, but, the thing is, er ... actually I don't know your name, I'm so sorry.'

'Edmonstone,' he said, 'Bill Edmonstone.'

'Lovely to meet you, Mr Edmonstone. The thing is ...'

'Oh, do call me Bill,' he said, as a great commotion suddenly erupted in the dining room.

Polly looked over her shoulder to see Digger running round the room, barking enthusiastically, his lead trailing, in hot pursuit of a very elegant lurcher. Bringing up the rear was the man who'd been lunching with Bill Edmonstone, tall and lean like his dog.

'Stop it, Artie,' he was shouting, 'you wretched animal. Come here!'

Horribly aware that Digger, as the pursuer, seemed to be the main aggressor in the situation, Polly judged the dog's speed and launched herself at him on his next circuit of the room. She timed it so well she managed to down both dogs, and lay on the floor panting, holding on to them tightly.

From this inelegant position she looked up at Bill Edmonstone's stepson.

'I'm so sorry,' he was saying, taking hold of his dog by its collar. 'I'm afraid I accidentally released your dog, trying to untangle him from Artie. They'd got all muddled up somehow.'

Polly stared at him and wasn't sure if it was her jaw that dropped or his eyebrows that went shooting up first.

'Chum?' she said, trying to move into a less humiliating position, whilst not letting go of Digger.

'Hippolyta?' he responded.

Polly nodded, getting to her feet with the help of Chum's hand, which he'd extended to her.

'How great to see you!' he said.

'What are you doing here?' asked Polly simultaneously, and they both stopped, laughing.

Bill came over, leaning heavily on his stick.

'So you and Edward know each other?' he said. 'How splendid.'

'We were at St Andrews together,' said the man whom Polly had only ever known as Chum. 'I haven't seen Hippolyta since 1988, when I graduated.'

'Now, that's a lovely name,' said Bill, turning towards her. 'Rarely heard these days. But you go by Polly?'

She nodded.

'I got called Hippo at school,' she said, 'which rather put me off my full name, so I became Polly, but when I got to St Andrews I wanted to be more mysterious, so I went back to Hippolyta. Then I got sick of spelling it out for people. Polly's much easier.'

'Well, Hippo certainly doesn't suit you. Edward doesn't like being called Ted either, do you?'

Polly tried not to stare at Chum. Of course he was older – nearly twenty-five years older, blimey! – but he was still so much the same. The wide mouth that split into such a schoolboy grin, teeth slightly gappy, dimples in each cheek, the slightly bemused expression. Cheekbones even her mother would approve of. Dark brown hair – now silver at the temples – that stood on end when he ran his hand through it, just as he was doing now.

He had opened his mouth to say something else when the dogs kicked off again. Digger made a sudden leap towards the lurcher, who responded with loud barking and jumping backwards and forwards.

'Stop it, Digger!' said Polly, pulling him back with a sharp tug. 'I'm so sorry, he's not very well trained. I think I'll have to get him out of here.'

She could hear other diners starting to mutter and saw the maître d' on his way over, with a pained expression on his face.

'It was lovely to see you, Ch– er, Edward,' she said, turning back to him.

'You can still call me Chum, *Polly*,' he said, emphasising her name as though it had inverted commas around it, his face split by his widest grin. 'All my old friends do. It's just Bill who doesn't like it. He thinks it's immature.'

Polly smiled back at him. He still had that same easygoing charm. The nickname – derived from his preposterous surname, Chillington-Hanley-Maugham – had always suited him. Better than the daft triple barrel. And she'd thought her full family name was a mouthful.

Then she remembered what the more socially ambitious girls at St Andrews used to call the Hon. Edward Cliddington-Hanley-Maugham: 'Pedigree Chum'. Wasn't there a stately home or something?

'And you can call me Hippolyta,' she said. 'It's rather nice to hear it again.'

She was glad to see that the maître d' had been distracted en route by one of the other diners, but before she could say anything else, Digger made another determined tug on the lead and nearly pulled her over.

Chum steadied her arm and, looking down at Digger in embarrassment, Polly noticed the crested signet ring on his left pinkie and had a sudden flashback, remembering that ring from all those years ago.

'He's got plenty of spirit,' said Chum, leaning down to pat Digger, who responded by jumping up at him with an enthusiasm Polly greatly feared was about to lead to some vigorous leg-humping.

'Well, that's one word for it,' said Polly. 'I must remove him before he does anything else appalling. Lovely to see you, Chum. Hope to run into you here again some time.'

She turned and began to walk away with as much dignity as she could muster, dragging Digger behind her. Then she remembered Mr Mitsouko – realising she was always going to think of him as that.

'Bye, Bill,' she said, turning.

'Goodbye, Hippolyta,' he said, raising his stick in a salute. 'Lovely to see you.'

With Digger a dead weight on the end of the lead, desperate not to leave his new canine pal, Polly got just close enough to the table where Daphne and Lucas were drinking their coffee for Lucas to be able to hear her. Daphne had her compact out and was retouching her lipstick, apparently oblivious to it all.

'Lucas,' she hissed, 'I've got to take this bloody dog outside. Can you get Granny moving as quickly as possible? We must get going.'

He nodded and Polly picked Digger up and practically ran out of the dining room, smiling apologetically at the pursed-lipped diners as she passed, although one nice lady thanked them for the show.

Polly headed outside and while Digger ran round and round the monkey puzzle tree in the middle of the lawn, fuelled by lady-dog excitement, she leaned against her car and absent-mindedly lifted her wrist to her nose. She'd sprayed it again the night before with Guy Webber's oddly intriguing The Darkest Hour and, as the surprisingly complex lingering notes hit her nose, she realised she'd forgotten to give Mr Mitsouko his perfume.

She took the small box out of her bag and put it in the glove box. Next time.

Then she found herself wondering if Chum might be there the next time as well. How strange it had been to see him again after so long, and in such an unexpected context. How strange, and how surprisingly lovely.

FragrantCloud.net

The scent of ... university days

I have such happy memories of university that it can throw me into a swoon of nostalgic poignancy just to think about them. I went to St Andrews and it was a particularly romantic place to spend four years: an ancient grey stone town on the east coast of Scotland.

My years at St Andrews were a glorious whirl of parties and balls, crazy nights, handsome beaus and amazing teachers, who inspired my love of studying. And it really adds something to your appreciation of history when you spend your days among buildings dating back to the twelfth century.

But while I adored my university years, there was one thing I had to get used to, which was the large proportion of 'Yahs' – people so called because that was how they said 'Yes'.

For example:

Two young men wearing dark red cords, navy-blue Guernsey sweaters, brown brogues, Barbour jackets and gold signet rings – always on the little finger of the left hand – meet on North Street. They are both nineteen years old.

'Oh, Rupert, hi. Good man.' They shake hands. 'Are you going to the point to point on Saturday?'

'Oh, yah, hi, Tarquin, yah ...'

They were quite something.

I was already familiar with these throwback upper-class types, with their very particular codes of dress, speech and behaviour – and very loud voices – from the streets of Cambridge, where they also proliferate. (My father used to do hilarious imitations of them.)

But being thrust among this caste in my day-to-day life was another thing altogether. En masse they were quite terrifying.

They all seemed to know each other from the very small network of elite public schools they'd attended, and what I couldn't get over was how blisteringly confident they were: a combination of the accident of their privileged births and those bloody schools. What do they do teach them there?

I'd been to a very good selective girls' day school myself, but this secret inner world of the old-school-tie brigade was new to me. As was knowing people with genuine triple-barrelled surnames.

My own double-barrelled name was completely artificial, made up by my mum, who'd wanted to hold on to her professional name - Daphne Masterson - as well as take my father's name.

The Yahs also had very identifiable Christian names, and as an only child, very well skilled at fitting in, I immediately started introducing myself by my birth name of Hippolyta - my father's choice, after a character in an eighteenth-century play he loved - rather than the more manageable Polly (or 'Hippo', as the girls at school had immediately dubbed me).

'Hippolyta Masterson-Mackay' slipped very nicely into that new milieu - far better than Polly Mackay might have done - and I soon found myself part of the main Yah set, which was great, because they did seem to have a much better time than anyone else.

The other notable thing was that a lot of them were incredibly good-looking - that Eddie Redmayne look for the chaps, Cressida Bonas for the girls - which I figured was from a combo of selective breeding (rich men can choose the most beautiful wives) and all the sport they'd played at school.

I fell in love a lot.

Getting to know such a particular – and sometimes downright peculiar – strand of British society was a great adventure, although it made me feel oddly cagey about my own background, which had never given me cause for concern before. I remember I didn't want anyone to know who my mum was. A model didn't seem the right thing for a mother to be.

How silly we can be when we're young.

I think that sense of 'otherness' might be why I haven't stayed in close touch with many of my Yah pals, though I wouldn't have missed my larks with them at St Andrews for anything.

My smells of university are the tarry wax on Barbour jackets and the oily wool of a Guernsey jumper. Fiendish fruity Pimms made in plastic dustbins for summer parties, with sickly sweet lemonade, fragrant with slices of apple and cucumber and handfuls of mint. The wasps were as mad for it as we were.

The chemical residue on breath tainted by the cheapest instant coffee (cappuccinos were still an exotic concept experienced only on European holidays).

Cigarettes – Marlboro specifically – scented everything. We all smoked. While we worked, while we walked, while we sat in the pub, while we danced – and after sex, of course, like we'd seen them do in French films. A lot of the time it felt like we were playing at being grown-ups in that way, which adds further poignancy to the memory of it all. We were babies.

If it wasn't the ciggie smoke, it was ashtrays piled with fag ends. It sounds awful, but that mix of stale smoke with sweat on morning-after clothing has a surprising appeal to me now.

As a counterpoint to all the staleness, there were the salty, biting North Sea breezes, the slightly fishy sweetness of cold damp sand and the sharp grass that grows in it. In summer the manicured grass of quad lawns and night-time bonfires on the beach.

A kiss in the dunes from a dashing young chap with beer and ciggies on his breath, and a faint whiff of horse on his shirt.

My scents for university days are:

Anaïs Anaïs by Cacharel
Lily of the Valley by Yardley
Obsession by Calvin Klein
Sel Marin by Heeley
Wood Sage and Sea Salt Cologne by Jo Malone London
Bas de Soie by Serge Lutens
Cuir de Russie by Chanel
Peau de Bête by Liquides Imaginaires

COMMENTS

MissingDior: I like the sound of those dashing young men smelling of horses! But what did the girls smell like?

> **FragrantCloud:** Anaïs Anaïs mostly. It was everywhere then. I wore Lily of the Valley, which is why I've included it on my list. It was so reasonably priced I could spray it on liberally every day rather than having something more expensive and saving it for special occasions, although I did sometimes steal my mum's perfumes and take them back with me!

LuxuryGal: St Andrews is so beautiful! You were so lucky to go there. I love Scotland. Are you a golfer?

> **FragrantCloud:** I love Scotland too, but I'm not a golfer. Too many other fun things to do up there.

Agatha F: What did you study? I studied geography.

FragrantCloud: History. A long way from perfume, I know, but the historical context of perfumes is very interesting.

ClemmieMedic: A kiss on the beach, eh? You'll have to tell me more!

FragrantCloud: Ha, ha, only if you'll tell me some of your uni stories! Or maybe better not ...

PerspiringDreams: Cambridge certainly smells a lot nicer since Clemmie has started bringing back samples from you! Thanks so much xxx

FragrantCloud: You are very welcome, Talitha. I've got some new things for you x

EastLondonNostrils: I bet it was bloody freezing. I'm surprised you could smell anything.

FragrantCloud: Guy, is this you? I've just put this together ...

Tuesday, 19 January

Polly smelled him before she saw him. As she walked into the elegant panelled function room of Connolly's department store, with the esteemed French perfumer she was interviewing for a special event, her head snapped round to scan the audience.

Somebody there was wearing the Great Eastern Fragrance Company's Half Past Eight. There was no mistaking that burned-lemon-peel accord. As her eyes scoured the room, she saw Guy Webber's face, grinning behind his thick black beard, clearly fully aware of what had caught her attention. He looked like a cheeky ten-year-old, waggling the fingers of one hand in greeting, his thick black eyebrows raised in mock innocence.

Polly gave him a hard stare. He knew exactly what a faux pas it was to wear a pungent scent by another house to a fragrance event – especially one featuring an eminent nose – and he'd done it anyway. In fact, he'd almost certainly done it deliberately, she thought, trying to gather her thoughts as she sat down opposite Lucien Lechêne, hoping Guy's very particular fragrance wasn't going to put her off her stride.

She raised her left wrist to her nostrils reflexively, trying to ground herself back in the task at hand via Monsieur Lechêne's most famous creation. She saw the perfumer notice and smile at her. But the moment Polly put her wrist down, Half Past Eight filled her nose and her consciousness once again.

Damn Guy Webber and his tricky antics! He'd cancelled the appointment for her to interview him for the blog and had then sidestepped all her efforts to organise another one, via text and email, with lame excuses like needing to go to the dentist.

It had been so enervating she'd been torn between thinking he could stuff it and just turning up unannounced at the shop. She thought he was being very unprofessional, not to mention downright rude, but the two perfumes of his she'd smelled were so interesting she desperately wanted to find out more about them and the rest of the range – and him. She couldn't help herself.

She lifted her wrist again.

'One of mine?' asked Lucien Lechêne, in his strong French accent, and Polly nodded, offering her arm to him. He took her hand very delicately in his, leaning his nose towards her skin, and smiled again. 'Ah, La Flâneuse, an excellent choice, thank you. I caught it before and I thought it was you, but now I can smell something else very strong in this room. Is this why you are referring to your wrist?'

'Yes,' said Polly, sighing.

Lucien pursed his lips.

'So we are here to talk about my two new fragrances with your readers, who have paid to come this event and have made the effort to come out on a wet winter night, and this odour ...' – he pronounced it in the French manner *odeur*, which made it sound very similar to ordure – '... while quite interesting, in its way, is very distracting. It is distracting my trained nose, so I think it will be very hard for our guests to be able to appreciate the *nuances* of my work, *non*?'

'I totally agree,' said Polly, her heart sinking. Because she knew the person who had so outrageously hijacked the air with his own perfume – and strongly suspected he'd done it solely to get a rise from her, and succeeded – it made her feel somehow responsible.

'I think I can fix it,' she said decisively. 'Give me a moment.'

She got up from the raised dais where they were going to do the interview and walked over to where Guy was sitting, looking even more amused than before.

'Hello, Guy,' she said brightly. 'Can I have a word? Outside?'

'Of course,' he said. 'Lead on.'

Polly turned and walked out of the door of the function room, holding it open behind her to be sure Guy was following. By the time he came through it and joined her on the landing of the store's side staircase he was shaking with laughter.

'It's not funny, Guy,' said Polly. 'The whole room reeks of Half Past Eight. How am I supposed to think about Lucien Lechêne's sophisticated *nuances* with your perfume punching me in the nose? Not forgetting my readers, who have paid to come to this event – and Connolly's, who have put it on, organised champagne and canapés and all that, done the promotion and sold the tickets and paid me to do the interview. You've put me in a very difficult position.'

Guy was leaning against the wall laughing.

'I'm sorry, Polly,' he said, 'but I just couldn't resist. It was pure vain curiosity. I wanted to see if you'd even notice and then if you'd recognise it.'

'How could I not bloody notice? Did *you* not notice that everyone in the room was looking at you as the clear source of the all-pervading aroma? Which most of them would have known was most certainly not one of Monsieur Lechêne's offerings? He's known for his subtlety, a concept I'm beginning to think is entirely lost on you.'

'I'm sorry, Polly,' said Guy, looking as crestfallen as he had previously looked mischievous. 'I get carried away sometimes. It seemed like a brilliant plan when I was on my own in the shop.'

'Oh, the shop,' said Polly, feeling increasingly irritated. 'The shop you don't seem to want me to write about – although I think you are a regular commenter on my blog. Is EastLondonNostrils you?'

He raised his eyebrows in faux innocence again, then grinned. The naughty schoolboy again. It infuriated Polly.

'What's with you, Guy?' she said. 'You comment on every blog I post, then when you have a chance to get your business featured on it, you make up excuses on a level with "The dog ate my homework", if you even return my calls, and then you turn up here smelling like you've poured a bottle of your *parfum* over your own head to see if I notice.'

'I do want you to write about the shop,' said Guy, but when I'm ready.'

'Well, that's good, because despite all this, I do want to interview you, but right now I'm going to have to ask you to leave this event. Lucien is not happy and I can't think about his perfumes with yours staging an armed occupation of my olfactory bulb. I'll refund your ticket myself.'

'That's fine,' said Guy. 'Please don't – and let me make it up to you. Are you rushing off afterwards? Could I buy you a drink to apologise? Or perhaps you're having dinner with Lucien ...'

'No,' said Polly, thinking that all she had to do after the event was go back to an empty house. Lucas had left for

Brighton that morning. She was dreading going home. 'Yes, a drink would be nice. I've got your number, I'll ring you when we finish.'

'Great,' said Guy. 'I'll await your call.'

He started off down the stairs and Polly was about to go back into the event when something occurred to her.

'Guy,' she called after him, her voice echoing down the stairwell, 'tell me one thing before you go – how did you get the sillage of your fragrance to be quite so pervasive?'

On the landing below, Guy's face cracked into a smile again.

'Smoked it,' he said, and headed off.

When she walked back into the function room, the windows were open and Connolly's head of PR and her team were waving their clipboards, trying to send Guy's smell out and bring some fresh air in.

Lucien was charming the crowd, apologising for the cold and promising them it would be worth it – which wasn't hard for him to do with his classic French perfumer look. They all seemed to have that dark floppy hair and sensuous mouth thing going on, and it never failed to amaze Polly what a uniform they adopted: the perfectly cut dark suit, the immaculately crisp white shirt worn unbuttoned just enough to reveal a hint of tanned chest.

Polly was convinced that for many of her readers the eye-candy factor of the perfumers was as big a part of the appeal of these events as the fragrances. Most of these men were classic Euro playboys, but Lucien was more interesting-looking than many, with an aquiline nose that added extra intrigue, and keen dark eyes brooding above it.

As she sat down opposite him, one of the Connolly's PR team came in with some cups of ground coffee, which she handed to members of the audience to smell and pass on.

'I've got them sniffing coffee, to clear their noses,' said Lucien quietly to Polly, as she tapped her iPad and scrolled down her list of questions. 'It doesn't work, it's just another strong smell, but they think it will, so this is the same thing, *non*?'

Polly smiled at him. She still felt mortified about what had happened, but her decisive action with Guy had clearly impressed Lucien, who turned out to be the most amenable interview subject, sharing wonderful stories of his years in the business, and describing his creative process, from the very first briefing for a new perfume, in fascinating detail.

It was a great relief for Polly, as Lucien had a reputation for being tricky, even when events were designed solely to promote his own brand, as opposed to the many leading design houses he also created fragrances for.

He was even rumoured to have created the signature smell of a leading brand of fabric conditioner, which had provided the funds to start his own house, but Polly had been warned by a French perfume blogger she'd met online not to mention that in any circs.

So she kept the focus entirely on his exquisite – and eye-wateringly expensive – eponymous range, raving with all sincerity over the two new ones that were being introduced this evening. Lucien's ultra-sophisticated French style was her very favourite kind of scent. He was known as the King of Chypre, which was – as Guy had so astutely worked out – her favourite perfume 'family'.

The interview was followed by questions from the audience and enthusiastic applause, but after they'd all left – heading down to the perfume hall to make use of the discount cards they'd been given for Lucien's range – he didn't seem too keen to rush off.

He was filling Polly in on the latest gossip in the perfume world – an eminent nose was leaving his role at one of the world's leading luxury brands to work exclusively on his own line, which Estée Lauder had just bought – when his assistant came over to remind him he had a dinner booking.

'Polly,' he said, putting his hand gently on her upper arm, 'would you care to join me? I would love to continue this conversation with you over dinner. It's such a pleasure for me to talk to someone who is as passionate about chypre as I am.'

Polly hesitated. Did she want to join him? One of the leading perfumers of the world, who knew everybody in the industry and was very entertaining in his own right, not to mention as suave as only a Parisian perfumer could be? Of course she wanted to have dinner with him – but she'd agreed to meet Guy, dammit.

Lucien noticed her pause.

'You have plans already?' he asked.

Polly took a breath.

'Well, I didn't, and I would love to have dinner with you, Lucien, but I agreed to have a drink with the guy we had to throw out ... he's a new perfumer. I felt sorry for him. He has quite an interesting shop in the East End.'

'And he's trying to impress you?'

'I think so,' said Polly, feeling embarrassed. 'He's a bit of a character and I'm quite interested to know his story.'

'Are all his fragrances so ...' Lucien rotated one elegant hand in the air and pursed his full lips as he sought the right word, 'so impactful?'

Polly laughed.

'Well, I've only smelled two so far, but yes, judging by the shop – which I could smell right down the street – he likes his creations to make a big impression.'

Lucien looked dubious.

'Do you?' he asked quietly.

'Not normally,' she said. 'I adore your style, as you know, but there's something wacky about the guy that quite intrigues me.'

'Well, why don't you ask him to join us?' said Lucien.

'Really?' said Polly, surprised he'd consider sharing her attention with another perfumer, even one just starting out.

'For coffee,' he added, raising one eyebrow and smiling.

Polly laughed.

'Great,' she said. 'I'll text him.'

She felt mean tapping out the words. She wouldn't normally drop someone like that after making an arrangement, but the chance of dinner with Lucien was an opportunity too special to turn down – and after what Guy had done, arriving at the event deliberately reeking of his own perfume, she felt he deserved a taste of his own medicine.

And if he wasn't too miffed to accept, the chance even just to have coffee with the great nose would be a marvellous opportunity for him too. Any wannabe perfumer would leap at the chance to sit at a table with Lucien Lechêne. It was like offering a young musician a gig hanging out with Mick Jagger, or an aspiring tennis player a quick knockabout with Roger Federer.

But from her experience of the inflated yet fragile egos of even the average perfumer, she wondered whether the snub of 'just for coffee' would be too much for him. It was his choice, she decided, and tapped 'Send'.

> Hi Guy really sorry but it seems there is a dinner organised. Lucien has suggested you join us for coffee? Polly

To her surprise, his reply came immediately.

> Great. Let me know where and when. Guy

Polly had assumed that the Connolly's PR head and Lucien's team would be coming for dinner too, but when they got down to the shiny black car waiting outside the store everyone else seemed to melt away and it was just Lucien and Polly who slid onto the sleek leather seats.

Lucien was clearly well known at his chosen venue, Scott's, and they were led to a table for two in an intimate corner. Polly wondered momentarily where Guy would sit when he arrived for coffee, but then put it out of her mind, relishing the faultless service, flattering lighting and starched tablecloths that came with this ultra-sophisticated end of London's restaurant spectrum. Treats that she'd never experienced until she became involved in the perfume world.

Her social life for years had been based round lively dinners in friends' kitchens, and big afternoon parties with everyone's kids running around. Although once their children were old enough to be left on their own, she and David had started going out to the theatre a couple of times a month, eating beforehand at the interesting new casual places in Soho, which he seemed to prefer to bigger parties. The last couple of years she'd increasingly found herself going to those on her own.

When she first started her blog, inspired only by wanting to explore and share her lifelong fascination with perfume, she'd had no idea it would lead her into such a glamorous new world – and since her social life with David had become so quiet, it was one of the things she most loved about it.

As the waiter snapped open her napkin and laid it across her lap, offering her the menu with a slight bow, and the sommelier popped the cork on the bottle of Veuve Clicquot that Lucien had ordered, Polly sent up a little prayer of thanks. Amid the inexplicable weirdness David was inflicting upon her, the thrilling world of perfume felt like a glorious safe haven, and she didn't know how she would have coped without the distraction.

Lucien was very entertaining company, regaling her with stories about the great names in the perfume world, which he could never have shared in public, and adding background to some of the anecdotes he'd told at the Connolly's event, some of it so salacious Polly's eyebrows were nearly at her hairline.

'So, my dear FragrantCloud,' said Lucien, after finishing an account of how one nose had bribed a lab technician to sabotage the work of a younger rival. 'Let us raise a toast to the civilised world of international perfume.'

Polly clinked her glass against his, giggling, as the waiter appeared at their table.

'Would you like coffee, madame?' he asked Polly, but before she could answer, Lucien jumped in.

'I don't think we want coffee, do we, Polly?' he said, his eyes glinting as he raised his wine glass again and drained it. He turned back to the waiter. 'I think we would like to see your list for some armagnac.'

Polly felt a bit uncomfortable. She hadn't given Guy a thought during the whole of dinner, she'd been having too good a time. But if they weren't having coffee, how was she going to make good on her earlier offer?

Guy had behaved very badly, but she couldn't just

abandon him – he was probably sitting somewhere waiting for her text. But how could she bring it up with Lucien? Especially as he had invited her to dinner and was clearly going to be paying for it.

She found it hard to concentrate on what Lucien was saying after that, wondering if she should mention Guy – but her attention snapped back when Lucien took hold of her left hand.

'So you are married, Miss Polly,' he said, tracing the top of her wedding ring with his forefinger.

Polly felt very uncomfortable with the way Lucien was holding her hand, especially as his finger movement developed gradually into whole-hand stroking, his fingers creeping up towards her wrist as he smiled at her. That was awkward, but almost worse was the question about being married, because that would lead inexorably to the subject of her husband, which was to be avoided at all costs.

Slowly and, she hoped, subtly, she pulled her hand away, sitting back in her seat and touching her hair, hoping to give the impression that was why she'd moved it.

'Yes, I've been married for twenty-four years,' she said. 'We have two children. Our daughter's doing Medicine at Cambridge and our son has just started at uni too, he's doing Music—'

'So you have an empty nest,' said Lucien, cutting her off. 'And does your husband not mind you having dinner à deux with another man?'

Polly froze. Her husband clearly didn't give a damn what she did, as long as he didn't have to see her doing it. She forced her brain into overdrive, not wanting to be drawn any further into a discussion of David, trying to think of an answer that would simply close the subject down.

'He's away at the moment,' she said quickly – too quickly. 'He's an academic and he sometimes has to go on long research trips. Sometimes I go with him, but this time I didn't.'

'So with your babies gone and your husband away, you are all alone,' said Lucien. 'You must get very lonely, in the house on your own ...'

His hand reached out and covered hers again. Then he lifted it and brought the inside of her wrist up to his nose. She could feel his warm breath as he smelled it, his eyes closed in concentration. He's only smelling his own perfume, Polly told herself, but then the sniffing became his lips, gently nibbling against her pulse point and starting to progress along her arm.

She panicked, snatching her hand away.

'I really must go to the loo,' she said, standing up and staggering slightly, a combination of the suddenness of her move, her high heels, and the champagne, wine and brandy she'd consumed in quick succession. She steadied herself, grabbed her handbag and headed determinedly towards the lobby.

Down in the ladies' loo, she leaned her forehead against the tiled wall, feeling slightly dizzy, mildly sick and very fuzzy-minded. Part of her wanted to make a run for it, up the stairs, out of the door and into the first passing taxi, but what would she do about her coat? Lucien had the bloody cloakroom ticket; she'd noticed him pocket it. And wasn't that an embarrassing overreaction?

He hadn't actually lunged at her – and after all, he was French; they had different ideas about that kind of thing. If she'd been a chic Parisienne, she probably would have returned the gesture with some expert footsie action under the table, taking Lucien's advances as nothing more than a compliment to her womanhood.

He probably didn't mean anything more than that, Polly told herself. She was just a frumpy North London housewife who didn't understand the ways of the sophisticated world into which she'd accidentally propelled herself by writing about perfume.

And then, on top of all that, David came marching into her head. David as he used to be, in his brown brogue boots, worn-in jeans and chunky fisherman's jumper. Reading the Sunday papers at the kitchen table, his heavy tortoiseshell glasses perched on his nose, his chin stubbly, grabbing her hand as she walked past with a big basket of laundry and pulling her onto his knee. Holding her tight and kissing her passionately there in the kitchen, until Lucas had come in and made loud retching noises.

David was such a good kisser.

Polly felt a sob escape her. The alcohol had loosened her inhibitions, and all the thoughts about David she'd worked so hard to keep locked away – all the wonderful things about him which she missed so badly – came rushing into her head.

David coming home with flowers because it was the anniversary of the day they'd met. David building tree houses for the kids, one in each tree in their small London garden. David's strong hands wielding the hammer, his chunky watch and hairy arms. David intently absorbed in choosing the music to play while they made Sunday lunch together. David in bed, broad shoulders and flat stomach, kept in shape at the university gym. David pressing against her, his lips nuzzling her neck as his hands explored her body.

Polly sobbed again and knew she was on the brink of a full crying jag. She couldn't let it happen. Not in Scott's, with Lucien Lechêne waiting for her upstairs.

She had to pull herself together. However embarrassing she might find his behaviour, she couldn't make a scene with one of the world's most admired noses in one of London's chicest restaurants. Apart from the general shame, it would disastrously compromise her reputation in the rarefied milieu that was keeping her together amidst all the domestic madness.

She needed her perfume life to survive her real one. She couldn't risk anything that might damage it.

Standing up straight, she closed her eyes and did some slow breathing until she felt more clear-headed, then checked the extent of the mascara damage in the mirror over the sink and reapplied her lip balm. She smoothed down her hair and picked up her bag.

Then, just as she was about to open the door to go back upstairs, she had an idea. She pulled out her phone and quickly tapped out a text to Guy.

We're in Scott's if you're still around. Come soon! Polly x

When she got back to the table Lucien was cradling a fresh balloon of armagnac and didn't look the slightest bit perturbed. Was he one of those men who just got off on the chase, she wondered, who didn't really want to get it on? Or was he one of those who hit on every woman he met, in a kind of elephant-gun approach? And weren't there some operators who got a particular thrill out of seducing married women?

Who knew? She'd heard all kinds of stories about the antics of men from her yoga girls over the years. Something about the 'sacred space' of the studio seemed to make people open up about such personal stuff.

Whatever was going on, she was going to make this be all right, she told herself, sitting down at the table and picking up her own glass of brandy. Hopefully Guy would show up. If not, she'd make enough conversation to move on from the previous oddness, then say she had to get home to her dog.

She raised her glass and Lucien smiled in that lazy, confident way he had. He was a very good-looking man, she had to admit, and so elegant, with gold cufflinks in the turned-back cuffs of his perfect white shirt. It wasn't like he was some hideous old sleaze. Then she glanced at the front of that shirt and noticed that it seemed to be open a couple of buttons lower than before she'd gone to the loo. She could clearly see the curve of his pectoral mound.

Polly just stopped herself laughing out loud. It was as unsubtle as those dresses film stars sometimes wore on the red carpet, where you could see the line of their underboob.

He leaned forward, putting his forearms on the table and treating Polly to an even less obstructed view of his muscular brown chest, clearly about to say something, when their waiter appeared again – with Guy in tow.

'This gentleman is asking for you, Monsieur Lechêne,' he said.

Polly couldn't believe how quickly Guy had got there, and felt as though the cavalry had arrived. She was so grateful to have the tension broken she had to stop herself from springing to her feet and throwing her arms around him.

She glanced at Lucien, whose brows had knitted together into a deep frown.

'Oh good,' said Guy, 'I see we've already segued from coffee to brandy. I'll have what he's having.'

He clapped the waiter on the back and pulled a chair over from the neighbouring table, which had just been vacated.

He sat down and put his right hand out towards Lucien, who took it with very little enthusiasm. Strong wafts of Half Past Eight were still coming off Guy. Perhaps Lucien didn't want to get tainted by it, Polly thought.

'Guy Webber's the name,' he said. 'I'm so sorry about arriving at your event wearing my own fragrance before. It was really bad form. I just wanted to impress Polly and I got carried away.'

Lucien said nothing, his only response being to tilt his head backwards, quickly raising and lowering his eyebrows in dismissal. A very clear Gallic expression of 'whatever'. Polly was glad the waiter returned at that moment with Guy's drink.

'Well, it was a shame you missed the interview,' she said. 'Lucien told us the best stories, and I think you would have particularly appreciated hearing about his creative process.'

'Yes, you might have learned something,' said Lucien, then swilled his brandy balloon and buried his nose in it, breathing deeply.

Guy glanced over at Polly and pulled an 'oops' face. She shook her head at him. It was like being in primary school with him around.

Lucien raised his eyes, his nose still in the glass.

'Do you like armagnac?' he asked Guy.

Guy nodded. 'Very much. My father drinks it.'

One point Webber, thought Polly.

'Perhaps you would like to tell us what you get from this one?' said Lucien. 'It's a Baron de Sigognac XO.'

Guy swirled his glass and stuck his nose inside it as Lucien had done. He moved the glass away and then went back down for another sniff.

'Christmas-cake spiced fruits, vanilla – I'd even say custard – with hints of rose and violet,' he said.

Lucien looked back at him steadily and nodded.

'Hmm,' he said. 'You're quite good. For an Englishman. Perhaps you'd like to smell my new fragrances? Seeing as how you missed out earlier.'

'I'd love that,' said Guy, apparently unperturbed by Lucien's patronising tone.

'Polly, do you mind opening your bottles?' asked Lucien. 'I will make sure you get fresh ones.'

Polly pulled two boxes out of the heavyweight carrier bag Lucien's PA had given her as they'd left the event. She took off the cellophane and the outer sleeves with Lucien's name on them in classic black engraver's type, then opened the shiny black boxes within, to reveal the chunky crystal bottles. Their gold tops were in the shape of acorns: a play on his name, which meant 'oak' in French, and also a reference to oakmoss, one of the classic ingredients of his signature chypre style.

Guy watched the process with the concentration of a cat eyeballing its intended prey, as Lucien pulled some blotters out of his jacket pocket.

'Do you always have those in there?' asked Polly.

'Of course,' he said, picking out three and pushing one between each lower knuckle of the fingers of his left hand, holding them away from the table and spraying them with one of the perfume bottles.

With great ceremony he then waved the blotters in the air to disperse the alcohol, and handed one by its unsprayed tip to Polly, then another to Guy.

Polly brought hers slowly up to her nose and closed her eyes, letting the magic of Lucien's artistry unfold. It was a classic chypre, exactly what Lucien was known for, and she adored it.

She knew the ingredients from the interview, but what came crowding into her mind now were her own associations with the smell – Hermès Kelly bags, camel coats, Catherine Deneuve smoking a cigarette in a Paris café, a perfect French manicure, parquet floors, a lazy Persian cat ... gorgeous.

Without thinking, she opened her eyes, found the bottle and sprayed it liberally onto her left inner arm, waiting for a moment and then bringing it up to her nose to see how it smelled on her skin.

She glanced at Lucien to see him smiling at her, his lids half-closed. He was a very attractive man, she thought, there was no denying it. If she'd been single like many of her yoga girls, she would have felt much less confused about him. He was, as Shirlee would have said, 'a hot patoota'. Just not for her.

Meanwhile, Guy was in the zone, eyes closed, a beatific expression on his face as he slowly fanned the blotter back and forth under his nose, taking alternately one long then one shorter breath in. Polly and Lucien watched him as he opened his eyes.

'Another classic for the history books, Monsieur Lechêne,' he said. 'Superb.'

'Thank you,' said Lucien very seriously. 'And what do you get?'

'Your classic chypre base at the heart, of course,' said Guy. 'Oakmoss, patchouli, bergamot, labdanum, in the balance you constantly shift and nuance like a conductor, but dancing on top of that tonka, a hint of leather and a cheeky reference to Miss Dior, with some carnation. I think there will be ambergris and sandalwood in the dry-down, and I can't wait to see how it smells in the middle of the night.'

He picked the bottle up from the table and, pulling his shirt forward, liberally sprayed his chest with it, squirting a bit down his back for good measure.

Lucien laughed. 'But what if you like the second one better?' he asked.

'I'll be going back to Connolly's to buy them both tomorrow,' said Guy, 'so I can try each of them again and again. How did I do with my guesswork?'

Lucien's eyes narrowed.

'You did very well,' he said. 'Especially given you had to identify my work over the still somewhat overbearing presence of your own *mélange*. Let us try the second one.'

He went through the same ritual with the blotters, then Polly and Guy closed their eyes and inhaled.

Again Polly remembered all the notes in this perfume from the event earlier, and enjoyed waiting for each one to register in the olfactory bulb in the front of her brain, while her imagination did its own thing. The neroli, jasmine and sandalwood transported her to a summer night in the south of France, wearing a crisp white shirt – this was a much fresher chypre than the first one. Then she remembered she'd sprayed this one on her wrist during the event earlier and lifted it to her nose to see how it had developed since then. Suddenly, out of nowhere: David.

Her eyes snapped open. Coal tar?

'Has this got guaiac wood in it?' she asked Lucien, not caring if it interfered with his testing of Guy.

Lucien smiled broadly.

'Yes,' he said, 'but very, very deep inside, it's a basenote, as you would know. Your nose is very good, Polly.'

Guy grasped her wrist and brought it to his nose. 'It's just under the bergamot and before the honeysuckle,' he said, opening his eyes. 'I do like this one more, actually. It seems simpler than the other one, but it's actually more complicated.'

Lucien regarded him coolly, pushing out his lips.

'Impressive,' he said. 'You have a nose, Mr ... what was it again?'

'Webber,' said Guy. 'Guy Webber. But my house is called the Great Eastern Fragrance Company. It's based in the East End.'

'You are very good – for a beginner – Mr Webber. If I am ever in that part of London, I will come and see you. I would like to smell your work – just not in the strength in which we experienced it this evening.'

They all laughed, and without missing a beat, Guy pulled a business card out of his pocket and handed it to Lucien.

'It would be a great honour, sir,' he said.

Lucien took the card and put it in his pocket, then looked at his watch, which Polly had already noticed was a Baume et Mercier. She'd come to know about such things since she'd been doing the blog.

'Oof,' he said. 'It is late, and tomorrow I have to see Harrods and Selfridges and explain to them why I gave the exclusive for the new perfumes to Connolly's, and why they should keep selling the rest of my range ... It's not all smelling beautiful things, what I do. I must go. You can both stay and have another drink if you want to. It's all on my account.'

He stood up and shook Guy's hand and then, inserting himself firmly between Guy and Polly, he put his arms around her in a tighter clinch than was normal for a social farewell kiss.

He smelled heavenly. Associations crowded into Polly's mind, which she did her best to bat away.

It got more difficult to do as he whispered very quietly into her ear.

'I'm tired of this,' he said, 'but I'm not really so tired. I am staying at Claridges. It's not far. Room 212.'

He paused to fish the cloakroom ticket out of his jacket

pocket, threw it on the table, gave her one last lingering look and left.

Polly immediately sat down again. She really needed to finish her brandy. Lucien's closeness had gone through her like a lightning bolt, making her feel something she'd almost forgotten: extreme arousal. There was no denying it. She experienced a frisson remembering his smell and what he'd said, and took a big swig from her glass.

What was happening to her?

'Well, that was intense,' said Guy, wafting the scent up to his face from his shirt. 'Mmm, it gets even better as it warms up. God, he's clever. How annoying.'

'Didn't you like him?' asked Polly.

'It's not a matter of liking, it's more that I sensed he might challenge me to a duel at any moment. I don't think he appreciated my turning up when I did ... I have a feeling that was your doing and he wasn't expecting me.'

Polly giggled, she couldn't help it.

'I'm glad you did,' she said.

'Was he hitting on you?' asked Guy.

'Of course not,' lied Polly. 'He knows I'm married.'

Guy laughed again. 'He's French. That just makes it all the more appealing. *Belle de Jour* and all that caper.'

'He's just intense,' said Polly, now desperate to change the subject. 'But I am glad you came, I felt bad letting you down earlier. Tell me, though: however did you get here so quickly?'

'I was in the pub round the corner,' Guy said blithely.

'That was a lucky coincidence,' said Polly.

'Nothing coincidental about it,' said Guy, draining his glass. 'Shall we have one more? I'll pay for it. I'm not jumping on Lucy Lechêne's bill, despite his kind offer.'

'OK,' said Polly, thinking the night had been so weird already she might as well keep going. And she welcomed anything that would put off the moment of opening the door to her house, to be greeted only by Digger, who she hoped wasn't already howling. He'd accepted being left at home for a few hours now, but it was always at the back of her mind. So even if she had fancied a trip to Claridges, she couldn't have left Digger.

Then what Guy had said just before sank in. The booze had given her brain-lag.

'What do you mean it was no coincidence you were round the corner?' she asked him.

'I followed you from Connolly's. I found the exit with the limo waiting outside it and sat in a cab behind it.'

Polly thought back.

'I did see a cab,' she said.

Guy grinned at her, then turned round to attract the waiter's attention.

'Why on earth did you do that?' she asked him.

'I thought he might try to stiff me, and if he did, I was going to swoop on you when you left the restaurant.'

'Oh, that's not at all creepy and weird, Guy,' said Polly, suddenly uneasy. It was very creepy and very weird, and it was the last thing she needed after Lucien's carry-on. First a seducer and now a stalker. Between them and a psycho husband, she really knew how to attract the crazies.

In that moment, exhaustion overtook her and the prospect of Digger's uncomplicated welcome was suddenly very appealing. It was probably a night for him to have upstairs privileges again. She really didn't want to be on her own.

'I'm really tired, Guy,' she said as the waiter appeared at the table. 'I won't have another armagnac after all. It's surprisingly enervating doing those interviews. I'm going home.'

'OK,' said Guy, and turned to the waiter. 'Can you bring over another armagnac and I'll come back for it after I've put my friend in a taxi?'

Guy waited while the doorman hailed her a cab, then walked her over to it. She told the driver she wanted to go to Archway, not saying the full address because she didn't want Guy to hear it. That stalkerish behaviour had made her wary.

Then she got in and looked out at him through the open door.

'Goodnight, Guy,' she said. 'It was fun. Let's get that interview in the diary, yeah?'

He nodded, but didn't shut the cab door immediately. Fishing in his jacket's inside pocket, he pulled out a small sample vial and a blotter.

'This is why I've been putting off seeing you,' he said, handing them to her. 'I wanted to finish this first. It's for you.'

She looked down at the tiny bottle of golden liquid as he slammed the taxi door shut and they drove away. Polly turned on the cab's inside light to examine the vial more closely and saw a round sticker on the side with two letters written on it: 'PM'.

She assumed it was his name for the new scent. It fitted in perfectly with his time-of-day theme – but it also happened to be her initials and he'd said the perfume was for her. Was that what he'd meant? Had he named it after her?

The small bottle had a spray closure, so she picked up the blotter, gave it a good wetting and waited for the alcohol to evaporate, then brought it up to her nose and breathed in.

She smelled it again. And again.

It was a chypre and it was even better than either of Lucien's. It was a masterpiece.

Wednesday, 20 January

'*Namaste*,' said Polly, smiling, as everyone in the class put their hands in prayer position and bowed, repeating it back to her.

After a night as strange and intense as the one she'd just experienced – which had also left her with a stonking hangover – this class had been exactly what she needed, making her feel grounded back in reality. Sometimes she thought she should be paying her pupils rather than the other way round.

Everyone was gathering up their bits and pieces and heading off, but Shirlee went straight to the kitchen for what had become their regular post-yoga breakfast. Since she'd come to her aid with Lucas, Polly had begun to see Shirlee very much as a friend and really looked forward to their jolly morning hangouts. Sometimes they invited other people from the group, which Shirlee had dubbed the 'yogi bears', but often it was just the two of them, with Maxine on the three mornings a week she now came to the class.

Polly smiled as she heard the kettle go on and cupboard doors being opened and banged shut. If anyone else had been so presumptuous in her house, she would have been outraged, but Polly found Shirlee's total lack of regard for other people's personal space lovable. Living as she was, creeping around the truth, being with someone who said and did whatever she liked was a great comfort.

One by one everyone else left, until it was just Maxine with her in the yoga studio, helping put the belts and blankets away. Suddenly super loud music boomed out of the speakers, making them both jump. Chaka Khan at ten past ten on a Wednesday morning, was a bit surprising. The volume went down and they could hear Shirlee laughing in the kitchen.

'Sorry, guys,' she yelled. 'Turned the wrong knob there.'

Polly and Maxine looked at each other and laughed.

'What is she like?' said Maxine.

'Like no other,' said Polly. 'If it was anyone else, I'd be appalled, but somehow when it's Shirlee, I don't mind.'

'She's a life force,' said Maxine. 'Not everybody gets her, though, and I'm glad you do. I've known her a long time, how about you?'

Polly thought about it.

'Well, she's been coming to my classes for a couple of years, but I've only got to know her properly recently. Since that first breakfast on Jan 1. She's become a friend now, although we don't see each other much outside this room. How did you meet her?'

Maxine's eyes flicked away for a moment and then back to Polly's face.

'I met her professionally, too,' she said.

'Oh,' said Polly as they walked into the kitchen together. 'What do you do?'

'She's a shrink,' said Shirlee with glee. 'She put my head back together twenty years ago and I haven't let her out of my sight since, in case it falls to bits again.'

Polly smiled at Maxine, understanding her earlier reticence.

'What kind of therapy do you do?' she asked. 'If that's not an infringement of your professional discretion?'

'I'll tell you what worked for me,' said Shirlee, waving a wooden spatula in the air. She had two of Polly's frying pans on the stovetop. 'This!'

She turned and whacked the spatula down hard and repeatedly onto the cushion on one of the kitchen chairs. Dust flew everywhere and Polly expected feathers to follow at any moment.

'*Boom!*' yelled Shirlee. 'This is for all the kids who called me fat in high school. *Boom!* Uncle Marv, you pervy old bastard. Wanna see something? How about this? *Boom!* Teachers who told me I was dumb. *Boom!* Mom, who thought sons mattered more than daughters. I could go on ...'

Polly looked at Maxine, who was laughing.

'Shirlee did respond well to role play,' she said.

Polly went over to the cooker and turned on the extractor fan.

'Sorry about the noise,' she said.

'Good idea,' said Shirlee, 'plenty of carcinogens in this breakfast – yeah, mama – but they're organic death foods, so that's OK, isn't it? And I've got my kosher lamb bacon. I felt bad about eating the piggy stuff that time.'

'What are the sausages today?' asked Polly.

'Venison,' said Shirlee. 'Freedom eggs, organic sourdough, organic tomatoes, organic butter made by virgins with no mercury fillings ... That clean-food freak Chiara can come back and blog this baby. This is the Clean English, à la Shirlee.'

The Clean English was delicious – just the thing for Polly's hangover – and she relished having company while she ate. Too often these days, meals were something grabbed out of the fridge and eaten standing up at the kitchen counter. She couldn't bear sitting alone at the table where they'd eaten all their meals as a family together. Laying it for one nearly killed her – and eating off her lap in front of the TV was almost worse.

'So, tell me, Shirl,' she said, sitting back in her chair. 'Now I know what Maxine does for a living – I never like to ask people in a yoga context, because they come here to get away from all that – but how about you? You've been coming to my classes for yonks and I've still got no idea.'

'Not much,' said Shirlee. 'I'm a lady of leisure. How do you think I get to come to yoga five mornings a week and then hang around jawing with you?'

'So is there a Mr Shirlee, slaving at a coal face somewhere to fund your leisure? Or a Mrs Shirlee?'

Shirlee barked with laughter.

'There's no Mrs Shirlee at the moment, although I have had a few memorable trips to the island ...'

Polly put her head on one side. 'The island?'

'Lesbos,' said Shirlee. 'Some very comfortable accommodation there.' She grinned, waggling her eyebrows suggestively.

'As for Mr Shirlee, what man could stand to be around me? I'd pussy-whip him to death. Or sit on him. No, it's just little old me. I have the odd dangerous liaison – a few old friends with benefits who come and go – but mostly I'm happy on my lonesome. And if you're wondering how I afford it, I have my aunt to thank for that. She had no kids and left me the house. Five bedrooms in Highgate. I quit my job, converted it in into three flats, sold two and live in the ground floor and basement, with enough change in the pot to survive.'

'What was your job?' asked Polly.

Now she'd started being nosy, she couldn't stop. A look crossed Shirlee's face that surprised her. Regretful.

'I worked with autistic kids,' she said. 'Art therapy. It was great. I really miss it. I loved those kids.'

'Couldn't you go back?' asked Polly.

'Naaa,' said Shirlee. 'I got off the bus and it's not that easy to get on again, at the level I worked at. Ideas about how to work with kids change all the time and it's weirdly political. People guard their patch very closely. I chose to quit and I've got to sit with that decision.'

Polly was about to ask her if she couldn't volunteer somewhere, but Shirlee got in first.

'So how's Lucas doing?' she asked. 'You said his finger's healing up nicely, but how about whatever he was numbing with the excessive boozing?'

Polly stopped with her mug halfway to her mouth.

'He's OK as far as I know,' she said tentatively. 'He only went back to uni yesterday.'

Maxine's face was fixed in gentle inquiry – her professional mask, thought Polly.

Shirlee, of course, showed no such restraint.

'Well, what could possibly go wrong there?' she said, laughing heartily. 'No kid ever drank too much at college – except all of them. Know anyone nearby who can keep an eye on him?'

Polly shook her head.

'I'm going to FaceTime him every day,' she said, 'and so is his sister. We reckon if we can actually see his face, we'll have a better idea how he is.

'And what can I do?' she continued. 'He's not a little kid any more. He's at that age when he's going to do his own thing no matter what I say. You know how they egg each other on ...'

But as she said it, she remembered how drunk he'd got at the country-house hotel with her mum. He hadn't had any friends to egg him on there, and she'd practically had to drag him up to his room after dinner, when he'd started ranting about how his father had left them.

'Don't you want that sausage?' asked Shirlee, her fork already hovering over Polly's plate.

'Oh, no,' said Polly, snapping back into the moment. 'You have it, I'm really full. It was delicious. Thanks so much, Shirlee.'

'Yeah, and thinking about your kid's killed your appetite, huh?'

'Something like that,' said Polly, enjoying the feeling of being real about something for once. 'It *is* a worry. You're right. Most young people drink too much – it's become a student rite of passage – but Lucas seems to be taking it to extremes.'

'And your husband's not here to support you,' said Shirlee. 'That must make it much worse. What does he think about it?'

That was too much reality. Who knew what David thought about Lucas, or about anything? Who knew who David was any more, let alone where he was.

Hot, stinging tears sprang into Polly's eyes. It was good to talk freely about Lucas, but there was no way she could open up about David, not even to these people who didn't know him. If she exposed herself like that to anyone apart from Clemmie, she wouldn't be able to carry on.

She got up quickly and walked out of the kitchen, calling out behind her in the cheeriest tone she could muster that she was just nipping to the loo.

She locked herself in the small downstairs cloakroom and sat down on the loo seat, controlling her breathing, re-earthing herself. After a while she felt calm enough to stop the tears that had threatened to engulf her. That was a relief, because she knew she wouldn't have been able to hide post-blubbing eyes from those two – and it would have inevitably led to more probing questions from Shirlee.

Polly waited for what felt like a suitable length of time, then went back into the kitchen. She could tell immediately they'd been talking about her, but they put on a good front and even Shirlee kept her lip zipped for once. Polly wondered if Maxine had told her to rein it in a bit. Whatever the reason, Polly was grateful.

The conversation had returned to a pleasant level again, as they discussed the possibility of doing a yoga break together in Greece later in the year, when the phone rang.

'Is this Mrs Masterson-Mackay?' said a woman's voice when Polly answered it.

'Yes,' said Polly. Ms, actually, but she couldn't be bothered to make the point.

'Oh, good morning, this is Julia, I'm the duty manager at Rockham Park. Don't be alarmed, your mother is fine, but we just needed to ring you to discuss something that happened this morning.'

'OK ...' said Polly.

Julia had said Daphne was all right, so why did she have that guarded tone in her voice? Like she was about to break bad news?

'Well, the thing is, your mother was a little bit confused today and we've called the doctor just to be on the safe side. We thought you'd want to know. She's all right, as I said, she's in her apartment and one of the staff is with her, but we thought you should know, in case you'd like to be here when the doctor comes.'

'When you say "a little confused" – what do you mean exactly?' asked Polly.

Out of the corner of her eye, she saw Shirlee and Maxine exchange a look. They probably thought it was about Lucas.

'Well,' said Julia, 'she came down for breakfast dressed in an, er, evening gown and lots of beautiful jewellery, and asked the waiter when he was going to dance with her. She got rather upset when he declined.'

Polly closed her eyes, the scene all too easy for her to picture. She turned her back to Shirlee and Maxine and lowered her voice.

'Did she say why she was wearing the dress?' Polly asked, praying Daphne had been trying it on for a forthcoming modelling job and just needed someone to zip up the back. If she had been sent a designer dress to try on for size, it would be typical of her to want everyone at Rockham Park to see her in it.

But even as she thought this, Polly knew it was unlikely. Daphne's booker always checked in with Polly first these days. There'd been a terrible mix-up one time, when Daphne had been expected at a shoot and hadn't turned up because she'd forgotten all about it.

'She said she'd come for the party,' said Julia, sounding embarrassed. 'She was just a bit muddled, and she's done a few other things recently that were a little unusual in this way. We all appreciate Mrs Masterson-Mackay's wonderful personality, but this seemed a little more, er, extreme, and when we tried to escort her back to her apartment, I'm afraid to say she got very distressed.'

'OK,' said Polly. 'I'll come right away. Thank you so much for letting me know.'

She sat down at the table, feeling like she'd been hit over the head with the frying pan.

'You OK, honey?' asked Shirlee. 'Is it something to do with Lucas?'

'No,' said Polly, tears filling her eyes again. This time she didn't fight them. 'It's my mum. She seems to think the dining room at her retirement village is the embassy ball. I've got to go and see what's going on.'

'Dementia?' asked Shirlee, with her usual tact. 'Loopy-loop?'

She circled her forefinger next to her head. It was so appalling Polly had to laugh.

'I wouldn't use the medical term "loopy-loop" at this stage,' she said. 'But she has been acting a little strangely recently. She rings me in the middle of the night to ask random questions, and she forgets a lot, but this seems like it's cranked up to a whole new level. Can dementia come on that quickly?'

She addressed the question directly to Maxine. She had a shrink here, she might as well make the most of it.

'Well, dementia is a very broad term,' said Maxine, slowly and carefully. 'It can be an early sign of Alzheimer's, or it could be just mild vascular dementia, which progresses much more slowly. If you are concerned, you'll need to get a diagnosis. But there are many other factors that could be in play here – she might just be dehydrated, or not eating properly, or taking medication erratically. I'm sure her doctor will check all those things and then probably do all the standard tests.'

Polly stared at Maxine as it sank in. Tests. That word made it seem so formal. She'd known Daphne's night-time calls were peculiar, but she'd tried to convince herself it was just the disjointed sleep patterns of the elderly. Of course, it had occurred to her that they might be an indication of something more serious, but she hadn't wanted to face up to it. No choice now.

'It's not an immediate life sentence, Polly,' Maxine continued. 'Some people have a little episode like this and then get right back to how they were before. It can even be a good thing, because it gets them some treatment at an early stage, which can do a lot to slow the pace of deterioration. If she was living alone, with no one to notice what she was doing, it could easily have developed too far to treat, so I think it's good this has happened, in a way. Try not to worry too much. I know that's hard, but the doctor will explain all this to you.'

'Holy shit,' said Shirlee. 'Now you've got your mom to worry about as well as your boozing son, and your husband off fuck-knows-where. We'll do the washing up, sweetheart, you go and get dressed, so you can leave quickly to see her.'

For a split second Polly's instinct was to say oh no, she couldn't possibly let them ... but she pushed it away as fast as it came. She could let them and she was going to. Shirlee was right, she needed help, and she was going to take it.

'Thanks, Shirlee,' she said, getting to her feet and smiling at them, 'and thank you, Maxine. Some help with the washing up would be absolutely brilliant. I'm so glad you two stayed today. It would have been very hard to handle that call about my mum on my own.'

She ran upstairs and got changed. When she came down again, the kitchen was immaculate and Shirlee was vacuuming the sitting room while Maxine dusted.

'Now *that* you don't need to do,' said Polly.

'We want to,' said Shirlee. 'Get going. We'll just finish up here and we can shut the door behind us.'

Polly hesitated.

'Are you sure?' she said.

'Hush yo' mouth and git gone,' said Shirlee in a fake Southern accent, laughing.

'OK, Missy Shirlee,' said Polly. She went out to the hall and sorted through the muddled pile of keys sitting on the side table, pulled out a set and took them back into the sitting room.

'Here,' she said, handing them to Shirlee, with one key singled out at the top. 'Do the mortise lock with this one when you leave – and I want you to keep them. Then you can let yourself in on yoga mornings.'

'Cool,' said Shirlee, putting the keys in her pocket and smiling broadly. 'Thanks, Poll. Now you get off to your mom, and text me to let me know when you're able to take classes again. It's fine if you need to skip a few – send me your contacts list for the regulars and I'll email them all.'

'You are an angel, Shirlee,' said Polly, giving her a big hug, before heading for the front door.

Maxine followed her out and handed Polly a card.

'Here are my numbers,' she said. 'You can call me any time if you need my professional opinion about anything to do with your mum, or with your son – Shirlee told me about that, I hope you don't mind – or if you just need to talk about anything, Polly. No charge, just as a friend. I'd be happy to do it for you.'

Polly hugged her and went out to the car thinking how lucky she was to have such great yogi bears.

Polly could smell Fracas halfway along the corridor outside Daphne's flat. She couldn't help smiling. What else would Daphne put on if she thought she was going to a party?

But Polly wasn't smiling when she got inside and saw her mother propped up in bed – her bare arms as scrawny as a plucked chicken, her face still in the heavy make-up she must have applied to go with the ball gown, except that now her mascara had run and her lipstick was smeared across her cheek. She looked like a Halloween fright mask.

Polly's heart turned over. Daphne would be mortified if she could see herself like that. Especially as the doctor taking her pulse was rather a strapping young man.

'Hey, Mummy,' said Polly, leaning across the bed to give her mother a kiss.

Daphne turned her head, not lifting it from the pillow, and looked at Polly as though she could hardly see her.

'Hello, darling,' she said weakly. 'This charming man is asking me a lot of questions but I'm so tired ...'

She closed her eyes and seemed to sleep.

'Hello,' said Polly to the doctor. 'I'm her daughter, Polly.'

'I'm Dr Adebayo,' he said, shaking her hand. 'I'm just checking your mum over. It seems she's been a little confused, and she does seem very tired, as she said. Is that normal for her these days?'

'Not really,' said Polly. 'But she doesn't seem to sleep much. She often rings me in the middle of the night ...'

Her voice petered out. She was talking about her mother like she wasn't there and couldn't speak for herself. Wasn't that what people did with patients who had dementia?

'Are you awake, Mummy?' she asked gently. 'I'm just talking to Dr Adebayo here, OK?'

Daphne didn't stir. Polly wanted to get that make-up off her more than anything. Her eyes lingered on Daphne's face, with its extraordinary bone structure still as glorious as ever, but looking so grotesque. She pulled herself up and turned back to the doctor.

'I'm sorry,' she said, 'but it's a shock to see her like this. She's very particular about her appearance. She used to be a famous model – well, she still is, if you know about that sort of thing.'

Why was she blabbing on about that? She'd be telling him about 'darling Cecil' next.

'So this is a sudden change of behaviour?' asked the doctor.

'Yes.' said Polly. 'Yes and no. She's pretty forgetful these days and I look after her money for her now, because she finds that too much. And she does rather live in the past – it was so glamorous, it must be hard to accept it's gone – but she normally knows what's going on. It's just the night-time phone calls that have been unusual, and they're getting more frequent.'

'Does she ring for any particular reason?' he asked.

'It varies. Sometimes it's to ask when I'm coming to see her, or where I've put her biscuits.'

He looked at her inquiringly.

'Her crispbreads,' said Polly. 'She loves them and she always keeps them in the same place, on top of the fridge, but sometimes she can't find them and she rings me.'

'Biscuits.' said Dr Adebayo. 'Do she think she's eating properly? She looks very thin.'

Polly turned to her mother again. Her arms looked like bony little twigs. How had she not noticed that? Daphne had always been very slender, but this was alarming.

She looked over at the ball gown draped across the chair. Primrose-yellow duchess satin. It was a Dior couture piece the house had presented to Daphne when she'd retired from doing their shows in what, 1960?

How the heck had she fitted into that? Polly had been trying to get Daphne to donate it to the Victoria & Albert Museum for years. Polly used to try it on herself when she played dress-ups and it hadn't fitted her since she was twelve. There was no way her mother was going to wear it again.

'She has lost weight,' she said. 'I just hadn't noticed how much. She's always been very slim and it must have happened incrementally, but I can see now how desperately thin she is. I feel awful.'

She picked the dress up and showed him the size of the waist.

'She was wearing this.'

'I think your mother definitely needs to eat more,' said the doctor. 'I'm going to take some blood and test for anaemia, and she's probably dehydrated as well, which can trigger an episode of confusion in an older person. It's very important she drinks enough water.'

'But I can't understand how she's got so thin,' said Polly, starting to feel seriously distressed. 'She has lunch every day in the dining room here – three courses – and sometimes she goes down for dinner as well.'

So she can show herself off in two different outfits, she thought.

'But does she actually eat it?' asked the doctor.

Polly remembered the meals at the hotel. Lucas, who had an insatiable appetite, had eaten most of Daphne's food. Polly had been so concerned about him that she hadn't considered the implications for her mother's health.

'Of course, because of her profession, she's always been very careful about what she eats,' Polly said. 'But now you mention it, I think she has got worse. She appears to be eating a meal, but she just plays with her food, really. Pushes it round the plate.'

'I'm just going to take her temperature and a few more things, but what I think your mum needs is some fluids and nutrition intravenously. As long as she can have someone around to keep an eye on her, I would like to get the district nurses to put a drip in here and to make regular follow-up visits. Hospital admission is better avoided if possible for a patient at this stage.'

What stage was that, Polly wondered, not liking the sound of it, but relieved he was trying to keep Daphne out of hospital. She'd read the stories about old ladies abandoned in wards, too weak to ask for help.

The moment Dr Adebayo left, she reached into her pocket to pull out her phone. It wasn't until she was about to hit the number that she fully realised the person she'd been going to ring was David.

She sat down quickly on the sofa as it sank in. It hadn't been a conscious thought, just a purely spontaneous response to being so upset about her mum. He was her go-to for those moments. Still.

For a second she felt something like pure desolation. How could he just disappear from her life like this? Then she pulled herself together. She couldn't fall to bits, she had to be strong for her mother – for herself.

After a moment's thought, she rang Clemmie.

A five-minute chat with her daughter – who was particularly comforting because she understood the situation from both a personal and a medical point of view – made Polly much better and she went back into the bedroom to take the awful make up off Daphne's face.

Daphne hardly seemed to notice as Polly gently wiped it away, but when she followed up with her mother's moisturiser, smoothing it on in an upwards direction, Daphne smiled.

'Thank you, darling,' she said very weakly. 'A little bit more on the neck, please.'

Polly kissed her forehead, relieved to see Daphne's vanity intact. That was a very vital sign in her case.

An hour or so later, a knock on her mother's front door announced the arrival of the district nurses, two lovely, smiling women, who had come about Daphne's drip.

Leaving them to get on with it, she took the opportunity to check on Digger, who she'd had to leave in the car.

As he sprang out and went running round the monkey puzzle tree, in what had become a bit of a ritual for him, Polly wondered how she was going to manage the dog for the next few days. One of the conditions for Daphne to be treated at home was that Polly needed to stay with her full-time while the drip was in. Obviously Digger didn't fit into that scenario.

Polly walked round to the other side of the tree to see what Digger found so fascinating about it, savouring the fresh January air on her face after Daphne's rather stuffy apartment. It felt like a salve for her overactive brain, like a cool rinse on the scalp at the hairdresser.

The grounds were nicely laid out and Polly continued round the side of the building, breathing deeply to enjoy the notes of wet leaves and bare earth, while she pondered what to do.

The best she could think of was to ask her doggy neighbour if she could look after him for a few days, and if she said yes, drive him there and then come straight back to her mother. Nearly a two-hour round trip. What a palaver, but what choice was there? And if the neighbour couldn't have him, she'd have to ring Clemmie.

Damn you, David, she thought. Damn you for adding a whole new level of complication to my life, without a second thought for what effect the non-negotiated sole custody of a rescue mutt would have on me.

But then Digger came running over to her with a stick in his mouth and dropped it at her feet, front paws forward, bottom back, tail wagging furiously, looking up at her expectantly.

She looked down at the scruffy dog, with his rufty-tufty black fur sticking up like Sid Vicious's hair, and found she couldn't resist him. Yes, having to look after him was a massive pain, but it was beginning to feel more than worth it.

She threw the stick for him for what seemed like the umpteenth time, while texting the neighbour – and then Shirlee, to ask if she wouldn't mind emailing the yogi bears as she'd so kindly offered. What a help that would be.

Noticing the battery was running low, Polly went back to the car to get her travel charger. When she opened the glove box she saw the perfume she'd brought last time for the man she still thought of as Mr Mitsouko, who had turned out to be the stepdad of Chum from St Andrews. That had been surprising, to see Chum again after so many years. Surprising and nice. She'd always liked Chum. She wracked her brain to remember what his stepdad's name was ... Bill, that was it. She couldn't remember the surname and hoped that would be enough to identify him.

She grabbed the perfume box and, whistling for Digger, headed back inside.

Julia, the nice manager who had rung Polly about her mother, was on the front desk and quickly identified Bill – and was happy to tell her which apartment Mr Edmonstone lived in. Polly set off with Digger on the lead, hoping he'd behave himself. She couldn't bear to put him back in the car just yet.

Bill's face broke into a broad smile when he opened his front door to them.

'Hippolyta!' he said. 'What a lovely surprise. Do come in.'

'Is it all right if Digger comes in too? He's not usually as badly behaved as he was that day in the dining room.'

'Of course he can come in,' said Bill, reaching down to pat him. 'That was just as much the fault of Edward's dog Artemis as this little chap. Artemis is not at all well behaved. Do come through and sit down. Would you like a cup of tea or coffee?'

Polly was about to say no, then thought better of it. He lived alone. She understood what that meant now and how much he might enjoy having a chat with someone.

'Some tea would be lovely, if it's not too much trouble,' she said, sitting down in the comfortable armchair he had indicated.

'Excellent,' said Bill. 'I've just made a pot. Is strong Indian all right?'

'Just what I like best,' said Polly, jerking Digger's lead as he made a lunge for Bill's passing slippers.

'Sit,' she hissed quietly at the dog, 'and behave yourself.'

Digger looked up at her dolefully and settled himself on the floor, his head resting on his front paws.

Polly looked round the room, which in terms of layout was a mirror image of her mother's sitting room, but looked so different in every other way. The walls were painted dark red and it was rather overcrowded with mahogany furniture and gold-framed paintings, and some well-stocked bookshelves. A silver tray on a side table held two decanters and some whisky tumblers.

But more than the furnishings, it was the smell that struck her. Old books and whisky combined with the unmistakable spice of cigar smoke. Sure enough, she spotted a humidor, a large ashtray and a heavy lighter with an onyx base. Bill was clearly fond of a smoke. The combination of all these distinct elements was cosy and reassuring.

Floris No. 89, thought Polly, or the most classic men's cologne. Or perhaps Penhaligon's No. 33 for the cigar smoke.

Bill came back in with a tray, which he put down on the coffee table. Polly took in the silver teapot, strainer, milk jug, cups and saucers, the plate of biscuits and two small tea plates. He must have had it all ready for his own afternoon cuppa.

'Do you think Digger would like a drink?' he asked.

'I'm sure he would,' said Polly. 'He's just been doing some intense stick-chasing. The stick won, mostly.'

Bill laughed and went back into the kitchen. Polly heard him put the tap on, then he came back into the doorway holding something out in his hand.

'Digger,' he called, 'would you like one of Artemis's treats? And some water from her bowl?'

Digger's head quickly came up, hearing his name and smelling the treat, and Polly let go of his lead so he could pad off to the kitchen.

Bill walked back into the sitting room, sat down opposite Polly and poured the tea.

'Would you care for a shortbread?' he said, holding out the plate of biscuits. 'Edward brings these for me. He says they're all butter, which they seem to have decided is good for us again. Lucky I never stopped eating it, eh? I like it on a cream cracker.'

Polly smiled as she picked up a shortbread finger.

'How nice it is of you to call,' said Bill, the saucer perched on the fingers of his left hand, the handle of the cup delicately gripped with the other hand, little finger most definitely not raised. He leaned forward and picked up a cube of sugar with the tongs.

'Do you take sugar?' he asked.

Polly shook her head, fascinated as he dropped the cube into his cup and then stirred it noiselessly. It was like watching some kind of elaborate tea ceremony. Daphne had gone over to teabags and mugs years before, but Polly was pretty sure Bill did this every afternoon.

'Have you come to visit your mother again?' he asked, carefully putting the silver teaspoon on the saucer – no rattle – and taking a sip from the cup.

'Yes,' said Polly, wondering how much he might know. Did they gossip in a place like this? Was everyone laughing at Daphne, coming down in her ball gown and trying to dance with the head waiter? If they were, she didn't think Bill would join in, but he'd probably heard about it.

'She had to have the doctor to see her,' continued Polly, 'so I came to hear what he had to say.'

'Everything's all right, I hope?' he said.

'Well, it seems she was dehydrated,' said Polly, 'and she hasn't really been eating, which isn't a great combination for anybody.'

Bill nodded, taking another sip from his cup and putting it back on the saucer again.

'It made her go a bit potty,' said Polly suddenly. There was something about Bill's face that was so kind it made her want to confide in him.

'Ah, yes,' said Bill. 'I've heard that we wrinklies – as Edward calls me – have to drink plenty of water, and not just in tea, because that's a diuretic. I really prefer my water with a tot of whisky, but that doesn't count either, apparently.'

Polly laughed.

'It was so nice to see Ch– Edward the other day,' she said.

'Call him Chum, if you want to,' said Bill. 'I'm just an old fusspot who insists on calling him Edward. Yes, he said the same about seeing you. You should meet up here some time. That was a Monday, wasn't it? He normally has lunch with me on a Friday. When your mother is feeling better, perhaps you'd both like to join us.'

'That would be lovely,' said Polly.

'Although you and Edward will probably have things you want to remember without the old wrinklies hanging about. Gay days at university and all that.'

Polly smiled.

'And it would do Edward good to have some congenial company,' said Bill, looking at her quite beadily. 'He's had a bit of a rough trot recently.'

'Oh, I'm very sorry to hear that,' said Polly.

'Yes. People feel sorry for us poor old crumbling geriatrics, but I think mid-life can be a very difficult time too. You start to feel like you've chosen your track and that's it, there's no chance that the signals will change. Full speed ahead in whatever direction you're pointed in, heading into a tunnel and hoping you don't come up against the buffers at the other end.'

He laughed and Polly joined in, but said nothing. Was that how David was feeling? Stuck on the tracks in one direction – with her – and starting to think he was never going to be head of department at King's? Just the black hole of old age to look forward to?

Digger came back from the kitchen, having a good sniff of everything he passed en route, clearly looking for the source of the delectable odour wafting from the shortbread. As his head moved towards the table, Polly snapped her fingers at him.

'Stop sniffing, Digger,' she said, 'it's rude. Sit down. Actually, all that sniffing has reminded me why I came to see you, Bill – I mean, I would have loved to come anyway, but there was a particular reason.'

She pulled the small, beautifully decorated box out of her handbag and passed it across to him.

'I want you to have this,' she said. 'With all the work I do in the perfume industry, I'm given more of it than I could ever use.'

Bill looked down at the box then back up at Polly.

'Is it Mitsouko?' he asked.

Polly nodded, smiling.

'Are you really sure you can part with it?' he said. 'Let me look at this beautiful box.'

He picked up a pair of spectacles that were on the table and put them on, examining the packaging.

'It's eau de parfum,' he said. 'Isn't that the very best?'

'I'm sure that's what your mother would have worn,' said Polly.

Bill looked at her steadily for a moment and then down at the box.

'What a lovely kind girl you are,' he said.

Before Polly could answer, her phone pinged to announce a message.

'I'm so sorry,' she said, 'but with what's going on with my mother, I think I'd better look at that. I wouldn't normally.'

'Of course,' said Bill.

She pulled her phone out and groaned reflexively when she read the message.

'Is something wrong?' asked Bill.

'Oh, I'm sorry, it's just that I need to stay here with my mum a few days and the friend who looks after the dog when I go away can't have him, so I'll have to get my daughter to come from Cambridge to get him. He can't be in the flat while Mummy has the drip in—'

'I'll have him,' Bill interjected. 'It would be lovely to have some company. As long you don't mind, eh, Digger?'

Digger raised his head at the mention of his name and stood up and trotted over to Bill to make a fuss of him.

'Really?' asked Polly.

'Of course,' said Bill. 'I'd love to have him. As long as you can take him out now and again. I can take him down for his morning and evening wees, but I'm not up to doing much more walking than that.'

'Oh, that would be so kind,' said Polly. 'And please don't worry about taking him out, I'll come and get him at least three times a day. But if you really don't mind him being here that would make things so much simpler.'

'I'll enjoy it,' said Bill. 'I miss having a dog. Mine died before I moved here and they have rather tedious rules about residents getting new dogs. Perhaps you could just leave me your phone number, in case something happens and I need to call you.'

Polly fished one of her FragrantCloud business cards out of her handbag and passed it to him.

'I'll pop back later with some food for him,' she said.

'You don't need to,' said Bill. 'I have dog food. Artemis stays sometimes, so I've got everything he'll need. I take it he's not a fussy eater?'

Bill's eyes danced with merriment as he said it, and Polly laughed.

'No, quite the opposite. In fact you'd better put those shortbreads in a safe place or he won't be able to stop himself.'

Polly finished her tea and told Bill she'd fetch Digger's blanket from the car, so he'd have something familiar to sleep on. Bill went to show her out, and just as Polly had walked through the door she turned back and gave him a spontaneous kiss on the cheek. It felt like the right thing to do.

As she did so she caught the smell of old-fashioned shaving foam and cologne, mixed with the cigar smoke that had permeated the cashmere of his cardigan, and a back note of whisky.

Daddy.

The combination was like falling through a gap in the space-time continuum. As she walked off down the corridor, tears sprang into Polly's eyes, as they seemed to so often these days.

This time she wasn't sure if they were sad or happy.

FragrantCloud.net

The scent of ... a dog

I wish I could see all your faces as you read the title of today's post!

I can see that the smell of a dog might not be a very appealing prospect, but that's partly why I wanted to write about it, to make the point that smell associations can be really abstract, but still meaningful.

My dog is called Digger – although it still feels odd to describe him as 'my dog'. Ever since he arrived in our lives a couple of years ago, from the rescue centre, he has very much been my husband's dog.

It was my husband who went looking for a pet to adopt in the first place; I wasn't that keen, in all honesty.

I didn't grow up with pets because my mum refused to have them in the house, so all I could envisage when we first brought Digger home was the 'mess' she used as an excuse, and the extra responsibility I was sure I would get landed with.

But to be fair to my husband, he looked after all the dog care and discipline from the start. He even took him to work most days. I was just the person who occasionally gave Digger some food if the all-powerful Pack Leader happened to be absent.

My husband is an academic, and it wasn't until he left recently on a long research trip for a book that I really bonded with Digger.

At first I found all the responsibilities a bit of a pain, but after a while I could feel a really tangible bond had grown up between us. He didn't just seem happy to see me because I was the one with the food-cupboard privileges, I really felt he was responding to me. And it worked both ways. If this is a delusional state shared by all dog owners, it's a very powerful one!

Digger is a classic mutt, a real Heinz 57, with scruffy black fur sticking up in spikes, but I've grown very fond of him. Hearing the sound of his claws clattering along the wooden floors of the hallway makes me smile.

There are a few things I don't like about Digger, though – and they are all connected with smell. For one, he gets bouts of flatulence that could clear the Albert Hall they're so pungent.

During our walks on nearby Hampstead Heath, he has a penchant for rolling in fox poo, which has a uniquely rank odour. The best description I've heard of it is 'burned bacon', but I think that's insulting to bacon.

Sometimes his breath gets a bit gamey too, but I got him some special chews which really help with that.

So, putting aside the yucky ones, the positive smells of a dog for me are the next-day cold-stew smell of his meaty food, and the aroma of a roasted chicken right out of the oven, which will have him running to the kitchen like a rocket. The dry seed and hay hum of a pet shop, and the sickly rotting meat of his treats.

Grassy fresh air and mud on long winter walks. The rubbery tang of the toys he likes to brutalise. The worn-in leather of his collar and lead. The sweet, musty smell of his velvety ears, which I love to stroke, and yes, I admit it, I kiss them.

My scents for a dog are (a bit of a challenge in all honesty, but it's fun to stretch yourself sometimes!):

Barbour For Him by Barbour
Grass by The Library of Fragrance

Dirt by The Library of Fragrance
Cuir de Russie by Chanel
Piper Leather by Illuminum
Mûre et Musc by L'Artisan Parfumeur

COMMENTS

AgathaF: I don't have a dog, I have a cat. Can you do write about the scent of a cat?

> **FragrantCloud:** Hi Agatha, I don't have a cat and I've never had one, so it would be a bit hard for me, but if I can think of a friend with a nice cat, I'll try. What are the scents of a cat for you?
>
> **AgathaF:** She smells a lot of fish.

EastLondonNostrils: You've lost me here, dear. What next – the smell of a tramp's coat?

LuxuryGal: What breed is your dog? I have two shitzus! Ting Ting and Tong. They are sooooo spoiled, but we love them. They smell mostly of the spray from their groomers. They have a comb out every week when I'm getting my nails done. I always say their beauty parlour is right next to mine! They come back smelling gorgeous. Sometimes I spray them with my own perfume! And sometimes I paint their claws! They are so cute.

> **FragrantCloud:** Gosh, they really sound like pampered pooches. The only time Digger gets sprayed with perfume is when I'm trying to block out one of his own special 'blends'.
>
> **EastLondonNostrils:** Not helping.

PerspiringDreams: Digger sounds like a character. Clemmie says he once ate a whole block of butter.

FragrantCloud: I'm afraid that is true. We left it out on the kitchen table when we went out and the smell just got the better of him ... I wish I had his sense of smell!

AnnaBandana: You should do an event with Digger, to show how amazing a dog's sense of smell is.

FragantCloud: A lovely idea, Anna. What could possibly go wrong?

Friday, 22 January

Swimming a lap of backstroke in the Rockham Park pool wearing one of Daphne's swimsuits, Polly gazed up through the glass roof at the grey January sky and smiled to herself. She was rather loving her stay here.

In three days she'd already established a bit of a routine. Whenever the nurses came to do their check-ups, or she could get one of the retirement village staff to cover for her, she'd collect Digger from Bill for a romp around the grounds, or nip down to the pool. The rest of the time she worked on her blog, using Daphne's dressing table as a desk, while her mum dozed. When Daphne was awake Polly sat and chatted to her, going through old photo albums and old copies of *Vogue*, which made her mother very animated.

On her way back up to the apartment, after a post-pool stint in the steam room, Polly's phone rang.

'Hello, Mummy,' said Clemmie. 'I'm just ringing to see how you're getting on at Crumbly Towers.'

'I'm having a ball!' said Polly, waving hello to two nice ladies she'd chatted to in the coffee lounge the day before.

Clemmie laughed. 'Really?'

'Really,' said Polly. 'I've just done twenty lengths of the pool, I get all my meals sent up from the dining room, and the rest of the time I doodle around on my laptop – I'm across every perfume-related website in existence – and I'm loving staying in a brand-new apartment. I've never lived anywhere new in my whole life. I think our house pumps dust and cobwebs out of its walls.'

'How's Granny doing?' asked Clemmie.

'Much better,' said Polly. 'She's got a lot more colour in her cheeks. The blood tests showed she was very anaemic, so they're giving her iron in the drip. She's still a bit confused when she wakes up to find the drip and catheter in, but once she comes to, she's fine, getting perkier every day. My main job now is getting her to eat properly.'

They chatted a bit more and Clemmie promised to come and see Daphne as soon as she could.

As Polly let herself back in through the sleek front door of Daphne's apartment, she acknowledged another thing she was enjoying about staying here, something she hadn't wanted to mention to Clemmie.

Rockham Park had absolutely no connection with David.

He'd only been there once, when they'd moved Daphne in, whereas every tiny corner of the family house was impregnated with memories of him. It was such a relief to be away from it – especially now she had to constantly walk past the gaping hole she'd made in his office door. Staying at her mum's place, she was able to put all that out of her mind. That was like a spa break in itself.

After lunch – salmon en croute for Polly, soup for Daphne – the doctor was due for a check-up, instead of the usual district-nurse visit. Polly would miss taking Digger for his normal afternoon walk, as she wanted to hear his assessment.

She was happy to hear he thought Daphne was making good progress and after he'd gone, she rang Bill to explain and say she'd come to get the dog as soon as she could arrange someone to sit with Daphne. But every time she phoned reception to see if they could send a staff member up, the line was engaged. She was about to call Bill again when there was a knock on the door. She opened it to find Chum standing there, with Artie and Digger.

'Oh,' was all she could say.

'Hi, Hippolyta,' said Chum, smiling slightly shyly, eyebrows raised. 'Bill said you were coming to take Digger out shortly and I thought perhaps we could walk the dogs together. They've bonded rather.'

Polly looked down at Digger, who was not in the slightest bit excited to see her, he was so preoccupied with trying to get behind Chum to be nearer his canine pal.

'I see what you mean,' she said. 'I'd love to, but I can't leave my mum until I've organised someone to watch her and I can't get through to reception for some reason.'

'That's because Bill was hogging the line,' said Chum, 'organising someone to cover for you. Ah, look, here she comes now.'

Polly followed his gaze down the corridor and saw one of the friendly cleaners who often helped out with Daphne, walking towards them.

'That's brilliant,' said Polly. 'I'll tell Mum what's happening and get my jacket.'

Five minutes later she was in Chum's Land Rover, the two dogs lying happily together in the back, being driven terrifyingly fast along small country lanes she'd had no idea were so close to Rockham Park. She always came straight off the motorway along the main road to the nearest town.

The mud-splattered four-wheel drive was just as messed up and stinky inside as the one Chum had driven at St Andrews.

Although she didn't remember that old heap smelling quite as bad as this, with wet dog and other odours she couldn't immediately identify and, for once, didn't want to. Fish guts? Dead rodents?

She rolled her window down a crack and pulled her polo neck up over her nose.

Chum laughed.

'Bit gamey for you, is it?' he asked.

'You could say that,' said Polly through the wool, glad she'd sprayed herself liberally with Guy's PM that morning. It developed so beautifully, as the luxurious rose and jasmine mid-notes entwined more deeply with the oakmoss, bergamot and labdanum of the chypre base. Polly was wearing it for the third day in a row, which was very unusual for her.

'I should get one of those traffic-light car fresheners,' said Chum. 'Hang it off my mirror.'

'That would be even worse than the eau de dead things smell,' said Polly. 'At least it's natural, like manure and horse wee. I actually like those smells, but the cheap fake ones give me an instant migraine.'

'That's unusual,' said Chum, 'liking horse wee. It's Chanel No. 5 to me, but townies are normally repulsed by such things.'

Polly groaned inwardly, hating such un-nuanced labels, while acknowledging simultaneously that she was feeling pathetically glad she was wearing her Barbour jacket, even though it was London black, rather than one of the green ones Chum and all his pals had worn at St Andrews. And he was wearing now.

She couldn't believe that all these years later, she still felt that need to fit in with the Yah set's social mores, and that made her equally glad she was wearing trainers. No Hunter wellies for her. Chum was wearing them, of course, or something along those lines.

'There's a nice wood not that far along here,' Chum was saying. 'We can let the dogs have a good romp around in there.'

'That would be great,' said Polly. 'Digger and I have explored every corner of the Rockham Park grounds. I did try walking out of the gate in pursuit of something more interesting, but that road is absolutely treacherous, with all the cars headed for the motorway.'

'Isn't that kind of terrain pretty normal in London?' asked Chum, glancing at her, then looking back at the road.

'Where I live, I'm not too far from Hampstead Heath,' said Polly, 'which is quite wild if you know where to go, so I take Digger up there whenever I can. He finds plenty of fox poo to roll around in, so that keeps him happy.'

Chum laughed, and without warning pulled the car abruptly off the road, into a gap next to a gate leading into a field. Polly couldn't see many trees, just hedgerows and fields.

'Is this it?' she asked, looking around. 'I thought you said there was a wood.'

'Yes,' said Chum, unbuckling his seat belt and opening the car door. 'We have to walk to the wood.'

He pointed to the left and Polly could see a clump of trees in the distance. The quite far distance.

'Looks more like a spinney than a full-blown wood,' said Polly, jumping down onto the muddy ground and having to grab the door, not to go flying. It was slippery underfoot. 'Or is it a copse? Isn't that what you hunting types call them? I remember all that from reading *Flambards*. They were always flushing foxes out of spinneys and running them to ground in copses.'

Chum snorted.

'I would call it a small wood,' he said. 'I'm not a hunting type, thank you very much. Don't make assumptions.'

'Well, don't call me a townie, then,' said Polly.

'Fair enough,' said Chum, laughing.

'But I do remember you as being super-horsey,' said Polly grabbing hold of Digger's collar before he could catapult himself onto the road.

'I still am,' said Chum, 'if you want to use that technical term, but that doesn't mean I chase terrified furry animals for sport. There are plenty of other things you can do on horses. I'll climb over the gate first and you can pass the dogs over to me.'

He gave her Artie's lead and climbed over in two neat movements of his long legs and a jump down. Polly couldn't help hoping he wouldn't be watching when she did it. She picked up Artie, then Digger, and passed them to him over the chained and padlocked gate, then just managed to clamber over herself, without falling face-first in the even deeper mud on the other side.

As she landed, she glanced back at the Land Rover blocking the entrance, and then over at the field, which had clearly been recently ploughed.

'I hope we're not going to piss off the farmer,' she said, as Digger and Artemis romped off, clods of mud flying around them. 'He might want to get into his field and I don't want him coming after us with a shotgun.'

'Don't worry,' said Chum, 'this is my family's land. If anyone comes at us with a weapon, I can call him off. Or her.'

'Oh,' said Polly, feeling as stupid as she always seemed to around people like Chum. Of course it was his land. She should have guessed. He probably owned the whole of Hertfordshire. She wondered who the 'her' might be. His wife presumably.

'So are you an equal-opportunities land owner?' she asked.

'No,' said Chum, starting off up a line of churned-up wet earth the colour of milk chocolate, in the direction of the wood. Turning his head over his shoulder towards Polly, he said, 'But my sister-in-law probably thinks she is.'

Before Polly could answer – and she couldn't think of anything to say anyway – Chum set off at a fast pace, whistling for the dogs, who had veered off to the left. She trotted a few paces, trying to catch up with him. She had pretty long legs herself, but Chum's stride was fast leaving her behind, and she wasn't finding it very easy in the mud in her trainers.

'Hey, Usain,' she called out, 'can you slow down a bit?'

Chum stopped and when she caught up with him he was grinning. He clapped her on the shoulder.

'Sorry, dear,' he said. 'I'd forgotten you townies don't know how to walk on the raw earth.'

'Very droll, Mr Super-Horsey,' she said. 'I suppose you've got hooves, rather than feet?'

'No, but I do wear proper footwear.'

He pointed at her trainers, which were now caked in mud. She could feel it oozing over the top, onto her socks. She wasn't feeling quite so smug now about not wearing wellies. She did have something more practical in the car that she wore for walking Digger on the Heath, she'd just wanted to make some kind of stupid point.

'And appropriate hats,' he added. 'You can't even see out from your hair.'

He reached over and brushed aside a stray lock that had blown into her face and was stuck to her lip balm.

'Hang on a minute.' He reached into the inner pocket of his waxed jacket – the game pocket it was called, Polly remembered, hoping there hadn't been any dead pheasants in there recently – and pulled out a tweed cap, which he put on her head.

'Suits you,' he said, pulling the peak right down over her

eyes, before turning and starting to walk off at the same brisk pace.

'Come on,' he said. 'Let's get some country air into your polluted urban lungs. Hampstead Heath indeed. There's probably a gift shop.'

Polly adjusted the hat as he strode off, then took it off and sniffed it: not too stinky, she was relieved to find. Not stinky at all, really.

It smelled of a man's head, all right, but not a nasty greasy-hair smell, more a light male musk, quite pleasant with that warm horsey accord, a residue of lanolin on the tweed, and a faint trace of something cologne-y. She wondered if Chum ever wore aftershave, but didn't feel she could ask him; it seemed too intrusive.

Just at that moment he turned round, looked at her and burst out laughing.

'What *are* you doing?' he asked.

'Checking for dead animals,' said Polly.

'You're smelling my hat,' he said, in faux outraged tones. 'I realise we've known each other a long time, Polly, but really, a man's hat is a very personal item.'

'Well, you did put it on my head.'

She stuck it back on there – she'd just copped another mouthful of windblown hair – then caught up and fell into step beside him. The dogs were out in front, zigzagging back and forth, sniffing, chasing each other, and occasionally looking back to check that Polly and Chum were still there.

'Do you often sniff people's property?' asked Chum.

'Absolutely,' said Polly. 'All the time. It's kind of what I do.'

'Really?' said Chum. 'Perhaps you can explain – and I do hope it isn't too offensive, my old hat.'

'It's fine,' said Polly, 'or it wouldn't be on my head.'

'So tell me why you smell things.'

'I'm a perfume blogger. I write about perfume, for my blog, on the internet.'

'I do know what a blog is, Polly,' said Chum.

'Oh, do you get the interweb out here, then?'

'Yes, West End Girl, we do. It's quite a crap signal, actually, but we do get it. I listen to *Farming Today* on the BBC iPlayer doodah on my iPad when I'm having my coffee, because I'm too arse-lazy to get up at five forty-five when it's on live.'

'So you're a farmer these days?'

'Sort of. I mainly do horsey things – you were right about that. But tell me more about being a perfume blogger.'

The way he said 'perfume', as though it were in inverted commas, reminded her that his lot had always said 'scent'.

She remembered how crushed she'd felt when she'd complimented a female Yah on her perfume while they were both refreshing their lipstick in the loos at a university ball.

'Oh, you mean my *scent*?' she'd said. What a cow. She was one of the girls who'd called Chum by the 'Pedigree' nickname behind his back.

Polly hadn't been able to stand Anaïs Anaïs ever since. She'd only said she liked it to be nice.

Well, sod them. If Coco Chanel and Jacques Guerlain and Frédéric Malle and Lucien Lechêne called it *parfum*, 'perfume' was good enough for her. And she was sure Estée Lauder and Tom Ford would agree.

She couldn't believe how quickly all that stuff was coming up after spending such a short time with Chum again. Surely caste divisions in the UK had moved on since she'd last seen him in 1992? Yet the class-markers of tribal clothing and specific words were still jumping out at her like booby traps in one of Lucas's computer games. 'Super Mario 3D Yahs'.

As she was having these thoughts, which were slightly spoiling the walk and the novelty of his company, she became aware that her feet were feeling seriously damp and cold.

Glancing at her watch, she saw they'd already been out for more than half an hour. She could easily give the excuse of needing to get back to her mother, but Digger was having such a lovely time she couldn't bring herself to suggest they turn back yet. And she didn't really want to. The wind was cold, but the air smelled so fresh, the rawness of the churned-up soil adding a lovely earthy layer.

Chum looked round at her.

'Are you sniffing again, Hippolyta?' he asked.

'Yes,' she said, realising she'd never answered his question about perfume blogging – or scent blogging, to use his term. 'I can't help it. I've always been obsessed with how things smell and how they make you feel, and the vivid associations between the two. I started writing a blog about smell and perfume a couple of years ago, just for fun, and it's become a bit of a job. It's great.'

'How is it a job?'

'I have a lot of subscribers who are very loyal to me and they pay to come to my perfume events – I know you call it "scent", Chum, but in the perfume world, it's very much known as perfume.'

'I don't care what you call it,' said Chum, looking mystified.

'OK,' said Polly, a bit embarrassed. That was clearly her issue, not his. 'Anyway, they come to themed events I put on, such as "Perfume and Love", "Perfumes of the 1970s", "The History of Perfume", that kind of thing, and now department stores and brands are paying me to do events for them. Say a famous nose – that's the term for someone who creates perfumes – has a new range out, I'll do an interview with him, or her, in front of a live audience. I did one a few days ago for Connolly's.'

'That sounds rather jolly,' said Chum. 'Is there a lot to say about scent – perfume – then?'

'You've no idea how much,' she said. 'It's one of those worlds within worlds. The more you delve, the more you find it opens up into deeper and deeper chambers, dragging you in.'

'Like the *Daily Mail* website?' suggested Chum.

Polly laughed.

'Just like that,' she said. 'So tell me more about what you do. What kinds of horsey things?'

He glanced quickly away, Polly noticed, as if looking for a distraction, then turned back to her.

'Oh, it's pretty dull stuff, really,' he said, sighing deeply. 'Looking after other people's horses mainly. It's not glamorous like what you do, but I like it. I just love being around the animals. I enjoy their company, which probably sounds crazy, but I do. I particularly love their smell.'

'So do I,' she said. 'It's one of the great smells, actually, and traces of it are used in perfumes. It's called an animalic note.'

'Gosh,' said Chum, 'I wouldn't mind some of that. What's it called – Eau de Nag?'

'Well, it's more of a hint deep inside a very complex blend of different smells, although one niche company does make a perfume called Stable.'

'I wear that all the time,' said Chum, sniffing the sleeve of his Barbour. 'Here, have a whiff.'

Polly took hold of his arm and brought it up to her nose. It did smell of horse, mixed with the wax on the jacket and a hint of diesel.

'Nice,' she said, smiling at him.

Chum smiled back, looking genuinely gratified, and they walked on in silence for a while. Not an awkward silence, but easy and comfortable, and Polly was happy to enjoy the peace, the only sounds the breeze whistling past her ears, the squelch of her trainers in the mud, birds calling and the dogs yapping at each other.

She made a conscious decision not to think as she walked, to treat this as a form of meditation, but it was hard to stop the memories that kept jumping up unbidden, of times she'd spent with Chum before.

Images from the past kept flashing through her head like a slide show. Chum at a dinner table, roaring with laughter. Chum in black tie at a university ball. Chum's face by the light of a bonfire. Chum's eyes gazing into hers.

It was so odd being with someone you'd known such a long time but hadn't seen or spoken to for years. They were strangers really and yet she felt oddly connected with him still. Maybe it was because the time they had shared together – peak youth – was such an intense period of anyone's life. Perhaps friendships from that time never faded.

All this turning over in her head, Polly was almost relieved when the peace was suddenly broken by the sound of a pheasant flying upwards, flushed out by Digger. Chum immediately raised his arms as though he were holding a gun and swung over to the right.

'*Bang!*' he said. 'Damn, missed it. Good gun dog you've got there.'

'Is that a form of ritual killing you do go in for?' asked Polly, feeling the cultural chasm opening up again.

'Yes,' he said, 'it's another part of my job, and I do enjoy shooting, but don't hate me for it. I eat what I shoot, or other people do. It's not just killing for the sake of it. You're not vegetarian, are you?'

'No,' said Polly. 'But my daughter is.'

'That's a phase they go through, isn't it?' said Chum. 'How old is she?'

'It's not a phase with Clemmie,' said Polly. 'She's twenty-three and has been a veggie since she was fourteen, so it's not just a pose. And it seems to suit her, she's very healthy. I've got a nineteen-year-old son as well. He's a big carnivore, so they slightly cancel each other out. Do you have kids?'

'No,' said Chum. 'I've got a nephew I adore, but I don't see him nearly as much as I'd like to. Probably why I'm so soppy about animals. Artie is my child, and Sorrel – that's my horse – is my wife. Not in a creepy way, but because of the importance she has in my life. No, that still sounds creepy, so you'll just have to believe me: I'm not a pervert, I just love my horse. OK, that's no better, I'll shut up.'

Polly laughed, but felt a pang of sadness for him. If his horse was his wife, it sounded like he didn't have a human partner. Single and childless? That was nuts. It was so crazy when she thought of all the women she knew who would have loved to have had kids with a guy like Chum. Not because he was posh and closely related to the large field they were walking through, but because he was nice and funny and tall and good-looking, and all those boxes women want to tick. And probably rich too, if that was your thing.

She wondered if he'd ever been married, but didn't feel she could ask. Unlike some of her St Andrews contemporaries, she hadn't kept up a daily patrol of the 'Births, Deaths and Marriages' column of the *Daily Telegraph* after she'd left. Anaïs Anaïs probably had them all in a scrapbook. Cross-referenced.

Polly had heard about plenty of engagements over the

years, but she didn't remember hearing Chum's name come up. Maybe the single-and-childless scenario was why Bill had said he was having a rough time.

She decided to keep the conversation on safe ground. Also, not asking him about his marital status would make it less likely he would ask about hers.

'Sorrel is a lovely name for a horse,' she said. 'Did you choose it?'

'Yes,' said Chum. 'I bred her, so I got to name her when she was born. Sorrel was the name of William III's horse – as in William and Mary? The house was built in his reign, although it was King James who bestowed the title.'

He said it all so casually it was rather endearing. She liked the way he'd said 'the house', without feeling the need to explain further. He wasn't showing off, or trying to put her in her bourgeois place. He was who he was and he was perfectly comfortable with it. She couldn't remember what the title was, or what the house was called, and didn't want to ask him. She didn't really care.

Preoccupied with all that, Polly had hardly noticed that they'd reached the wood. The dogs disappeared into it at great speed and she heard Digger's familiar bark in the distance – his happy bark, as she thought of it.

Even though there were no leaves on the trees, it felt wonderful to be enclosed by the canopy of branches, the huge trunks forming a kind of architecture around them. Polly closed her eyes and breathed in deeply. It was mossy and woody, with a green dampness. Glorious.

'How's your sniffometer?' asked Chum, who'd clearly noticed again what she was up to.

'My sniffometer is on ten,' said Polly. 'Full power. There are thickets of trees up on the Heath, but it's not like this.

They're like cardboard trees from a stage set by comparison. This feels primal.'

Chum grinned, clearly pleased she liked it.

They walked on in silence, the dogs crashing around in the undergrowth, the odd bit of early birdsong. Polly felt calmer than she had in weeks. Being at Rockham Park was a lovely remove from the constant reminders of home, but being out in raw nature took that sense of release to another level.

Suddenly there was the blare of a klaxon. Polly jumped in surprise.

'Sorry,' said Chum, 'that sound's a bit brutal. It's my reminder that we've been going for thirty-five minutes and we need to turn round. Bill arranged for that carer to stay with your mum for an hour and a half. About turn.'

He spun one hundred and eighty degrees on the spot and started walking back the way they'd come, whistling for the dogs as he did.

They came crashing out of the bracken, tongues lolling, ran round Polly and Chum a couple of times then sprinted off in the direction in which the humans were now walking.

'That's a good system,' said Polly. 'A walk-stop call, rather than a wake-up call.'

'Yes,' said Chum, 'I do it every time I go out for a walk or a ride, or I'd just keep going till I fell off the end of something. I get into the zone and forget about everything, which is the whole point, of course.'

'It has rather zonked me out,' said Polly. 'All this beautiful fresh air.'

Chum grinned.

'That's the whole point, Hippolyta,' he said, 'to get the brain into off mode. Do your London walks not have the same effect?'

'No,' said Polly. 'I thought they did – well, they're better than being stuck inside – but compared with this, they're the low-fat version. Not fully satisfying. There is one thing that does make me feel like this, though: yoga. That's my other occupation. I've been a yoga teacher for over twenty years. This gives me a similar buzz to a yoga meditation and I'm getting aerobic exercise too, so double score.'

And there was another element, thought Polly, apart from nature in all its glory, that had made this walk so enjoyable: having someone to talk to. Normally it was just her and Digger, so it made such a nice change to have someone else there she could chat with while they walked. It was also nice when they weren't talking. Companionship, that was what it was – sharing space comfortably in silence.

'We should do it again,' said Chum. 'I know lots of great walks around here. Been walking and riding this country all my life. When your mother's better, perhaps we can set my stop-walk alarm for longer and then you'll really feel the benefit.'

'That would be great,' said Polly. 'And Digger would love it too.'

'I have lunch with Bill every Friday, so that's always a good day, but I don't live far away and I can come over any time, really. I'll give you my number and you can text me if you feel like another walk.'

'I will,' said Polly, and as they came out of the wood and back into the field – the Land Rover visible in the distance, the churned muddy earth shining in the low winter afternoon sun and a hawk wheeling overhead – she realised she was already looking forward to it.

'How about Monday?' she said.

Thursday, 28 January

Daphne was supervising as Polly did her nails.

'Just use the emery board in one direction,' she was saying. 'Don't saw at the nail, you'll weaken it.'

She was definitely better, Polly thought. Daphne had been off the drip for a couple of days, and with Polly's encouragement was eating more, taking various supplements and drinking two jugs of water a day. Polly had pointed out how good water was for the skin, rehydrating from the inside, which had done the trick with her mother.

She was going home that afternoon, but was so pleased to see her mother back to her old self, her former dottiness greatly reduced, that she'd been happy to indulge her by agreeing to this beauty-care tutorial before she left.

'Can I take this mud mask off now?' she asked. 'It's making my face itch.'

She washed it off and then rejoined Daphne at her dressing table as she demonstrated her facial massage techniques and Polly tried to copy the moves.

'Always up, darling,' Daphne said, elevating her extraordinarily long neck like a well-coiffed ET, and patting the cream onto it in little sweeping upwards movements, using the fingers of both hands like stiff little flippers.

'Round to one side, up to the jaw, along, then repeat on the other side.'

'How often do you do this?' asked Polly.

'Every morning and every night,' said Daphne, as though it were a ridiculous question. 'I've done it all your life, so I'm surprised you haven't noticed.'

'Well, I do remember you doing all your patting,' said Polly, 'but I didn't realise it was twice a day. My neck's tingling now, is that all right?'

'That's exactly what you want!' exclaimed Daphne. 'It means you're stimulating the blood flow, moving it around, carrying away impurities, refreshing the cells.'

Polly didn't think that statement would stand up to too much scientific examination, but said nothing. Daphne did have wonderful skin and a very firm jawline for her age, so maybe there was something in it.

With that done, they moved on to another ritual involving a serum that was smoothed on, followed by another cream, which had to be lightly pressed on over the top. Polly had hummed the Hokey Cokey as she did it.

'In out, in out, rub it all about,' she sang.

'Even after the serum, your skin is very dry,' Daphne said, peering at Polly's forehead through a magnifying glass she kept on her dressing table. 'It's quite papery. What products are you using?'

Polly struggled to remember. It was something Clemmie had left behind. Before that she'd had a nice pot of cream a beauty PR had given her at an open day, but she couldn't remember what the brand was. Sometimes she just used coconut oil.

'Oh, this and that,' she said, taking the magnifying glass from Daphne and looking at herself through it in the mirror. Her cheeks were bright red, probably an allergic reaction to the mud mask, she thought, although the second walk she'd taken with Chum on Monday had been pretty bracing. It had started sleeting before they'd got back to the Land Rover and her cheeks had felt frozen. That couldn't have been great for the complexion.

'You need to take your skin more seriously, Polly,' said Daphne. 'You've been lucky so far, good genes, but you're at the age now when it will suddenly deteriorate beyond repair unless you start looking after it. I use Sisley, as you know. You should go and have a consultation at one of their counters.'

Polly didn't know, although the white and grey pots did look familiar.

'They send it to me, of course,' said Daphne, regarding her reflection with satisfaction. 'Because I did all those campaigns for them. I'll ask them to send me some products for you, see what they have for premature aging.'

After that there'd been a make-up lesson, involving way too much powder and that awful coral lipstick again, then finally Daphne wanted to supervise Polly painting her freshly filed nails.

Daphne's hands weren't steady enough to paint her own nails now – she had them done every week at the on-site beauty salon – but she showed Polly how much varnish to load onto the brush and how to press it down lightly at the base to release it and then pull it up the nail. She also told Polly to do her right hand first, with her left, to reduce the chance of clumsy left-hand slips at the end.

'There,' said Daphne, when Polly had carefully done the final layer of top coat. 'Don't they look lovely? Now you look finished.'

Polly couldn't stop admiring her fingers. On her older hands, the polished nails looked very sophisticated, not overdone as they could look on young women.

It wasn't the first time in her life she'd painted her nails, she just hadn't done it for years because David loathed it, as he did all make-up, and she hadn't cared enough to spend time debating it. Now she thought she might start wearing nail varnish all the time. She could see it would look better at events when she was holding up perfume bottles and handing round blotters to the audience. She might even have a proper manicure once in a while; that would please her mum.

She turned to look at Daphne, engaged in tweaking her already perfect hair with the end of a tail comb. Polly put her arms around her mother's bony frame and gave her a gentle hug.

'Thanks, Mummy,' she said, 'for making a proper woman of me.'

'You're welcome, darling,' said Daphne, patting her shoulder. 'Thank you for looking after me. I'm very lucky to have you for a daughter – and your children are very lucky to have you for a mother.'

Polly was so pleased and surprised at the unexpected compliments she couldn't think what to say, so she gave her mum another hug.

~

'Look who it is, Digsy!' said Bill, opening his front door to Polly. 'Time for your walk.'

'Actually, it's time for us to go home,' said Polly with a tinge of regret. 'My mum's fine now and I need to get back. This is to say a massive thank you for looking after him.'

She held out a bottle of single malt.

'Oh, dear girl,' said Bill, 'you really didn't need to do that. I loved having Digger. We're great friends, aren't we?'

He leaned down to pat the dog, who looked up at him, tail wagging vigorously, glancing over to Polly and then back at Bill, clearly wondering where his loyalty lay. Where his next meal was coming from, more like it, thought Polly.

'Well, it was very kind of you to have him,' said Polly. 'You really got me out of a tight spot. Please take it.'

'You're very generous, and I would be delighted,' said Bill, taking the bottle and looking at the label. 'Aha, Ardbeg. A good peaty one. Lovely.'

'My father used to drink it,' said Polly, thinking how lucky it was she'd found it, unopened, at the back of one of her mother's kitchen cabinets. 'He was a Highlander and liked a lot of peat in his dram.'

'As do I,' said Bill.

'I know,' said Polly. 'I spotted your bottle of Talisker.'

Bill laughed.

'Will you come in and have a cup of coffee before you go?'

Polly hesitated. She didn't want to turn him down, if it would be nice for him to have some company, but now she was able to leave, she really wanted to get going. There would be so much to see to at home after a week away.

'Edward's coming for lunch,' he added, glancing at his watch. 'He'll be here in half an hour or so. You could say hello to him.'

Happy to be reassured that Bill wasn't going to be lonely, Polly couldn't resist the urge to flee another minute.

'Oh, that would have been lovely,' she said, 'but I need to get off. Please say hi to, er, Edward for me. It's been great to see him again and I've so enjoyed our walks.'

'So has he, dear,' said Bill, patting Polly's arm. 'A bit of stimulating company is exactly what he needs. Do let me know when you're next visiting, because I know he'd like to see you. He can pop over any day, really.'

'I'll do that,' said Polly. 'I've got your number, and I'm sure Digger would like to see you again too.'

Polly drove out of the gates of Rockham Park singing along with the radio, thinking what a relief it would be to be back in her own place.

It wasn't.

From the moment she walked through the front door and inhaled its very particular smell, she felt desolate. Nowhere could make you feel lonelier, she thought, than an empty place that was once full of life.

Leaning against the front door, she closed her eyes and almost thought she could hear the kids' voices, as they were when they were young, echoing down the hallway to her from the kitchen.

'Mum! Mum!'

Of course it was deadly silent. She wondered if she was actually going mad.

She glanced around the hallway, noticing there wasn't any post. Then she saw a vase of fresh lilies on the side table, with a postcard propped up against it: a nice cheerful Matisse interior. She picked it up and read it:

> Hi, doll. Came by a few times while you were away, to keep the place looking lived in. I've put your post on your desk. I got your text about coming back and there's milk (cow) and stuff in the fridge. Let me know when you want to start classes again and I'll message the yogi bears.
>
> Shirl xxx
>
> P.S. No pressure. Well, a bit ha ha.

What a good friend Shirlee was. Polly felt quite choked up with gratitude and sent her a text to confirm there would be a class in the morning.

Opening and responding to the large pile of post on her desk pleasantly occupied most of the afternoon and really cheered Polly up, especially all the invitations to perfume events. By the time she'd sorted and replied to them all, she had a pretty full diary for the next three weeks. That was great news. The more often she could be out of this horrible empty house, the better.

But she had a problem with one of the most enticing invitations. OM Beauty were launching a new men's fragrance, and rather than an intimate dinner for key media, or a 6 p.m. cocktail gathering, they were holding a proper big glamorous party. And the invitation was 'plus one'. It said: 'Polly Masterson-Mackay – and a man who loves the Great Outdoors'.

It would be so nice to be able to take someone with her, but who? David wouldn't have gone even if he'd been around. He'd have muttered something about how perfume was a bourgeois trifle, although he did wear the Yohji Homme she'd given him because he liked its distinctive liquorice note. David loved liquorice; it was one of his little quirks.

She sat at her desk admiring her red fingernails as she tapped them against the stiff card invitation, wondering who on earth she could invite. Clemmie had come along to a few things, which had been fun, but mostly Polly just arranged to meet up at the event with other perfume bloggers she'd got to know on the circuit, who were also invited. They were mostly women, and for this she needed a bloke. Plus she wanted to go to this party *with* someone, not just hook up once she got there.

She put the invitation down on her desk and walked through to the kitchen to make a cup of tea. As she filled the kettle, the perfect candidate for 'a man who loves the Great

Outdoors' suddenly became obvious: Chum. Although she was certain he would never call it that – 'country' was the word he used. But whatever you called it, she didn't think she'd ever met anyone who was as attuned to it as he was.

She'd seen it on their walks; as soon as he got his boot soles onto the bare earth he seemed to inhabit his own body in a more complete way.

But while he was clearly the one for the real 'Great Outdoors', she was fairly sure he'd be mystified by the idea of trying to capture it in a bottle. 'Why not just go for a walk?' he'd say. Plus, she wasn't sure he'd feel comfortable at such an event, and he lived miles outside London. And she hardly knew him well enough to ask him anyway. They'd known each other so long ago; a couple of walks didn't make them close friends again.

So, definitely not Chum, but who else could she ask? Sitting back down at her desk with her mug of tea, she warmed her hands round it, admiring her nails from another angle, thinking.

As she looked at them, the light from her laptop screen caught her wedding ring and it made her blink.

She'd worn it for so many years she never gave it a moment's thought these days, but suddenly she wondered about it. There she was, walking round with that potent symbol on her finger advertising her marital state when in fact she'd been living alone for weeks. What did it even mean any more?

Slowly, she slid it off her finger and put it on her desk. She held her fingers out straight and they looked so odd. They felt funny too. Her ring finger was even a bit shrivelled below the knuckle, where the ring had been all that time. Should she leave it off as a statement, until David came back?

She wanted to, but then thought of the kids. It would upset them, especially Lucas, and she didn't want to trigger another binge from him. She and Clemmie were still monitoring him from a distance and thought he was being more sensible; she certainly didn't want to set him off again.

She turned her attention back to the invitation. Who could she take?

Then, as she lifted the mug of tea to her lips, she had a strong waft of the perfume on her wrists – PM, as it so often was these days – and realised Guy Webber was the perfect person.

Wednesday, 3 February

Polly took a glass of champagne from a tray held by a strikingly handsome young man, wearing a plaid shirt unbuttoned nearly to his navel, with tight khaki cargo pants, tucked into chunky walking boots.

He was dressed for the Great Outdoors, all right – or at least a pastiche of it, as were the other waiters, clearly recruited from a model agency – but all the guests were dressed very much for Mayfair. Polly was glad she'd painted her nails again, blow-dried her hair and put on a dress and high heels. Maybe that saying that every woman turned into her mother eventually had some truth in it after all.

She took a sip from her glass and mentally toasted the idea. There was a lot about Daphne to aspire to.

Waiting to stash her coat in the cloakroom, she looked around for Guy, who had walked into the venue with her and promptly vanished. She hoped it hadn't been a mistake to invite him. But then he reappeared, walking slowly towards her with three lavish cocktails carefully clasped between his hands.

'Sorry, Poll,' he said, 'I got distracted by the drinks options. They've done something rather clever and I wanted to check them all out. Ditch that champers and try one of these. Quick, before I drop them and make an arse of myself.'

Polly looked regretfully at her glass of golden bubbles and reached out and took one of his cocktail glasses.

'Smell it first,' Guy was saying and Polly lowered her nose to the ice-cold flute. Pine cones, thyme and a general air of greenness.

'Good, isn't it?' said Guy. 'They've themed the cocktails with elements from the fragrance and other notes that fit the outdoors theme – like this crazy decor.'

He nodded at a pile of what were clearly prop house papier-mâché rocks, with real flowers climbing up them.

'Don't spare the budget, do they?' he said. 'So, anyway, that one you've got has the strong pine accord in it, this one has an ozonic hint, so ...'

Polly put her hand on his arm to stop him in mid-flow. She could hear a tantalising hum of talk and laughter coming from the floor above and didn't want to hang around while he expounded on the other two mixes.

'Come on, Guy,' she said, 'let's get into the party. You can tell me about the cocktails on the way up.'

Although it was a cold February night outside, the rooms upstairs were lit with golden filters, which made it feel more like May, and the tribe of plaid-shirted hotties were circulating with platters of delicious – and suitably rugged – canapés.

Polly and Guy stood on the far side of the main room, taking in the scene.

'You can see why I haven't had a launch,' said Guy, chewing on a piece of practically raw steak. 'I could never compete with something like this.'

A major footballer who even Polly recognised had just walked in and Guy had already pointed out a Formula One driver and a famous jockey. It was the most glamorous perfume event Polly had been to yet. Checking out the crowd, she could also see a good-looking academic who presented a popular TV show about the British landscape, a well-known mountaineer, a survival expert who hosted a celebrity reality show, and one of the faces from the BBC's most loved nature programme, which had more viewers than *The X Factor*. Clever call by OM Beauty, she thought.

'I think they've got every man here who has ever appeared on British television in speciality outdoor footwear,' said Guy, grabbing a mini-burger from a passing rent-a-hunk. 'Football boots, walking boots, riding boots, whatever weird boots racing car drivers wear ... See that tall bloke there, Rupert Everett type, sort of a flat head, like something off a Roman coin? He's a famous dressage dude. You know, that cringey horse dancing?'

Polly glanced over to where Guy was indicating and flinched in shock. For a moment she thought it was Chum. Surely it couldn't be? She peered, trying to see more clearly.

'Are you all right?' asked Guy.

'Oh, sorry,' said Polly. 'It's just the dressage bloke looks so much like a friend of mine – although this is really the last place I would expect to see him. He is a big rider, though, so perhaps it *is* him ...'

The man had turned his head away but she couldn't stop staring. From the back he looked about Chum's height and build, but it was hard to visualise Chum in such a nice suit. Apart from his dinner jacket at St Andrews, she'd only seen him in his old tweed jacket and his Barbour.

'Let's swerve past,' said Guy. 'I'd liked to circumnavigate the room, check out the rest of the joint, see where the ack-shon is.'

He led on and Polly followed behind, finding her heels oddly easier to walk in after a couple of cocktails. She'd just finished one with a more floral tone to it, something a bit bluebell-ish.

Guy led her right past the Chum look-alike and then came to an abrupt halt, pulling her round to face him – giving her a direct sight line to Non-Chum, as she now saw he was. But still so like him it was quite uncanny.

Non-Chum noticed her staring at him. That was embarrassing. She smiled broadly, hoping he would think she was a big dressage fan recognising a hero, and he smiled back, which made him look even more like Chum. He had the same deep creases on either side of his mouth, right down to his chin, though he didn't quite have Chum's bemused look, or the endearing gap between his front teeth.

Polly turned on her heel and walked off fast, Guy appearing immediately at her side, laughing.

'Not your mate, then?' he said.

'No,' said Polly, 'and he saw me staring like a freak. Oh, never mind.'

She stopped a passing lumberjack and grabbed a glass of champagne. She'd had enough of the scented cocktails. Her mouth was starting to feel like she'd eaten too many cheap sweets. She loved wearing perfume, but wasn't so keen on the idea of drinking it, although it occurred to her Guy would probably think nothing of swilling it down neat.

She leaned in closer to him and sniffed.

'Mmm,' she said, 'you smell lovely tonight, Guy. It's quite subtle for you. Is it one of yours?'

He laughed.

'Dammit,' he said, 'rumbled. No, after that stupid stunt I pulled on our last outing, I thought it would be polite if I wore someone else's work tonight. Can you recognise it?'

Polly put her nose close to his shirt collar and breathed in again.

'Something with a lot of lovely iris root,' she said. 'Gotta love that earthy "orris", as you probably call it, being a poncy perfumer ... It's not Miller Harris and I don't think you'd wear Crabtree & Evelyn. It's not Prada ...'

'You say iris, I say orris,' said Guy. 'Potato, pot-art-o ... Do you give up?

'No,' said Polly, closing her eyes and concentrating on what she could smell apart from the glorious powdery waves of iris root – which she so loved. Then she got it. There was a metallic edge to it.

'Iris Silver Mist,' she said, smiling at Guy. 'Serge Lutens.'

'Damn right,' said Guy, putting out his hand to shake hers. 'Good call. I'm glad you like, what I call orris. It's what I want to work with next, so I'm studying around it.'

'Stepping even further away from the power orientals, then?' she asked. 'First the chypre, now iris ...'

'Yes,' said Guy, smiling. 'I've got the message. It was very nice of you to wear PM tonight, by the way.'

'I'm wearing it a lot,' she said. 'I'd probably be wearing it even if you weren't here. I love it, it's fascinating.'

Guy looked delighted.

'Well, I did make it for you, so I'm glad you like it, and I'm very grateful that you set me on that course, because it's flying out of my shop. Doesn't scare them off like the others.'

'You mean to tell me you're selling it to other people?' said Polly in a mock outraged voice. 'I thought it was exclusively for me.'

'Well, I did name it after you, Polly, but I'm afraid it is still a commercial venture.'

Polly smiled. 'I'm very touched you've named a perfume after me, and especially one I adore so much – but you'd better not let some other blogger write about it before I do.

When are we going do that interview, Guy? I know I was away for a bit, but you keep dodging the subject and it's driving me nuts. I want to blog about you before someone else stumbles across you.'

'Soon,' he said, 'really soon. I just want to build up a little more critical mass through the word-of-mouth thing, and I promise I won't talk to any other bloggers before you. Ooh, listen, there's a band playing in the next room, let's go and see what they're like.'

Polly was certain he was changing the subject, but wasn't in the mood to push it. She was loving the party. It was the best time she'd had for ages and she wanted to revel in the fun of it.

The band were great, and after spotting a beauty magazine editor she knew on the dance floor, Polly went and joined her. Guy came too and soon there was a little gang of them in the centre of the mêlée, getting down to the great cover versions the band were playing of American rock bands, mostly from the 1970s.

It was great fun dancing to the endearingly cheesy tracks, and Guy turned out to be one of those people who could be hilarious through dance moves. His interpretative shapes during the slow part of 'Hotel California' made Polly laugh so much she thought she might wet herself.

She left the dance floor to find the loo and on her way back made a detour to grab a glass of water. As she turned away from the bar, Non-Chum walked up.

'Oh, hello,' she heard herself saying, as if she knew him. He looked so much like Chum she felt as though she did.

'Hello,' he said, looking a little puzzled, probably wondering where they'd met.

'Sorry I was staring at you earlier,' said Polly, realising as she said it that this was a conversation she would never have had without several cocktails and a lot of champagne inside her. 'It's just that you look so much like a friend of mine, I thought you were him for a moment, and I wondered if you might be related.'

'Well, I'm Rollo Cliddington,' he said, putting out his hand to shake hers. 'Does that help?'

Polly's champagne-addled brain tried to work out if it did. Hang on ... Cliddington.

'Well, possibly,' she said. 'My friend is Edward Cliddington-Hanley-Maugham, so the Cliddington bit's the same, and you look so like him. I call him Chum.'

Rollo grinned, but then a sad look came into his eyes.

'So do I,' he said. 'He's my cousin. I'm really Cliddington-Hanley-Maugham too, but I shorten it. Our dads were brothers. Poor old Chum. Have you seen him recently?'

Poor old Chum. There it was again. Bill had said he'd had a rough time and now this from his cousin. How odd. He'd never let on that anything was badly wrong on their walks. Mind you, neither had she. That was one of the things she enjoyed about them, no deep and meaningfuls, just easy company and fun talking about old times. And as long as she didn't go prying into his private life, it was less likely that he'd ask questions about hers.

'I saw him last week,' she said. 'We were at St Andrews together and we ran into each other recently, because my mum lives in the same place as his stepfather, Bill.'

'Ah,' said Rollo. 'How is Bill? Lovely chap. He's been very good to Chum.'

'He's great,' said Polly, rather vaguely, distracted by yet another hint that Chum needed extra emotional support for some reason.

'Well, do give them both my love next time you see them,' said Rollo. 'I don't get back to see that side of the family much these days. It's difficult in the circumstances, and I'm so busy training at the moment.'

'Oh, yes,' said Polly, wondering what these 'circumstances' were. 'The dressage. Are you going to the Olympics?'

'Yes,' said Rollo, with a slightly cool expression. 'I'm Captain of the British Equestrian Team.'

'Of course you are,' said Polly. Oops. 'Silly me, too much champagne. Well, good luck with that. Fantastic. I'll be cheering you on. In front of the telly, of course ...'

She really did need to shut up.

'Thank you. Good to see you,' he said, turning away and clearly about to head off.

Suddenly she couldn't resist.

'Just one thing, Rollo,' she said, touching his arm. She could feel the hard muscle of his forearm even through his suit jacket. All that horse-restraining. Crikey. 'Why do you say "poor old Chum"?'

Rollo looked at her with slightly narrowed eyes. He clearly thought she was sensationally stupid, too nosy, or not to be trusted in some way. A gold-digger? A title-hunter?

He hesitated for a moment before answering.

'Google it,' he said and walked off without saying another word.

Thursday, 4 February

Early morning Downward Dog was more of a challenge than usual with a thumping headache – especially as Polly had stayed up when she got home the night before to write a blog post about the party. She'd wanted to be the first person to do it and a strong black coffee had sobered her up enough to do a decent job.

She'd opened her site with some trepidation that morning, in case it was an embarrassing drunken rant, but written so close to the event, while she was still on a party high, she thought it conveyed the fun of the evening rather well. She was quite pleased with herself – and delighted when she saw that the head PR for the brand had commented with lots of kisses.

Polly's good mood lasted right through the 8 a.m. yoga class and on to breakfast with Shirlee and Maxine.

'I'm starving,' she said, hovering over Shirlee's shoulder as she cooked bacon simultaneously in two pans – the kosher lamb variety for herself, the classic version for Polly and Maxine. 'Don't turn the gas off, I'm going to fry some bread in that fat when you've finished.'

'Good night, was it?' asked Shirlee. 'I thought I detected a bit of a glow around you this morning. If you weren't a happily married woman, I'd think you'd gotten yourself laid.'

'Oh sure,' said Polly, sarcastically. 'My Wednesday night lover. Thursday's in the gym right now, getting revved up.'

'Friday's getting his crack waxed,' added Shirlee.

'Saturday's child works hard for his living,' threw in Maxine.

'Verrrry hard,' said Shirlee, chuckling.

'Very funny,' said Polly, pinching Shirlee's bottom. 'No one got laid, but if I've got a glow, it was from the dancing. It was so fun. A live band – you know how that makes it even better?'

'That's great, Poll,' said Shirlee, sitting at the table. 'You don't have enough fun.'

Polly said nothing for a moment, thinking about what Shirlee had just said as she put slices of bread into the now-empty frying pans, and feeling oddly winded by it.

'You're probably right,' she said, once she'd gathered herself. 'I hadn't thought about it before, but do many adults really have much fun? It gets squeezed out by real life, doesn't it?'

She lifted the slices of golden, crispy bread onto a plate, took them over to the table and sat down.

'I think it's why so many people drink,' said Maxine. 'It enables them to transcend everyday cares without making any effort – apart from opening the bottle, or ordering at a bar – and they feel like they're having fun. Of course that can be beneficial if it's only occasional. It's when they start reaching for that instant distraction every day that the balance shifts and rather than easing their real-life worries, it creates more of them, which quickly becomes a downward spiral. More worries, then more drink and so on—'

'Well, thank you for that uplifting thought this morning, Sigmund,' said Shirlee, cutting her off. 'One minute we're talking about having more fun, then Dr Shrinkhead here starts going on about descent into alcohol dependency. Lighten up, lady. Anyway, you don't have to drink to have fun. I *find* fun. I go looking for it. You can sniff it out anywhere if you try. I think having breakfast with you two is fun – except when Maxine goes off on one ...'

She stuck her tongue out at her and Maxine laughed.

'Sorry,' she said, 'it becomes a habit, doing what I do. Pathologising everything.'

'Well, why don't you pathologise this?' asked Shirlee, putting a bit of bacon on the end of her fork and flicking it at her. It sailed over Maxine's shoulder and hit the floor. Digger was over in a moment to snaffle it.

Polly smiled at them, dropping another piece of bacon for Digger to 'find', but she was still thinking about what Shirlee had said. She didn't have much fun, it was true. She hugely enjoyed all the perfume events she hosted and attended, but they stimulated her, rather than being fun.

The night before had been different. There'd been a joyous abandonment to it that had left her feeling renewed. It was hard to think when she'd last let go like that. Not since Lucas had gone back to college, certainly. They would spontaneously dance together in the kitchen, if the right track came on. Sometimes it would turn into a full-on Dinner Time Disco, as he called it, with the two of them taking turns to choose the next track. How she missed her boy.

'So how do you randomly find fun?' she asked Shirlee.

'It's a bit like looking on the bright side, I guess,' she replied. 'Your glass might be half-empty or half-full, whatever – I'm wearing mine on my head, juggling it, making it into a percussion instrument. It's not what you're doing, or where you go, or who you're with, but what you make it into.'

Polly remembered being in Emergency with Shirlee that time. How Shirlee had got chocolate bars and coffee and made jokes with the staff. Whittington Hospital Emergency Department at four in the morning was one of the grimmest places Polly could think of, but with Shirlee there, it had been fun in a bonkers kind of way.

'But talking of laughs,' said Shirlee, 'it can't be a load of fun being here on your own all the time, in what used to be your laughter-filled family home. Any sign of that husband coming back? Or do we need to start lining up those lovers for real?'

Polly put her knife and fork down. She hadn't been expecting that. Far from creating fun, with one serve too many of her over-intrusive questions, Shirlee had snuffed out Polly's good mood in an instant. And to do it at Polly's kitchen table, lounging back in her chair like she owned the place, wiping her fat finger along her plate to pick up the last bit of egg yolk, was the limit.

Polly felt a flash of hot indignation go through her.

'I don't know where he is,' she snapped, the words out of her mouth before she could check herself.

Not good. She shouldn't have said that. That was somewhere she really didn't want to go with these two.

They were both looking at her steadily, as though they were waiting to see what she would say next.

Polly looked back at them, feeling cornered and not happy about it. She got up from the table and started briskly gathering up the plates.

'He's off on some boring research project, like I told you,' she said, snatching Shirlee's plate from under her still-scavenging finger. 'Some of the places he goes have very poor communications, so I don't always know exactly where he is. Academics get long study breaks and he's researching an important new book. It takes a while.'

That was a downright lie, she acknowledged to herself, as she noisily stacked the dishwasher. The first she'd told anyone about David's absence. Up until then she'd relied on half-truths and evasions, but Shirlee had caught her unawares.

Polly normally found Shirlee's brutal forthrightness refreshing and amusing. Not this time, though.

She glanced back over her shoulder to check if there was anything left on the table to clear, and saw Shirlee leaning across towards Maxine, mouthing something. Maxine's eyes were open wide and she shrugged, grimacing, spreading her hands. Just at that moment Maxine noticed Polly had seen and quickly looked down. Shirlee swung round towards Polly, who whipped her head back towards the dishwasher.

What the hell was going on, thought Polly. She stalled for time, fiddling with plates, trying to look busy, and to her great relief, when she turned back, Shirlee and Maxine were both standing up, pushing their chairs under the table.

'See you tomorrow, yoga goddess,' said Shirlee, in a slightly deflated attempt at her usual bonhomie, kissing Polly on the cheek as she moved towards the door.

Polly gave her shoulder a squeeze, in what she hoped was a silent reassurance that it would all be fine, and followed them though to the hall. Then she blew them a kiss from the front door, closing it firmly behind them. She was already halfway to forgiving Shirlee, but for the time being she was glad to see them go.

After a moment standing in the hall to gather her thoughts, Polly set her shoulders then headed to the study. A day of solid work was what she needed, getting stuck into researching her next event.

It was themed on the subject of chypre, her favourite fragrance family, which had a fascinating and quite vigorously debated history; some people in the perfume world loved a bitch fight. Chypre's origins went back to Roman times and took in Marie Antoinette's personal perfumer, long before you got to 1919, when Jacques Guerlain launched Mitsouko, the greatest chypre of them all.

Polly was mentally rubbing her hands with glee at the thought of getting stuck into it. Historical research examining the still undecided question of which were the true base notes of the style, combined everything she'd loved about academia with her perfume passion. Heaven.

Before starting that, she did a quick check of her email inbox and clicked immediately on a message from Lori, which had a row of exclamation marks in the subject line.

As she read it, Polly's good mood evaporated for the second time that morning.

> Poll doll!!!! Get the French on ice – we're coming over! April – so not far off. Yay!!!!
>
> Rich has got some research to do and this is one field trip I'm happy to tag along on.
>
> Can we stay? It's just us, no kids, and he'll be going off on loads of (boring) research missions, so it'll mostly just be me. I'll get back to you when I know the exact dates. So excited!!
>
> Lozzer xxxxxxxxxx

Polly couldn't think of anything she would love more than having Lori and Rich to stay – normally. But how the hell was she going to explain David's absence to them?

There was no fudging the details of a historian's research trip to another historian and his wife. And if there was anyone on earth who would see through her act, it was Lori. She'd know something was going on the moment she laid eyes on

Polly. That was one of the reasons Polly had been avoiding Skyping or FaceTiming her since their last call.

Polly pushed her laptop away and put her head down on the edge of the desk in despair. How the hell was she going to handle this?

Something like panic started to rev up in her head, closely followed by a flash of white-hot anger. There was nothing she would love more than seeing her wonderful, vibrant, life-affirming friend Lori and again – yet *again* – David's crazy disappearing act had ruined it before it had even begun.

Polly got up, feeling charged with furious energy. She felt like punching the wall, but knew it would hurt, if not actually break her hand. She tried to calm herself down, to breath through it, as she usually did, but it was hopeless. This visceral anger needed to be vented.

She glanced round the room and her gaze fell on David's badminton racket in the corner. Remembering what Shirlee had done with the wooden spoon that time in the kitchen, she picked it up and brought it down onto the cushioned seat of the nearest armchair. It was surprisingly satisfying and she did it again – harder.

'That's for leaving the kids!' she shouted. *Thwhack*. 'That's for leaving me!' *Thwack*. 'And making me lie to my friends and my mother! And this is for turning our beautiful son into a lush! And for making Clemmie collude with you! And for deserting Digger! And this is for being the most selfish man on earth!' She banged the armchair repeatedly, until the clouds of dust made her cough and she had to stop.

She stood for a moment, her chest heaving, feeling almost dizzy from the violence of her hits, but there was still a bit more to let go. She threw the racket onto the ground, jumped up and down on it a few times, until she heard a satisfying crack, and then kicked it into the corner.

Sod him and his namby-pamby arsehole badminton racket. Bugger his selfish bastarding shittiness. In fact, basically, fuck him. Polly had had enough.

Without bothering to close it down properly, she slammed the lid of her laptop down. She'd answer Lori's email when she was feeling calmer – and had some idea how she was going to handle the situation.

Meanwhile, she had to get out of the house.

She needed some proper head space to digest this latest complication – and that meant one thing. A walk.

Chum was waiting for her in his Land Rover when she pulled up outside Rockham Park. Digger immediately started barking and whining, his paws up against the car windows. Could he smell Artemis through the glass? Probably.

Polly turned off the engine and leaned down for a moment, pretending to grovel around in her handbag on the passenger seat. She felt momentarily shy. It had been pure impulse texting Chum to ask whether he had time for a walk with her that day, and she'd been quite surprised to get his immediate reply saying he'd love to.

Another text had followed right after it: Long walk or short?

Looooooooong, Polly had replied, and here she was, having jumped straight into the car, not even showered.

She was still pretending to grope around in her bag when the car door opened. She turned to see Chum's smiling face and was glad when Digger seized his opportunity to make a break for freedom, jumping heavily onto her lap and then out of the car door.

'Whoa,' said Chum, stepping back and laughing. 'Looks like you're not the only one who needs some exercise. You said a long walk, Polly – did you mean that?'

'Yes,' she said, pulling out her lip salve and holding it in the air, as though that was what she'd been looking for all the time. She slicked some on for good measure.

'Have you got some proper footwear with you this time?' asked Chum, looking at her trainers as she got out of the car. 'This is going to be serious walking. The other two we did were nursery slopes.'

'Yes,' said Polly, and then leaning against the side of the car as she pulled her boots on, she couldn't help smiling when she saw how suspiciously Chum was looking at them.

They were black, with biker-style straps around the ankle and top.

'I know they look like city boots,' she said, 'but they really are waterproof. I've waded into ponds in these to drag Digger out. Boots don't have to be green to be waterproof.'

Chum laughed.

'Got it,' he said, 'and I've already learned Barbours don't have to be green either, when you're wearing one.'

'I've got a hat too,' she said, pulling a brown corduroy butcher-boy cap out of her pocket and putting it on. 'So I won't need to borrow your tweed number.'

'Very fetching,' said Chum. 'I even approve of the material. It might be related to my trousers.'

Polly laughed, climbing into the Land Rover, and they set off at Chum's customary terrifying speed down the country lanes.

'It's a bit of a longer drive to the start today,' said Chum, 'but it'll be worth it and we've got a few hours, which is great.

It's only just after twelve and it won't get dark until five. Have you eaten anything?'

'I had a big breakfast … bit of a hangover.'

'Oh yes,' said Chum, 'you met my cousin Rollo at some swanky party.'

Polly looked at him, her mouth open in surprise. She shut it quickly.

'Did he tell you?' she asked. But she hadn't told him her name, so how could he have?

'No. I read it on your blog this morning,' said Chum, turning towards her for a moment with a very cheeky grin.

Polly looked at him with her mouth open.

'You read my blog?' she said.

'Well, if you chat up my cousin at parties, you've got to expect me to keep an eye on what you're up to.'

How embarrassing. It had never occurred to her that Chum would look at FragrantCloud.

'I didn't chat him up,' said Polly, feeling herself going pink. 'But I did ask him if he was related to you.' She started to giggle. 'He looks so like you … a slightly younger version.'

She play-punched Chum's bicep and found it was as firm as Rollo's forearm had been.

'And better dressed, no doubt,' said Chum. 'Better looking, richer, more famous … You should be on a walk with him.'

'I haven't got enough legs,' said Polly, 'and I wouldn't look good doing that sideways dancing thing.'

Chum laughed. Proper laughter, head back, loud noise. Polly felt shy again, though happy she could make someone laugh like that.

'So what did he tell you about me?' he asked after a moment, sounding more serious.

'That your fathers are brothers – so you're cousins.'

He glanced at her again, eyes narrowed.

'That was all?' he asked.

Polly hesitated for a moment. 'He said I should google you.'

Chum laughed again, but more of a snort than the lovely free guffaw earlier.

'Did you?' he asked.

'No,' she answered. 'It was only last night and I've had a busy morning.'

He turned to her again – she wished he wouldn't, as they hurtled towards a blind bend – smiling, but with a wistful look in his eye.

'I'll save you the bother,' he said. 'If you want to know anything about me – just ask.'

Polly hesitated for the moment. There were lots of things she wanted to know. Like, why does everyone keep saying 'poor Chum'? Why aren't you married to a lovely horsey posh woman? Why don't you have lots of lovely horsey posh children? How come you're free to go for a walk with me on a Thursday morning with one hour's notice?

But tempting though it was, she knew such a line of inquiry would inevitably lead to a similar interrogation about her own life and she really didn't want to go there. The whole point of this walk was to block out all the complications and confusions of the David mess that Lori's email had brought back into sharp focus. Not to have to answer questions that would force her to think about it.

'OK,' she said, 'tell me what you love about working with horses.'

He turned quickly to look at her again and then grinned. He'd clearly been expecting something different and was just as relieved to be off the hook as she was.

'Do you ride?' he asked.

'I did, a bit, as a girl,' said Polly. 'I had pony posters on my walls when I was ten. The normal thing.'

'Well, then you'll know how satisfying it is when an animal so much bigger and stronger than you are understands what you would like it do to – and does it. Happily. Then scale that up to working with them from when they're very young. Having a relationship with an animal that close is very rewarding. And I just like being around them. They're so much less complicated than human beings.'

'That makes sense,' said Polly. 'I'm starting to feel like that about Digger.'

'Starting to?' said Chum, and Polly realised she'd accidentally put herself in dangerous territory. The last thing she wanted to get into was why she was suddenly spending more time with the dog.

'Oh, you know,' she said hurriedly. 'I just love the stinky old mutt more and more, that's all.'

'Got it,' said Chum. 'So tell me about your work. I know you go to very glamorous parties, but what else does a perfume blogger do?'

She gave him a very potted version, which he seemed satisfied with, but even before she'd finished talking, she was processing the idea that Chum had read the blog and wondering which posts he might have looked at.

She did a mental run-through of the most recent ones and then it hit her: the one on university days. Oh, no! All that stuff was about his crowd. And him.

Her head whipped round to look at him and he glanced back with his bemused, slightly sad smile. He hadn't read it, she decided. He would have said something or teased her about it if he had.

That was a relief. Big time. Especially because of the last bit, about the kiss. That time they'd kissed. In the sand dunes, the night of the beach bonfire.

A secret tryst, while everyone else was skinny-dipping, distracted with tearing off their clothes and racing into the sea.

'Come with me,' he'd whispered, taking her hand in the dark.

She shivered, remembering.

'Are you cold?' asked Chum, snapping her back into the present. 'Too bad if you are, because the heating's pretty much broken in this thing, but the walk will warm us up. It's mostly uphill. A big hill.'

'No, I'm fine,' said Polly, hoping he'd forgotten it had ever happened. He'd been such a heart throb up there, he probably kissed so many girls it was all just a blur to him. And it had been just a kiss between them, nothing more – although not a peck on the cheek by any means: a full-on snog on the damp sand. She could so clearly remember the softness of his shirt and that slight smell of horse ...

She sat up straight, consciously putting the brakes on that line of thought. It was a sweet memory of youthful days, but they were different people now.

It was a relief when he pulled off the road, a couple of minutes later, into what Polly was surprised to see was a proper car park containing other cars, with National Trust signs and public loos. There were lots of dogs too; it was clearly a popular spot.

'Don't worry about the people,' said Chum. 'I know all kinds of paths through here they've got no idea about. We'll have our own private bespoke walk.'

He jumped out, then paused, tapping his phone.

'Setting your turn-back-now-or-die alarm?' asked Polly.

'Yep,' he said. 'Ninety minutes each way. Can you hack it?'

'Lead on,' she said.

For the first fifteen minutes or so they passed a lot of other walkers, mostly with dogs, so there was endless stopping for butt-sniffing, and Polly couldn't help feeling a bit disappointed, despite what Chum had said.

They were out in lovely unspoiled landscape, not farmland like the other two walks they'd done. But with all the people and the fussy signposts telling them how far they were from the next fussy signpost, it felt oddly suburban. The air was beautifully fresh, were surrounded by proper ancient deciduous woodland, but it wasn't getting her in the zone.

Maybe the first two walks had been a fluke, thought Polly, suddenly regretting her impulsive decision to text Chum. The novelty of seeing him after so many years had suspended them in a little bubble of their shared youth before; now she couldn't help feeling she was just out for a slightly peculiar walk with a total stranger she had very little in common with.

She plodded on, trying to look as though she was enjoying it, until after a few more minutes Chum suddenly struck out to the right, up a steep bank.

'Are you all right?' he said, turning to look at her. 'I know it was a bit dreary back there, but it gets better from now on. Trust me. I know this country.'

'Is this family land again?' she asked.

'Used to be,' said Chum. 'I roamed all around here as a boy, on horses and on foot. My brother and I used to go on great expeditions.'

'But it's not your land any more?' asked Polly, more to make conversation than anything.

'No, my father sold this part off to the National Trust years ago. Nothing tragic, he just didn't feel we needed it. It wasn't productive and he wasn't one of those landowners who believed in having as much acreage as possible, no matter what was on it. If he couldn't grow something, or graze something on it, or see it from the house, he thought it was better to put the care of it into other hands for the public to get the use of it. He was forward thinking like that.'

'Presumably, he could have shot things on this land,' said Polly, as a bird flapped out of a tree ahead of them.

Chum laughed.

'Way too many trees for shooting,' he said. 'You wouldn't be able to see anything.'

'I wouldn't know,' said Polly. 'The only dead birds I have any dealings with are plucked and wrapped in plastic.'

'You should come on a shoot sometime,' said Chum.

'You should come to a fragrance launch,' she said and he turned to look at her, clearly checking to see if she was joking. She was.

'Good point,' he said. 'Fish out of water and all that.'

As he spoke, they came out of the trees onto a bridle path, looking out across the tops of the woods they'd just walked through, no one else in sight. Polly stopped for a moment, savouring the silence and feeling the sense of ease she had so craved coming over her again.

'Oh, this is more like it,' she said.

Chum grinned at her.

'I should have warned you about the Surbiton part of the walk. Is that what Hampstead Heath is like? Nature in check?'

'Well, you do pass other people and dogs, but it has an odd kind of wildness to it, because it's open country on the edge of a major city. It's hard to explain, but if you know where to go, you can feel like you might run into a highwayman at any moment.'

Chum smiled.

'That's a quaint image,' he said. 'Perhaps you'll take me and Artemis for a walk up there one day. I'd like to see it with a local.'

Polly was surprised.

'That would be my pleasure,' she said. 'Let me know when you're heading down next. Do you come to London much?'

'A bit,' he said. 'I'll come up to town occasionally to see friends, or buy something, although you can do so much of that online these days. Mostly to see lawyers, really.'

Polly smiled at 'up to town'. It was always 'up' to his lot, she remembered, even though Hertfordshire was north of London.

Then the last thing he'd said sank in. Lawyers. What was that about?

She had a strong suspicion it would be connected with 'poor Chum', but she wasn't going to ask. This walk was a refuge from reality – his and hers – and she had a strong inkling he appreciated that as much as she did. Determined to stay in the zone, she concentrated on the rhythm of her feet, one in front of the other, as the going got harder up the gradual incline.

'It gets a bit steep here,' said Chum. 'Not too much for you?'

Polly shook her head.

'I want to know what's at the top,' she said.

The vegetation was thinning out and she was aware of a wider expanse of sky opening up ahead. Finally there were no trees, just grass, bushes and big rocks, and she could see the apex they were aiming for and then, at last, they reached the summit.

'Wow,' she said, coming to a standstill.

Spread out before her was the most amazing view: miles of rolling countryside, crossing what looked like a glacial plain to more hills in the distance.

'Good, isn't it?' said Chum.

'You really do know all the best walks,' said Polly. 'This is fantastic.'

'Do you want to have a seat for a moment?' he asked. He checked his phone. 'We've got twelve minutes before we need to start back, so we can have a breather.'

He reached into his pocket and pulled out a small square of plaid with waxed cotton on the back, and spread it on the ground in front of a boulder, gesturing towards it gallantly.

'Sit on that and you won't get a wet bum,' he said.

'What about you?' she asked.

'I'll pull my jacket down and hope.'

Polly sat on the rug and shifted over to the edge.

'There's room for you on here as well,' she said, patting the space beside her. 'One buttock, anyway.'

'Well, if you insist,' said Chum, and sat down next to her.

Polly was aware how close they were – their bodies touching from the shoulder to the hip – and tried to ignore it.

'Want one of these?' asked Chum, pulling two apples out of his inside pocket.

'Were they in your dead-animal holding zone?' she asked him.

''Fraid so,' he said, poking around on the other side. 'And this.'

He passed her a water bottle and she unscrewed it and took a deep drink before giving it back. Then she leaned against the rock, blood still humming in her veins from the long stretch uphill, and gazed out over the view, thinking about nothing at all. Just the clear air, the view, the crunch of Chum eating his apple, and his warm shoulder against hers.

For a moment she felt she just existed, like the rock she was leaning against and the grass she was sitting on. No thoughts. No whats, hows or whys. Just being.

Then, as she looked out over the miles of splendid country laid out before them, something caught her eye. A huge grey stone building in a kind of U shape, with other buildings coming off it. A veritable forest of chimneys.

It was a house, she realised. A very big house.

Could it be *the* house? The one Anaïs Anaïs cowbag and her friends at St Andrews had been so so obsessed with? The famous 'stately'?

'Is that your family's house?' asked Polly, pointing.

'Yes,' said Chum, a tightness coming into his voice.

'Gosh,' said Polly, 'so it really is the full-on stately deal, then? I remember some people at St Andrews getting very excited about that. Girl people. I never really understood what they were talking about. Or cared. Sorry.'

She took a bite out of her apple and turned to look at him. It felt so good to be real about all that.

'That's what I always liked about you,' said Chum. 'You weren't looking people up in *Burke's* bloody *Peerage* like some of the girls up there.'

'I did consult it a couple of times,' said Polly. 'In the university library. I was writing an essay about the Civil War and needed to know the dates of certain investitures.'

Chum laughed.

'You must have been the only person there who used it as an academic resource. Did you notice how well-thumbed it was?'

'I did, actually,' said Polly. 'I thought a lot of other historians were using it.'

Chum smiled. Polly had another drink of water and they carried on eating their apples.

'So, go on then,' she said, 'tell me about it. What's it called? When was it built? What's it like to live in a house with – let me see – one, two, three major wings and two smaller ones?'

'It's called Hanley Hall. It was built in the early seventeenth century, and growing up in a house like that was ... well, I don't know what it would be like to grow up anywhere else, but it was pretty bloody good.'

'And your dad was an Earl or something?'

'Yes,' said Chum. 'My father was the ninth Earl. He died when I was twenty-five and my mother married Bill.'

They were silent for a moment, Chum looking straight at the house, a fixed expression on his face that Polly hadn't seen before.

'So you don't live in it any more?' she asked tentatively. He'd clearly brought her up here to show it to her; it seemed only polite to ask questions about it.

'No,' he said, slowly, not looking at her.

'So who's the Earl now, then?' she said.

'Well, my brother was,' said Chum, sighing deeply.

'Was?' said Polly, then, seeing the expression on Chum's face, she stopped. The conversation had gone very quickly from being a pleasant chat to clearly being highly distressing to him.

He got to his feet and put his hand out for her.

'I think we've just about had our twelve minutes' break, we'd better start back.'

She let him pull her up and when she was on her feet he didn't let go of her hand immediately, holding it in his own for a moment, looking down at it. Then he gave it a gentle pat and let go, briskly zipping up his jacket.

'All that stuff ... the house, my family,' he said, looking very tired for a moment. 'I know I said if you wanted to know anything about me, just to ask, but now we're up here I really can't be arsed to go into it. Rollo was right – google it.'

Chum dropped Polly back at Rockham Park and she decided to go straight up and surprise her mother. They could have dinner together, perhaps look at some more photos, and she'd stay the night. It would be fun.

Daphne answered the door in her silk kimono, a green face mask on, her hair freshly done.

'Oh, Polly, how lovely. I didn't know you were coming, did I?' she asked, just a hint of uncertainty in her voice.

'No,' said Polly. 'I thought I'd surprise you for fun.'

'Well, that's very sweet,' said Daphne, 'but I'm afraid I'm going out this evening. I'm just getting ready.'

'That's good to hear,' said Polly, happy to know Daphne had a social life, but just a little concerned it might be another imaginary embassy ball. 'What's on?'

'We have a film night every Thursday,' said Daphne, heading into her bedroom and standing at the wardrobe, flicking through her options. 'It's very interesting, because one of the chaps who lives here used to be a film reviewer for the papers and he gives us a little talk beforehand about the making of the film, the actors and all that, and then afterwards we have a glass of wine and discuss it. He's got some very good stories, and it turns out we've known some of the same people. It's great fun.'

She pulled out a dress and held it up against herself in front of the wardrobe's mirrored door, smiled with satisfaction and laid it on the bed.

'Now I've just got to take this mask off. I won't be a minute. We can chat while I do my face.'

Daphne bustled off to the bathroom and Polly made herself some tea then sat on her mother's sofa, staring into space and wondering what to do now.

She'd been looking forward to spending an evening with her mum – partly to get a proper good look at her and make sure she was still eating and drinking, but also because she really couldn't stand the prospect of another evening in her own empty house. After the tension with Shirlee and Maxine that morning, and then the problem of how to answer Lori's email, going back there felt like some kind of prison sentence.

The walk, and Chum's company, had done their usual brilliant job of blocking out all her unthinkables for a few hours, but now it was all rushing back into her head. She needed people around her, she now understood, because the minute she was alone, it became unbearable.

She got to her feet and paced up and down the room, feeling itchy inside her own skin. It wasn't surprising she needed company. She'd never lived alone before, not in her whole life.

Daphne very clearly hadn't invited Polly to join her at the film – so what to do?

She sat down again, picked up her phone and scrolled through her 'Favourites' list: David – yeah, right – Clemmie, Lucas, Shirlee, her dog sitter and a couple of friends she didn't see much of any more.

She tapped on Shirlee's number. She'd send her a text just to make it clear there were no hard feelings over what had happened that morning. Polly needed the few friends she still felt comfortable with more than ever.

> Hi Shirlee, sorry if I was a bit short this morning. It was the hangover. I'm not used to galivanting! I'm just up at my mum's but wondered if you fancied seeing a film later? P xxx

She sent it off, hoping Shirlee would reply right away. If Daphne was having a film night, she might as well do the same thing.

After ten minutes, she'd finished her tea and Shirlee hadn't texted back. Daphne was still in the bathroom, and Polly checked the time on her phone and was pleased to see it was still only ten past six. She could be back in London by seven and in Mayfair by eight, easily.

She tapped out another text, this one to Guy:

> Hello Fred Astaire. How are you feeling after the perfumed cocktails??? There's a whole menu of them at the new bar in the Langton Hotel that I want to write up for the blog. I thought I might head down there later. Fancy a hair of the dog? Polly x

She read it over again twice and then deleted it, sighing. Had she lost her mind? She was still hung over from the night before – not to forget the physical exhaustion from Chum's uphill walk. And how did it look for a married woman to go out dancing with a younger man one night and then ask him out for drinks again the next? It looked desperate, that was what.

Polly's hands flew up to her face, as sobs started to wrack her body. She couldn't hold it in another minute. The weirdness, the hurt, the anxiety, the loneliness all came surging to the surface at once.

Daphne rushed into the room and came straight over to her, sitting on the sofa and putting her arms round her.

'Oh, my poor girl!' she cried. 'I know what's wrong. That rotten man has done this to you.'

She rocked Polly in her arms, stroked her hair, kissed her head and carried on talking.

'Have a good cry. You've every right. I'm so angry with that man, but I haven't wanted to talk about it to you. I thought you were going through enough as it was.'

She carried on rocking her, saying 'Shhhhh' over and over as you would to a baby. It was exactly what Polly needed – and such displays of physical affection were so rare from her mother she found she was crying more.

'Oh my poor love,' said Daphne. 'I did wonder whether I should talk to you about it when we were in that hotel with Lucas, but I could see you had enough on. Has David asked for a divorce?'

Polly managed to stop the choking sobs and pull herself back a little, using her sleeve to wipe away the tears that had soaked her face.

Daphne fished around in the pocket of her dressing gown.

'Use this, darling,' she said, handing Polly a lace-edged hanky, 'but gently, you know how delicate the skin around the eyes is – and tell me everything.'

Polly started crying again, but now it was more from the relief of being able to let it go – and being reminded of all the times in her childhood when Daphne had suddenly switched like this, from being entirely self-absorbed to showing Polly that she really did care and noticed what was going on with her. She was a loving mother, really, just in her own particular way.

'Tell me about it, darling,' said Daphne, taking Polly's hands in hers and gazing into her face. She reached up and pushed some stray hairs behind Polly's ears, but she didn't comment on it for once. 'Is there another woman?'

'I don't think so,' said Polly. 'He's having some kind of a breakdown and he's gone away. I don't know where he is, or whether he's ever coming back.'

'Is he in touch with the children at least?'

Polly shook her head.

'Not really,' she said. 'He made Clemmie tell him when I'd be out, so he could come to the house and get some things. She was having lunch with me when he went there.'

Some more tears escaped. That betrayal still got to her.

Daphne looked appalled.

'That's horrible,' she said. 'How dare he put Clemmie in that position, how dare he do that to you. The selfish pig.'

She stopped for a moment, looking thoughtful, and Polly could tell she was making a decision. She sighed deeply and then spoke.

'I've got to tell you something, darling.'

Polly froze. What now?

'I've never liked him,' said her mother. 'I've never liked David. I feel wrong saying it because he is the father of your children and I love them with all my heart, but I didn't care for David from the moment I met him. There's a coldness to him. I know he loves you, but it always seemed to be on his terms.'

Polly was so surprised she didn't know what she thought. About this, or anything else.

'Do you remember your wedding?' Daphne continued. 'How he insisted that you had it in London and kept it very small and casual, and we weren't allowed to invite your cousins or any family friends? It was all about him, wasn't it? And he didn't want you to wear a proper wedding dress, when I'd saved mine for you.'

Polly nodded. It was true. She had always imagined she would get married in the extraordinary chapel of her father's college, wearing her mother's couture wedding dress, with the choir singing, and all her lovely Scottish cousins there, as well as her father's gang of university friends who she'd known all her life. But David had been dead against it all.

He was stupidly resentful of the whole Cambridge connection. Polly's father could have put in a good word for him in very helpful places, but David had done his first degree at Leeds and was withering about Oxbridge privilege. The fact that her father had got into Cambridge from his state school in Scotland didn't sway him one bit.

'You're right,' said Polly, 'but I didn't mind about the wedding so much at the time, because I was young and in love ... and while of course I'm furious with him now for what he's done, he is still the father of my children, and up until now he's been a wonderful husband, and I do still love him ... and he must be really in a bad way to have left the kids like this ...'

She started crying again.

'There, there,' said Daphne, stroking Polly's head. 'Men can go very peculiar at his age. It's the hormones.'

After a couple more minutes, which Polly was finding very comforting, she could feel Daphne twisting her arm, and she opened her eyes to see that her mother was trying to look at her watch.

Business as usual, then, thought Polly. A short burst of parenting and then back to the me me me. Well, at least she knew what her mother was like. She was used to it and very grateful for the times when Daphne did rise to the occasion.

'What time does the film start?' asked Polly.

'Not until seven-thirty,' said Daphne, 'but I like to get down there early to chat to people before it starts.'

At the front, thought Polly. Where everyone can see you.

'But I'm not going to leave you like this,' said Daphne. 'I can miss one week.'

'Don't worry, Mummy,' said Polly. 'I'll be fine. I feel so much better just for telling you about it.'

'You could always come to the film with me,' said Daphne, standing up and heading for the door, but Polly knew she was just being polite.

'It's OK, I'll stay here and watch TV and chill out, if that's OK. I'm too exhausted to drive. What's the film tonight?'

'I can't remember,' said Daphne, smiling brightly. 'It's always a nice surprise when I get there. Come and talk to me while I do my face.'

Polly obediently followed her into the bedroom, and watched with a fascination that never lessened as Daphne stepped into the elegant grey wool sweater dress she'd chosen earlier and then stood up straight, half-turning to look at herself in the mirror.

At eighty-five, she still had it. If you couldn't see her face, you'd have no idea she was in her eighties, she held herself so straight.

'You look fabulous, Mummy,' Polly said, and Daphne rewarded her with a beaming smile. Polly could almost hear shutters clicking.

'Oh thank you, darling,' said Daphne, choosing a belt from the rail inside the wardrobe door and buckling it round her neat waist. 'I know I'm a terrible old hag these days, but I do like to make an effort. I do it for myself, not for other people, that's what I wish I could make you understand.'

She moved the belt up a little so it was above her waist, then loosened it so it dropped down to hip level, her eyes always on the mirror. Then she put it back on the rail.

'Better without,' she said, sitting down at her dressing table – Polly wondered how many hours she'd spent at it over the years – and opened a drawer, taking out various necklaces and holding them up against her neck, before settling on several strands of chunky beads.

'I bought these in Kenya,' said Daphne. 'I was doing a *Vogue* shoot with Parkie. Before you were born. I wore a pink, orange and white one-piece and a marvellous cartwheel hat, and there were flamingos in the background. I must see if I have that issue somewhere.'

Daphne started the ritual of her preparations, patting on her creams, then applying the layers of make-up that transformed her already beautiful face into a beacon of loveliness, without ever looking overdone.

'I see you've got your nails painted again,' she said, looking at Polly in the mirror. 'They look lovely.'

'Yes,' said Polly. 'I do finally see the point of that. It's fun.'

'It makes you feel good, doesn't it?' said Daphne. 'There's a reason they call it nail "polish".'

Polly smiled at her.

'I think that's another influence David has had on you,' Daphne continued, deftly defining her arched eyebrows with powder shadow on a small brush. 'He loves your beauty, but he doesn't like you to make the most of it. It's as though he doesn't want you to show yourself off – you're just for him.'

Polly pulled a face, feeling a bit got at, but there was something in what Daphne had said. She'd come to think not wearing make-up was her own choice, but perhaps it had just been easier to go along with what David preferred. Whenever she'd tried to take her mother's advice and wear mascara, a bit of blusher and some lipstick, he'd always grizzled and she'd given up on it.

'I think you're right,' said Polly, sighing deeply.

Nearly twenty-five years she'd been with the man, and she'd thought they were happy, but now she was beginning to see there were all these little ways in which he'd undermined her – and it was so strange finding out at this late stage that her mum had never liked him. Had her father hated him too?

'Tell me, Mummy,' she said, 'and I want the truth: did Daddy dislike David as well?'

Daphne looked at her thoughtfully from her reflection in the mirror. For once her eyes stayed on Polly and didn't flick straight back to her own face.

'Your father respected him,' she said, 'for his brain and his commitment to his work, but he was concerned David was a little too earnest. He always said a great academic must also have a sense of humour or they become too separated from the human condition.'

Polly could so imagine her father saying that, her eyes prickled again. If only he were here now, to ask for his carefully considered advice.

She remembered how wonderful he'd been when she was deciding whether to give up her PhD. He'd sat in his office with her for a whole morning talking about it. When she'd asked David for his advice on the same subject, he'd just told her to do what felt right for her, which hadn't been very helpful at all.

She blinked and shook her head. She didn't want to do any more crying.

'But that wasn't all, Polly,' said Daphne, turning on the stool to look at her directly. She put her hand on Polly's knee and patted it. 'Your father told me not to say anything to you about my misgivings at the time, because it was so apparent how much in love you were with each other – and he was right, you were. Whether you still are is something for you to think about.'

Daphne looked at Polly very tenderly, her head on one side. Polly nodded, sighing, and Daphne patted her leg again, before turning back to the mirror.

'Now, which lipstick, I wonder,' she said, opening the drawer and surveying the many options.

Once her make-up was finally finished, Daphne made the all-important adjustments to her hair, roughing it up a bit all round, then snapped on some chunky gold earrings, which Polly could see perfectly offset the grey of the dress and the different shades of brown in the necklaces.

Then she ran her finger, with its French-manicured nail, along her collection of perfumes, stopping at Givenchy III and squirting it behind each ear and on her wrists, which she then rubbed together. Polly made a mental note to tell her about that some time; it was one of the few aspects of her mother's elaborate preparations she could advise her on. One point Polly.

Then Daphne opened one of the dressing-table drawers, took out a fresh handkerchief, sprayed it with the scent and dropped it into her handbag.

That was something Polly could use on the blog. Game to Daphne.

'There,' she said, leaning on the dressing table to lever herself back to her feet and turning her head from side to side in the mirror, as she always did. 'All done.'

She padded back to the wardrobe – Polly thought there would soon be a track worn in the carpet – and took out her favourite high-heeled pumps.

Slipping her feet into them, Daphne stepped back to check her reflection once more and staggered, starting to fall. Polly leaped over to catch her.

'Mummy!' she said. 'Those bloody shoes! You're not safe in them. Either wear flats or use a stick. You're going to kill yourself in those stupid heels. You don't even need them, you're so lovely and tall, it's really not worth it.'

Daphne's mouth set in a stubborn line.

'OK,' said Polly. 'How about I help you down to the film now in your stupid shoes and then I'll come back for you at the end – but only if you promise in future to make a choice between low heels or a stick.'

'I promise to give it some serious consideration,' said Daphne, pulling herself up, her swan neck seeming to lengthen as she did so. 'And I would love you to come down with me – I can show you off – but only if you brush your hair and put on some lipstick first.'

Polly laughed and sat at the dressing table to do as she was told. When she'd finished her face and hair – she even did her eyebrows, as she'd watched Daphne do hers – she considered the tempting array of perfumes. She picked up Daphne's bottle of Fracas and sprayed herself with it, liberally.

'Will I do?' she asked, coming over to her mother and putting out her arm. 'Madame?'

Daphne threaded her arm through Polly's elbow and patted her hand.

'You look beautiful,' said Daphne. 'I'm very proud of you, and although I may not always show it demonstrably, you know I love you very dearly. I will support you as best I can through this difficult time. You must always ring me if you're unhappy.'

Polly gave her mother a light hug – she didn't want to risk spoiling her hair – and they headed out of her front door towards the lift.

'And another thing,' said Daphne, getting up a good pace along the corridor as she leaned on Polly's arm. 'Next time you come up, bring your highest pair of heels with you. I may have to give them up myself, but I'm going to teach you how to walk in them first.'

Thursday, 18 February

Polly and Clemmie were back in the Shoreditch restaurant. After that special moment of connection with her mum, Polly had felt an almost visceral need to see her own daughter, but it had been a frustrating couple of weeks before Clemmie could take time away from her studies.

Much as she admired Clemmie's diligence, Polly couldn't help wishing she would loosen up a bit sometimes. She'd been incredibly busy herself over that period, with four events of her own, on top of the usual launches and showroom open days, but these weren't normal circs. They needed each other.

Although Clemmie was the only person Polly could talk to in depth about the David situation – it had been great to tell Daphne, but she didn't want to go into all the details with her mother – Polly was determined to keep the conversation off David for as long as she could this time. She just wanted to enjoy her daughter's company for a while before that subject took over.

'I've got some jolly news,' she said, as the waiter put their food in front of them. 'Lori and Rich are coming over.'

Even as she said it, Polly realised there was no escape. Her attempt to talk about something fun and upbeat was inevitably going to lead to a discussion of how to handle the visit of their closest family friends if David still hadn't come back.

'Oh that's brilliant!' said Clemmie, her face lighting up. 'Are the kids coming too? I'd love to see Poppy so much, but she'd probably have let me know if she was going to be here.'

'It's just Lori and Rich this time,' said Polly. 'I can't wait to see her.'

She could tell by the expression on Clemmie's face that she was already thinking about the complications.

'Are you going to tell them, before they arrive?' she asked quietly.

Polly felt her shoulders slump.

'I don't know what to do,' she said. 'There's no one – apart from you, of course – I'd rather talk to about this craziness than Lori.'

'I thought you might have told her already,' said Clemmie, butting in.

'I've been very sorely tempted,' said Polly, 'but there's the complication that Rich is in the same field as your father. You remember how he was particularly vehement about that – how we mustn't contact the university, or let anyone know it's anything other than a normal research trip? If I tell Lori what's really going on, she'll tell Rich. It's unrealistic to think she wouldn't. Then it will inevitably get round the academic world, which is very small as you know, and of course they'd hear about it at King's. I can't imagine what your father means by all that – what did he write? "It could create profound difficulties for us." But he was so adamant I don't want to risk it.'

She paused for breath and had a drink of water. She knew she was rattling on, but it was such a relief to say it all out loud. Clemmie didn't reply, so she continued.

'How can I keep pretending David's on a research trip when I don't even know where he is – and to them, of all people? I'm not a good enough actress. And anyway, I really don't want to lie to my best friend. So, there we are. I can't think of anything I'd love more than a visit from Lori and now it's become something to dread.'

She put her fingertips on her temples and shook her head from side to side.

Clemmie forked in some of her lunch and chewed silently for a while. It contained copious amounts of kale and looked like it would need an awful lot of masticating, Polly thought. Her own appetite had fled. She poked her food with her fork. It was a very tasty barley risotto thing, but she couldn't face it.

'When are they coming?' asked Clemmie, after finally swallowing.

'Second week in April,' said Polly.

Clemmie took a long drink from her water glass and looked down at her plate with something like trepidation.

'Do you want my barley?' asked Polly. 'I had a big breakfast with Shirlee this morning and I'm really not hungry.'

'Are you sure?' said Clemmie, taking the offered plate and tucking in. 'Mmm, that's so much nicer that what I ordered. I'm coming to understand why kale was only used as cattle feed for a long time. Now where were we – you said mid-April for Lori?'

Polly nodded.

'Well, that gives us a deadline, doesn't it?' said Clemmie.

'A deadline for what?' asked Polly.

'What I mean is,' said Clemmie, 'how long is a reasonable time to allow Dad to have this freak-out, before we actively start looking for him?'

Polly still didn't get it. Clemmie leaned across the table towards her.

'When did he go?' she asked. '20 December?'

Polly nodded again. It wasn't a date she was ever going to forget. And a Merry Christmas to you too.

'So that's very nearly two months,' said Clemmie. 'Which will make it three months on 20 March. That's long enough.'

'But he said he had six months' research leave,' said Polly.

Clemmie rolled her eyes. 'Who cares what he said? He might want to dress it up as a period of formal research leave, but he's basically gone missing, and I think three months is long enough to indulge him. There might be something seriously wrong. So let's give him the three months and then start asking questions at King's, see if anyone there knows where he is.'

'Despite all his dire warnings in that letter about not contacting them?' said Polly.

'Yes,' said Clemmie. 'We can find a subtle way to do it. And if they can't help us get in touch with him, I think we need to involve the police.'

Polly felt her eyebrows shoot up.

'The police?' she said, stupidly. This whole conversation was making her feel as though her IQ was dribbling out of the end of her fingers.

'Yes, Mummy,' said Clemmie, firmly. 'And we can formally register him as a missing person right now. I've been looking at some websites about it and there are specialist organisations we could talk to that might be able to help us find out more.'

Polly sighed. The thought of Clemmie sitting at her computer, typing the words 'missing person' into a search engine made her feel desperately sad.

'I don't feel ready to do that, yet,' she said. 'I think we should wait the three months, like you said.'

'OK,' said Clemmie. 'We have a plan. If we haven't heard from him properly by 20 March we will start actively looking for him, and it will give us two or three weeks to make some progress before Lori and Rich arrive.'

'Er,' said Polly, sitting up straight. 'What do you mean by heard from him "properly"? Have we heard from him at all? Apart from that time when he wanted to sneak into the house?'

Clemmie looked down for a moment, clearly anguished, then at her mother again. She nodded.

'He's in touch with you – and you haven't told me?' said Polly, hardly able to believe this was happening. 'Perhaps you'd like to explain, Clemmie.'

'He texts me once a week.'

'From where?'

'I don't know. I always try ringing the number back straight away, but it's always just off, no message thing.'

'So what does he say in these cosy little texts?' asked Polly, feeling the rush of anger that seemed to be a new part of her world. '"Having a lovely time, glad you're not here"? God! Every time I think I'm starting to cope with this insanity, something else comes up!'

'I know, Mum,' said Clemmie, sounding desolate. 'I didn't know whether to tell you or not, but I have now.'

'Well, here we go again,' said Polly, throwing the piece of bread she had been playing with onto the table, 'with this restaurant working its usual magic. Every time we come here we have an upset.'

She stopped herself from saying anything else, closing her eyes for a moment and taking some slow, calming breaths. Don't lose it, she told herself. Don't do it to Clemmie – and don't do it to yourself.

'I'm not going to fall out with you, Clemmie,' she said after a few seconds, feeling more in control. 'I wish you'd told me about these texts, but it's not your fault at all – it's David's, yet again, for singling you out for this responsibility. Just like with his sneaky house visit, it puts you in such a difficult situation. I'm just glad I know now. So tell me, what do these texts say?'

Clemmie smiled at her, clearly very relieved.

'They all say, "I'm OK, don't worry. Dad." That's it.'

'"Don't worry"?' repeated Polly, laughing bitterly. 'That's a cracker even by David's current standards. But at least we know he's still alive. I think I'm glad about that, but I can't be sure any more.'

They sat in silence for a few moments. Polly's head was spinning from it all. But then something began to bubble up inside her. She could feel herself beginning to giggle, and once she'd started she couldn't stop until it turned into a full-on belly laugh.

After a moment's puzzled surprise, Clemmie's face broke into a grin and she joined in. Within moments they were both laughing uncontrollably, bent over the table, then throwing their heads back. The more Polly thought how crazy it was to be laughing about it, the funnier she found it.

'Oh! This is ridiculous,' she said, gasping for air, 'but it's all so nuts, it suddenly seems hilarious.'

They had tears streaming down their faces and people at tables nearby were looking at them curiously.

'"Why are you laughing, lovely ladies?"' said Clemmie in a fake sleazy voice. 'Well, kind sir, you see, my dad's a nutter and he's run away from home and he texts me once a week to tell me he's not dead. It's hilarious!'

This only set Polly off again, making her bang the table with her hand, until gradually they started to calm down, tiny snorts escaping. Polly caught the waiter's eye and ordered two glasses of champagne.

'I've come to the conclusion,' she said when the drinks arrived, 'that the only way to survive this is to have a good time doing it.'

'I'll drink to that,' said Clemmie, and they clinked their glasses.

'To you,' said Polly, 'for helping me survive this nightmare.'

'To you,' said Clemmie, 'for being the best mum ever, who doesn't deserve this crap.'

After that, they were finally able to chat generally for a while, enjoying the drinks then ordering more of them, plus a portion of steamed raspberry sponge and custard with two spoons.

'*This* kind of trauma I can deal with,' said Clemmie, wiping her mouth on her napkin before taking another sip of champagne.

Polly reached over and held Clemmie's hand again, sending up a silent prayer of thanks for her wonderful daughter.

When they'd paid the bill and were gathering up their things to leave, Polly realised she couldn't bear the idea of parting with Clemmie again so soon.

'Do you have to rush back to Cambridge right away?' she asked, as they shrugged on their coats and started for the door.

'Not immediately,' said Clemmie. 'Is there something you want to do?'

'Well, I'm going to do an interview and take some photos for a blog post – there's an interesting new perfumer who's opened a shop just off Brick Lane, down the road – and as you seem to be more interested in perfume these days, I wondered if you'd like to come and do it with me. It will make a change from the inner ear, or whatever it is you're "boning" up on at the moment.'

She nudged Clemmie with her elbow.

'Very funny,' said Clemmie, pulling out her phone and checking the time. 'It sounds fun – and I can torture Talitha about it. She's being insufferable about how she's a perfume blogger now. Let's do it.'

They set off, walking arm in arm, chatting as they went, enjoying the vibrant bustle, until they were standing outside Guy's shop in Cheshire Street.

'This looks sprauncy,' said Clemmie, taking in the glossy black shop front and the window featuring a pyramid of crystal bottles, with the Baccarat chandelier visible behind them. 'Very posh for Brick Lane.'

'Isn't it?' said Polly. 'I've got to know the owner, we're friends, really. He's quite a character, but weirdly cagey about the set-up – like who's funding all this. I've been trying to interview him for a blog post for weeks, before anyone else does it, but he keeps cancelling on me, so I thought I'd just ambush him today.'

'So he doesn't know you're coming?' asked Clemmie.

Polly shook her head, smiling, and pushed open the shop door. The old-fashioned bell tinkled and Guy appeared immediately, swishing through the bead curtain behind the counter.

'Pollissima!' he said, sounding delighted. 'I'm so happy to see you. I've nearly finished the iris scent and I want to see what you think.'

'Great,' said Polly. 'I can add it to the blog post – because that's why I'm here today, Guy. I won't be put off any longer.'

Guy's face fell, but he quickly recovered himself and came out from behind the counter.

'And who is this lovely creature you have with you, Miss Polly?'

He took Clemmie's hand and raised it to his lips.

'Are you by any chance Polly Junior?' he asked, still holding her hand, clasping it between both of his.

'I'm Clemmie,' she said, looking a bit flustered. She glanced at Polly and widened her eyes.

'This is my wonderful daughter,' said Polly, putting an arm around her and pulling her closer, so Guy dropped her hand. 'Clemmie, this is Guy, who we are going to be interviewing today about his lovely shop and his wonderful perfumes.'

'Oh, come on, Polly,' said Guy, 'leave off with the interview thing. Why don't I make some tea and we can have a lovely natter and I'll show you the iris? Do have a sniff around, Clemmie, I'd love to know what you think of my perfumes.'

He set off towards the back of the shop, turning as he went.

'Think of some good goss for me,' he said as he disappeared back behind his curtain. 'Won't be a minute.'

Clemmie looked inquiringly at Polly.

'He really doesn't seem keen on the interview idea, does he?' she said. 'And does he always kiss people's hands like that?'

Polly laughed.

'Guy's a piece of work,' she said, 'but he's great fun – and seriously talented.'

She went over to the shelves and took down the tester for PM, sprayed some on a testing blotter and handed it to Clemmie.

'That's nice,' she said. 'It smells like you.'

'Well, I have been wearing it a lot recently,' said Polly.

She sprayed another blotter with The Darkest Hour.

'How do you like this one?'

Clemmie grimaced.

'Yuck,' she said, just as Guy walked back in.

He roared with laughter.

'Oh, you must tell me which one that was,' he said. 'I love it when I see a strong reaction, even if it is "Yuck".'

'The Darkest Hour,' said Polly. 'Clemmie's a fresh, green kind of a girl. She doesn't like strong fragrances, but she loved PM. Clemmie, tell Guy what you think PM smells like.'

'It smells like Mum,' said Clemmie.

Guy grinned.

'That's wonderful,' he said. 'You couldn't pay me a higher compliment, because I created that perfume for your mother – and named it after her.'

'PM,' said Clemmie, picking up the bottle. 'For Polly Masterson-Mackay. Cute. It should be PMM really, though.'

'Clemmie's a science brain,' Polly explained. 'She's studying medicine and she doesn't do poetic licence. Facts only, please.'

Guy smiled and gestured for them to sit on the black velvet sofa, while he perched in his usual elevated position on the stool, pouring the tea in a long stream from the elaborate silver pot and offering around a plate of baklava.

'So this is all connected to your Iranian roots, I assume,' said Polly, taking a honey-dripping triangle from the silver platter Guy was holding. 'When did your family move to the UK?'

Guy said nothing, offering the platter to Clemmie, then taking a piece for himself, chewing it and following it with a sip of tea.

'Did you say something, Polly?' he said, one black eyebrow raised.

'You know I did,' said Polly.

'Well, it sounded to me as though you were talking in a sort of interview-y language that I don't speak,' he said. 'Can't we just have our tea and a nice chinwag? Where are you studying, Clemmie?'

'At Cambridge,' she said.

'Oh, like your grandfather,' said Guy. 'Although, of course, your mum went to St Andrews, with all the Yahs. They sound awful.'

'So it was you!' said Polly. 'EastLondonNostrils, I bloody knew it, although you never fessed up.'

Guy stuck the very end of his tongue out at her and pulled a face.

'The same to you,' said Polly, sticking her own out back at him. 'So how come you're allowed to know all about me and my family, which you've stalked off my blog, but I'm not even allowed to ask you one question about yours?'

'Well, you've just answered that yourself,' said Guy. 'All your personal info is sitting where you've chosen to put it, out into the blogosphere for the great wide world to read – and very interesting it is too, for fellow perfume nuts like me. But you will notice that I don't have a blog, or even a Facebook page. I'm not on Twitter, Instagram or Snapchat. I'm just not into that public persona thing. I would love it if you would do a blog post about my perfumes and the shop – but not about me.'

'But your perfumes are part of you,' said Polly. 'People will want to know who created these wonderful scents. It's part of the experience.'

'Why?' said Guy. 'It never used to be. Women have been buying Chanel No. 5 since 1921 but only recently has it become widely known that it was created by a bloke called Ernest Beaux. Everyone thought designers like Coco Chanel and Christian Dior made their perfumes themselves. They didn't know about noses; perhaps they imagined the designers mixing them up in old jam jars in their ateliers, between fittings. Some people probably still believe David Beckham and Kim Kardashian make their own perfumes when all they do is sign the contract, choose one of five samples and bank the money. All the smell work is done by a wonk in a lab. It's a new thing for the perfumers themselves to be known.'

'So don't you need to be at the vanguard of that?' asked Polly.

'I don't want to be some kind of pseudo-celebrity like that pompous git Lucien Lechêne, I just want to make smells so beautiful they make people sigh and then sell a shitload of them.'

Polly laughed.

'Lucien is a bit of an arse,' she said, 'but he's a very successful arse.'

'Well, I want to try to achieve that success on the strength of my perfume alone. I aspire to be Jacques Guerlain – not Tom Ford. I'm not going to have my flat in magazines, or be photographed next to my bottles. When every semi-celebrity on earth has their own fragrance – Star Wars characters have perfumes now, for God's sake – I think it's really tacky to put your face to a scent. I'm going to go incognito.'

'Perhaps you should get a wig with a fringe to cover your entire face, like Sia,' said Clemmie. 'And ask an eleven-year-old to act as your persona.'

'That's an excellent idea,' said Guy. 'See, Polly, your daughter gets it, even if you're stuck in some kind of *Celebrity Big Brother* mentality.'

'All right, mystery man,' said Polly. 'I'll do a blog just about the shop and the smells. Let's have a whiff of this new one, then.'

Guy swished off through his curtain again.

'He's brilliant,' said Clemmie. 'I love him. Is he gay?'

'I don't know,' said Polly. 'I thought he was when I first met him, but he's never mentioned a boyfriend or a husband – or a wife or girlfriend – so I've got no idea. As he says, he's very private about his personal stuff. We mostly talk about perfume and I just like him because he's such a laugh. We've been to a few events together and it's always a riot.'

'Next time you're doing that, can I come?' asked Clemmie.

'Of course,' said Polly, 'I'd love that. Would you come back from Cambridge just for a party?'

'If I didn't have any big tests coming up,' said Clemmie. 'Definitely.'

'What about Bruno?' said Polly, thinking that a huge rugby player with a flattened nose would have fitted in at the Great Outdoors launch, but not at any others she could think of. 'Would you bring him too?'

Clemmie quickly looked away. Polly saw she was biting the inside of her lip. She put her hand on her daughter's arm.

'Is everything all right with Bruno?' she asked quietly.

Clemmie closed her eyes and shook her head.

'We broke up,' she said, in barely a whisper.

'You broke up?' said Polly, shocked. 'When?'

'It hasn't been great for a while. I thought bringing him home for Christmas would make things better, but it didn't, and when we got back to Cambridge we had one more big row and it's over. He's moved out.'

'Oh sweetheart,' said Polly, 'and you've never said anything to me. Why didn't you tell me?'

'I thought you had enough on,' said Clemmie, and Polly pulled her close and kissed the top of her head.

'My poor love, I'm always there for you. Whatever's going on for me, you still come first, and you must always tell me if something bad happens. Always. OK?'

Clemmie nodded.

'And I'll find some really amazing parties for us to go to soon, OK?'

Guy came back with a plain spray bottle, a pile of blotters and some kind of metal gadget. It had several hinged arms coming off a central spindle, with clips on the ends. He splayed them out and put blotters in three of them.

'Ooh,' said Clemmie. 'Very Edward Scissorhands.'

'It's my blotter holder,' said Guy, spraying the blotters lavishly then proffering the gadget so they could each take one.

Polly already loved the smell in the air, and as she lifted the card to her nose for the first time she sighed involuntarily.

'You sighed!' said Guy, jumping off his stool and doing a happy dance.

'Mmmmm,' said Clemmie, 'I think I sighed too. This is lovely. It's not the sort of thing I wear, but I do love it. It's posh, but there is a kind of freshness to it … not lemony, but …'

'Pennyroyal,' said Polly, looking at Guy, who pointed his left forefinger at her as he swung back onto his stool. 'Mint. I normally hate mint in anything, but it works here.'

'Bang on it. Just a tinge of toothpaste among all the earthy stuff to freshen it up, that was my thought.'

'And a very soft rose,' said Polly. 'I think there's a lot more to come, this is a very quiet beginning for you. What are you calling this one?'

'First Light,' said Guy. 'I went for rose because they are one of the flowers that smell best in the morning – but not too much, because it's really all about what comes next. Do you like the name? I was going to call it Dawn's Crack, but thought better of it. But what is going to come through next is lots of lovely orris root, which has that musky morning bed smell to me – and it all just said "waking up in the morning after serious hanky panky", so I went with that. And then there's the idea that you can experience first light after a long night without sleep, which I also like.'

'Well, I love it,' said Clemmie. 'It's not cloying like that other one I said "Yuck" about and it's not old-lady like the things my mum loves.'

'Old lady?' said Polly. 'Excuse me!'

'All your favourite perfumes smell the same,' said Clemmie.

'I think she might mean they're variations of chypre,' said Guy, grinning.

'It's bloody rude, whatever she means,' said Polly

'Do you think you would wear this, Clemmie?' said Guy.

'Can I try some on my skin?' she asked, holding her wrist out to him.

'You've trained her well,' he said to Polly, spraying Clemmie's arm.

She waited a moment and then lifted it to her nose.

'I think I might wear it,' she said. 'Like I said, it's very different from my usual perfumes, but I think I might be ready for something a bit more grown-up now.'

Polly picked up the bottle and sprayed some on her own arm, took a sniff and then left it alone, so the scent could develop on her skin.

'You look serious, Polly,' said Guy. 'What are you thinking?'

'That I need to see how it progresses, like I said.'

'You're right,' said Guy. 'And of course, this is only a first mix. I need to leave it to sit for at least month to macerate, to see how it all settles in.'

'Is that what you have to do?' asked Clemmie.

'It's like a stew,' said Guy. 'The longer you leave it for the flavours to mingle, the better.'

They drank their tea and chatted until Polly decided to go in for another smell. Guy was watching her intensely. She brought her arm up to her nose again and breathed deeply.

'Well?' said Guy, leaning towards her.

'Hmmmm,' said Polly. 'This is an interesting one. The rose is lovely and subtle and now I'm getting the orris root and classic patchouli and I think some suede, but then ... I can't put my finger on it quite, but it's as though something is missing. It starts off so quietly and beautifully, moves on enticingly, but then it drops away, just when I would expect – going on your other perfumes – something else surprising to unfold. I hope that's not rude.'

Guy was looking at her steadily.

'How interesting,' he said. 'Because I did take something out. Maybe I need to put it back in again.'

He jumped off his bar stool and strode over to the door, turning the sign over to 'Closed'. Then he pulled a set of keys out of his pocket and double-locked it.

'Shall we go and have a play?' he said.

Polly and Clemmie followed Guy behind the counter and through the bead curtain to a small hallway with stairs going up, and next to it a closed door, with three locks on it.

'Blimey, is it Fort Knox?' asked Polly.

'Something like that,' said Guy.

He opened the door, which Polly could see was reinforced with metal, and flicked on a light that revealed another staircase, going down.

'Are you sure you're not going to lock us up in here?' said Clemmie, as he stood at the top of the steps and ushered them down.

Guy laughed.

'Don't give me ideas. I just have to close the door up here

before we open the one at the bottom. Wait for my signal, OK?'

When he gave the go-ahead Polly pushed open the door to reveal what looked like a laboratory. Guy ran down the stairs, rushed past them then took a fresh white coat out of a drawer and put it on.

'Hey, Dr Strangelove,' said Polly, starting to giggle.

'You may laugh,' said Guy, 'but if you knew how much these ingredients cost, it might wipe the smile off your face. I can't risk contamination from anything – not even air or light.'

He handed them each a lab coat.

'Put these on, please, and don't touch anything unless I hand it to you, OK?'

He started opening a wall of locked cupboards behind them, then turned and handed Clemmie a plastic spray bottle and a cloth.

'You must be used to lab rules,' he said to her. 'Can you wipe down the bench, please?'

Clemmie set to and Polly watched as Guy took an array of things out of the cupboards and lined them up very precisely on the work top. There were scales and liquid measures, pipets, a bottle of liquid labelled with a number, and five empty test tubes, which he set up in their own brackets.

'OK,' he said, rubbing his hands together, 'let's make magic happen.'

He put on a pair of latex gloves, opened the bottle and used a pipet to put a few drops of the liquid into each of the empty test tubes.

'That's my master mix for First Light,' he said. 'What you smelled upstairs.'

He turned round and took a notebook out of the cupboard, flicking over the pages and then putting it down, open, on the work bench.

'I do this old-school, because I'm sentimental,' he explained. 'I write it all up on my laptop afterwards in spread sheets, but I like to pretend I'm Jacques Guerlain with a notebook when I'm concocting.'

'I had no idea you did all this yourself,' said Polly. 'I thought you would tinker about, but send the serious stuff to a professional lab.'

'I learned how to do it in a lab,' said Guy. 'I've got a BSc in Chemistry and when I graduated I went to work for Givaudan.'

'That's a huge international flavour and fragrance company, Clemmie,' said Polly. 'They create everything from perfumes for elite and celebrity brands, to smells for chewing gum and washing powder.'

'I worked on tastes for cheap sweeties,' said Guy. 'Which are just smells, really. Possibly mixed some of the deadlier ingredients you would have consumed as a child.'

'Where did you do your degree?' asked Clemmie.

Guy smiled, looking her straight in the eye.

'Cambridge,' he said.

'Get out!' said Clemmie. 'What college?'

'Oh, let's not talk about all that now,' said Guy, spinning round and regarding the contents of the cupboard, which contained row upon row of small vials, all neatly labelled. 'We've got a perfume to perfect.'

'Did you know that?' Clemmie whispered to Polly, while Guy was preoccupied, humming to himself and picking out some vials, which he threw from one hand to the other like a cocktail barman. 'That he went Cambridge?'

'No idea,' said Polly. 'As I told you earlier, I know nothing about Guy, apart from the fact he has this shop and makes beautiful perfumes – but almost nothing would surprise me.'

Guy turned back to them and consulted his notebook.

'So, we have the quiet opening of the rose, which I tempered with patchouli, as you picked up – because remember this is the morning after the night before, so she would have been wearing her pulling perfume ...'

'Do you always make up stories to go with your perfumes?' asked Clemmie.

'Of course,' said Guy. 'I have to create a scenario, a whole world. Sometimes I give the people in the stories names.'

'Has this girl got a name?' asked Clemmie.

'Not yet,' said Guy. 'Now, so remember I'm putting this on top of a base I buy from the lab I work with in Grasse, which is a secret recipe, although I'm sure it has lavender in it, because there's a smooth freshness at the bottom of it that is redolent to me of beautiful white sheets. So we just have to imagine those sheets in a lovely tangle.'

'So she's had quite a night, this girl of yours,' said Polly.

'Oh, yes,' said Guy, grinning. 'Very much so. That's why I put the civet in, to evoke the man. A nice bit of armpit. Then I flung in the pennyroyal – mostly to show off, because no one uses it, but there's also the thought of a bit of emergency chewing gum, to freshen the morning breath, or wiping toothpaste on your teeth with your finger, because you haven't got your toothbrush with you.'

Polly and Clemmie laughed.

'You sound quite experienced in this area, Guy,' said Clemmie.

'I don't know what you mean,' he said, with a faux innocent expression on his face. 'Now, let's smell it again.'

He dipped the blotters in the test tube and handed them each one.

'That's where it dies down,' said Polly. 'After the pennyroyal, before the civet. You need something to amp up the animalic there, to keep it really smooth and sexy.'

Clemmie frowned.

'I'll have to take your word for all that, Mum,' she said, 'but I do know what you mean about dying off. It starts so amazingly and then it sort of stops.'

Guy had his eyes closed, lost in the zone.

'You're right, Polly,' he said, opening them again and gazing at her with his head on one side. 'But what to use?'

He picked up a couple of the bottles and looked down at them in his hand.

'I wondered about more patchouli, because it's such a good carrier, but it's too obvious.'

'Another spice note?' suggested Polly.

'Yeah, maybe they had a curry on their way back to his place,' said Clemmie, sniffing the blotter again. 'Or some chicken tikka crisps ...'

'I could try putting the anise back in,' said Guy. 'That's what I took out. Not many people like it, but I thought it might be interesting.'

'Had they been drinking ouzo?' asked Polly.

'All right,' said Guy, 'I was showing off to myself. Orris and anise was a classic renaissance accord, but it didn't work for this. Perhaps something gourmand. Chocolate might be good.'

He took another small vial out of his cupboard and put a tiny drop from it into one of the test tubes containing the original blend, which he then stoppered and slowly tilted back and forth to mix. Once he was satisfied, he prepared three blotters and they all sniffed.

Polly burst out laughing.

'So not,' she said. 'That's just awful. It's like you've put a Snickers bar in there, it's so caramel and nutty.'

'That is basically what I did put in there,' said Guy. 'I

thought a cheap chocolate accord, with a toffee element, would work better than the eighty per cent cocoa solids style.'

They tried black tea, absinthe and blackcurrant – on a whim of Polly's – but none of them worked.

'Let's recap,' said Clemmie. 'So they met at a party. She was wearing her heavy oriental pulling perfume – what was he wearing?'

'David Beckham Instinct,' said Guy, chuckling. 'I'm serious. I put in some bergamot for that.'

'That's their scents covered, then,' continued Clemmie. 'So they go back to her place – or is it his place?'

'Hers,' said Guy. 'The nice white sheets, remember? He would have polycotton.'

'Is he a bit of rough?' asked Polly.

'Sporty,' said Guy, winking at them.

'So they have a big old night of how's-yer-wotsit,' said Clemmie. 'And you've got that sweaty animal thing covered by the civet musk?'

Guy nodded.

'Well, it's obvious what's missing, then,' said Clemmie. 'Cigarette smoke.'

Guy looked at her for a moment, then clapped his hands.

'You are so right, Miss Clemmie,' he said, spinning round and peering into the bottom shelf of the cupboard. 'Cigarette smoke in her hair the next morning. That's exactly what it needs. Here we are, this should do it.'

He added the essence to a fresh test tube of the original blend, mixed it and then prepared the blotters.

'On three,' he said, handing them across the bench. 'One, two, three.'

Polly raise the sliver of card to her nose and inhaled.

'Aaaaaaah,' she said.

She turned to Clemmie, who was beaming.

'Works for me,' she said. 'What a difference. I had no idea one ingredient could transform a perfume like that.'

'That's precisely where the magic is,' said Polly, smelling her blotter again. 'This is seriously sexy now. Do you like it, Guy?'

His eyes were closed again, nose down to the smell, and he made a noise in the back of his throat, almost a growl.

'I love it,' he said, opening his eyes and grinning at them. 'Obviously I'll need to fine-tune the exact proportions, but that was definitely the missing link. Let's all skin it.'

Polly and Clemmie held out the arms they hadn't tried the first version on and Guy dropped a tiny bit of the mix on them, then on his own.

'Works for me,' said Polly, waving her arm in front of her nose and taking deep sniffs of it.

'And me,' said Clemmie. 'I would definitely wear this. In fact, I think it's going to be *my* pulling perfume.'

~

Clemmie went straight to Liverpool Street Station from Guy's and Polly went home and tried to distract herself from missing her, and feeling horribly alone by writing the blog post about Guy's shop. She'd have to go back another day to do the photos, there'd been too much going on, but she wanted to get the words down while it was all fresh.

She was chewing her lip, trying to work around the fact she couldn't give any information about the nose who created these new perfumes she was raving on about when her phone pinged.

It was Chum asking for her email address. She sent it straight back to him, wondering what it was that he couldn't just put in a text. Then she turned her attention back to Google, where she'd been researching what Guy had said about the orris root and anise combination he'd experimented with being a classic Renaissance combination. Then something occurred to her: she still hadn't googled Chum.

He'd given her permission himself, but every time she'd thought of it, she'd been distracted by something else and didn't remember to go back – or was it more Freudian than just forgetting? Perhaps she didn't really want to know what all the sad 'poor Chum' stuff was about?

Apart from that moment on the top of the hill, when he'd suddenly clammed up, she always found him such good company on their walks. She didn't want to go poking around into something that might start her seeing him in some kind of a downer context. She had enough negative complications in her own life without going to look for them in someone else's.

Of course he knew some stuff about her because he'd looked at the blog. Just as she knew he was attached to that extraordinary house she'd seen from the top of the hill, and did something to do with horses and pheasant shoots. With the rich vein of their shared youth to talk about, that seemed like enough.

Her fingers hovered over her keyboard for a moment, should she do it? Just tap in that silly cumbersome name and see what all the 'poor old Chum' was about, once and for all? But she couldn't do it. She didn't want to.

She turned her attention back to the piece about Guy's shop when the irony struck her. Of the two men she was spending the most time with during the absence of her husband, one was an intriguing character she really wanted to know more about and the internet had yielded nothing – and then there was Chum, who'd told her himself she could find out all about his life online and she didn't want to look.

If only it were the other way round, she thought, frowning at the screen. Writing about Guy's shop and perfumes without any context was proving to be even more of a challenge than she'd thought. It made her look as if she wasn't doing her job properly. She read what she'd written again and closed the file. If Guy wasn't prepared to be a bit more forthcoming, she was going to have to park it.

She decided to send him an email to tell him that he had one last chance to co-operate or the FragrantCloud post was off. Then she saw she had a new message in her inbox, from chum@mail.com.

Hi Hippolyta,

Thanks for giving me your email address. I can't stand doing long texts. At least I can use two fingers on my laptop.

I just wanted to tell you I'm coming up to town tomorrow morning for a meeting and I was wondering if you and Digger would like to take Artemis and me for one of your walks on Hampstead Heath. We could be with you around eleven.

Sorry, it's a bit last-minute, but I didn't know I was coming until just now.

Chum

Polly found she was grinning at her computer screen. Only one way to reply to that: Yes, how lovely, here's my postcode … She started typing, her earlier low mood completely lifted now she had something to look forward to. A couple of hours of light-hearted respite from the uncomfortable aspects of her real life. That was all it took.

Friday 19 February

The next morning Polly felt oddly nervous about Chum's visit. Shirlee and Maxine seemed to stay longer than usual for breakfast, and by ten-fifteen, much as she enjoyed their company, Polly was starting to feel edgy. She didn't want to have to explain to them who Chum was and why she was going on a walk with him. And she dreaded to think what questions Shirlee might ask if she had to introduce him.

After another five minutes she told them as casually as she could that she had to go and get ready for a meeting, and was very glad when they took the hint and left.

By five to eleven, she was dressed and ready – trying not to fussily tidy the house, or pretentiously untidy it, to make it look less suburban. Why would he care what her house was like? They were only going for a walk, she reminded herself.

She forced herself to sit in front of her computer and read another perfume blogger's new post, but found it very difficult to pin herself to the chair and was very relieved when Digger's frantic barking started even before Chum rang the doorbell.

'Can you smell Artemis through the wood, Digger?' she said, pulling him back from the door by his collar so she could let them in.

Digger's excitement on actually seeing Artemis resulted in a great deal of yapping and jumping.

Polly was glad of the distraction. She'd taken one look at Chum and realised she felt incredibly shy. Her cheeks started to burn.

'Come in!' she said, over-brightly. 'You found it, then.'

'Trusty phone,' said Chum.

'Do you want to set off right away, or would you like some coffee first?' She stood in the hall, feeling like her arms had become longer and she didn't know where her hands went.

'I'd really love a cup of tea, Hippolyta,' he said.

'Come through,' said Polly, thinking as she spoke that it was a phrase she'd never used before in her life. Come through to the relaxing kitchenette with its extensive Formica facilities.

Digger and Artemis nearly knocked her over, chasing each other down the hall.

'They're happy to see each other, as usual,' said Chum, laughing. 'How joyously simple to be a dog.'

Polly made the tea, feeling oddly pleased he liked it just as she did – strong English Breakfast, no sugar – and brought it over to the table.

'Would you care for a biscuit?' she asked, feeling like some kind of 1960s housewife. Pardon me while I locate the doilies.

Chum's face broke into his big smile, the gap between his front teeth on full display.

'Never more,' he said.

Polly smiled back and grabbed the biscuit tin off the top of the fridge, putting it on the table in front of him with the lid off.

'Have as many as you want,' she said. 'My son is the cookie monster in this house and he's away at uni now. They might be a bit stale, actually.'

Chum was already rummaging through the tin.

'Hobnob!' he cried triumphantly, holding up a round biscuit then dunking it in his mug, before putting it into his mouth. 'Mmmm ... that's better. Snack of the gods.'

He chewed contentedly, finishing the Hobnob while continuing to inspect the tin.

'Bourbon,' he said, holding up one of Lucas's favourite chocolate sandwiches. 'Another fine species in the biscuit genus.'

He dunked that one, chewed, dunked again, put the rest of the biscuit in his mouth and continued to go through the contents of the tin, pulling out a few more, which he piled up in a small tower next to his mug.

'Can't seem to find a Garibaldi,' he said, 'but it's the only classic absent from this tin. Your son is a fine biscuiteer. And no vile custard creams.'

'Are Garibaldis those squashed-fly ones?' asked Polly.

'The very same,' said Chum. 'Crispy on the outside, with a chewing factor that's almost a pastry style, and not oversugared, just the perfect balance of sweet and squashy from the raisins. It's like sending your mouth on holiday.'

'There aren't any of those because Lucas has eaten them all,' said Polly. 'He likes to remove a whole layer of them from the packet and eat it in one go – he doesn't break them up into individual biscuits.'

'A classic manoeuvre,' said Chum. 'The full slab. I've been known to do it myself. Or you can stack 'em. Break up a slab, stack them into a pile of five and eat it in one go as a multi-storey biskwit sandwich. I bet he does that too.'

'He does actually,' said Polly chuckling. 'And he calls them biskwits.'

She hadn't seen Chum so skittish before, but it was a welcome distraction from how strangely shy she felt.

'I had no idea you were such a sugar shocker,' she said.

'Prep school,' said Chum, sliding down in his chair, an expression of bliss on his face, as he nibbled round the edges of another Hobnob, turning it round and round as he went, so it kept its circular shape until the last mouthful. 'I was eight. Biscuits were my comfort, purchased in bulk from the tuckshop. It's amazing I'm not toothless and obese, but I discovered sport and that saved me. And then puberty brought other means of self-comfort, of course ...'

He grinned at Polly, popping a bourbon into his mouth, whole.

'But, still, whenever I feel in need of instant comfort, a couple of bourbons and a slab of Garibaldis will do the trick as well as anything. I'd rather have a Hobnob than a glass of wine any day.'

Polly picked up a bourbon and bit the corner off it.

'They are pretty delicious,' she said, 'although I try not to eat too much sugar, and I'm sure they're full of deadly trans fats.'

She took another bite and then a sip of her tea.

'Mmm, they are good together, aren't they?' she said. 'I'd forgotten.'

She ate the rest of the biscuit wondering if she should ask him the question that was pressing into her mind: why did he need 'instant comfort' at that moment?

But just when she decided to plunge in with 'So, why ...' Chum started talking.

'So, where ...' he said.

They both laughed.

'We keep doing that, don't we?' said Chum. 'What were you going to say?'

Polly shook her head.

'It doesn't matter – were you going to ask where we're going for our walk?'

Chum nodded.

'Well,' said Polly, 'we've got a choice. We can jump in one of the cars and park right by the Heath or we can walk from here. It will just mean that the first fifteen minutes will be on pavements before we get to the proper walk. How does Artemis feel about being on a lead?'

'She's not very impressed with it as a concept,' said Chum. 'But we've already had a longish drive and there's another one to get home, so I vote for starting out on foot to maximise her activity. I don't want her jumping about in the back while I'm driving.'

It took until the end of Polly's street before they could stop the dogs constantly jumping around and getting tangled up, although Chum still had to stop intermittently, jerking Artemis back, until she settled down and he could catch up with Polly and Digger again. Polly would then have to grab Digger by the collar, to stop him from getting overexcited at being reunited with his canine gal pal after a thirty-second separation.

'This is relaxing,' said Chum, as he yanked Artie's lead yet again and stopped, holding her by the collar. 'Not. Heel, you infernal hound.'

Polly laughed.

'It's another ten minutes,' she said. 'I could go ahead and you could follow by sat nav, if you like.'

'It's OK,' said Chum. 'I'll put up with my appallingly trained dog for the pleasure of your company. It's my own fault. Artie is only used to country life. If I have to go into town – I mean the small town nearest to where I live – I leave her in the car. She's a farm dog, really, but I got too fond of her and made her into a pet, without pet training.'

'Naughty Chum,' said Polly, in a dog-admonishing tone. Chum whimpered back.

'Digger's pretty good on the street, isn't he?' he said. 'Did you train him?'

Polly froze mentally, her head suddenly full of images of David in the back garden, his pocket full of treats, trying to get Digger to stop sniffing his trousers long enough to learn anything. It had been an arduous exercise, but David hadn't given up until Digger knew how to stop, stay, come, roll over and walk to heel.

'He was a rescue dog,' she said, hoping it was enough to answer Chum's question without prompting any more discussion.

'Good for you,' he said. 'Battersea Dogs Home? I've always wondered how anyone could come away from there with just one dog. I'd want to take them all.'

Polly laughed.

'I know what you mean,' she said, once again hoping it was enough of a response not to prompt further inquiries, without appearing as vague as it really was.

It seemed her ploy worked, because Chum stopped talking about dogs and turned his head to look at the houses they were passing.

'They're all the same, but different,' he said after a few moments. 'I mean, all the houses are roughly the same size and format, so if you were to drive down this street at night, you'd think they were all the same, but when you see inside, every one is different.'

Polly nodded. It wasn't exactly a revelation to her.

'Have you ever lived in London?' she asked him.

'No,' said Chum. 'I've never lived in a town. Except for my first term at St Andrews, when I was in Sallies.'

Polly smiled to herself. Of course he'd been in St Salvator's – or Sallies, as they called it. That was the Hall of Residence all the Yah guys were in. She'd forgotten.

'Then I got offered a place in a house out towards Crail and I lived out for the rest of my time there. I only came into town for lectures and to go to the pub.'

'I'm not sure one academic term in a hall of residence at St Andrews even counts as living in a town,' she said. 'I remember now, you lived out in that big farmhouse, didn't you, with lots of other people? How many of you lived there?'

'Ten, I think,' said Chum, 'with a few more in the wing over the garages. Mind you, you never knew who'd be at the breakfast table.'

Polly glanced at him, laughing, and saw he was already looking at her. It could have been me at that table, she thought. Was that what he was thinking?

'I always thought you hearty types were nuts,' she said quickly, 'living miles out in the country like old people while you were at university. You missed out on so much, with all that boring designated driver and sharing lifts stuff you had to do. All the really great times happened spontaneously.'

She turned to look at him again and found he was smiling at her. Not the broad, gappy-toothed schoolboy grin, but the eyebrows-raised, closed-mouth one. Slightly knowing. A man's smile.

'But I didn't miss out on everything, though, did I, Hippolyta?' he said, holding her gaze for a moment longer, until he tripped over Artemis, who had stopped dead in front of him, fascinated by a smell in the bottom of a privet hedge.

'Arse!' he cried out. 'Bloody dog, you nearly killed me. Walk! Stop sniffing everything. Is it much further, Polly, to the grassy bit where we can let the hell-hounds off their leads?'

'Just at the end of this road,' she said, trying not to laugh, although she was secretly glad Artemis had distracted him. That look had made her feel as uncomfortable as she had in the hall. More.

'I tell you what,' said Chum, 'I'm going to run ahead with her, and if I don't know where to go, I'll just stop until you catch up and can tell me.'

'It's straight ahead,' said Polly. 'See that green bit at the far end of this road? That's the entrance to the Heath. I'll see you there.'

Chum and Artemis set off at a jog, which made Digger yank so hard on his lead it almost pulled Polly over, but she managed to calm him down and found she was glad of a few moments alone with her thoughts.

There was something she had to think about, which she'd been pushing to the back of her mind with all of the other subjects that seemed too hard – it was getting to be a big pile – but she couldn't ignore this one any more.

The shy awkwardness Chum inspired in her. She knew exactly what it was. And from the way he'd looked at her just before Artemis tripped him up, she was fairly sure he felt the same. Remembering that night in the sand dunes, she wanted to kiss him again.

Did she have a full-blown crush on him? Or did seeing him again after all those years just make her want to go back to where they'd left off? To do what they never had and take it on to the next stage – or even just to see if that kiss had been as heavenly as she remembered it?

She slowed up as she walked along – despite Digger pulling on the lead – wanting to think it through before she caught up with Chum again.

She didn't have a crush on him, she decided, because she wasn't obsessing over him twenty-four/seven the way she remembered you did when in the throes of such a passion. She hardly thought of him between walks, but whenever those opportunities came along, she always looked forward to them hugely and then really enjoyed spending the time with him.

The physical self-consciousness, though, the blushing and awkwardness, was a new development. And crush-like, she had to acknowledge.

Great, thought Polly, gazing down the street at Chum's lanky figure already standing by the gate into the Heath. Something else peculiar to worry about.

Because if she did have a crush on him, what was she going to do about it? Stop seeing him until the inappropriate feelings went away – when the walks with him were one of the few comforts in her current life?

Obviously she couldn't try to defuse it by acting on her impulses. She couldn't go around kissing random men just because she fancied them, or had kissed them when she was twenty. She was still a married woman.

Or am I, she thought, as she drew closer to Chum and his face broke into one of those broad smiles, the one with the deep creases at the edges of his mouth, his eyes crinkled up, and her stomach turned over.

They stepped round the metal swing gate onto the grassy expanse of the Heath and released the dogs from their leads. As they stood side by side, watching the animals bound off together leaping with joy, Polly had to stuff her hand into her jacket pocket to stop herself from reaching out to take hold of Chum's.

She glanced over at him just in time to see him do exactly the same, and wondered if it was for the same reason.

Something told her it was, and she started walking. Fast.

Monday, 29 February

Polly was still doing her early-morning meditation when she heard Shirlee arrive. The front door opened with a great crash, followed by huffing and puffing and plenty of swearing as she carried large bags of food towards the kitchen, kicking the front door shut behind her as she went.

Her concentration shattered, Polly glanced over at the bedside clock. Seven-twenty. Shirlee was coming earlier and earlier, but Polly didn't mind. These days she had the studio all ready by the time Polly came down – mats out, windows open, candles lit – and it was such a help. She even brought fresh flowers a couple of times a week, which was lovely.

She'd insisted on taking over the bookings as well and in return, she received all her classes for free. Shirlee was brilliantly organised, and her help left Polly with more time to concentrate on the blog, which was very useful because it was really getting noticed. She was actually having to turn events down.

Polly took a moment to check her phone for texts and emails. She knew she shouldn't do this before class, in case there was something that would distract her and affect her concentration – it wasn't fair on the class if her attention was wandering. But with everything that was going on she couldn't help herself.

It was barely a month until the deadline she'd agreed with Clemmie for doing something proactive to find David, and they were keeping in close touch. Supporting each other to hold their nerve. Between that and checking up on Lucas – who seemed to be OK back at uni, with no mishaps so far, but she wasn't going to leave it to chance – she had a lot to keep an eye on.

And there was another reason she couldn't resist checking: to see if Chum had been in contact. She was trying to suppress the inappropriate feelings she was having for him – she'd even said she was too busy the last time he'd suggested a walk – but any contact with him was like a bright spark in her day. Sure enough there was an email. No content line as usual, just a blank email with a *New Yorker* dog cartoon copied into it.

Two dogs watching a man throwing a stick, one saying to the other: 'I can't believe we do this for a living.'

Polly grinned and closed it. Later on she'd spend a happy few minutes looking for one to send back to him. There wasn't any harm in that, surely? Just two old friends cheering each other up.

She arrived downstairs to find Shirlee putting a jug of yellow tulips on the kitchen table.

'Oh, how lovely,' said Polly. 'A breath of spring. You are such a pal.'

She put her arm round Shirlee and kissed her on the cheek.

'You're welcome,' said Shirlee. 'You've got to spoil the tribe.'

'So how many yogi bears do we have this morning, oh organisational guru?' asked Polly, pouring the warm water left in the kettle over the slice of lemon still in her empty glass. 'Do you want one of these?'

'Is there vodka in it?'

'No vodka until breakfast,' said Polly, smiling.

'Spoilsport – but go on, then, I'll have some tooth-enamel-stripping lemon water, and to answer your question, there's the usual famous five regulars, plus two more occasional dropper-inners – and one new bug.'

'Oh, that's good. We love a new bug. Where did she come from?'

'He,' said Shirlee, raising her eyebrows. 'It's a male bear.'

'Really?' said Polly. 'Well, that'll make a nice change. Did you warn him he'd be the only one?'

'Yeah, he seemed cool about that.'

'Great. I used to have lots of blokes in my classes when I worked in yoga centres and gyms – do you remember that chap in Highgate with the terrible smelly feet?'

Shirlee laughed. 'How could I forget? And do you remember how he stopped coming quite suddenly?'

She grinned, showing her teeth.

'What did you do?' asked Polly, putting one hand on her forehead.

'Gave him the card of a local podiatrist. Told him it could be a symptom of a serious health condition. Mentioned the word stilton.'

Polly shook her head. 'You are appalling,' she said, laughing, 'but I can't say I missed him. Perhaps if this new bloke likes the class, he'll bring some pals. It would be good to have a mix again. What's his name?'

'Roger,' said Shirlee, giggling like a teenager.

'How old are you?' said Polly. 'Fourteen? Twelve? Don't you dare make any comment about "Roger by name, roger by nature" or anything along those lines, do you hear me?'

'Yes,' said Shirlee. 'But not promising.'

'Did he say how he heard about the class?'

'Your Facebook page – something about a friend of a friend,' said Shirlee, shrugging.

'Great, the more the merrier.'

Polly headed towards the hall, talking over her shoulder as she went.

'Did you check if he was single? That's the only thing all the other yogi bears are going to want to know.'

'He is,' said Shirlee.

Polly stopped in her tracks and turned round to look at her friend, hands on her hips.

'Are you kidding me? You really found that out already?'

'Sure,' said Shirlee, putting her tongue in cheek and moving it around, suggestively.

'You are a piece of work, Shirlee Katz,' said Polly.

Shirlee responded by turning round and waggling her ample rear end at Polly.

'That's Twerk-asana,' she said. 'Upward Minaj.'

'I'll incorporate it into the Sun Salutation,' said Polly and headed for the studio to get her head in yoga gear.

Maxine was the next to arrive, closely followed by everyone else, but there was no sign of Roger.

'I guess Mr Yogi isn't coming after all,' said Shirlee, when they were all settled on their mats cross-legged.

Polly said nothing, not wanting the rest of the class to be distracted. She glanced at the clock that she kept turned towards her on a shelf so her pupils couldn't see it, and waited until it clicked over to eight.

'Let's start,' she said. 'Lie down on your mats, legs straight, arms at your sides, and close your eyes ...'

She had them all settled, slowing each breath, when the doorbell rang.

'Ooh,' said Shirlee. 'Roger the Dodger, I'll go.'

She jumped up and was out of the room before Polly could say anything, so she carried on with the class as though nothing had happened, asking them to lift their knees to their chests and circle them slowly, first one way and then the other.

She could hear Shirlee talking to someone in the hall and the deeper tones of a male voice answering that he had no injuries or health issues. Shirlee then came back through the door, followed by – Guy.

Shirlee sat down, looking very pleased with herself, and Polly just stared at him in disbelief. He had the same expression on his face as when he'd turned up at Lucien Lechêne's event drenched in his own perfume: like a little boy who has just successfully put a frog down the back of a girl's dress.

'Welcome, Roger,' said Polly, putting a firm emphasis on the name. 'I've been looking forward to meeting you. Everyone, this is Roger.'

He put up his hand in greeting and nodded at all the women who had turned to gawp at him.

'Have you done yoga before, Roger?' asked Polly.

'A little,' he said. 'But mostly Ashtanga, Hippolyta.'

'Well, this is Scaravelli yoga, Roger. You'll find it much slower, but deeper. I hope you enjoy it, Roger. And do feel free to call me Polly. Everyone here does, Rog.'

She could see Shirlee looking back and forth between her and Guy as they spoke, a little frown line between her eyebrows. She could clearly tell something was going on and Polly knew it would be killing her not knowing what it was. She hoped Shirlee could at least restrain herself until the session was over.

After that, Polly did her best to concentrate on the class, managing to resist the temptation to include postures that would cause maximum stress to Guy's testicles, but Shirlee was in full flow.

'Been Downward Dog so long it seems like up to me,' she chirped as Polly had them hold the pose for some extra breaths.

Guy – 'Roger' – laughed heartily, which only encouraged her.

'Funny-looking eagle,' she said, as Polly showed them how to entwine their lower arms, palms together, in Eagle Pose, then flicked her eyes left to see if 'Roger' was laughing. He was.

'I think this eagle is taking a poop,' said Shirlee, as Polly demonstrated how to entwine one leg round the other at the same time, knees bent.

She struck again as Polly moved them into Camel Pose, which involved kneeling with their spines arched back, hands resting on their heels behind them, abdomens and chests pushing upwards.

'Hey, Miss Polly,' said Shirlee, whose own back arched so beautifully she could nearly get her head down to her feet, 'one of your camels ain't got no humps ...'

Guy let out a shout of laughter and the entire class collapsed in hysterics.

'I'm a dromedary,' said Guy.

You're a massive arsehole, thought Polly.

'Very funny, Shirlee,' she said, feeling and sounding like an Edwardian school teacher. 'OK, let's do some balancing poses.'

That'll shut them up, she thought. Even Shirlee would have to keep her trap shut to concentrate on Lord of the Dance, which involved standing on one leg and pulling the other one up behind your head with both hands. She hoped Guy would sprain his groin doing it. What was his game, she wondered, pulling her own leg easily up behind her.

'Use your strap if you need to,' she said, dropping hers to the floor. 'And put one hand on the wall, if you can't balance ...'

That was directed at Guy, who was wobbling like a baby giraffe.

Good. She'd had enough of his carrying on. He'd already pulled a stunt that could have done her serious damage at a very important event; he'd been so maddeningly uncooperative about the blog post on his shop she'd had to give up on it, and now he'd tricked his way into her yoga world.

What did he want out of these shenanigans? They got on so well and always had such a fun time when they went out to events together – and that day with Clemmie had been great. Polly just couldn't understand why he had to keep pushing her boundaries the rest of the time.

With all these frustrations rattling around in her head, even she was finding Lord of the Dance a bit of a challenge so she segued quickly on to Tree Pose and was very glad when it was time to settle them down for the final meditation, snug under blankets, like a class of toddlers having their afternoon nap at nursery school.

Guiding them through the deep breathing and loosening of joints, Polly could feel them all going under. She always found it very satisfying. There was a moment when you could see the tension leave their faces, and seeing Guy's jaw slacken she felt a small sense of triumph.

Thought you'd surprise me at my yoga class, did you? Well, who's in control now, smart arse?

She supposed it was a harmless lark, really, his idea of a bit of fun, and wasn't sure why she felt so intruded upon. Because of the way he'd gone about it, she decided. He could have asked her straight out if he could come to a class, and she would have been quite tickled by the idea, but instead he had to do it under a false name and leave her on the back foot – literally – in front of all her regulars. Oh, he was a tricky customer.

She glanced at her hidden clock again and saw it was time to bring them round. Chiming her little temple bells, she sat up straight, realising she'd allowed herself to slump with the negative thoughts she'd been having. Naughty yoga teacher.

After everyone was up in a sitting position she led them all in the usual bow and '*Namaste*', only to have Shirlee chip in at the end with 'and have a nice day'.

Polly could have gladly thrown her chimes at Shirlee's head, but at least everyone was laughing, which distracted them from noticing Polly slip out of the room. She normally hung around to chat and take the money, but Shirlee could do that today. Polly didn't want the whole class to see her interacting with their new friend 'Roger', because she couldn't trust herself to keep her cool.

She nipped to the bathroom upstairs, hoping he'd be gone by the time she came down again, but when she walked into the kitchen all the regulars were in there, comfortably seated at the table – with 'Roger' installed at the head.

'We asked Rog to stay,' said Shirlee, a beady expression in her eye, clearly relishing the prospect of finding out what the beef was between him and Polly.

'Hello, Guy,' said Polly.

'Hello, Hippolyta,' he said.

'Why are you calling him a guy?' said Shirlee, looking confused. 'Do you call all guys "guy"? "Hello man, hello male person".'

'His name is Guy,' said Polly, taking the kettle out of Shirlee's hands. It was her bloody kitchen, she wanted a cup of tea, she was having the kettle. 'Cap G. Not Roger – Guy.'

'Hippolyta and I are old friends,' said Guy.

'Who's Hippopo ... ita?' said Shirlee.

'Me,' said Polly. 'It's my real name, but everyone – well, most people call me Polly. It's easier.'

'So why did you tell me you were called Roger?' asked Shirlee.

'It was just a joke,' said Guy. 'I wanted to surprise her.'

Shirlee beamed.

'That's funny,' she said, 'I like that. You must have had a big shock when he walked in, hey, Hippityhiphop – however you say it.'

'You pronounce it Polly,' said Polly.

'Hip*pol*yta,' said Guy, exaggerating the middle syllable like an Italian lothario.

'Polly is fine, thank you,' she said, starting to feel really irritated.

Her father used to call her Hippolyta, and there were just two people alive who called her that now and she wanted to keep it that way. Bill and Chum. It was special to them. She didn't want it bandied around as some kind of joke name.

She turned round from filling the kettle, to make sure they'd heard her, and saw Guy and Shirlee exchange a complicit look. Shirlee had her eyes crossed and her mouth pursed up.

Great. They were partners in crime already.

'So, what do you like for brekkie, Rog – I mean, Guy?' asked Shirlee. 'I make a great full English, with kosher bacon, but I don't think you're a Jew ...'

She regarded him shrewdly, with narrowed eyes. 'It's halal, if that's good for you.'

Polly turned discreetly to look at Guy. Shirlee – and her complete lack of tact – had her uses, and she saw Guy flick a look back towards herself. Interesting, he was aware he might be giving something away with his answer to Shirlee's customarily intrusive question.

'Kosher halal bacon would be great, thanks,' said Guy, 'but I should warn you I only eat phoenix eggs – organic, free-range, biodynamic phoenix eggs. Aquarius.'

Shirlee laughed.

'With the combined food neuroses of this crew, that wouldn't surprise me. Anyone brought any of that gluten-free crap to poison us today?'

Damn, thought Polly, he'd dodged that bullet. She'd have to get him to come to another class and prime Shirlee first to get the information she wanted out of him. She would respect his wish not to put it all on the blog post – if she ever did one – but her curiosity was still raging to know how he'd funded such a high-spec business. All that gear he had in the basement would have cost a fortune. Some of those perfume ingredients were as expensive per ounce as gold.

She was also genuinely interested to know more about his family. He'd mentioned he was half-Iranian the first time she'd met him, but she'd never been able to get anything else out of him about it since. He'd told her she knew too much already, whatever that was supposed to mean.

Polly took her tea and sat down at the other end of the table from Guy, quietly cradling the mug and taking in the scene for a few moments. Shirlee was frying up a storm, with Maxine as sous chef, and everyone was chatting and laughing, clearly excited to have a man at breakfast for a change. It was a very happy gathering for a Monday morning, and Polly decided she needed to get over herself and just enjoy it. She'd be on her own the rest of the day.

'Hey, Groger,' said Shirlee, 'get over here, you're head waiter.'

He got up from the table and she handed him two plates.

'OK, this one's for Louise – she's veggie so it's just eggs, mushrooms and tomatoes – and this one's for Annie – semi-paleo, no nightshades, so it's just eggs and bacon for her. So go serve and then straight back – and remember their orders for next time.'

Guy – or Groger, as everyone was now calling him – served the food with great aplomb, a tea towel over his left arm, never forgetting a name, or which plate was for who.

When it came to Polly's turn, he took advantage of the moment to whisper in her ear.

'Sorry, Poll. I only did it for a laugh, please don't be cross with me.'

'You're fine,' said Polly, patting him on the back. 'The girls love you. Make the most of your novelty status.'

'Service!' yelled Shirlee.

'Coming, sir! Yessir!' said Guy.

The rest of breakfast was very entertaining, with Shirlee showing off even more than usual. And she didn't show any signs of slackening off when everyone else started peeling away. She even let Maxine leave without her, until finally only Guy and Shirlee remained.

'So, Groger,' said Shirlee, sitting back in her seat and regarding Guy with another of her appraising gazes, 'are you gay or straight or what?'

'What,' said Guy.

'I said are you gay or straight?' said Shirlee.

'You asked if I was gay or straight or what – and I replied. I'm what.'

'Very funny,' said Shirlee. 'So what are ya?'

'What are you?' said Guy.

Polly watched with interest. It was like King Kong versus Godzilla and she wondered which of them would break first.

Shirlee burst out laughing, head thrown back.

'I'm what too,' she said. 'You're funny. What ... that's a classic. I'm a what. I'm gonna use that.'

She extended her hand across the table to Guy and he took it. They shook on it, whatever it was – a new confederation of very maddening, lovable people? Polly didn't know.

'Well, it's been real, Groger,' said Shirlee, 'but I've got to head off now to bully a few tradesmen. I'm getting my flat spruced up, did I tell you, Poll? Anyhow, I hope you're going to come and do some more classes with us, Grog. It's good to have a guy around, mixes up the energy a bit.'

'I'd love to,' said Guy, 'if Polly will let me.'

He turned and gave her his most appealing smile, big black eyes wide, like one of those cheesy urchin paintings.

She rolled her own eyes. She was beginning to find the pair of them exhausting.

'Of course,' she said. 'But you'll do whatever you want anyway, so it doesn't really matter what I say, does it?'

'Do you mind if I hang around for a few more minutes now?' he added. 'I've got something to ask you.'

'Fine,' said Polly, 'I'll put the kettle on again.'

Shirlee left and Polly was glad to be fussing about making cafetière coffee for Guy and hot water for herself. She was trying to keep her English Breakfast habit to one a day, to help with her sleeping, which was increasingly fitful.

'Are you still mad at me?' asked Guy.

'No,' said Polly, 'I'm getting used to you, but please don't play any more of these childish tricks on me, Guy. I know you think it's hilarious, but I find it enervating. A lot of the point of the yoga and meditation I do is to find a place of calm in my life, and your pranks don't help with that. I suppose I'm just not a great fan of surprises.'

And I've had way too many of them recently, she thought. Perhaps if he had any idea what was going on in her life he wouldn't spring these things on her, but she certainly wasn't game to tell him.

'I'll try to rein myself in,' he said, 'but life's so boring. I like to keep it interesting.'

'You and Shirlee are soul mates,' said Polly. 'It's her life's work to make everything fun and interesting. She considers it her human obligation to make standing at a bus stop a life event.'

'Goals ...' said Guy, pushing the plunger down on the coffee pot.

'Sorry I don't have a hookah for you,' said Polly.

'Oh, I'm over all that,' said Guy.

Polly looked at him, puzzled.

'I thought it was part of your Iranian identity,' she said, 'smoking your grandfather's hubba bubba.'

'I made all that up,' he said, pouring coffee into a mug and stirring in two spoonfuls of sugar.

'It wasn't your grandfather's pipe thing?'

Guy shook his head. 'I bought it in Edgware Road,' he said, grinning at her.

Polly dropped her head into her hands.

'Here we go again,' she said. 'Was any of it true? The grandmother with the roasted preserved lemons ...?'

'No,' said Guy. 'I made all that up. I thought it enhanced the Great Eastern Fragrance Company if I had a real oriental connection, but now – thanks to your brilliant insights – I'm moving away from that and getting into more sophisticated styles of perfume, so I've dropped it.'

Polly couldn't think of anything to say. She was certainly glad she hadn't put all that in her blog piece and posted it.

'Is that why you've been so cagey about the blog thing?' she asked.

Guy nodded. 'Yeah, I knew I was moving on from that angle and I didn't want to make you look bad.'

'Well, thank you,' said Polly. 'At least I understand what that was all about now. It did seem a bit peculiar. So can we do the interview now, with your real story?'

'Not really,' said Guy, taking a slow sip of his coffee.

'Why not?'

'I haven't decided what it is yet,' he said.

Polly just shook her head.

'You're a one-off, Guy Webber,' she said eventually, 'if that is even your name. It could be Harry Potter, for all I know. You do my head in, but I'm just going to go ahead and run my piece about the shop and your perfumes, without any background – in fact, I'm going to make your mystery part of the story – because while you drive me mad with all your posturing and silly games, your perfumes are simply brilliant and I can't ignore them any longer. I want my readers to know about what you do – even if I've got nothing to tell them about the person behind it all.'

'Great,' said Guy, 'that's exactly what I'd love you to do.'

'OK,' said Polly, 'we have a deal.'

'There's one more thing I want to ask you about,' said Guy.

'Fire away,' said Polly.

'I'm going to do an ad campaign – print and online, beautiful black-and-white pictures – and I want your mum to model for it. She's got exactly the iconic sophistication I want to confer on the brand, so that people will associate it with the heritage houses, even though it's actually newly minted.'

'She'd love that,' said Polly, with genuine enthusiasm. 'There's nothing Mummy enjoys more than getting in front of the camera, and she's still really good at it. Did you see the Céline campaign she did a couple years ago?'

Guy nodded enthusiastically.

'I loved it. I've always loved her work. I've got an original print of one of Cecil Beaton's *Vogue* pictures of her.'

'Oh that's nice,' said Polly. 'Did you have that before we met?'

'Yes,' said Guy. 'I bought it a while ago at auction. I've collected old copies of *Vogue* since I was about eleven. My mum – and this is true, I'm not making this up now – used to buy it every month and I loved looking at them and that made me really interested in magazines. Then one summer holiday I found some old copies in the attic and realised I liked them even more than the new ones. I had to have the floor in my drawing room reinforced last year to take the weight of my collection. You know how heavy magazines are.'

His drawing room? thought Polly. Reinforced? She'd never been into Guy's flat over the shop, but now she really wanted to get up there – to see if any of this was true, apart from anything. She wasn't going to take anything he said at face value now.

'And going through all the old magazines,' he continued, 'I got really fascinated spotting the models who kept appearing in different issues – and your mum was always my favourite. So when I looked at your blog and read that you were Daphne Masterson's daughter I was really keen to meet you. You can imagine how excited I was when you came into the shop – my favourite perfume blogger, also the daughter of my favourite model.'

'Well, it's always nice when someone knows who she is,' said Polly, quite briskly.

Was this nice, or was it creepy? She wasn't sure, but she did know Daphne would be thrilled to get another ad campaign, especially for a luxurious niche perfume brand.

'I'll give you her agent's number.'

'Can't I just arrange it through you?' asked Guy.

'No,' said Polly, firmly. 'She has an agent and all bookings go through him. I'll go and get his number for you.'

She got up from the table and walked through to her study. She actually knew the number by heart and there was a pad of scrap paper in the kitchen, but she wanted a moment to think.

Did she want Guy to meet her mother? Hadn't he already intruded on her life slightly too much?

He was in regular touch with Clemmie now, sending her samples of his perfumes to give to her friends and then getting feedback on how they were received. He'd even offered to pay her a commission on any online sales he made as a direct result of her introductions. And Clemmie had asked Polly a couple of times when they were all going to go out together to some fun at a glamorous event.

So, thought Polly, he'd infiltrated himself into her blog life and her yoga scene, he'd met Shirlee, as well as already being matey-matey with Clemmie – and now he wanted to work with her mother. Was it too much?

She pondered for a moment, tapping a pencil against her lip, and decided she couldn't see what harm it could do. Doing the campaign – and being worshipped by somebody who would thrill to all the stories Polly had heard a million times – would make Daphne so happy it would be mean to turn the opportunity down. She scribbled the agent's name and number down and took them back to Guy.

'Thanks so much, Polly,' he said, carefully tucking the piece of paper away. 'I'll ring him as soon as I get back to the shop. But I wonder if I should also meet your mum before we do the shoot. Then she'll be more relaxed with me – and I won't be all shy and star-struck with her.'

Polly didn't reply immediately, pretending to do something to the cafetière and considering what he'd said.

'That's a great idea actually,' she said eventually. 'There's nothing she likes more than talking about her glory days – and she adores perfume as well. She's still got some of the bottles the great designers gave her when their perfumes were first launched – they're empty now, but it's pretty amazing to know that Christian Dior himself gave her that particular flacon of Miss Dior.'

Guy's face was rapt with interest.

'Yes,' he said. 'I read about that on your blog. It's so amazing to think that she actually knew them all.'

'And there's speculation – and I got this from some research I was doing, not from her – that she was the inspiration for Jean-François Volant's 1955 perfume La Cygne.'

'Of course!' said Guy, sitting up straight with his mouth open. 'Her legendary swan neck. Wasn't La Cygne her nickname?'

Polly nodded.

'How amazing,' said Guy. 'Oooh, I'm so excited about meeting her I could pass out. When can we do it?'

'Whenever you can take a day away from the shop and I don't have anything on. We'll go up to where she lives and have lunch. It's just under an hour from here. She can be a bit dotty at times, just to warn you, but she's mostly OK, as long as she's been eating and drinking enough, and I'm sure the prospect of meeting someone who admires her work will perk her up no end.'

'Oh, I know she'll be just wonderful,' said Guy, then he stood up, pulled Polly to her feet and whisked her round the kitchen in a polka.

'I'm going to meet, Da-a-aphne,' he sang, in time to their steps. 'I'm going to meet a le-e-gend ...'

Polly had to laugh. Guy drove her nuts, but she couldn't help loving his company. Like Shirlee, he seemed to make the sun come out – and she had to take her fun wherever she could find it.

Monday, 14 March

As she pulled up at Rockham Park, Polly wondered how her mother would receive Guy. Would she be waiting on the sofa in reception in full regalia, possibly a fur, legs entwined, one elegant hand extended out, the other on her hip?

Or perhaps she would throw open the apartment door, in profile, head back laughing, for maximum amazing neck impact.

'This is swanky,' said Guy, as Polly pushed the entrance buzzer and they were admitted by the receptionist. 'Is it a hotel?'

'This is the new age of assisted living for the well-derly.'

Guy raised an eyebrow.

'Well-off, pretty fit and elderly,' explained Polly. 'It's like a hotel: there's a dining room, a bar and a café, a pool and a hairdresser, but they all have apartments, with a front door and a letterbox. Mummy won't let me call it a flat. It's an apartment.'

Guy chuckled. 'I love her already.'

The receptionist told them Miss Masterson was waiting for them in the library, and Polly led the way, curious to see what tableau her mother would have created for herself in there.

They walked in to see her standing with her back to them at a three-quarters angle, looking out of the floor-length window, her slender frame perfectly outlined against the light in an immaculately cut little black dress, her hips forward, feet – in her favourite heels – in fourth position, holding a champagne flute in one hand, the fingers of the other resting lightly on its base. Her head was turned fully towards the view, extending the famous neck.

Guy gasped. It was a perfect rendition of an iconic shot Mark Shaw had done of her for *LIFE* magazine in 1958.

'The Crillon session,' he said under his breath, in awed tones.

It was all Polly could do not to laugh. Daphne had a print of that very photograph in her flat/apartment. Polly had known it all her life and this wasn't the first time she'd seen her mother re-create it. God, she was funny.

Hearing Guy's exclamation, Daphne turned – impossibly slowly – towards them, breaking into a delighted smile, as if surprised to see them there. Guy rushed over and took her right hand in his, bringing it to his lips, as he had Clemmie's, except this time he also bent his right knee.

Polly stood back and watched the show. A pair of posturing peacocks together.

'Miss Masterson,' he said, breathily, 'I'm so very honoured to meet you.'

'Oh, do call me Daphne, darling,' she said.

'Guy Webber,' said Guy, kissing her hand again before letting go of it.

Polly saw her mother's eyes giving Guy the once-over, warm with approval. He was looking particularly sleek, in one of his immaculate bespoke suits. This one was a dark navy, lined with bright orange silk, and he was wearing it with a crisp white shirt, no tie, but a burgundy and white polka-dot silk square in his breast pocket. He had a cashmere muffler, in a slightly darker orange than the suit lining, draped around his neck.

'Hello, Mummy,' said Polly, bringing up the rear and kissing her mother's delicately proffered cheek. Daphne's sculpted face looked even more beautiful than usual. She must have been getting ready for days.

'Hello, darling,' said Daphne. 'Would you like a drink before lunch? I'm just having a little coupe. Let's ring for a bottle.'

Polly had to stop herself from rolling her eyes at the thought of ringing for drinks, and headed for the bar. She could imagine that someone probably had come and brought that glass of champagne to her mother. Dazzled by her glamour – or perhaps just too kind to let an old lady down – the staff at Rockham Park did indulge Daphne.

When Polly came back with the drinks, Daphne and Guy were roaring with laughter. They hardly seemed to notice she was there, they were so engrossed in discussing what it had been like to work with Mark Shaw.

'Oh, he was heaven,' said Daphne. 'I adored Mark. When he took your picture it was as though there was no camera in the room, you were just having a private moment with him. He was so young, when a lot of the photographers then were so much older than I was – of course I loved Cecil Beaton too, but he was an Edwardian, really, and even Parkie – you know, Norman – was twenty years older than me. And with Mark being an American, he had that lovely easy manner. It was so sad how he died so young.'

'He was only forty, wasn't he?' said Guy.

Daphne nodded, taking a delicate sip from her champagne flute.

'I have some of his pictures in the apartment,' she said. 'Original prints. You must come up after lunch and see them.'

'I would love that,' said Guy. 'I collect Mark Shaw's photographs myself ...'

They carried on like this, apparently oblivious to Polly's presence, and she resigned herself to a lunch spent mostly with her own thoughts. But she couldn't resent it, as they were both clearly having a wonderful time.

Checking her phone to see if there was anything she could look at on Instagram to pass the time, Polly noticed it was already ten past one.

'We need to go through to the dining room,' she said. 'They'll be wondering where we are.'

Guy helped Daphne up and put out his arm for her, and they set off in state for the dining room, with Polly following on behind as usual.

As they entered the room – which was full, except for Daphne's table in her special corner – everyone turned to look at her on the arm of the striking-looking man, with a thick black beard, in a beautiful suit, hair slicked back like a matinée idol. Polly felt like the village idiot, trailing in their wake wearing jeans and a sweater. She hadn't thought to dress up.

She was so mortified at the way everyone was staring at them that she didn't notice until she was right alongside the table that Chum was sitting with Bill.

It wasn't a Friday, when he always had lunch with Bill, so it hadn't occurred to her that he might be there. Oh, why hadn't she checked beforehand when she made this arrangement? It didn't matter, she told herself, but somehow she felt embarrassed to see Chum when she had Guy there. Two worlds colliding.

'Hippolyta!' said Chum, sounding delighted to see her. He got to his feet and she went over to kiss him and then Bill, horribly aware her cheeks were burning. It was all too confusing.

'How lovely to see you both,' she said. 'I'd better keep up with Mummy, she's with my, er, friend.'

'Perhaps we'll see you in the coffee room afterwards,' said Bill.

'That would be great,' said Polly.

'Artie's in there already,' said Chum. 'Is Digger with you?'

'Yes,' said Polly, 'but luckily he's in the car this time.'

'Perhaps they can have a bit of a run around together after lunch,' said Chum. 'Outside, I mean, not in here again. If you can ...'

He glanced at Guy, who Daphne was introducing to some of her friends at a nearby table. He was kissing their hands. Polly cringed.

'Yes,' said Polly, 'that would be great. That's my friend Guy. He's come to see Mummy.'

She felt like she had to explain him somehow.

'Well, he's certainly not dressed for dog walking,' said Chum.

Polly smiled at them both and then turned away to catch up with Guy and Daphne, only to see they had stopped for more introductions.

'Guy has very kindly invited me to model in his new advertising campaign,' she could hear her mother saying. 'He's a very distinguished *parfumeur* ...'

She wondered how the other women at Rockham Park put up with her. It was a miracle they hadn't poisoned her lunch.

'I think we need to get to the table, Mummy,' she said, touching her gently on the arm.

Then she caught Guy's eye and spoke to him in a low voice. 'They get thingy if you're late. It's not a proper restaurant, it's a lunch service.'

He nodded and steered Daphne on at a brisker pace, preventing her from making any more introductions. She made do with nodding from side to side, like the queen she was.

'We can go through to the coffee lounge after lunch,' said Polly, 'and you can introduce Guy to everyone else then.'

The meal progressed just as Polly had expected, with Guy and her mother locked in conversation about photographers and fashion designers and Paris in the 1950s, then a long discussion about perfume, which at least Polly could make some contribution to, before Guy finally got onto talking about the shoot.

'So the thing is, Daphne,' he said, 'seeing you framed in the window like that is making me think we must shoot it in Paris. How do you like that idea?'

'Oh, that would be marvellous!' said Daphne. 'I haven't been for so long. We shot the Céline photographs in a big studio in a rather ghastly bit of London, which was disappointing. I would adore to go to Paris again.'

'I wish we could do them at the Crillon, to really recreate the Mark Shaw photograph,' said Guy, 'but they're closed for renovations, so I'll get the shoot manager to find a location that looks like the Crillon – with those gorgeous long windows. We'll stay at the Ritz, of course.'

'Of course?' thought Polly. Where did he get his funding? Oh well, Daphne looked beatific with happiness, that was the main thing.

'Oh Guy, darling, how wonderful,' Daphne was saying. 'I used to stay there so often, I always had the same room and they always made sure there were white roses for me. I wonder if they'll remember me?'

Guy turned to Polly and winked at her. He'd make sure they 'remembered' her, she was sure of it, and the white roses would be there too.

'And you'll come, won't you, Poll?' he asked.

'I'd love to,' she said. 'What a treat.'

Not adding that she would never let her eighty-five year old sometimes-confused mother go to Paris without her. Especially not with him.

Lunch finished and they headed to the coffee lounge. It was pretty full up, because with their late arrival in the dining room and all the talking Daphne and Guy had been doing – not to mention Daphne's torturously slow eating of very little. Everyone else had finished before them.

There didn't seem to be any free chairs, and Polly was delighted to see Chum waving at her. He stood up and came over.

'We've saved three seats for you,' he said, 'and you'd better come quick, because it got a bit ugly holding on to them just now.'

He turned to Daphne and put out his hand.

'Hello, Mrs Masterson-Mackay,' he said. 'I'm Edward Cliddington-Hanley-Maugham. I was at St Andrews with Hippolyta. My stepfather, Bill Edmonstone, lives here, I think you know him.'

'Oh, you're Bill's son,' she said. 'How lovely to meet you.'

Chum then put his hand out to Guy, who was looking at him a bit coolly, Polly thought. Adding to the awkwardness, it was hard for Guy to shake it because Daphne had her arm tightly round his right elbow.

'Edward Cliddington,' said Chum.

Polly remembered his cousin shortening his name, in the same way.

Guy waved at him with his trapped hand. 'Guy Webber-Tango-Foxtrot,' he said, nodding curtly and then walking Daphne towards the empty seats.

Polly was so mortified by what Guy just said she felt rooted to the spot, but Chum didn't seem to care. He gave her a conspiratorial smile, and put out his left elbow for her to take. She smiled back at him and threaded her arm through it, willing her cheeks not to flame up again.

'Artie's dying to see you,' said Chum. 'I don't think Bill can hold her back much longer.'

As he spoke, Artie broke free and bounded over to them, jumping up at Polly. She fell to her knees and rubbed the dog's lovely head, patting her back and submitting to some thorough face licking.

'Oh, do stop that, Artie,' said Chum. 'I can't take you anywhere.'

'Hello, you lovely thing,' said Polly. 'I've got someone with me today who'd love to see you, but I'm not going to say the name, because you'll go bonkers.'

'Shall we skol the gruesome coffee and head out with them?' suggested Chum, when Polly stood up again.

'Let me just make sure my mum and Guy are sorted, so I can leave them for a bit,' said Polly, 'and then, yes, please.'

She sat down and Chum took orders from them all for coffee, which was laid out on a sideboard at the end of the room. He headed off and Polly turned her attention to the other three.

Bill was asking Guy how he came to be a perfumer. Nice going, Bill, thought Polly. Maybe he could get an answer out of him.

'I always loved playing with my mother's perfume when I was a kid,' he said. 'My parents went away a lot when I was young, so I used to go looking for my mum's smell.'

Bill beamed at Polly.

'I think we can all relate to that, eh, Hippolyta?' he said.

'That's pretty much how it started for me,' she agreed.

'What perfume did your mother wear?' Guy asked Bill.

'You can ask Hippolyta about that,' he replied. 'I still want to hear how you went from liking your mother's scent to making a profession out of it. How did you train to make them? It must be a very complex operation, I've often wondered about it. It must be a bit like painting with invisible paint. So how did you learn to do it?'

Go, Bill! Thought Polly. Shame she now knew the answer to that part of it. Perhaps if she left them to it, Bill could find out how he funded it all, but before Bill could pursue his interrogation, Chum arrived back with a tray of cups and a large plate of biscuits.

'Here you are, Hippolyta,' he said, putting a cup and saucer in front of her. 'Are you sure you only want hot water?'

'So how come you and Bill are allowed to call her Hippolyta?' asked Guy, looking at Chum pointedly. Polly could have thrown her hot water right over him.

'I've always called her that,' said Chum, looking right back at him and biting into a ginger nut.

'Well, I'm only allowed to call her Polly,' said Guy, turning to look at her. 'Why can't I have special naming privileges?'

'Because I haven't known you since I was nineteen,' said Polly. 'And in the perfume world – and my yoga classes – I'm Polly and I'd like to keep it that way.'

'But these two are allowed to call you the full Hippolyta?' persisted Guy.

'It's such a lovely name,' said Bill, 'and so rarely heard, I'm afraid I insisted upon it.'

Polly glanced at her mum and saw that her eyes had closed. She was having a micro nap, something she'd started to do recently – particularly if the conversation wasn't about her.

'Your coffee's here, Mummy,' said Polly, with a gentle nudge, hoping to wake her before the others noticed she'd dropped off. However annoying he was, she didn't want Guy to be put off using Daphne in his ad campaign. She really wanted her mother to have that treat.

Daphne came to and immediately fixed her face into its most radiant beam. Polly hoped the coffee would stop her nodding off again.

'Guy has asked Mummy to appear in his advertising campaign,' said Polly to Bill, to turn the conversation back to Daphne.

It worked, and Bill started asking Guy and Daphne interested questions about what that would entail. Polly caught Chum's eye and he smiled at her. Artie saw the contact between them and stood up, walking over to Polly and putting an elegant paw on her thigh.

'Shall we take them out while this lot are chatting?' said Chum, nibbling on a bourbon biscuit.

Polly nodded, hoping she could make it out of the room without running. She stood up.

'I'm going to check on the dog,' she said, 'give him a breather. Will you be all right for twenty minutes or so, Mummy?'

'Of course,' she said. 'Guy will look after me, and if we finish down here before you get back, he can come and see my photographs.'

'Great,' said Polly. 'I'll see you up in the apartment, then.'

'I'll come out too,' said Chum, as though it had only just occurred to him. 'Artie needs to stretch her legs as well.'

'Have a nice time, *Hippolyta*,' said Guy, with an infuriating smirk.

'Thanks, Roger,' said Polly, and followed Chum out.

'That was strangely tense,' he said, as they walked along the corridor towards the reception area.

Polly rolled her eyes.

'Guy's a bit of a number,' she said. 'He's a sweetie really – and very clever – but he likes to make everything into a ... oh, I don't know, a thing.'

'How do you know him?' asked Chum.

'I went to check out his perfume shop one day and we became friends. He's a really gifted perfumer and it makes up for a lot of his silliness. Now he wants to use my mum in his swishy ad campaign and it will be such a treat for her to be taken to Paris and stay at the Ritz and have a bit of a taste of the life she used to live. Guy was already a big fan of hers – which is a bit creepy, frankly, but he collects vintage fashion photographs and he's got some of her and he wants to reproduce them for the—'

'He's gay, then?' said Chum.

Polly laughed.

'What an assumption! I don't know what he is. He never talks about his love life. I'm not sure he has one.'

'I know how he feels,' said Chum. 'Artie doesn't, though, look at her.'

The moment they'd stepped out of the main door into the car park, Artie had bolted towards Polly's car. She jumped up and put her paws on the window, barking. Polly could hear Digger's answering woofs from inside.

She rushed to let him out, glad of an excuse to have a moment to think about what Chum had just said. He was definitely single, then. Not just unmarried. Why did that knowledge please her? She wasn't. If anything, knowing he was single just made things worse.

Digger and Artie went bouncing off together onto the grass, chasing each other round the trunk of their favourite monkey puzzle tree.

'There isn't really anywhere much to walk here,' said Chum, leaning back on his heels and surveying the scene. 'Shall we take a turn around the lawn, ma'am? See what flowers are up? I saw some primroses on the way over, which always makes it feel like spring is starting to stir. I love this time of year.'

He put his arm out again and Polly was happy to take it. Too happy. They set off past the tree where the dogs were still playing, stopping as they went to admire the daffodils and crocuses. The garden turned round the side of the building, and there was a bench set into a lovely old wall, which must have surrounded the garden of the old house that was knocked down to build the complex. On either side of the bench were two beautiful clouds of yellow flowers.

'Oh, look,' said Polly, 'the mimosa's out, how lovely. Let's go and smell it.'

They headed over and as they got closer the scent of the fluffy yellow blooms filled the air.

'Ah,' said Polly, breathing deeply. 'Some of my favourite perfumes are based on this smell. It reminds me of my time in Australia. It's a native plant there. They call it silver wattle.'

'Shall we sit and enjoy it for a moment?' said Chum.

They settled themselves down on the bench and the dogs raced past, glancing over at them as though checking in to make sure Chum and Polly were still there and letting them know that they were, too.

'Hey, Artie!' Chum called out, and the dog came to a sudden halt and turned to look at him, her elegant head on one side. 'Nothing, just kidding, as you were.'

Artie seemed to sense she wasn't really being summoned and ran off to catch up with Digger, who had stopped and turned round, searching for her.

'Rotten tease,' said Polly.

Chum grinned at her. 'I like to keep her on her toes – well, her paws. Remind her who the pack leader is.'

'OK, Mr Dog Whisperer,' said Polly.

'So you lived in Australia,' said Chum. 'Lucky you. I've always wanted to go. Did you like it?'

'I loved it,' said Polly. 'We were only there two years and it broke my heart to come back after such a short stay. The kids were little and it was just heaven for them.'

'So why did you come back?' asked Chum.

'My husband got offered a really good job,' said Polly.

She'd started the sentence without thinking, but by the time she'd finished it, she felt almost sick. That word 'husband' hung in the air between them. Like a bad smell, thought Polly.

What used to be one of the most positive things in her life – her happy marriage – now seemed dirty and tainted, with too many unhappy and confusing associations. And now complicated even more by the inappropriate feelings she was starting to have for another man. The one she was sitting in this garden with.

'Has he still got that job?' asked Chum.

Polly thought for a moment, looking Chum right in the eye.

'I don't know,' she said very quietly.

'Do you want to tell me about that?' asked Chum, gently, as though he was speaking to a frightened animal.

She felt tears fill her eyes and tried to blink them away.

'Possibly,' said Polly. 'One day. Not right now, but some time soon, yes.'

After that looming deadline she'd decided on with Clemmie had passed and she might actually know something. It was only a week away now. Ugh.

Chum looked away for a moment, brushing his hand over the mimosa bush, so more of the glorious scent was released into the air, then turned back to her.

'Have you googled me yet?' he asked her.

Polly shook her head, wiping a tear from her cheek, but smiling.

'I'm not going to,' she said. 'I don't want to do that to you. It doesn't seem right. I've got a lot of my life out there on the internet, because I put it there – but I only broadcast what I'm happy for people to know. I don't think the stuff you're referring to is something you put on a blog, right?'

Chum laughed.

'You're so right,' he said. 'And I do heartily wish it wasn't out there for all to see. It doesn't turn into chip paper any more, all that stuff, that's the problem. It's all there to be picked over forever like a dead gazelle in the Kalahari.'

'That's why I don't want to look at it,' said Polly.

'Thank you,' said Chum, laying his hand gently on hers, where it was resting on the seat of the bench. 'It's very thoughtful of you, but I do want to tell you about it some time. You'll understand me more when you know what's gone on, and then, when I've done that, if you like, you can tell me about your skeletons.'

'I'll think about it,' said Polly. 'But probably, yes.'

He gave her hand a squeeze and lifted his off again.

'I tell you what,' he said, 'I think they're saying it's going to be nice weather again next week—'

'Your friends at *Farming Today*?' said Polly.

'The very ones,' said Chum. 'You should listen. They had a gripping item today about paddock eggs. But I mean it – if the weather is good and you're free, let's do a really long walk. I've got just the one in mind – it would take all day.'

'I can't think of anything I'd like more,' said Polly.

And she meant it.

Thursday, 17 March

Polly and Clemmie were sitting in the kitchen trying to work up the courage to ring the police about David. It was three days before their deadline of 20 March, because they hadn't realised that was a Sunday. It seemed important to do it in the working week.

'Please, you call them, Clemmie,' pleaded Polly, throwing a piece of orange peel at her. 'It was your idea.'

'He's your husband,' said Clemmie, throwing it back.

'He's your father,' said Polly.

'Who's her father?' asked Lucas, coming into the kitchen scratching his tummy, his hair standing up on his head in a tangled mess that reminded Polly of Digger after a particularly rough exchange with a hedge.

'Have we got a new one?' he continued. 'We seem to have lost the other one.'

Polly and Clemmie looked at each other. They'd been hoping that Lucas would spend most of the day asleep to give them space to start making inquiries. They hadn't wanted to tell Lucas about it until they were sure he was all right.

Lucas had only arrived home for the Easter vacation late the night before, so Polly hadn't had a chance to talk properly with him, to be sure he was really OK and hadn't just been putting on a good FaceTime front to her and Clemmie.

Polly glanced at the clock – not even midday. Practically dawn by his standards – that had to be a good sign in itself.

'It's the same father,' she said. 'The one we haven't seen for three months ... I'll make you some coffee and we can all talk things through.'

'Oh, are we talking about it now?' said Lucas, sitting down at the table and massaging his temples with the heels of his hands. 'I thought there was some kind of super-injunction against discussing it, because every time I've tried to bring it up before, it's like I've been struck mute and nobody can hear me.'

'There kind of was a total news blackout,' said Clemmie. 'That's what Dad wanted for some unexplained reason, and it seemed best to go along with it at first, but it's been three months now, and Mum and I have decided we've had enough of his nonsense and we're going to find him.'

Polly busied herself with making the coffee and a pile of toast for Lucas. She was more grateful for her level-headed daughter at that moment than she could possibly express.

'Ooh, thanks, Mum,' said Lucas, as she put the toast on the table, followed by the butter and various jams and spreads.

Clemmie reached out and took a piece.

'Oi!' said Lucas. 'I need that. That was going to be my Nutella slice. I was going Marmite, peanut butter, raspberry jam, Nutella – starter, main course, pudding, petits fours – and now I've only got three slices, I can't run my full gamut.'

'I'll make some more,' said Polly, thinking a nice pile of buttery toast would be comforting for all of them. She felt like she was going to need some props to get through this. She still had Lucas's old sniffy blanket stashed away somewhere in the house and right now the thought of sucking her thumb while cuddling a bit of old ragged wool was quite appealing.

The toaster popped up and Polly piled the hot slices onto a plate and went over to the table, so happy to be sitting at it again with three-quarters of the family present at least.

But thinking about what they had to discuss – and do – quickly drained all the joy out of her again. She froze with a piece of toast halfway to her mouth and put it down on the plate. Her mouth had gone dry; she couldn't eat anything.

Clemmie reached over and took her mother's hand.

'Are you OK, Mum?' she said.

Polly couldn't answer immediately. She didn't want to break down in front of them; she was supposed to be the strong one, to help them through it. That was what mothers did, wasn't it? But she felt so tired from it all.

'It's just so nice to have you both here,' she said, kissing Clemmie's hand and letting it go.

'So,' said Lucas, licking a stray smear of peanut butter from the corner of his mouth, 'do we know where he is?'

'No,' said Clemmie.

'But we think he's still alive,' said Lucas with his usual forthrightness, though Polly could see the uncertainty in his eyes. He was acting gung-ho, but inside he was as confused and hurt as she was.

'We know he's alive,' said Clemmie.

'He texts her once a week,' said Polly.

Lucas frowned. 'He never texts me,' he said.

'Or me,' said Polly. 'But we mustn't be cross with Clemmie about that, it's not her fault. You know Dad. He's always thought Clemmie was the sensible one, like him, and you and I are more …'

'Fuckwits?' asked Lucas. 'Air heads?'

'I don't think he would put it that harshly, but at any rate he thinks Clemmie's the right one to text.'

'So what do these texts say, oh chosen one?' asked Lucas.

'Just that he's all right and not to worry,' said Clemmie. 'Which is not very helpful, so don't envy me the texts too much.'

'Can I see them?' asked Lucas.

It had never occurred to Polly to ask that, but now Lucas had, she desperately wanted to see them too.

Clemmie picked up her phone and handed it to Lucas. He looked at it for a few moments, scrolling up and down with his finger, then handed it to Polly.

'You're due one today,' he said.

Polly looked at the screen, feeling queasy. There seemed to be so many of them, it just showed how long he'd been away. The first few had desperate replies from Clemmie, begging him to answer his phone, or call and tell her what was going on, but there were no replies to them, just the same thing repeated:

I'm all right. Don't worry. Dad

Could he not have varied it a bit? And couldn't he have put a kiss on the end or something? It was so stark and cold.

'How do you work that out?' asked Clemmie. 'That I'm due one?'

'He sends them every Friday at 2 p.m. You'll be getting one in a couple of hours.'

Clemmie grabbed the phone from Polly and stared at the screen.

'Oh, my God, you're right,' said Clemmie. 'Why didn't I notice that?'

'What were we saying about air heads?' asked Lucas.

'Of course,' said Polly, smacking her hand against her forehead. 'That's just what he'd do. You know how he likes his routines. You could set a clock by when he leaves – used to leave – the house every morning. He always works to a timetable, right down to his stupid texts.'

'Can we use that in any way, Sherlock?' asked Clemmie, looking at Lucas. 'To find him?'

'If we were the police we might be able to,' said Lucas. 'They could probably put a track on his phone, or MI5 could, but there's no way we can trace it. He's probably bought the cheapest handset possible pay-as-you-go £15 job ... they're untraceable, that's why crims use them. I assume you've tried ringing the phone he sends them from?'

Clemmie nodded, pulling a face.

'Of course, I have,' she said. 'It's always just that recorded message that says the phone isn't switched on.'

They sat in silence for a moment. Lucas looked up at the ceiling, scratching his head, then turned to Polly.

'Have you rung his work phone?'

Polly shook her head slowly. She hadn't. Why hadn't she? She tried to unscramble her thoughts.

'He said he was going away on a research trip,' she said, 'so that was the last place I thought he'd be.'

'You didn't ring the department to find out if they knew where he was on that mission?' Lucas persisted.

'Well, no,' said Polly, 'because just before he left he sent me an email setting it all out, and saying that it would somehow be disastrous – for all of us – if the university found out his absence was anything other than a normal research trip. So I didn't feel I could ...'

Her voice trailed away as she said it. She felt so stupid.

'What's the number?' said Lucas, picking up Polly's phone. 'Of the History Department?'

Polly stared at him for a moment, taking it in. He was going to ring them.

'It's in my contacts,' she said, 'under King's College.'

Lucas fiddled with the handset and Polly glanced at Clemmie, who looked as surprised as she felt at Lucas's sudden authoritative manner. He put the phone to his ear and after a few moments handed it to Polly.

She lifted it to her head to hear the familiar voice of the History Department Administration Manager.

'Oh, hello, Maureen,' she said, gathering her thoughts on the hop, 'it's Polly Masterson-Mackay here – David's wife ...'

'Hello, Polly,' she said, 'are you looking for him?'

'Er, yes,' said Polly, her voice rising in panic. Did they know he was missing? But Maureen sounded relaxed and normal, not how you would speak to the wife of a missing person.

'Here you are,' she said.

'Hello?' said a man's voice. It was David.

Polly was so surprised she froze.

'Hello?' said David again.

Polly couldn't speak. Then she heard him ask Maureen who was supposed to be on the line for him, and was so freaked out when she heard Maureen answer 'your wife' she hung up.

The hand holding the phone dropped to her lap. She felt dizzy.

'Are you all right, Mum?' said Clemmie, jumping to her feet. 'You've gone white.'

Polly thought she might be about to faint.

'Put your head between your knees, Mummy,' said Clemmie, gently pushing her down. Polly surrendered to it, gasping for breath, until she felt calm enough to sit up again.

Clemmie crouched beside her, rubbing her back and looking at her with great concern. Polly peered up at Lucas to see him lifting the phone to his ear.

'It's Lucas Goodwin,' he said, after a moment. 'Very well, thank you. Um, my mum just rang for my father, but they got cut off – can I speak to him, please?'

There was a pause and the expression on Lucas's face darkened.

'OK,' he said, 'I'll catch him on his mobile, we couldn't get through on it before, I think it's gone a bit dicky. Thanks, Maureen, bye.'

He ended the call and sat down heavily opposite Polly.

'The utter twunt did a runner,' he said. 'What a cock knob. What a pathetic feeble bollock blister. He realised it was you on the phone, Mum, and suddenly found he was urgently needed elsewhere. I can't believe my own father is such a coward.'

Clemmie handed Polly a glass of water, which she took gratefully.

'So he's in London,' said Clemmie, slowly, as though she were thinking it through as she spoke, 'and going in to work. How did Maureen sound?'

'Absolutely normal to me,' said Polly, then turned to Lucas.

'Same,' he said. 'He'd clearly left her office in a big rush after Mum hung up on him, but Maureen didn't sound like she'd just seen him again for the first time after a three-month absence. It seemed perfectly humdrum for him to be in there talking to her, a normal working day.'

They sat in silence for a few moments.

'He might have been there all the time,' said Polly eventually. 'Maybe that's why he was so adamant about me not contacting King's, because he knew he was going to be there all along and didn't want us to find him.'

She could see by their expressions that her kids found that revelation as profoundly upsetting as she did. It was so coldly calculated. Sly.

Polly sat with this new idea, turning it over in her mind, as if looking at an object from different angles, before reaching a conclusion. Yes, this was worse. Somehow the idea of his actually going away wasn't quite as bad as pretending to be away, so they wouldn't even try to find him.

'What a bastard,' said Lucas, standing up. 'I'm going to have a shower and then – with your permission, Mum – I'm going to ransack his study to see if I can find any clues as to why he's behaving like a sociopath.'

'Feel free,' said Polly. 'I've already gone through it several times. As you'll remember, I jemmied a big hole in the door after he locked it, but please have a look. You might spot something I haven't.'

Lucas paused and then came back and leaned down to give his mother a big hug.

'Everything will be all right, beautiful Mummy,' he said, rocking her from side to side and kissing the top of her head. 'We'll find out what's going on with him and we'll sort it out. We'll never let you down – will we, Clemmie?'

'No way,' she replied. 'We are here for you one hundred per cent and we're all going to get through this together.'

'Thank you, my beautiful darlings,' said Polly, and as she spoke she had an idea. 'Just give me a moment,' she said, and went through to her study.

Yes, there it was in her diary. An invitation to a big party that night for the launch of Sent, the first perfume by pop music's hottest R & B superstar, Quirk. It was going to be a really big night, with Quirk playing a set.

Polly read the details on the invite. 'Polly Masterson-Mackay plus one', it said, but that was no problem, she knew the PR well and had done her a big favour recently with another brand. One phone call would fix it.

Polly Masterson-Mackay would be going to that party. Polly Masterson-Mackay plus three.

'Yassss!' said Lucas. 'Replay, free game, oh yay ...'

He did a spin and high-fived himself.

'How are you going, Guy?' he asked. 'Game over?'

Guy lifted one hand momentarily from the side of the pinball machine and gave him the finger, before getting back to frantically pressing the buttons.

'Oh, look, Lucas,' he said, 'I've got multi-ball. Bring it on. Come to Papa, you little critters.'

Crazy lights flashed and the pinging noises on the game Guy was playing got even more frantic. Polly shook her head at Clemmie, who was sitting opposite her in a booth.

'Boys,' said Polly.

They were in a bar in Shoreditch that had a side-room full of old pinball machines, staging what Lucas had dubbed 'the Pinball Olympiad'. Polly and Clemmie had tired of it after a few games and left them to it.

It had been Guy's idea to meet there before heading to the launch, which had a late start, in keeping with Quirk's pop-star style. She wasn't expected to make an entrance until 11 p.m. Plus Guy had told Polly he wanted to 'bond' with Lucas before they went into full-on party mode.

Polly had been a little concerned that any kind of party mode with bottomless supplies of free drink might be too much of a good thing for her son, even if he had seemed to be on top of his drinking, but a conversation in the cab on the way over had put her mind at rest.

When she'd asked him if he could promise not to hit the booze too hard at the Quirk event, he'd waggled his scarred middle finger at her.

'Don't fret, Mama,' he'd said. 'Don't fret 'cos I'm on da fret ... My guitar fret, get it? I nearly lost a crucial playing finger that night and it freaked me out. It's still a bit sore when I play and I'm not getting stupid-drunk any more.

'It took a while to sink in, how stupid I was being, but when I got back to uni and saw the guys and we tried to rehearse and I couldn't play, then I got it. Big-time. I haven't gone dry – I'm nineteen, I'm at uni, I'm a musician – but I'm not going to put my fingers at risk like that again, ever.'

Just to be sure, Polly had taken the precaution of filling him up with lasagne before they left home, so there would be no empty-stomach scenario and so far, he'd been as good as his word, still nursing the first beer Guy had bought him when they'd arrived at the bar. She just hoped he'd be able to keep it up when faced with the ever-circulating trays of cocktails and champagne that would be laid on at the launch party.

It took the Uber driver several wrong turns before they arrived at what seemed to be the venue: a warehouse building so far out east it was practically in Essex – and not an old brick warehouse of real-estate fantasies, but the nasty corrugated-metal type on a stark industrial estate.

'Well, this is scenic,' said Guy, lowering his window and looking out. 'This is it, according to the postcode on the invite, but I'm not sure I want to get out until I'm certain. It's a long walk back, even to E1.'

He turned to the driver.

'Would you mind taking us a bit further, so we can be sure?' he asked, and the car inched along until they went round a bend and saw 'Sent by Quirk' projected on the other side of the building in bright pink light. The video for her latest single, 'Sliding By', was playing on a huge screen next to it. Now they could hear loud music coming from inside too.

'Well, we're clearly in the wrong place,' said Lucas, opening the car door and jumping out, 'but let's see what's happening at this party.'

The answer to that was: a lot. There were great DJs to dance to, and then Quirk made her entrance, sliding down a helter skelter onto the stage, and performed three of her biggest tracks, ending with 'Sliding By', during which her new fragrance was pumped into the air.

Lucas was almost glowing he was having such a good time – but he wasn't drunk. Merry, yes, legless, no, and during Quirk's set he got right up to the front and Polly could see how closely he was watching the musicians.

She was so glad she'd brought him and Clemmie with her. It was exactly what they all needed after that horrible shock earlier in the day.

But thinking about that, even for a moment, was a mistake. Remembering the surprise of hearing David's voice again instantly dented her happy mood and she was suddenly aware of how much her feet were hurting in her heels.

She leaned in to Clemmie's ear to shout over the loud music that she was going to the loo, then headed away from the crush towards the back of the space, where there were some tables and chairs. She sat down and took her shoes off, wondering as she did if it was a mistake. She might never get them on again.

All the energy of the pinball bar, the cool crowd, the cocktails and the great music drained out of her as unwelcome thoughts about discovering David in the History Department pushed themselves back into her mind.

She rubbed each foot, wondering what the hell she thought she was doing, flouncing around like a twenty-something party girl. She was a grown-up. A wife – in theory, at least – and the mother of adult children, yet here she was gadding about in a far-flung warehouse in the middle of the night in silly shoes.

It was a Thursday night in March. She should have been at home binge-watching Netflix, drinking a glass of merlot and knitting something tasteful in grey cashmerino, instead of acting like some middle-aged clubber. It was sad. Tragic. She'd be asking around for drugs next.

She got out her phone and looked at the time. It was nearly one and she had to teach a yoga class at eight the next morning – no, actually, that morning. The kids could stay on if they wanted to – and that included Guy – but it was time for her to go.

She tried to put her shoes on again, but sure enough, released from their bindings, her feet seemed to have swelled up several sizes. She was squinting at the floor, trying to decide if it would be too treacherous to walk in bare feet, when Clemmie came up.

'There you are,' she said. 'I've been looking everywhere for you. Come and dance again, we're having such a good time. Guy's an amazing mover, isn't he?'

'He is,' said Polly, 'but my dancing is over for tonight. I can't get my shoes on. I'm just trying to determine how much broken glass there's likely to be between here and the exit.'

'Ah,' said Clemmie, 'it's fatal to take them off, isn't it? But don't worry, I've got a solution – stay here.'

Polly was quite happy to do that. She pulled another chair out from the table and put her feet up on it, wondering if she could line up a third one in the middle and have a little lie down.

She closed her eyes, trying to block out all the thoughts about David, and must have drifted off, because she was aware of nothing until a hand touched her shoulder.

'Hey, Cinderella,' Guy's voice said. 'I've got your glass slippers.'

She opened her eyes to see Guy crouched next to her, a concerned look on his face.

'Are you OK?' he asked. 'Clemmie says you've got high-heel fatigue and she's sent me over with these. She had them in her handbag.'

Polly looked down to see him pulling a pair of fold-up ballet flats out of a mesh pouch.

'Handy you're the same size,' he said.

Polly put them on and stood up, wiggling her toes then taking a few tentative steps.

'Oh, what heaven!' she said. 'It's like having little duvets for each foot after wearing those excruciating heels.

'Do you think you can dance again?' asked Guy, picking up her party shoes and putting them into the bag the flats had been in.

'I'm not sure, but I'll enjoy watching the rest of you.'

'This might help,' said Guy, picking a martini glass up off the table behind her. 'It's got a shot of coffee in it.'

The combination of the espresso martini and Clemmie's flat shoes gave Polly a second wind. Quirk was on the decks now, serving up brilliantly mixed tracks, and every new one that came on made it impossible to stop dancing, with the euphoric energy of the crowd seeming to power Polly along.

Guy was up to his usual dance-floor antics, posturing around like Freddie Mercury when 'We Will Rock You' came on, throwing shapes to Daft Punk, singing along to 'A Little Less Conversation' with appropriate actions and facial expressions.

They all danced together, then Guy took turns to whisk Polly and Clemmie around, while Lucas did his thing – on his own, with Clemmie, with his mum, and with a succession of attractive young women.

'Tune!' he yelled to the opening riff of 'Groove Is in the Heart', launching into moves that made him look like a freaked-out funky chicken.

When they announced the last track just before 2 a.m., Polly joined in the cries of 'Booooo …' then, as the very distinctive opening bars of Quirk's mega-hit soul ballad played, Guy grabbed her arm and pulled her towards him.

'Will you have the last dance with me?' he asked her.

She smiled, and without thinking took his right hand in the classic ballroom dancing position, her other on his shoulder.

'Relax,' he said. 'Don't think, just be.'

Closing her eyes, Polly allowed herself to go consciously limp, like in a yoga meditation. She was still half-expecting Guy to throw her into some over-the-top dip or spin at any moment, as he usually did, but this time he just rocked back and forth, turning slowly with the music. It was very restful – and something more than that.

Polly opened her eyes to see Guy looking at her thoughtfully.

'Enjoying yourself?' he asked.

Polly nodded. She was enjoying feeling the warmth of someone else's body – a man's body – pressing against hers far more than she was prepared to admit, even to herself. She wondered whether it was entirely appropriate, and looked around for Lucas and Clemmie. She couldn't see either of them and was relieved. She hoped they both had someone nice to dance with.

She breathed in deeply. Guy always smelled gorgeous; one of the things she liked about spending time with him was that there was always something delectable in the air around him. She looked up at him again and found his dark brown, almost black eyes still gazing back at her. He licked his lips reflexively and she felt a twinge – somewhere she really shouldn't have.

'So, tell me,' said Guy, lowering his head so they were almost cheek to cheek. She could feel his warm breath on her face and she liked it. 'Do you and your horsey friend dance together like this?'

For a moment Polly didn't understand what he was asking. Then it sank in.

'Do you mean, er, Edward?' she said. She didn't want to say 'Chum' to Guy. He'd make fun of it.

'Fotherington-Thomas-the-Tank-Engine, or whatever his name was. The one at your mum's place who was looking at you like a hungry monkey eyeing a banana.'

'Oh, don't be ridiculous, Guy,' said Polly, pulling back from him.

'Well, you seemed pretty keen to go off for a walk with him.'

'We needed to take the dogs out,' said Polly. 'Digger and Artemis are very close.'

She knew it sounded ridiculous as she said it. Guy threw his head back and laughed.

'Woof!' he said. 'Oh, that's a good one – we're just good friends, it's our dogs who fancy each other.'

'Can you not be so childish?' said Polly, pulling her hand out of his. 'He's a very old friend, we went to uni together.'

She started to walk off and he ran after her, putting his hand on her shoulder.

'Please dance with me, Polly,' he said, 'I'm sorry, I was being stupid. It's the last song.'

'Well, that makes it a good time to ring for a car, then, doesn't it?' said Polly, shrugging him off and walking away. 'Before everyone else does.'

By the time the two Ubers drew up to take them home, Polly had mostly forgiven Guy. She gave him a kiss on the cheek, but his words still rankled with her as she looked out of the window at sleeping North London.

Why did he always have to go that one bit too far? She loved his company, he brought the fun into her life that was so lacking from it, but every time she felt herself relax into enjoying his friendship, he managed to push her buttons in some way.

Clemmie and Lucas had no such reservations.

'How brilliant is your friend Guy?' Lucas was saying. 'He's going to come and see the band next time we play. I've told him he's got to get on the dance floor – his dancing will fill it. He's such a cool dude. I want a suit like his. Can I have one for my birthday?'

'For a suit like Guy's I think you'll have to save up a while,' said Polly. 'They're bespoke – you know, specially tailored for him. Savile Row.'

'Like James Bond,' said Lucas. 'So is he minted, then?'

'If only I knew,' said Polly. 'He must be. He doesn't seem to have any backers for his perfume company and it's a very expensive business to start up. I've tried to find out where the cash comes from but he's cagey about it.'

'Have you googled him?' asked Clemmie.

'Of course,' said Polly. 'And there's absolutely nothing. He's proudly not on Facebook or any social media either.'

'Maybe it's a false name,' said Lucas.

Polly looked at him and blinked. Why had she never thought of that? It was exactly the kind of thing Guy would do. He'd called himself Roger when he booked the yoga class, so assuming another identity was clearly a concept he felt quite happy with. But why did he have to be so coy? It didn't make any sense, and she had quite enough mystery in her life already with David.

It was all still going round in her head as she climbed into bed at nearly 3 a.m., eagerly looking forward to even a few hours of blessed peace from it all under the covers. But when she finally got her head on the pillow, she realised the curtains weren't closed properly and a bright shaft of light was shining through the gap, right into her eyes.

She got up again and went over to the window to pull them shut. She deliberately didn't look at the moon, remembering the last time she'd gazed up at it, nearly three months before, on New Year's Eve.

As she jumped back into bed, she could vividly recall how raw with pain she'd been that night just eleven days after David's sudden departure – longing for the security of his strong arms pulling her to him, for his dry jokes and constant music.

Now she felt even more alone. Time hadn't lessened the pain of his absence at all; it felt worse the longer he was away. She felt cast adrift, unanchored without his grounding presence.

But was it really David she was missing now? There was no doubt she yearned for physical contact, that closeness of feeling attached to someone. The question was, if she could have her choice, whose arms would she really want to have around her?

She wasn't sure.

Monday, 21 March

'Service, Groger!' yelled Shirlee, back in her now customary position at the stove, several frying pans on the go. 'One veggie special for Miss Clemmie – eggs, tomatoes, mushrooms and beans – and you're up next, Lucas, so stop fiddling about with that stereo and sit down.'

'Wilko,' said Lucas, as the first notes of 'Weather With You' rang out.

Polly smiled. She was sitting at the table sipping one of Clemmie's bright yellow turmeric and ginger brews, taking in the scene, not sure what surprised her about it the most. She hadn't known Guy was coming to yoga until he turned up – Shirlee had 'forgotten' to tell her he'd booked and paid for ten classes in advance – and the very idea of Lucas up, dressed and lucid at twenty-past-nine on a Monday morning was off-the-scale astonishing.

She hadn't been expecting Clemmie to come home for the whole of the Easter holidays either, so that was a particularly lovely surprise. But, taking a moment to observe the happy scene – Maxine closely examining a crochet project Clemmie was stuck on, Shirlee and Lucas having a little dance as he made his way over to sit at the table – something struck her:

it felt completely normal and right to have this happy scene playing out in her kitchen.

Just three months before, she'd only known Shirlee as a regular yoga attendee, she hadn't even met Maxine, or Guy – yet now it seemed completely natural to have them all sitting in her house with her kids.

What had breakfasts been like before, she asked herself. Years earlier it had been fun like this, with all of them at the table, David making stacks of blueberry pancakes, lively music always playing. But once the kids had got older that had stopped, with everyone grabbing breakfast in their own time. During the week David had got into a routine of having toast at his desk, before leaving the house at exactly ten-past-eight. At the weekends they might still eat breakfast together, but he'd mostly have his face in the paper, loud classical music making conversation difficult.

This new regime, of breakfast as a fluid social gathering, was a revelation. She'd grown to love it in the weeks since Shirlee had first sprung the New Year's Day brunch on her, and having the kids there made it even more special – and now there was Guy too.

He was the last person she would have imagined fitting into such an ordinary domestic setting, but he did and they all seemed to love him. It turned out Lucas had set his alarm especially to be up for it after Guy had texted him the night before to say he was coming for yoga.

As she looked round at them all, chatting and laughing, enjoying their food, she couldn't help smiling to herself, and then a thought suddenly struck her: was she actually happier without David?

The idea was such a shock it made her feel almost queasy, and when Guy landed a plate of bacon and eggs on the table in front of her, she knew she was going to struggle to eat any of it. Her mouth had gone completely dry and her appetite had disappeared.

She clicked her fingers under the table and Digger came trotting eagerly over. She slipped him a rasher of bacon, and was just going in for a second one when Shirlee noticed.

'Don't like my bacon, Poll?' she asked. 'Too kosher for you?'

Everyone turned to look at Polly, and ridiculously, she felt herself go red.

'No, oh, I ...' she stuttered, but she just couldn't explain. How could she possibly tell them – especially her kids – this new truth? That she'd lost her appetite because, while the last three months had been the strangest and, at times, most miserable of her life, she'd just realised that she was probably happier without her husband of twenty-plus years than she'd been with him?

She couldn't tell them that, and suddenly it was all too much. Knowing she wasn't going to be able to keep herself together, she got up from the table and rushed from the room.

Even before she hit the stairs she was crying hard. Not the tears-rolling-silently-down-the-cheeks kind, but wracking, painful sobs, as all the suppressed confusion came rushing out. She ran into the bedroom and threw herself on the bed face down, howling.

On top of everything else, what had really made it too much to take was that she had been intending to keep this particular breakfast swift and then spend the morning with Clemmie and Lucas, devising the strategy about David they'd so hopelessly failed to make the week before.

They'd all been too hung over to do anything on Friday after the Quirk party, then it had been the weekend and

Clemmie and Lucas both had plans – so Monday morning had been Polly's deadline for them to sit down and decide what to do. Now it all just seemed too hard, and she felt like she was going to be stuck in this terrible limbo forever.

Even as she cried, she could hear voices on the stairs – Shirlee's unmistakable penetrating tones and Clemmie's quieter responses. Just behind them she could hear Guy's distinctive deep pitch and Lucas's emphatic delivery.

Were they all out there? The only one she couldn't make out was Maxine, who would probably have been the most helpful.

She groaned and reached up for a pillow, which she pulled over her head, but too late to avoid hearing a gentle knock on the door and Clemmie saying, 'Mum? Can I come in?'

Polly lifted up the pillow to see the door open a crack and Clemmie's head peep round the edge.

'Mum?' she said again, and Polly reached out towards her with her hand, to indicate she wanted her to come over.

'Shirlee wants to come in too,' said Clemmie, uncertainly.

'Not now,' said Polly. 'I just want to see you at the moment – tell the others I'm fine, I'll be down in a minute.'

Clemmie disappeared behind the door again and Polly could hear her telling the others to go back to the kitchen, then she came back into the bedroom, closing the door behind her and rushing over to the bed. She lay down next to Polly, stroking her mum's head.

'Poor, darling Mummy,' she said, 'it's all too much, isn't it?'

Polly nodded, loving her daughter with all her heart.

Clemmie took her hand away and Polly reached out for it.

'Don't stop,' she said, 'I like it.'

'You used to do that to me when I was little, do you remember?' said Clemmie.

Polly nodded, closing her eyes, trying to think of nothing but the lovely comforting sensation of Clemmie's hand gently stroking her head.

'Granny used to do it to me,' she said, remembering how Daphne had soothed her the exact same way when she'd opened up to her about David just a few weeks before – and that made her think about what her mother had said that evening about never really liking David.

Her comments about the wedding had stayed with Polly, quietly niggling away at the back of her mind. And about his dislike of make-up. All the little ways in which he had trivialised the things she enjoyed and quietly controlled her.

'What set you off just now?' asked Clemmie, breaking into Polly's thoughts. 'Is there anything in particular you haven't told me about?'

Polly thought for a moment. Yes, but she couldn't tell Clemmie she'd finally come to understand that she might be happier without her father. She might have to tell Lucas and Clemmie that one day, but not yet.

'I just felt overwhelmed,' she said. 'It was so lovely at the table with everyone there, having fun, and then I remembered we've still got to make a plan about what to do regarding your father, and it all just got to me. Nothing's ever simple at the moment.'

'I know,' said Clemmie. 'I saw lots of friends at the weekend, but I didn't enjoy myself because I knew we'd have to face up to all that this morning. I'm sure Lucas is feeling the same, although we haven't talked about it. It's all so unknowable it seems easier not to talk about it, doesn't it? But then it sort of eats you up and makes you feel crazy from the inside out.'

Polly nodded.

'That's exactly how I feel,' she said. 'I have such a good time here with Shirlee and Maxine and the other yogi bears, then I go out with Guy and that's brilliant, and I have all my perfume events, with some really exciting things coming up ...'

And I have my walks with Chum, she thought, but didn't want to have to explain that.

'So I'm having a ball at the moment in so many ways, but then underneath it all, the great unknown is still there. What on earth is going on with David now, and what's going to happen in the future?'

Clemmie suddenly sat up.

'I've had enough,' she said, turning to look at Polly. 'As of this moment I've officially had enough. I can't stand seeing you this unhappy and I can't take any more of it myself. We know he's in the country – or at least he was on Thursday. If he's flitted off in the meantime, someone in the History Department will know where he is. We need to find him and sort this out.'

She stood up. 'Have a shower and get dressed into something you feel good in,' she said. 'I'm going down to tell the others.'

'Tell them what?' asked Polly, sitting up herself.

'That we're going to find Dad.'

Clemmie headed out of the door and then put her head back round it.

'And put some make-up on,' she said. 'I've noticed you wearing it more recently and it really suits you. You looked like Granny on Thursday night – in a good way.'

In no time, Polly was dressed in her favourite jeans, with stack-heeled ankle boots and a black polo neck – and carefully made up as Clemmie had ordered, with her hair brushed and a good spraying of PM. The sound of the shower in the main bathroom and the music coming from Lucas's room told her that he and Clemmie were also getting ready.

She was relieved to find when she went downstairs that the others had already left. The kitchen table was bare, everything cleared up and put away. All that remained of breakfast was a plate next to the cooker, with tin foil over the top and a note propped against it. In Shirlee's giant handwriting, it said:

> Eat! Eat! You'll need your strength. Good luck sorting that man out. Go get him girl! Love Shirl xxx

Polly stood staring at it, taking it in. So Clemmie had told her and Maxine and Guy what they were going to do ... and presumably, the whole story behind it.

For a moment she was appalled at the idea, and then realised she didn't care any more. She had nothing to be ashamed of. David was the one with the secrets, not her. It was actually easier if people knew what she was going through.

She pulled the tin foil off the plate and picked up a cold fried egg. She was ravenous.

~

As they walked along the Strand from Charing Cross, Polly began to regret scarfing down Shirlee's food. Her stomach felt as though it was expanding like an air balloon and she couldn't stop belching.

'Have you got any gum, Lucas?' she asked.

He shook his head.

'I've got some peppermint oil,' said Clemmie.

They retreated into the doorway of a shop while Clemmie fished around for it in her handbag and Polly tipped a few drops of the strong liquid onto her tongue.

'Let's just run over the plan one more time,' she said, trying not to think about how many times David had trodden this same stretch of pavement from the station to the university. Thousands.

'We're going to go in and find Maureen,' said Clemmie, talking slowly as you would to a frightened child, which was exactly what Polly felt like.

'And we're sure she's going to be there?' said Polly. 'Haven't they finished for the Easter break like you two?'

'No,' said Lucas. 'I checked online. They finish on Thursday, and she's there. I rang the office from my mobile this morning and when she answered I pretended it was a wrong number.'

'OK,' said Polly, belching again.

'We're going to act very casual with her,' Lucas continued, 'like it's a completely normal thing for us to be doing.'

'Which is it,' added Clemmie. 'Then we'll go wherever she says he is and confront him.'

'What if she doesn't know where he is?' asked Polly.

'We'll think of something else,' said Lucas.

'Let's just get in there and see what happens,' said Clemmie. 'It can't be any worse than what we've been putting up with for the last three months, can it?'

'Let's do it,' said Polly.

Maureen was sitting at the same tidy desk where she'd always sat, the same spider plant on the windowsill behind her. She smiled broadly when they came in, seeming pleasantly surprised but not shocked to see them. That was good at least, thought Polly.

'How nice to see you, Polly,' she said, standing up. 'And this must be Clemmie and Lucas – all grown up and at university, I hear.'

'How are you, Maureen?' said Polly. 'Good to see you too.'

'I'm very well, thank you,' she said. 'Can't complain. So I presume you're here to see David? He's in his office.'

Polly felt her stomach lurch. He was there. Clemmie took her hand and squeezed it.

Maureen reached out towards her phone. 'I'll just—' she started, but Lucas practically leaped towards her.

'No,' he said, 'don't call him, we're here to surprise him – he doesn't know we're both home yet. We're going to take him out to lunch.'

'Well, I think he might be with a student,' said Maureen, frowning slightly.

'Don't worry,' said Lucas, and practically pushed Polly and Clemmie out of the room.

'Let's leg it down there sharpish,' he whispered in the corridor. 'We don't want Maureen to tip him off.'

David's office was on the same floor, just round the corner and along a bit. Polly could feel her heart drumming as they got close to it. And her belching was getting worse.

'Shall I go in first or—' she started to say, but all too soon they were standing outside the door.

Lucas didn't hesitate, grabbing the handle and pushing it open. The three of them fell inside.

'Surprise!' he said.

David looked up at them from behind his desk, over his heavy spectacles. A young woman sitting opposite turned round to see who it was.

'Sorry to interrupt,' Lucas said to her, 'but we've just come to see my dad and it's rather urgent. I'm afraid you'll have to come back later.'

David said nothing, pushing his chair back and starting to get to his feet, then slumping back in his chair.

Polly stood in the doorway staring at him, trying to work out what she felt. That face was so familiar; she even recognised the clothes he was wearing and, of course, the smell of coal-tar soap. It was all as familiar as her own hand, but somehow completely unknown as well. She felt dizzy.

The student was looking at David, clearly wondering what to do.

'We'd better leave it there, Miranda,' said David. 'I'm sorry, I forgot they were coming today. I'll email you the rest of my notes and you can phone me in the break if you get stuck again.'

So Miranda can phone him, thought Polly. But I can't?

The young woman gathered her things and left the room, and Polly closed the door behind her. Lucas was standing with his arms folded, glaring at his father. Clemmie was sitting on the sofa at the back of the office, tears running down her cheeks. David hadn't moved from his chair. He seemed frozen in shock. Polly leaned against the door, wishing someone would say something, because she knew she couldn't.

'Well, fancy seeing you here,' said Lucas, sitting down in the chair Miranda had just vacated.

'What do you want?' said David in a completely flat tone of voice.

Polly looked at him in astonishment. What did they want? Something inside her flipped.

'What do you think we might want?' she said in icy tones, stalking over to the desk. 'We want an explanation. Where you've been for the past three months, why you haven't been in contact with any of us – well, apart from to find out when you could come to the house without the horrible risk of seeing me – and what you plan to do next.'

'I asked you not to contact the university,' he said.

Polly straightened again and stared at him in disbelief.

'What gives you the right to make conditions, David?' she said, shaking her head slowly. 'You're a husband and a father, two roles that come with responsibilities – you don't get to check out of them for a while, with absolutely no explanation. We've all had enough. We want to know what's going on.'

Clemmie came over, crying harder now.

'How could you be so cruel to Mummy?' she asked. 'What has she done to deserve this treatment? You can't just leave us in the lurch like this.'

David said nothing, but got up from his chair. Polly thought he was going to come and comfort Clemmie, but instead he started putting things into his messenger bag. Then he took his jacket off the back of the chair and put it on.

Polly was so astonished she couldn't think of anything to say.

Still not speaking, he came out from behind the desk, stepped round Clemmie and Lucas – who had his arm round his weeping sister's shoulders – and walked out of the office door as though they weren't there.

'What the actual ...?' said Lucas, and set off after him.

Polly and Clemmie got to the door just in time to see Lucas grab his father by the shoulder and turn him round.

'Where the hell do you think you're going?' he shouted.

He was red in the face. Polly had never seen him so angry before.

David just stared at his son as though he didn't know who he was and started to turn away again.

'No, you don't!' said Lucas, and grabbing his father's shoulder again he landed a punch, right on his jaw. *Smack.*

Polly was so shocked she felt like she'd been punched herself, and started walking over to see if David was all right, but Clemmie put her hand on her arm.

'Leave him to it,' she said. 'He deserved that.'

David had recovered his balance and was rubbing his chin, blinking, clearly a bit dazed, while Lucas glared at him, his body tense, as if waiting for his father to respond. Instead, David looked at them all, with the same strange blank expression he'd had when they walked into his office, turned and walked very fast down the corridor away from them.

'That's right,' Lucas yelled after him. 'Walk away from us ... just don't expect us to be waiting for you if you ever decide to come back. Arsewipe!'

A man coming along the corridor behind them gave them a shocked look as he passed. They weren't used to such emotional scenes in the corridors of King's College.

'He's an arsewipe,' Lucas said to the man, with a fake polite smile, but behind his bravura Polly could see his face was pale.

She moved towards him, and as she put her arms out to embrace him, he started to wail.

'Muuuuum,' he said, bursting into tears and sobbing into her shoulder. 'I punched Dad. What have I done? I'm even more of a psycho than he is.'

Polly hugged him and kissed his head and Clemmie put her arms round both of them.

'You're a hero, Lukie,' she said, 'not a psycho.'

While they were still locked in a clinch, Polly heard footsteps coming along the corridor towards them. Lifting her head, she saw Maureen, clearly on her way to find them.

'Come into my office,' she said. 'I think you all need a cup of tea.'

Maureen sat them down and busied herself making strong mugs of tea – with two sugars for Lucas, who was clearly in shock. Then she handed Polly a biscuit tin, which Polly passed on to her son. He grabbed a handful of bourbons and smiled at her weakly, his eyes still red from crying. He reminded Polly so much of the emotional little boy he'd once been that she could hardly bear it.

'I kept my door open,' Maureen was saying, 'because I did wonder, when you all arrived just now, if it might lead to a bit of an upset.'

Polly and Clemmie exchanged a look.

'Why do you say that?' asked Polly, as casually as she could, dipping a ginger nut into her tea.

An image of Chum smiling as he dunked a biscuit flashed into her head, but she pushed it away. Not now.

Maureen sat at her desk with her hands clasped in front of her and sighed, clearly not sure how to answer her.

'Well, how can I put this?' she said at last. 'Dr Goodwin hasn't been quite himself recently.'

Polly took another bite of the biscuit and said nothing, hoping Maureen would elaborate.

Clemmie jumped in. 'How do you mean?'

'Well, I hope you won't find this intrusive,' said Maureen, 'but I rather had the feeling he's not living at home. I arrive about the same time as him each morning and I've noticed recently he always comes from the Kingsway direction. It always used to be along the Strand. I come across Waterloo Bridge myself. The Thames is different every day, I do so enjoy that.'

She paused and smiled at them.

'Also, one time there was a heavy parcel that needed to be forwarded to his home address, so I wrote the usual one on it, and I just happened to go down to the post room later that afternoon and saw the address had been changed. I asked one of the chaps down there about it and he told me Dr Goodwin had come in and done it himself.'

'What was the new address?' asked Polly, an idea forming.

'Judging by the postcode, not far from here. Somewhere in Holborn, or Bloomsbury. It was WC1. Does he have another office he writes in or something?'

'Not as far as I know,' said Polly quickly, an extraordinary thought dawning on her. WC1 had been the postcode of David's old flat, the one they'd lived in together before they bought the house.

Could he be back there somehow?

'Can I ask you something else?' said Polly. 'Has my husband been away on any research trips recently? He was talking about going to Nepal ... or Turkey.'

'No,' said Maureen. 'Well, a couple of days here and there visiting archives in regimental headquarters, but no big trips. Most of his research at the moment is in the Imperial War Museum.'

Clemmie looked outraged at this revelation, but Polly was glad Lucas seemed too preoccupied with inspecting the biscuit tin to pay attention.

'Have you noticed anything else different about my husband, apart from where he seems to be living?' asked Polly.

'Yes,' said Maureen. 'He's much quieter than usual. He's a very discreet man, as you know, but recently he seems to have gone into himself more. He doesn't come to any of the department's social events, and he doesn't have lunch or drinks with his colleagues any more.'

Polly smiled at her. 'You're really across this department, aren't you?' she said.

'Well, after thirty-five years you do get a feeling for things,' said Maureen. 'So when you arrived just now, I did wonder if things were going to come to a head.'

'Thank you, Maureen,' said Polly, 'for being so open with us. I can't tell you what a comfort it is to me to know that you've noticed things weren't quite right with him. It's been a very confusing time for us.'

'I tell you what,' said Maureen, 'why don't you give me your mobile number and email address, and if anything else crops up, I'll let you know.'

Polly gave her a card, and as the three of them got up to leave, Maureen came to the door with them. As Clemmie and Lucas were walking away, Maureen put her hand on Polly's sleeve.

'You've got my number, dear,' she said. 'You can always ring me. I'll keep a close eye on him for you now. You were always the nicest of the wives and partners.'

Polly gave her a small spontaneous hug and set off after her children, who were walking down the corridor with their heads hanging low.

The traumatic events had clearly taken their toll on them, but Polly suddenly felt much stronger.

FragrantCloud.net

The scent of ... a son

I have two children, a daughter and a son. I think I was alive before they were born, but I can't remember what it felt like not to have somebody else's – two elses', in my case – best interests always at the front of my mind. It shifts your whole world on its axis, in a way I had never understood until I first looked into my baby daughter's face.

Four years later I was looking down at another little stranger, my son. He's nineteen now and I'm still sometimes taken aback when I see a great big hairy leg sticking out from under his bedclothes, remembering the little sprite he used to be.

The particular poignancy of loving a son is knowing that the physical change in him will be so exponential. Obviously, it's a huge deal when your little girl starts to turn into a woman, but the change has a gently fluidity, so it seems to happen like time-lapse photography of a flower blooming.

Boys, on the other hand, go through a sudden transformation of werewolf intensity. From Dr Jekyll into the hairy, hormonally crazed Mr Hyde. When this hulking creature slopes into the kitchen in his size-twelve trainers, roaring, and eats the entire contents of the fridge, it can be really hard to associate it with the little boy who used to climb onto your lap and twiddle your hair while sucking his thumb.

It can be hard to deal with while the change is happening because boys seem to test their parents in ways that involve putting themselves at risk of serious physical harm, whether it's driving too fast – or drinking way too much.

There's also that revolting stage they go through, when somehow searching for an idea of masculinity, they seem to be attracted to everything nasty and vulgar in the world, from foul horror films, to horrendous music and even the terrible body sprays they all seem to use.

After these, at times, very testing years, it's a very thrilling moment when you realise that your boy really has become – in the best possible way – a man. Confident in his own giant, hairy skin.

Especially as every now and again, the little boy will suddenly reappear for a moment, in a grin, or a giggle, and your mother's heart will clench in poignant adoration.

My smells of a son are gummy sweeties, Play-Doh, Pritt Stick, poster paint and wax crayons. Earthy mud on polyester football kit. The sweet antiseptic of sticking plasters. Fruity bubble gum and the minty tang of chong – as he and his friends called chewing gum. Bicycle chain oil and rubber inner tubes. The chemical overload of Lynx sprayed profusely over sweat, hair gel and toxic trainers. Fried onions and meat on the breath. Tomato ketchup.

My scents for a son are:

I am Juicy Couture by Juicy Couture
Black by Bvlgari
L'Air de Rien by Miller Harris
Serge Noire by Serge Lutens
Rocker Femme by Britney Spears
Dirty by Lush
Africa by Lynx

COMMENTS

LuxuryGal: We don't have any sons but our pups are like sons to us and they are so naughty!

AgathaF: This is funny. I have three brothers and it was their bad smell which made me like perfume.

> **FragrantCloud:** That's a very good reason!

NoseFirst: I don't think this is really about perfume, I prefer it when you write properly about perfume. How can perfume smell of fried onions?

> **PerfumedWorld:** What exactly qualifies you to say that NoseFirst? I think it's beautiful, there's more to perfume writing than just copying what you've read on Fragrantica, which is what you seem to do on your so-called 'blog'. Think first is my advice to you.
>
> **FragrantCloud:** Come on, you two, this is only supposed to be a bit of fun.

WhirlyShirlee: Love that boy.

AnnaBandana: I love this.

> **FragrantCloud:** Thanks so much x

EastLondonNostrils: Lynx ha ha ha.

Wednesday, 23 March

Polly was walking very tentatively, one hand out in front of her, a red-and-white spotted bandana tied around her eyes. Her other hand was in Chum's, and she wasn't sure what was occupying more of her attention – walking blindfolded or the feel of his hand around hers.

They'd walked normally for a couple of miles, along the edge of fields, until they'd come to a thick stand of trees and Chum had insisted she put the blindfold on. She'd agreed, thinking it was a lark, but this game of blind man's buff was going on a bit longer than she'd expected.

And it wasn't the only odd thing about this walk: they didn't have the dogs with them either. When Chum had rung her the day before to firm up the loose arrangement they'd made at Rockham Park, he'd asked if she wouldn't mind leaving Digger behind for this one. It had seemed peculiar, but Polly had agreed, because after what had happened just a couple of days before at David's office, she needed the balm of one of Chum's walks more than ever.

'How much further?' she asked.

'Not far,' he said, 'don't be a wimp.'

With her sight shut off, all Polly's other senses felt heightened. It seemed as though the birds were singing louder than usual, and she could feel the glow of the spring sunshine more keenly on her cheeks. Most of all, she could feel the warmth of Chum's hand, and she could smell him.

The familiar wax on his Barbour jacket, the horsey tinge and the underlying musky male smell, with just a tinge of something woody on the top. She wished she could get closer to him and breathe it in deeply.

'OK,' he said at last. 'Stop here. I'm going to take the blindfold off, but keep your eyes closed until I say to open them.'

'Yes, boss,' said Polly, as he pulled it away.

'Open them,' he said.

Polly did, and after blinking a couple of times in the light, she gasped. They were standing right in front of a vast grey house, two wings going off to the back, a huge fountain in front, throwing a plume of water high into the air, a formal garden around it.

'Wow,' said Polly. 'It's so beautiful.'

She glanced at Chum to see him beaming back at her.

'This is your house, right?' she said. 'The one we saw from the hilltop?'

Chum nodded.

'My family's house, yes. This is Hanley Hall.'

'It's ... spectacular,' said Polly, taking in the way the sunshine was turning the grey stone golden on one side, the ranks of huge windows black against it. 'So beautiful. No wonder all those girls at St Andrews were obsessed with you.'

'I don't know why,' he said. 'I'm the younger son, I was never going to inherit it.' He paused, gazing at the building. 'Now I'm not even allowed to go into it ...'

'Is that what I would have found out about if I'd googled you?' asked Polly quietly.

Chum nodded. 'Yep,' he said. 'All that, but today we are going in.'

He turned and smiled at her and then, even though she didn't have the blindfold on any more, he took hold of her hand again and started walking towards the house.

He skirted round the front, along the right flank of the building, then round a corner, where there was yet another, smaller wing, which looked older. He stopped at a flight of mossy stone steps going down to a wooden door.

'Here we are,' he said, leading her down.

He turned the old metal handle, and with a hefty push from his hip, opened the door.

'Don't worry about the dark,' he said, leading her inside, closing the door behind him and taking hold of her hand again. 'I can find my way to the light switch without illumination. Couple of steps up here, bit of a landing, two more steps ... You OK?'

'Yes,' said Polly, thinking that as long as Chum was holding her hand, she'd feel OK anywhere.

She heard a click and a light came on, a bare bulb brightening a long flag-stoned corridor.

'We're in the back passages,' said Chum. 'It's too complicated to go in the front door, so this is easier. It's a bit of a walk to the main part of the house, but worth it.'

They carried on until the passage started to rise gently and they reached ground level, with natural light coming in between the gaps in old shutters on the windows.

After a few more twists and turns and a few steps up, Chum stopped in front of a door that was covered in green felty fabric.

'Is that an actual green baize door?' asked Polly.

Chum laughed.

'I suppose it is,' he said. 'We'll leave our boots on this side of it, anyway.'

Polly bent down to pull hers off and looked up again to see Chum pushing open the door, to reveal a marble hall, with pillars and a lavishly painted ceiling.

The walls were covered with huge paintings in gold frames: horses and battlefields – and people who looked quite like Chum. Several of them had his slender face, with a similar square jaw and wide mouth.

'Bit of a family resemblance thing going on, I think,' said Polly, peering up at an impressive fellow in full red and gold dress uniform, a feathered hat under one arm, a large sword on the other side.

'He's a great-great-great-great, I think,' Chum said.

Polly came to a halt again in front of a beautiful woman, black hair in soft curls around her face, smiling as though she knew a wonderful secret.

'I love her,' said Polly.

'Yes, she's a pretty one,' said Chum. 'Great-great, if I remember correctly.'

'Very great, anyway,' Polly said.

From there he led her into a room of bewildering splendour with vast brocade curtains held back with silk tassels, elaborate inlaid furniture, ornate carpets and huge vases. From there they passed into a dining room with a table long enough to seat a couple of football teams, silver candelabra along the middle, and then into library full of old leather-bound books.

'Now I see why you didn't want me to bring Digger,' said Polly.

'Well, we did always have dogs, growing up,' said Chum, 'but it seemed better not to risk our two going on a rampage today.'

'Is there anyone else here?' asked Polly, her only experience of such places being full of other visitors, guides and security guards.

'Just us,' said Chum.

'So no one lives here now?'

'Not at the moment.'

'And it's not National Trust? We're not going to run into a party of school children around the next corner?'

'Not today,' said Chum, 'although it will be full of children and other worthy visitors if I get my way.'

'More Google stuff?' asked Polly.

He nodded and she thought for a moment.

'So, if no one's living here, and it isn't open to the public, why isn't it all covered in dust sheets? Don't you have to close up a house like this?'

Chum beckoned to her with his finger, and she followed through a door in the panelling to what was clearly another servant's passage: there was a great pile of dust sheets in it.

'I took them off for you,' he said. 'And I got the silver out. Some of it.'

'Well, I'm very honoured,' said Polly.

'I wanted you to see it properly,' he said. 'Now I'll show you a room I really love.'

He led the way to a cosier one, with lots of squashy armchairs and sofas, small card tables and ottomans dotted around with old copies of *Country Life* on them. Decanters on a side table.

'Oh, this is nice,' said Polly.

'This is a family room,' said Chum. 'I love the staterooms, but this is my favourite. This is where we used to have Christmas.'

Polly went over to the window and looked out to see the more formal gardens changing to parkland in the distance, mighty oak trees dotting the landscape.

Chum came and stood next to her.

'Do you miss it horribly?' she asked him.

'Would you miss a leg?' he answered, looking at her sadly before rallying. 'I've still got to show you upstairs. Come on.'

They walked slowly up the stately staircase that swept up from the marble hall, and Polly paused at the top, gazing out at the fountain and the huge ornate gates beyond it.

'This way,' said Chum, and she followed him into a room off to the right.

Polly sighed when she walked in; it was so pretty – the walls painted with Chinese birds, ginger jars of different sizes dotted around, pretty white and gold furniture and a huge four-poster bed, nearly as high as the painted ceiling, hung with rich silk drapes.

In front of the central window were two chairs and a sofa with beautiful brocade seats next to a low table. On that was a picnic basket.

'Lunch,' said Chum. 'Do sit.'

'How lovely,' said Polly. 'Did you put this here?'

Chum nodded, starting to take things out of the basket.

'Isn't a house like this madly burglar-alarmed?' asked Polly, sitting down on one of the chairs. 'Are the police going to arrive just as I'm eating my first sandwich?'

'I know how to turn them off,' said Chum, lining up plastic-wrapped packages. 'There aren't any plates – although I suppose I could go down to the china store.'

'Don't bother,' said Polly. 'I'll catch my crumbs. I wouldn't want an old retainer to find them and rumble you – I presume there is a caretaker of some kind? And there must be loads of gardeners, it all looks so perfectly kept.'

'Yes,' said Chum. 'There's still quite a large number of people needed to keep the place up, but I had a word with the key ones. They don't mind my coming here – in fact they like it, most of them have known me since I was a little boy. No one's going to disturb us, Polly.'

As he said it, he opened the picnic basket again and pulled out a bottle of Taittinger and two champagne glasses.

'Shall we?' he asked.

Polly nodded enthusiastically.

'It will mean staying a while, if I have some,' said Chum, 'because of the driving thing after. Is that OK?'

Polly smiled at him. 'I'd quite like to stay here forever,' she said.

He popped the bottle and they toasted the joy of trespassing, then sat contentedly eating the sandwiches, sipping the champagne and gazing out at the view. Polly relished the slightly dizzy feeling as the alcohol hit her bloodstream, all her anxieties drifting away.

Chum held the bottle up in front of her empty glass with an inquiring expression. She nodded.

'You know something, Hippolyta,' he said, leaning over to fill her glass, then putting the bottle down, 'you're a bit too far away over there on that chair. Come and sit beside me on the sofa here, it will be so much easier for me to refill your glass ...'

He moved sideways and patted the seat next to him. Polly was there in a moment, sinking back and looking up at him, as he perched on the edge of the seat. He looked down at her and for a moment she thought he was going to kiss her, but he didn't. Instead he gazed thoughtfully out of the window for a few moments, before turning back to her.

'There's a reason I brought you here today,' he said. 'Apart from just wanting to show off.' He smiled.

'Well, you've certainly impressed me,' said Polly, reaching up to clink her glass against his and then taking a sip. 'So what's the other reason.'

'I'm very touched,' he said, 'that you didn't just jump onto Google to find out what my story is. It really a means a lot to me, that you respected my privacy, but now I want to tell you what it is myself.'

He reached for his jacket, pulled a piece of paper out of the pocket and handed it to her. It was a newspaper cutting.

'This is how it was done pre-search engine,' he said.

She unfolded it to see it was from the *Daily Mail* dated two years earlier. She read the headline:

EARL'S BROTHER STRUGGLES TO SAVE STATELY HOME FROM RUSSIAN OLIGARCH

She glanced back at Chum, who was looking pained.

'Just scan read it,' he said, 'and I'll fill in the details after. It just saves me going over it all again.'

Polly began reading:

> The Hon. Edward Cliddington-Hanley-Maugham, younger son of the eleventh Earl of Hampford and cousin of Olympic Equestrian Team captain Rollo Cliddington, has started legal proceedings against his late brother's widow, the Dowager Countess of Hampford, about the fate of the family's historic stately home, Hanley Hall.
>
> Mr Cliddington-Hanley-Maugham's elder brother, the twelfth Earl, died in a shooting accident on the family's

Hertfordshire estate five years ago. His then three-year-old son inherited the title, with his mother as guardian.

The Dowager Countess, former model Flavia Cardoso, wants to sell Hanley Hall, which is ranked as one of the top twenty stately homes in the country, to a private buyer, rumoured to be a Russian oligarch.

Although the house is held by a trust, the Brazilian beauty's lawyers have found a loophole that may allow her to sell the property, on behalf of her son.

'Oh, Chum!' exclaimed Polly, dropping the cutting onto her lap and putting her hands over her face. 'This is terrible. I had no idea.'

He pulled a resigned face.

'You can see why I couldn't bear to talk about it,' he said. 'I try not to think about it unless I really have to. Where have you got to?'

'Your brother dying and his widow wanting to sell this beautiful house to an oligarch.'

'Keep going,' said Chum. 'There's a choice bit coming up.'

Polly read on:

Even before the sale of the house – built by the first Earl in the seventeenth century and added to by subsequent generations – the Countess intends to sell the contents, with a separate sale planned for more domestic items and the contents of the extensive attics. Even family letters and photographs will be auctioned off.

Mr Cliddington-Hanley-Maugham, who is currently running a riding stable, has so far failed in all his bids to fight the sale. The house and grounds, which used to be open to the public, have had to be closed while the dispute is settled, seriously draining the estate's finances.

A successful farm shop business the late Earl's brother used to run has also had to be closed down, since the ownership of any of the produce or animals grown and raised on the estate is *sub judice*.

If the case continues for too long, the house may have to be sold anyway to settle debts against the estate. The late Earl's brother has been paying the wages of the estate's remaining members of staff out of his own pocket, as the Countess has failed to do so.

With support from a group of prominent well-wishers who have come together to help him save the house for the nation, Mr Cliddington-Hanley-Maugham is trying to persuade the National Trust to take the legal case on.

Mr Cliddington-Hanley-Maugham is making no claim on the property himself.

"I just want to preserve the house with its historical associations and important art collections for the nation," he said. "I'm not looking for anything out of it myself. It's what my brother and my father would have wanted and I feel I have a duty to protect it for them and all my ancestors – and for my nephew."

Polly sat staring down at the press cutting for a moment, not knowing what to say. Poor Chum, indeed.

'I can see why you don't want to make light conversation about this,' she said. 'It must be horrendously stressful. Have you got anyone to share the load with you? Do you have any other siblings?'

'No,' said Chum. 'It was just Charlie and me.'

'And your father must have died quite young ...'

Now she knew the details of his situation, Polly realised that, far from finding it off-putting, she wanted to hear all of it. So she could support him.

'My father was only sixty-two when he died,' said Chum. 'He had weak lungs from a childhood illness and a bout of pneumonia was too much for him. Mum married Bill a couple of years later; they'd known each other since they were young, and his wife had died, so that was lovely. They lived in the Dower House just a couple of miles from here and it was all great. I worked for the estate, running the farm shop and food brand, which was quite a big thing; we were in Fortnum's and Harrods and all that.'

'Hang on a minute – Hanley Hall, of course. I used to buy your marmalade.'

For David, she thought. It was his favourite.

Chum smiled. 'Ah yes, the award-winning marmalade. Even President Obama liked it. The British Ambassador gave him some – he was Charlie's friend at school, which helped – and we got a letter of thanks on White House writing paper.'

'So when your brother died that all just had to stop?' said Polly.

Chum nodded.

'Flavia closed it – well, her ghastly lawyers did, using the excuse mentioned in that piece, but really just to spite me – and I had to put a lot of people out of work. It was dreadful. I'm very lucky that an old friend gave me a job right away, running his livery yard, but a lot of the people I had to lay off are still unemployed. I lose a lot of sleep over that.

'I was offered other jobs in the bespoke food world, but I needed to stay near here,' he continued. 'I would have felt like I was abandoning the estate if I'd gone to live in Scotland, or Cornwall. I'm viscerally attached to this land and to the other people connected to it. I have to live on it, or at least near it.'

'Tell me about Flavia,' asked Polly. 'Is she really evil? What she wants to do – and what she's already done – is so awful, but I always find it hard to believe that people can be fundamentally bad. Can't she see there's a lot more to this house than being a valuable piece of real estate?'

'You're right, said Chum. 'She's not evil so much as easily influenced. And flighty. Very flighty. None of us really understood why Charlie married her – well, there were the obvious reasons, she's an exceptionally attractive woman and Charlie was always a sucker for that. He was blinded by her looks and she loved the idea of having a title and swanning around London being the Countess of Hampford. She wasn't a blatant gold-digger – that's come later – and she did genuinely love Charlie, but she doesn't have great judgment.'

He picked up the champagne bottle and held it up to Polly with his eyebrows raised. She nodded. Reading the press cutting had sobered her up rather and she hoped another glass might lift her mood again.

'We had an inkling things might be tricky when she insisted on having the wedding featured in *Hello!* magazine,' said Chum, thrusting the empty bottle back in the picnic basket upside down, as though it were an ice bucket.

'I couldn't believe Charlie gave in to that, but he just thought it was funny. I found it mortifying. I'm not being snobby, it was just so embarrassing. We had to pose for all these cheesy photos – hundreds of them – and my friends really roasted me about it. Every time I saw them for years afterwards, they'd shout "Hello!" at me. I was actually glad my dad wasn't around to see it.

'So she loved all that side of it – what she hadn't understood was how much living in the damp, muddy country there'd be, and she just didn't take to that. Mummy and Bill and I really did our best to get on with her, but once Charlie died, it all just fell apart. In her grief, she moved to London full-time, met some awful people, who introduced her to some even more gruesome lawyers, and the next thing we knew, the house was shut up and we were all thrown off the estate.'

'Is that why Bill lives at Rockham Park?' asked Polly.

'Pretty much,' said Chum. 'Mummy got cancer; I really believe it was the stress of all this, on top of losing her son. Bill couldn't really manage on his own and it was his idea to move to Rockham Park. He likes it. Is your mum happy there? She seems to be.'

'Oh, she's fine,' said Polly. 'But let's not get distracted. Now you've started to talk about it, I need to know everything.'

'Do you want to read another cutting?' said Chum, with a lopsided smile. 'It saves me having to spell out all the other grisly details. There is more.'

'Whatever works for you,' said Polly and he pulled another piece of paper out of his jacket pocket and handed it to her.

'This one is from *Tatler*,' he said.

Polly looked at the headline and intro:

THE TOP TEN TRAGIC (HOT – AND SINGLE) ARISTOS

> They're impeccably bred, entirely single, properly handsome and having a horrible time – could you be the one to comfort a tragic aristocrat?

'You're kidding me,' she said. 'Are they allowed to write things like that?'

'At least they've said I'm hot,' said Chum, laughing. 'But look at my entry – I'm not even top five. So rude.'

'I think the whole thing's rude,' said Polly, scrolling down until she found a picture of Chum. He was a on a horse in the full formal rig out – black tailored jacket, white stock and velvet riding hat. Hot indeed.

6. The Hon. Edward Cliddington-Hanley-Maugham

Thrown off the family estate (listed after Chatsworth in *Country Life*'s stately home rankings) by his widowed sister-in-law, who wants to sell it and everything in it, the younger brother of the late 12th Earl of Hampford, Edward CHM – Chum to his friends – knows pain on a Johnny Cash level.

Chum has embarked on a noble legal battle to save the estate for the nation and in retaliation, the dowager Countess closed down the internationally admired glamour food empire he built up – leaving him jobless and homeless.

Now the former model has also banned him from seeing his only nephew, the heir to the whole shebang, so Uncle Chum has started another legal suit against her about that.

The Countess has not remarried, but has been romantically linked to several men since her husband died, including a Canadian ski instructor, her fitness trainer, and most recently night-club owner Gary Atherton, owner of the Good Times chain of lap-dancing clubs.

'Lap-dancing clubs?' said Polly, turning to Chum.

He rolled his eyes and nodded.

'That's what I mean by easily led. She's quite innocent, really, that's what's so sad about it. If only she'd fallen in with decent people, none of this would be happening, but she got picked up by the dregs and she believes everything they tell her. Can you hurry up and finish reading that? I'm getting bored with myself and my dreary problems.'

Polly turned back to the cutting.

And there's more … all this came after this most tragic aristo lost his wife, Lady Arabella Melton, youngest daughter of the Marquess of Mowbray, in a car crash – although she had already left him for another man. Double doom.

Could you be the one to comfort sad Chum?

Tragic Aristo Ratings

House: 10

Cash: 3 (was 9, but the lawsuits are draining funds fast)

Looks: 9

School: Eton

University: St Andrews

Hobbies: Horses, shooting, fishing

Previous liaisons: married once, widowed

Children: none

Polly read to the end and felt overwhelmed by sadness.

'You really have had a shitty time, haven't you?' she said.

'That's one way of putting it,' said Chum.

'How do you cope with it all?'

'Just keep on keeping on, what else can I do?' said Chum. He turned to look out of the window for a moment, then looked back at her. 'Although I must say, the walks we've taken together recently have done a very great job of taking my mind off it all.'

Polly smiled at him, wanting to tell him it was exactly the same for her, but then she'd have to explain what it was she needed distracting from and it didn't seem the right time for that. After everything he'd just revealed, her problems seemed so petty. Her husband was having a bit of a funny turn – it wasn't like he'd died, or left her, or thrown her out of the house. All those things had happened to Chum, and more.

She would tell him what was going on in her life, she wanted to now, but it had to be at the right moment.

'Those walks have meant a lot to me too,' she said and very gently squeezed his hand.

He squeezed hers back and they sat for a while, their hands linked, saying nothing, just gazing out of the window, until Polly noticed the light was changing. The sun was on the other side of the house now and the temperature in the room was dropping.

Chum seemed to notice too. He took his hand away from hers and seemed to think for a moment before he spoke.

'You know, Hippolyta, it's about to get spectacularly cold in here and we can't put the lights on in this wing when it gets dark, because they'd be visible from miles away. But I don't feel like leaving yet, do you?'

Polly shook her head.

'Good,' said Chum. 'We'll go somewhere a bit more cosy, where we can have a nice cup of tea before we set off for the car. There's a quicker way back, I brought you the long way this morning to add to the drama.'

Chum led on, carrying the picnic basket, through a door set into the painted walls that let onto a back corridor, then up a couple of staircases, down another and along several more corridors.

'You could do your 10,000 steps a day just walking around this house,' said Polly.

'More,' he said, 'but not now, because we're here.'

He took her through a door into a small hallway with several doors off it, opening one of them into a delightful square room, with late afternoon sun pouring in through the windows.

It was very comfortably furnished, with bold floral wallpaper and a comfortable chintz sofa with lots of cushions on it, in front of a fireplace, with logs and paper all set to light. On the wall opposite, set into a wall of packed bookshelves, was an elegant desk, with a pen lying on it next to a sheet of headed writing paper. The air smelled spicy from a large bowl of pot pourri.

'What a lovely room,' said Polly.

'It was my grandmother's parlour – well, that's what she used to call it. I think the correct term is a morning room. This apartment was her special place in the house when she was the Dowager Countess. My brother didn't want her to move out to the Dower House, so she created a little spot for herself here.'

Polly didn't say anything, not feeling qualified to comment on any of those topics. She walked over to the marble fireplace to look at the collection of Staffordshire figures and other intriguing things on it. There was a stack of thick card invitations propped behind a small brass pug.

'That's all Granny's stuff,' said Chum. 'Even the invitations. Nothing was changed in here after she died.'

'Would she mind us being in here?' asked Polly.

Chum grinned. 'She'd love it. I often used to sneak in here to see her. She let me keep a pet lamb in here one spring, and when I was caught walking him round the house on a lead, Granny took all the blame.'

Polly followed his gaze to the wall between the two windows, where there was a portrait of a smiling woman. She didn't have the wide mouths of the ancestors in the marble hall, but her surprised-looking raised eyebrows were so like Chum's that Polly laughed.

'I take it this is her?' she asked, and he nodded.

'Right,' said Chum, rootling around in the picnic basket. 'I've got some milk in here and these ...'

He held up a packet of Garibaldi biscuits.

'I'll go and make the tea. If you need the loo, follow me.'

He showed her a door that led into a bathroom painted the prettiest sugar-pink. It was furnished with a painted armoire and a French chair with a needlepoint seat and back. The wash basin sat on a pretty white cupboard, and on the side was a large bottle of Joy.

Polly smiled. She liked Granny more and more.

When she got back to the sitting room, Chum had the fire lit and a tray of tea, with a teapot, was sitting on the ottoman.

'You know how to live, Mr Chum,' said Polly, taking in the scene.

'Well, Granny certainly did,' he said. 'She wouldn't have liked the mugs, but I can't be bothered with cups and saucers.'

Polly sat down on the sofa, a wave of shyness washing over her. It had been magical sitting in the grand state bedroom, but so disconnected from anything like real life for her that it hadn't made her feel awkward. But this felt so comfortable and domestic – so perfect – she felt almost panicky.

Chum sat down next to her and reached over to pour the tea.

'I know how you like it,' he said, passing her a mug.

She was happy for the distraction of the tea and the biscuits, but when that was all finished and Chum had stoked up the fire and sat back down next to her, they fell into a silence that seemed to roar in Polly's ears. All she was aware of was Chum's warm body next to hers and how much she wanted to crawl onto his lap and never leave it.

They sat for a little longer until Polly couldn't stand it and, with her head against the back of the sofa, she turned to look at him. He turned at exactly the same time, so their faces were practically touching.

'Hello, beautiful,' he said quietly, and reached up and smoothed a stray strand of hair.

Polly felt tears fill her eyes. She looked back at the fire and blinked madly trying to stop them, but she couldn't and felt one roll down her cheek.

Chum reached up again and very gently turned her face back towards him, wiping away the tear with his forefinger.

'What's the matter?' he said, so tenderly, Polly felt two more tears escape. He wiped those away too and then pulled a white cotton handkerchief out of his jeans pocket. 'Use this.'

Polly wiped her eyes with it, feeling like a first class idiot.

'Sorry,' she said, trying to hand it back to him.

'Hold on to it,' he said. 'But tell me – why are you crying?'

Polly thought for a moment and then she just had to say it. The truth.

'Because you make me so happy and that makes me feel guilty.'

'Because you're married,' said Chum.

Polly nodded, closing her eyes in shame. She felt Chum take her hand then lay his other one over the top.

'It's OK,' he said. 'I understand and I have to tell you something: I've never wanted to kiss someone as much as I want to kiss you right now – well, all day really, it hasn't just come over me, and long before that, if I'm really honest. Well, ever since the first time I kissed you, which really was an awfully long time ago.'

Polly couldn't help smiling.

'I didn't know if you remembered that,' she said.

'Are you serious?' he said. 'From the moment I saw you again lying on the floor at Rockham Park with dogs all over you, it's all I've been able to think about. Anyway, those were different days and, as much as I've wanted to, I don't make a habit of kissing married women. It's a fool's game.'

He paused for a moment.

'But I must also say,' he continued, 'that in normal circumstances I wouldn't have brought a married woman to this house and certainly not to sit on this particular sofa, which is very special and personal to me, but over the weeks we've been going on our lovely walks I've begun to feel, from the way you never mention your husband in conversation – well, just once – and how he never comes to see your mother with you, or features in your blog in real time ...'

He smiled as he said the last thing.

'I just started to get the feeling he doesn't seem to be in your life very much these days, so I had begun to wonder if perhaps one day I might feel I could chance my arm to see whether you might kiss me.'

'He's not in my life at all,' said Polly bluntly.

And then she told him the whole story, all the way from the email that had come out of the blue, with every detail, right up to the terrible moment when Lucas had punched David, and Maureen had come to their rescue and given them her invaluable insights into the situation.

'Well, I do like the sound of Maureen and her biscuit tin,' said Chum, 'and I can't help respecting Lucas for what he did. The question is, what are you going to do?'

Polly realised she had come to a decision about that, right then. Or perhaps it had happened after that horrible visit to King's College, but she hadn't quite been able to voice it in her head. She could now.

'I'm going to leave him,' she said, not quite able to believe the words as they came out of her mouth. 'Well, he's already left me, so that's not the right way to put it, but now I know where he is, I'm going to tell him I want a formal separation. A divorce.'

She paused for a moment, to breathe and swallow. She had to come to terms with what she'd just said. Chum made no comment, just looked at her steadily and held her hand firmly in his.

'Do you think that's awful?' she asked him.

'Definitely not awful,' he said. 'Of course I can't offer any impartial comment because – while I don't want to be tactless – I'm absolutely thrilled he's out of the picture. But I do have my own experience of being left. As you will have read in that charming *Tatler* article, my wife left me and it was just as sudden and unexpected as your husband's departure. I came home one day to find a note. She'd run off with a bloke we knew a bit from horsey circles. I didn't realise she'd got to know him rather too well while I was busy building the food business. So I do know what it's like having to deal with hurt and anger simultaneously. It's impossibly confusing.'

He paused for a moment, looking into the fire, before continuing. 'Then it got even more mixed up for me when they were both killed in that terrible car crash, with grief and even a weird sense of guilt that if I hadn't been away so much for work, she might not have felt the need for another man and she'd still be alive. After that I felt like some kind of whack-a-mole. Every time I came to terms with one element of it, I got hit over the head by other one.'

Polly blinked at him for a moment, taking in what he'd said.

'That's exactly it,' she said, 'that's why I've been so muddle-headed. I didn't know whether to be broken-hearted or furious, and somehow it doesn't seem possible to feel both of those things at once.'

She paused for a moment, collecting her thoughts.

'I do understand there must be some reason David is behaving like this.' She felt she had to say his name out loud, to make him a real person, not a vague concept of a 'husband'.

'Knowing David,' it felt good to say it, 'I don't think it's another woman. His other woman is his work. But he was acting so strangely when we saw him at the university, I can't help thinking he might be clinically depressed, or something awful like that, and I'm very sorry if that's the case, but – putting myself aside – I can't forgive him for the way he's treated the kids.'

She paused again. Now she'd started talking about it, she couldn't stop. 'Am I going on too much?' she asked Chum.

He shook his head. 'Not at all,' he said. 'I know how much better I feel for telling you my story. Let it out.'

'Well, it was my mum of all people who made me start to understand this,' she said. 'But since he's been absent I've come to realise just how controlling David has been throughout our relationship. It was great when I was younger, because he seemed to know everything and I looked up to him so much, but I see now he didn't want me to grow up from that. He's been very patronising about the blog, for example. And what you said about not coming to see my mum with me – apart from when we moved her in, he's never been there and he makes me feel I'm being unreasonable if I ask him to come with me. And our wedding ...'

Now she was really in her stride.

'This is what my mum reminded me about – I'd always thought I'd get married in the chapel at my father's college, it's so beautiful, but David insisted on a London registry office and minimum guests. He didn't even want me to wear a long dress and I'd always dreamed of wearing my mum's wedding dress, which was made for her in the 1950s by Christian Dior. But I just accepted it, because I was so infatuated I thought everything he wanted must be right. But looking back, that wasn't fair, and that's just one of many examples ...'

She came to a stop, suddenly feeling exhausted by it all. She sighed heavily.

'Phew,' she said, 'that turned into a bit of a marathon.'

Chum said nothing, just put his arm around her shoulder and pulled her towards him, so her head was resting against his shoulder. It felt like the most comforting place on earth to be, especially as she could smell him so well. She breathed in deeply, wondering if she would ever tire of that smell, with the hint of horse and ....

'Equipage,' she said suddenly, pulling back to look at him and then going in for another sniff. 'That's what it is. You wear Hermès Equipage. Of course you do. An aftershave by a company that started as a saddlemaker and has a horse on its logo. What else would you wear?'

Chum laughed.

'I don't wear it often, but I did put some on this morning for you. I thought it might make me more alluring.'

'You don't need any help with that,' said Polly and then, without thinking about it, she leaned towards him and put her lips on his. Very softly at first and then more insistently, until he took the lead, his tongue pushing gently into her mouth, entwining with hers – just as it had been all those years before, and just as wonderful.

As the kiss went on, slowly, then faster, Polly felt something inside her start up like the roar of a jet engine and she pulled herself up, kissing him hard, her hand round the back of his head, keeping him close, pressing her breasts against his chest. Until, like someone in the distance, she heard herself moan.

She pulled away, surprised at herself. Where had that come from? Well, she hadn't had sex for a long time; even before David had gone away it had been a while ...

But as soon as that thought came into her head, she pushed it away. Not that, not him. Not now.

'Sorry,' she said, feeling embarrassed. 'I got a bit overtaken ...'

'Don't apologise, Hippolyta,' he said. 'You can overtake me any time you like.'

He pulled her onto his lap, her legs stretched out along the sofa, so she was lying in his arms and he was gazing down at her, tracing the lines of her face with his fingers.

'You're so beautiful,' he said. 'You were always the most beautiful woman I ever kissed, and now I'm going to kiss you again.'

He did and then he put some more logs on the fire and lay down on the sofa next to her and they stayed like that, kissing and talking, reminiscing about all the times at St Andrews when they'd nearly kissed again, logging all the missed chances and misunderstandings, relishing the delicious nonsense. Then they'd kiss again, or just lie there gazing into each other's eyes.

This is what bliss feels like, thought Polly – and in that state, she didn't notice until Chum got up to tend the fire again, that it was completely dark outside.

'Oops,' said Chum, clocking the black windows at the same moment. 'We rather forgot the time.'

'What shall we do?' said Polly.

'We can't really walk back in the dark,' said Chum, going over to the windows and closing the curtains. He bit his lip, thinking.

'We could call a taxi to pick us up at the lodge at the end of the back drive,' he said. 'I wouldn't have it come to the house, or up the main drive. I do have to be a bit careful. That's only a couple of miles. We can use our phones as torches.'

'Or?' said Polly.

'Or we could stay here,' said Chum. He started to chuckle. 'It's not like there aren't plenty of bedrooms. Unless you have to get back to Digger, of course. Artie's fine, she's with one my stable girls. I can text her and say I'll be back too late to pick Artie up.'

Polly thought for a moment. Digger was fine – he was at home with Clemmie and Lucas. It was them she was thinking about.

She'd already lied to be there that day, telling them she was going to see a friend she'd met through the blog who lived in the country. If she stayed, she'd have to lie to them again, saying she'd decided to spend the night at the friend's house rather than drive back in the dark – which would be kind of true, but it would feel like a lie, because she had rather implied that the friend was female. She'd also have to lie to Shirlee, asking her to cancel the next morning's yoga class.

She couldn't do it.

'I think I'll have to go home,' she said.

Seeing the disappointment on his face, she got up and hurried over to where he was standing by the window, putting her hands up onto his shoulders and looking up at him.

'It's not because I don't want to stay with you,' she said. 'I'd love to stay more than anything, but I just can't lie to my kids. They're at home for the Easter holidays, and I'd have to make up some lame excuse why I didn't come home. I'd find it hard to do anyway, but with what their father's done to them, I just have to be the reliable one.'

Chum nodded and put his arms round her.

'I understand,' he said, 'and you're absolutely right. I'll call that taxi – but first, look at this.'

He turned her round and gently pushed her towards the window, pulling the curtain back. Polly looked out into the night, right up at the moon. It was just a crescent, but very bright in the clear sky, hanging above the dark outlines of the oak trees in the park, its light reflected in a lake.

'Oh, that's so beautiful,' she said, remembering how desolate she'd felt looking at the moon alone on New Year's Eve.

How good it felt to be gazing up at it now, with Chum's strong arms around her.

Sunday, 27 March

Three days later, Polly was in Shirlee's car on their way to have Easter Sunday lunch with Daphne. She glanced over her shoulder to see if Lucas and Clemmie were still behind them in her car. Lucas saw her looking and flashed the headlights.

It was pouring with rain and she hoped he would take extra care driving. Something else to be anxious about on a day when she was beginning to feel her head might start spinning round on her neck she was so nervous.

'It was real nice of you to ask me today,' Shirlee was saying. 'It'll be very interesting for me to see how a Christian family kill each other at a religious celebration meal, as opposed to the Jewish tradition, with which I'm already very familiar.'

She laughed heartily.

'But really,' she continued, 'I don't know when I last went to any kind of family thing, so it means a lot.'

'Well, you're kind of part of our family now,' said Polly, 'so I thought you should meet the *grande dame*. I'm so glad you could come.'

As she said it, she hoped she really meant it. She'd invited Shirlee on a crazy impulse while they were having breakfast after yoga a couple of days before, not thinking too clearly in the euphoric state she'd been floating around in since her time with Chum at Hanley Hall.

She hadn't seen him since – only three days, which felt like an eternity – but they'd spoken or FaceTimed several times a day since and arranged to meet 'casually' at Rockham Park for Easter Sunday lunch. They would both have been going there anyway, but now it felt like a thing.

Polly's stomach fluttered at the thought of seeing him, and she seriously hoped she'd be able to keep it together in front of her family and Bill. That was going to be hard enough, but she had to face up to it. Shirlee was another situation altogether, and she couldn't help wishing she hadn't been quite so hasty with the invitation.

'It's great I'm getting to meet your mom before the Paris trip,' said Shirlee.

Polly looked at her, confused.

'For the ad campaign,' Shirlee added, glancing at Polly, then turning back to the road.

'How do you know about that?' asked Polly. 'I didn't tell you.'

'I booked all the travel today,' said Shirlee, 'and I had to have this long conversation with the guest relations manager at the Paris Ritz about what to have in your mom's room for her on arrival. White flowers, champagne, a bowl of blue M&Ms – just kidding about that last one.'

'I still don't understand,' said Polly.

'I'm Guy's new assistant.' said Shirlee. 'And I'm coming with you on that trip, so that should be a riot.'

'Well,' said Polly, 'I don't think anything can surprise me any more, but I'm thrilled for you both. You'll be brilliant at it and you'll have so much fun, but I do hope you'll still be able to come to yoga and stay for brekkie. I'd miss that so much now.'

'On it,' said Shirlee. 'I'll still be at yoga every day, and I'll stay for breakfast whenever I can. It was a condition of my employment by the Great Eastern Fragrance Company that I have a late start at least twice a week, and he's coming to classes regularly now too, so some days you'll have both of us for brekkie. Be careful what you wish for.' She chuckled.

'Thanks, Shirl,' said Polly. 'I would miss you so much now.'

'Likewise, Polls, likewise,' said Shirlee, glancing in the rear-view mirror. 'Got some macho trucker moron tailgating me now, right up my butt, and I can't see if the kids are still with us.'

She slowed down and shook her fist in the rear-view mirror.

'Back off, asshole!' she shouted, lowering the window as the lorry overtook them, honking its horn. 'Yeah, drive in the fast lane, big guy, go kill yourself, but don't take us with you.'

Polly let her get on with it. Colourful interaction with other drivers was always a feature of being in the car with Shirlee – and she'd just had an idea.

'Now you're working for Guy,' she said, 'can you do something for me?'

'Sure,' said Shirlee. 'I owe you one for the intro. What do you want?'

'I want to know where the money for the business comes from and who his family are. He's so evasive about it all and he's fed me so much bullshit. He had me believing he was half-Iranian, with an exotic grandmother who was a great influence on him. The first time I met him he was smoking a bloody hookah. Told me it was his grandfather's and I totally believed him. He's so nosy about everyone else's life – he virtually stalked me to get to my mum – but then he's totally secretive about his own background, and I've had enough. So will you be my mole?'

'Are you kidding?' said Shirlee. 'Why do you think I took the job? Not really, but I do want to know all that stuff too –

and his love life. That's what I really want to know. I can usually work it out about people and it's bugging me. I've got a plan.'

'What? I've tried and tried to find out what the story is and he wouldn't give anything away.'

'I'll get him drunk,' said Shirlee. 'Old-school martinis.'

'I've been drunk with Guy,' said Polly, 'well, pretty tipsy anyway, and he still never told me about his family.'

'Ah, but that's the thing – you were drunk too. I'll get him drunk, but I'll stay cold-ass sober and pretend to be drunk. That's how you do it. But I should tell you there's another thing I already tried to get out of him and couldn't.'

'What?' asked Polly.

'Whether you two are getting it on,' Shirlee said.

Polly burst out laughing.

'You are kidding, aren't you?' she said.

Her laughter was genuine, but she felt her cheeks turning pink anyway, because while she wasn't getting it on with Guy, she most definitely was with Chum. Well, not fully on, but well on the way to on. Semi-on.

Had Shirlee noticed a change in her? Was the rosy glow she felt inside clearly visible on her face?

'There's no way I'm getting on anything of Guy's, apart from his wonderful perfume,' Polly continued. 'We're friends. He's hilarious and a brilliant perfumer, but he's much younger than me and he's a dingbat. I definitely don't have any romantic designs on him.'

'And with you being a married woman and all that ...' Shirlee turned to give her a sly glance. 'Or not. You've got virtual single status now, Polly. You've been through so much recently I think you should just enjoy it. Get something for yourself out of the situation that's been thrust – pardon the pun – on you. Your husband has thrown the rule book out, so why should you follow it any more?'

Polly looked quickly out of the window, needing a moment to think through what Shirlee had said. As she'd told Chum at Hanley Hall, she'd made her decision about David. Whether it was that awful time at King's or kissing Chum that had convinced her didn't matter. Her mind was made up. She was going to tell him she wanted to make the separation he'd created – without consulting her first – official. The Big D.

She was sure about that – just as she was certain she wanted to move things on to the next stage with Chum, to having a relationship with him. And to going to bed with him in the first instance.

So she knew what she wanted from both men. It was just the combination of the two momentous things that overwhelmed her. She could think calmly and clearly about both of them individually, but as soon as she put them together it became terrifying, especially with the thought of telling the kids.

What would she say? *I'm divorcing your father – and here's my new boyfriend, he's staying over?*

How could she do that to them? Lucas had been very badly affected by his father's behaviour, taking up that binge drinking. With support from her and Clemmie – and the fright about not being able to play the guitar any more – he'd got on top of it really impressively and seemed to have found a new strength in himself as a result, but if she started acting out of character as well, she didn't know how he'd cope.

And then there was Clemmie's relationship with her father to consider. She was furious with him and very hurt, but she was still fundamentally that little daddy's girl – still the chosen one who got the texts ... So while she might castigate her father herself, being told Polly wanted a divorce would doubtless make Clemmie feel very conflicted.

And now Shirlee was definitely on to her. She could tell Polly had something going on her life. Something male. Oh, taking her to this lunch was such a mistake.

The minute Shirlee met Chum she'd be watching them both like a surveillance camera and asking him inappropriate questions. Each one loaded with uncomfortable complications. Are you married? Do you have kids? What do you do? Where do you live?

Polly got her phone out, pretending to be looking something up to give herself time to think.

She did urgently want Chum to meet her kids, she reminded herself. That was very important; she needed to see how they got on together. If it wasn't comfortable she would have to think very hard about what happened next. Everything hung on that – so why the hell had she been so stupid as to invite Shirlee along to this crucial first meeting?

Polly realised she had to try to defuse this ridiculous situation she'd created before it happened. She tapped out a quick text:

Hello Mr Equipage. I forgot to tell you I'm bringing my friend Shirlee today – the one who helps me out with the yoga classes. She's great, but she can be very full-on and will probably ask you lots of intrusive questions. Just to warn you! Can't wait to see you. xxx

A reply came back immediately:

Don't worry, I won't notice anyone else. I'm already here. Hurry up. xxxx

She smiled at her phone and then flicked a glance at Shirlee.

'We might join up with some friends of Mum's and mine for lunch,' she said as casually as she could. 'It's a lovely man called Bill, who lives there, and his stepson Edward, who was at St Andrews with me. It's just the two of them, they don't have any other family, so we thought it would be nice if they joined us, make it a bit of a party for everyone.'

'Is he single?' asked Shirlee.

Polly groaned inwardly. Shirlee coming on to Chum was an even worse prospect than the inevitable third degree she would put him through. She also felt a pang of something she had to admit to herself was jealousy. Hands off, he's mine.

'I think his wife died in tragic circumstances,' said Polly.

'Single, then,' said Shirlee. 'Excellent.'

'But I think he's seeing someone,' said Polly quickly. 'Not living with her or anything, but you know, a sort of girlfriend thing.'

'She sounds dispensable,' said Shirlee, 'but if you were at uni together he's probably a bit young for me. Is he cute?'

Chum's wide-smile, eyebrows-up, faux-innocent amused expression flashed into Polly's mind and she realised she was grinning like a fool. Luckily, Shirlee was concentrating on the road, overtaking another huge truck that was spraying up great arcs of water from the wet road.

'I wouldn't say cute,' said Polly, 'but handsome in a horsey kind of a way.'

'He looks like a horse?' said Shirlee.

Polly laughed.

'No,' she said, 'but he works with them. He's one of those posh country English blokes. Tweed jacket, corduroy trousers, wellies, you know ...'

'Oh,' said Shirlee, 'a stiff. Glad you told me, I was getting my hopes up.'

Polly had to bite her lip to stop herself from saying something she would regret. About Chum's long legs and lean body, all muscle and sinew. His hands and forearms so strong from reining in big horses.

She felt a spasm of desire thinking about it, remembering his legs entwined with hers on that sofa, the hardness of his bicep and shoulder under her hand when it had strayed inside his shirt. How she longed to touch and see and smell all of him, beneath his clothes.

She shut her eyes for a moment and pictured his thighs tensing inside his jeans whenever he stood up from a chair. Then she remembered his slow kisses, with those exquisite pauses, and sighed deeply.

Relising what she'd done, she snapped her eyes open and sat up straight.

'Nearly nodded off there,' she said, trying to cover up. She hoped she hadn't moaned. 'Better stay awake so we don't miss the turn-off, it's not that far away. At least the rain's stopped, it's supposed to be nice for the rest of the day ...'

Keeping the conversation to small talk was the safest way to get through the rest of the journey, she decided. She cast around in her head for things to say.

'Do you know why Maxine hasn't been coming to class?' she asked. 'I miss her.'

'Yeah,' said Shirlee, 'she texted me, said she's really busy at the moment, might not be able to make it for a while. She asked me to give you her apologies – sorry, I forgot to tell you. I said we'd hold over the classes she's paid for, is that cool?'

'Of course,' said Polly, 'she's one of the inner circle. I hope she'll come back soon.'

Talking more about the yoga regulars and the trip to Paris for the photo shoot, Polly managed the rest of the journey without any mishap.

As they turned into the gates of Rockham Park, she glanced round to check on Lucas and Clemmie again, and could see Digger running backwards and forwards frantically on the back seat. No doubt he was already picking up the pungent smell of Chum's Land Rover, with the traces of Artie all over it.

'Well, hello,' said Shirlee, pulling up right in front of the entrance. 'Check out Mr Hottie here.'

'Oh, that's Chum,' said Polly, before she could stop herself. She was completely taken off guard by seeing him standing just outside the sliding glass doors, looking much smarter than usual in a white shirt and navy jacket. And absolutely gorgeous.

'Chum?' said Shirlee.

'I mean Edward – the guy I was at St Andrews with. Chum was his nickname at school, it's stupid. Edward ... he's called Edward, and that's his dog, Artemis ...'

Oh, Lord, was this going to be a total nightmare? It was looking that way.

'You said he wasn't hot,' said Shirlee, sounding outraged. 'That guy is smokin'.'

'I haven't seen him in a smart jacket before,' said Polly. 'He's normally really scruffy.'

No, no, there *is* no normally. Too much explaining. Shut up.

'I'd better help the kids with Digger,' she said. 'I can see he's going bonkers in the back of the car. He always gets excited coming here, and ...'

She started to get out of the car before she could say anything else incriminating, but Chum was already there, opening the door.

'Hello, Hippolyta,' he said quietly, and Polly felt her stomach turn to liquid as she looked up into his face. She couldn't think of anything to say – apart from 'I want to kiss you now, all over' – and was hugely relieved when Artemis tugged so hard on the lead that he was almost pulled off his feet.

'Whoa!' said Chum. 'I think we need to let the dogs say hello.'

'I'll let Digger out of the other car,' said Polly, very glad of an excuse to run away from Shirlee.

Before she could get over to her car, Digger was out of the driver's door, nearly knocking Lucas over in the process, and the two dogs were leaping in the air. They took off, running around the monkey puzzle tree, then rolling over and over in the grass together.

'Have they got rabies?' said Lucas. 'Digger started going mad before we even stopped the car. Does he know that dog?'

'He sees her when we come here,' said Polly lamely, 'and you know how he gets on car journeys ...'

But Lucas wasn't listening; his gaze was fixed over her shoulder, his head on one side, a questioning look on his face.

Polly turned round to see Chum had joined them. Oh, why hadn't she choreographed this better? Told him to meet them in the dining room or something? Or to pretend he didn't know her? Or just not come at all?

'Hi, I'm Edward Cliddington,' he said, raising his hand in greeting to Lucas, then opening the car door for Clemmie, helping her out like Prince Charming.

'You must be Clemmie,' he said.

She nodded.

'I'm Edward,' he said. 'That hell hound playing with Digger is my dog, Artemis. They go a bit crazy when they see each other.'

'Hi, Edward,' she said, glancing at her mother with a puzzled expression.

Polly felt something akin to pure panic. She had told Clemmie and Lucas other people were joining them for lunch, hadn't she? Or had she just run through how she was going to tell them hundreds of times in her head and not actually said it? Like she hadn't told Chum about Shirlee until they were nearly there. Oh, God. A few kisses with Chum and her IQ seemed to have evaporated. Digger was more intelligent.

'Edward and his father are having lunch with us,' said Polly, trying to sound as though it were the most normal thing in the world. 'Bill and Daphne are friends here, and Edward and I were at St Andrews together, so we thought it would be fun if we all sat together.'

'Will the dogs be sitting with us?' asked Lucas, watching them run round and round the tree again, yelping.

Everybody laughed, and Polly was relieved to feel a release of tension – but not for long. She hadn't noticed Shirlee coming up just behind her.

'Well, hello, *Chum*,' she said, looking up at him with narrowed appraising eyes, her mouth slightly open, pink tongue peeping out of one corner then running across her lips.

Chum put his right hand out towards her.

'Edward Cliddington,' he said, smiling.

Shirlee took hold of the proffered hand and didn't let go of it.

'Polly says your chums call you "Chum", Chum,' she said. 'I'm Shirlee Katz, but you can call me Coco.'

He smiled nervously, glancing quickly at Polly with his eyes wide.

She was so appalled by what was happening she closed her own in horror. Coco?

'Hi, er, Coco,' said Chum, pulling his hand gently away. 'Lovely to see you. Are you the one who helps Hippolyta with the yoga classes? She's told me about you.'

'Oh, "Hippolyta", is it?' said Shirlee, poking Polly in the ribs with her finger. 'So Chum has privileged naming rights, does he? He's one of the chosen few who can call you by your one true name. How very interesting.'

'It's just what everyone called me at St Andrews,' said Polly, trying to sound less fraught than she felt, 'because I thought it made me sound posher. And everybody called him Chum, because that's what he was called at school. It's just old habits. Everyone else calls him Edward and me Polly these days.'

'So you just have your cute little name game together,' said Shirlee. 'Isn't that adorable? Chum and Hippolyta, sitting in a ...'

'That's right, *Coco*,' said Polly, cutting her off sharply. 'Or should I call you Roger?'

To her great relief, Shirlee threw back her head and laughed heartily, then she linked her arm through Chum's and smiled up at him.

'OK, Edward,' she said, 'show Shirlee the way.'

Chum looked over at Polly again and she nodded very quickly, hoping he'd understand her message: Just get her away from me.

'I'll mind the dogs,' said Lucas. 'I'll exercise – and exorcise – them before we come in.'

'You're a brave man,' said Chum, tossing him Artemis's lead.

'So are you,' said Lucas quietly, as Chum turned away and walked Shirlee towards the entrance.

Polly stood for a moment, frozen with tension, not knowing whether to stay outside with Lucas and the dogs to recover herself, or follow Chum and Shirlee into the building for damage limitation and was still undecided when she felt Clemmie's arm go round her waist.

'Come on, Mum,' she said, 'let's go inside and find Granny.'

Polly started to walk with her and then thought better of it.

'Actually, Clems,' she said, 'you go in with Ch … Edward. I just need to get something out of Shirlee's car. Hey, Shirl! I need you to help me out with something here.'

Shirlee turned round and Polly gave her a very hard stare.

'I need something from your car,' she said, trying to sound natural while also conveying the importance of it. 'Can you open the boot, please? You go in with Edward, Clemmie.'

She practically pushed Clemmie towards him and was very relieved when the two of them disappeared through the door into the reception area together.

'Come here, quickly,' she hissed at Shirlee, sticking her head into the car boot as it opened.

Shirlee's face popped up next to hers.

'What gives?' she said.

'Very quickly,' whispered Polly. 'I don't want Lucas to hear. The thing is, Ch … Edward—'

'Chedward,' said Shirlee, grinning at her own joke.

'Whatever,' said Polly. 'That man.'

'The tall handsome one with the adorable smile and the incredibly strong arms I was secretly feeling up through his jacket a minute a go?' said Shirlee. 'That one?'

Polly nodded, tightly.

'Anyway. Like I told you, I was at St Andrews with him and we met up here a few weeks ago by pure chance, and the dogs just took to each other, and we've been going for walks, and …'

Tears filled her eyes and her voice cracked. Shirlee put her arm round her.

'It's OK, bubs,' she said. 'You like the guy, right? I don't blame you, he's seriously toasty. Go for it, girl. He's much better for you than Guy – and I can tell you, he's seriously got the hots for you.'

'Really?' said Polly, unable to help herself.

Shirlee chuckled.

'Oh, you have got it bad,' she said. 'It's just what you need, like I was saying on the way up here – get yourself laid, Polly.'

'I want to,' she said, 'believe me and ... well, if you can promise to keep this to yourself, Shirlee. Do you promise?'

'Yessir,' she said.

'Well,' said Polly, taking a deep breath. 'I've decided to tell David it's over. I want a divorce. I can't ever take him back after this.'

'Way to go, girl,' said Shirlee. 'I am so glad you've got to that place.'

'You think I'm doing the right thing?' asked Polly,

'No doubt – and a victory roll around with a guy as cute as that one is the perfect way to celebrate it.'

Polly smiled, although it didn't remotely reflect how she felt about him. It would be much more than a roll around to her.

'But it's the kids, Shirlee. I'll have to tell them my decision about their father and it doesn't seem fair to introduce the new man in my life at the same time – I have to think about their feelings. It's not just me.'

'Do they need to know?' asked Shirlee.

'Well ...' said Polly.

'You're an adult,' continued Shirlee, 'and entitled to a private life – emphasis on the word "private", as in no one needs to know, except me, of course, ha ha, and I do promise I won't tell anyone. You might find it hard to believe, but I can actually keep a secret if I'm asked to.'

Polly just looked at her, taking it all in.

'And your kids are adults too,' said Shirlee. 'They're not in kindergarten any more, Polly, they're grown-ups, and you don't have to keep your life on hold for them now. They wouldn't want you to.'

Polly thought for a moment longer, then she flung her arms round her.

'Thank you, Shirlee,' she said, hugging her tight. 'You've made me feel so much better about it all.'

'Happy to help,' said Shirlee, who was now reaching into the back of the boot and pulling out a large bulging shopping bag.

'Look,' she said, 'I brought Easter eggs. I wasn't sure how many we'd need, so I got ten big ones. Do you think that will cover it?'

Polly laughed. 'When have you ever under-catered?' she said. 'That was so kind of you – but can I just say one more thing about the, er, Chedward issue?'

'Shoot,' said Shirlee.

'Can we be cool at lunch?' asked Polly. 'I really wanted the kids to meet him, to see if they get on, but – for the reasons just discussed – I don't want them to know there's anything between us. Not yet. So none of your usual antics, OK? No more K.I.S.S.I.N.G.-ing or any of that nonsense.'

'I swear,' said Shirlee, chuckling. 'Now, you get in there and lust after that guy.'

FragrantCloud.net

The scent of ... Easter

When I was a kid we always had a special lunch on Easter Sunday, with the traditional leg of lamb, followed by rhubarb crumble.

My favourite ones were when we went up to Scotland and I'd get to spend it with my huge tribe of cousins – heaven for an only child. There would be cinnamon-y hot cross buns on Good Friday and fish for dinner, then the next day we would dye and decorate hard-boiled eggs with my granny.

On the morning of Easter Sunday we would climb up a hill near my grandparents' house and then roll our decorated eggs down it. The person whose egg rolled the furthest was the winner and they got the biggest chocolate egg.

I've kept those traditions going with my own family, and although my kids are grown up and at uni now, they still love it and both came with me this year to have Easter lunch with my mother at the retirement village where she lives.

We joined up with some friends, which made it so much more fun – family gatherings are always better when there are 'orphans', not just the nuclear family group in a claustrophobic bubble.

We took our New Yorker friend Shirlee and linked up with Edward, who is an old friend of mine from St Andrews days, and his dad Bill, who lives at the same place as my mum.

Bill surprised each of us with a beautiful hand-painted wooden Russian Easter egg and we had such a laugh rolling them down a hill – a very small one – in the grounds.

Lucas and Edward were neck and neck winners with their eggs, so we had to have a replay, but that went horribly wrong when I got overexcited and accidently let go of Edward's dog Artemis and she ran in and 'retrieved' his egg.

Then my daughter let our dog Digger go – deliberately for the sport of it – and it was absolute pandemonium with the dogs running around with the eggs in their mouths and the two chaps chasing them to try and retrieve them. I haven't laughed so much for years.

In the end Bill declared it a draw and the champions shared the biggest chocolate egg – which was funny in itself because they both have crazy sweet tooths.

To keep it 'fair' they sat opposite each other across a coffee table while they ate it, matching each other, piece for piece, while my daughter and my friend Shirlee, adjudicated.

I felt queasy just watching them eat so much chocolate, but they loved it, declaring they were ready for more at the end. I had to intervene when they started talking about having a 'choc off'.

My mum had a lovely time, relishing the company and highjinks, seeing her grandchildren, and being spoiled rotten by Edward and his father, who both have those old-school manners she loves, pushing in her chair for her, standing up whenever she did and all that caper.

Lucas was fascinated by it and told Edward he wants to have lessons in how to be an 'uppy downy' man, as he called it.

All in all it was the best Easter I can remember since I was a kid.

My Easter smells are the cinnamon and mixed spices in the hot cross buns, and the rosemary and mint sauce with the roast lamb. The grassy tang of rhubarb and real muddy wet grass from the egg rolling. And of course, lots and lots of milk chocolate.

My scents for Easter are:

Angel by Thierry Mugler
Anima Dulcis by Arquiste
Musc Maori by Parfumerie Générale
Blue North by Agonist
Opium by Yves Saint Laurent
English Pear & Freesia by Jo Malone London
La Tulipe by Byredo

COMMENTS

LuxuryGal: This is so cute. But who was the Easter Bunny?

FragrantCloud: That is catching on here now, but we didn't have that tradition when I was a kid, I think it's more of a US thing.

WhirlyShirlee: I'm never going to eat chocolate again. The Easter Bunny is a creep sponsored by dentists.

AgathaF: In Germany we also paint eggs and on Easter Sunday we light bonfires. This is also good fun. I love the smell of a bonfire. You should write about that.

FragrantCloud: Smoky perfumes are very interesting, I really like all the Comme des Garçons fragrances for that element.

PerspiringDreams: I loved this. It sounds like you had a great Easter. Has Clemmie talked to you about doing an event at our college?

FragrantCloud: She hasn't, but I'd love to.

EastLondonNostrils: Sounds like you had a great time. Well thanks for inviting me ... NOT.

Thursday, 31 March

Polly was standing just off a busy London street, staring at a strip of buzzers next to a heavy double door. All of them had names next to them except one, which just said 'Flat Seven'.

That was David's flat, where they'd lived together until just before Lucas was born. He'd always kept it anonymous like that – which made her think it was very likely that he still had the lease.

She wondered whether she should press the buzzer and see if he answered, but then, remembering how he'd behaved when they'd arrived at his office, decided he'd probably leg it out via the fire escape if she announced herself. So she put the key into the lock and opened the door.

How lucky she'd kept those keys all these years. It had been such a big deal when David had given her a set of keys to his flat, the first place they'd lived together, and when they'd moved to their house, she hadn't been able to part with them. She'd stashed them in the box where she kept his love letters and other mementos, still on the Big Ben key ring he'd given her.

She stepped into the lobby, which seemed pretty much the same as it had the last time she'd been in it. The carpet was different, but the mail boxes were still there, and the smell ... The smell was exactly the same: other people's cooking, a top note of cabbage and a distinct hint of garbage brought down in the lift. Polly had never got used to that smell.

She started up the stairs to the fourth floor, remembering how she used to carry heavy bags of shopping up there – and baby Clemmie – without a second thought. But then nothing's a problem when you're young and in love ...

She got to the door of Flat Seven and hesitated again. What if someone else lived there now and she just walked in on them? Knowing it was moronic, she put her eye to the peephole, and of course couldn't see a thing. Then, after glancing around to make sure no one was watching, she put her ear against the wood of the door to listen for any sign of life inside. Nothing. She thought about knocking, but if David looked out through the peephole and saw her she knew he wouldn't let her in. There was only one thing for it.

Taking a deep breath, she tried the key and it slid in smoothly, but the door didn't open because she'd forgotten about the deadlock below. Shuffling the keys, she found that one, unlocked it, then turned the upper key again.

The door opened.

With her heart hammering, she stepped inside and stood very still, listening for any sound of occupation. Nothing. She closed the door as quietly as she could behind her and looked around.

It didn't look the same, but how could it have? They'd emptied it when they moved, taking all the furniture from this flat to the house where they lived now – well, where *she* lived. So how could she know if this new stuff was his or if she had just let herself into a complete stranger's home?

Not moving from the door, she closed her eyes and breathed in deeply. Did it have David's smell? Coffee, for sure, and books. But both of them strongly overlaid by the sterile sting of cleaning products, so not a lot else. And while she didn't want to believe it, there was the undeniable hint of coal-tar soap. Not many people used it any more. Yet that wasn't evidence in itself. She'd have to go and look.

Walking tentatively along the hallway, she peeped into the bedroom and the bathroom as she went. There was no one there. The kitchen – which had been completely refitted – was also empty, leaving just the sitting room.

The door was closed and she paused outside it, feeling even more nervous than she had coming in through the front door. There was something so deliberate about the way the door had been left shut.

As she reached down and took hold of the handle, she almost hoped it would be locked like his office at home had been, but it opened normally. She was hugely relieved to find no one was inside.

Having established that David, or whoever lived there now, was out, Polly quickly went back into the other rooms to look at them more closely. Opening the bathroom cabinet, she had to admit to herself she was looking for signs of a woman – make-up, tampons, perfume – but there was nothing like that there. It was resolutely male, containing David's preferred shaving foam and Nivea Men face cream, which he also used.

That could be just a coincidence, she told herself. Millions of men used those products ...

But then she spotted the bottle of Yohji Homme. Of course it could be pure coincidence again, but when she picked it up and smelled the cap she knew immediately it was the original 1999 formulation, not the new version that was released in 2013.

She'd tracked the original down for him online after they'd discontinued it, because its unique combination of strong lavender and liquorice was the only the men's fragrance David had ever been really enthusiastic about. He loved liquorice.

Polly closed her eyes and put her hands on the basin, letting it take her weight as a wave of dizziness swept over her. That pretty much clinched it. He'd held on to the lease of this flat for over twenty years without her knowing. And now he was living in it again, without telling her why.

When she'd recovered, a quick flick through the kitchen cupboards – torturously tidy, with everything perfectly lined up – revealed they were stocked with David's usual staple foods, including a bag of his favourite strong coffee from the Algerian roasters in Old Compton Street.

Then she went through to the bedroom. The wardrobe was full of clothes she knew: shirts she'd ironed hundreds of times, sweaters she'd bought him.

How could you have that level of intimacy with someone, yet know them as little as it seemed she actually had?

She could remember packing everything they'd had in this flat up with him and then unpacking it in their new place – their family home – together. She'd been so excited. And now it turned out he'd come back and secretly refurnished this one. He'd even had the kitchen refitted! There was nothing casual about any of this. The whole time they'd been married he'd had a secret separate life going on.

Polly went back into the sitting room, wondering what she was looking for now. What more evidence did she need that he was not committed to his marriage to her in any normal way – and never had been?

It was pretty clear he wasn't shacked up there with another woman or another man. She would have been able to recognise someone else's clothes, another toothbrush. And there wasn't another person's smell. So it didn't seem to involve a third party, but she still yearned to find something, anything, to explain it all.

A quick glance round the room showed he had refurnished it with very little imagination, mostly from IKEA. As long as everything was neat and very clean, David had never cared about interior design. There was a sofa – the same as the one they'd moved out – a desk and, of course, bookshelves, all the books perfectly aligned to the front of the shelf, filed by genre and author names in alphabetic order.

She ran her eyes over the spines and it was all the usual stuff she would expect to find on David's shelves – academic history, some classic novels, the last few Booker Prize winners and some male-interest thrillers.

Feeling cheated that, after the courage it had taken to come into the flat like this, she still knew no more about why he was living in it, she sat down at the desk and pulled open the drawers, to find just odds and ends of stationery, bills, some receipts – nothing helpful.

She slammed the last one shut in frustration, deciding she'd had enough of David's creepy hideaway – and as she didn't want him to come back and find her here, it was time to leave.

Then, as she stood up to go, her eye fell on a business card propped up against a pencil pot. The name on it made her pick it up and look more closely.

It read, 'Maxine Thurloe, Psychotherapist', followed by a cluster of academic and professional acronyms.

She stared down at it, frowning. Wasn't that *her* Maxine, who came to yoga? Polly was sure that was her surname. The card had a Belsize Park address and she was a psychotherapist by profession. It must be her. But why the hell did David have her card?

After taking a quick photo of it with her phone, Polly carefully propped the card up again where she'd found it and turned to head out, pausing to look at a calendar on the wall next to the desk.

Of course. David always had a wall calendar. He'd never made the adjustment to online, saying he needed to see his life written down to remember it. This one featured photographs of deserted Cold War bunkers, such a typically bleak David subject that Polly almost laughed.

She looked at the entry for that day and read, in his distinctive small neat handwriting: '11 a.m. Maxine.'

So that was where he was at this very moment: with Maxine, presumably having a professional appointment. He bloody needs it, thought Polly, with his recent behaviour.

Leafing back through the pages, she saw the same entry on all the previous Thursdays in March, February and January. Then, flipping forwards, there it was again: the same appointment, every week.

She went back to the January page. Maxine had come to yoga for the first time with Shirlee for that special New Year's Day class, when they'd had the inaugural breakfast, so she particularly remembered the date. How odd to think she had then seen David the following week. Was that the first time?

She thought for a moment, then went over to the filing cabinet on the other side of the room and pulled open the top drawer, then the second, where she found what she was looking for: a file marked 'Calendars'.

Polly sighed. How well she knew his habits, yet how little it seemed she really knew him. She fished out the one from the previous year – Second World War tanks – and sure enough, practically all the Thursdays going back right through it had that same appointment with Maxine every Thursday. So he'd been seeing her for at least fifteen months – even when he was still living at home.

But the big question that was vexing Polly now was this: did Maxine know that her patient David Goodwin was Polly's husband?

She'd never taken his surname, she was still Polly Masterson-Mackay, so there wasn't that clue to flag it. So was it perhaps just a simple matter of London geography? Maxine lived and worked in Belsize Park, so Polly's yoga class was pretty handy. Ten minutes' drive, or you could walk it in half an hour.

But her clinic wouldn't be very convenient for David in his working week, she thought, even when he was still living at home. Then Polly remembered that for quite a while he had been going to the office later one day each week. He'd given her some reason for it, which she hadn't even taken in. She'd just accepted it. And yes, thinking back – it was Thursdays.

So he hadn't been going late to King's College every Thursday. He'd been taking the whole morning off, going to see Maxine at 11 a.m. and then going into work.

As she stood there at David's filing cabinet, all the possible scenarios started to jump around in her head. Had Maxine known from the outset that her yoga teacher was the wife of one of her longstanding regular patients, and had she come along with Shirlee despite that – or, for some reason, because of it? Or had she not realised until she'd been going for a while and then kept coming anyway? After all, how many historians with yoga teacher wives called Polly and kids called Clemmie and Lucas were there in North London? There's no way she wouldn't have made the connection.

Polly couldn't bear to think that Maxine might have been sitting in her kitchen knowing everything that was going on, when Polly herself hadn't – but equally, from what she knew of Maxine, she just couldn't imagine her doing something so deceitful.

Then something else occurred to her. Maxine hadn't been to yoga for two weeks. She'd suddenly stopped coming, claiming she had too much on. Was that all connected somehow?

For a moment Polly thought her head might explode from the pressure of all the things she didn't know. It was like living in a giant riddle and she didn't think she could stand it any more.

She reached into her bag for her phone, opening her Favourites list for Chum's number. Her finger hovered over his name. She longed to tell him where she was and what she'd just discovered – just hearing his voice would be a comfort – but she stopped herself. He wasn't the right person to talk to about it.

Not because she felt she owed David that respect – she felt she owed him less with every new thing she found out about his hidden life. But because she didn't want to taint her fledgling relationship with Chum with baggage from her last one. She wanted to keep that precious thing pure and special, as long as she could.

Before she threw the phone back in her bag, she checked the time. Twelve-fifteen. Shrink sessions always lasted about an hour, didn't they? Which meant David's would have been over at least a quarter of an hour ago; he could be back at any time.

She hastily pushed the calendar back into the drawer, closed the door to the sitting room behind her and rushed out of the flat – but as she was about to turn the key in the deadlock she paused for a moment, then went back inside.

Going straight to the bathroom, she grabbed the bottle of Yohji Homme out of the cupboard and stuffed it in her pocket. She hoped its strange disappearance would make him feel as bewildered as she permanently did.

Polly looked at the large glass of red wine on the table in front of her and wondered if she could down it in one. Her brain was still throbbing from the shock of confirming that David was living in his old flat – and then finding Maxine's card on his desk.

And it was the same Maxine, the one who came to her yoga classes and stayed for breakfast. Or used to. She'd checked her yogi bears email list as soon as she'd got home and confirmed Maxine's was the same as the one on the card.

She still didn't know where to file this latest revelation in her head and knew she wouldn't be able to until she had all the facts. In the meantime, it was yet another hole in the fabric of her life. It was beginning to feel like a string vest, there were so many missing bits.

She didn't know how she would have got through the rest of the day if she hadn't had this dinner with Lucas to look forward to, a treat at his favourite steak house, just fifteen minutes walk from home, before he went back to uni the next morning. He was going back early to do extra band practice. Clemmie had gone the day before.

Lucas had just texted to say he was going to be a few minutes late, and she'd resolved to spend it calming her mind by just sitting and being – not looking at her phone and trying not to think; she'd done way too much of that today already. The wine was helping, she decided, as she looked out of the window at the darkening street, the cars and buses swishing past, the street lights shining.

Lucas arrived in a flurry of long limbs, messy dark hair and the precious hugs a grown-up boy gives his mother. Just seeing him was like a balm for Polly's hectic mind.

'Have you ordered for me?' he asked.

'Rib eye, well done, no salad, extra chips, mayo on the side, Becks served in the bottle,' said Polly. 'Not yet, but I know what to ask for.'

Lucas grinned.

'Fillet, medium rare, no chips, extra salad, large red,' he said.

'That's me,' said Polly, 'medium rare.'

'I think you're very rare,' said Lucas. 'A jewel among women.'

They ordered their food and chatted about general things, Polly relishing the novelty of living in the moment and not having to analyse any element of it, everything open and at face value. Just loving her son's company and his stories about the band and what they were planning for their next step towards world domination, starting with his determination to get a gig at the university union. His vital young energy was so refreshing.

'So how was your day, Mum?' he asked, taking her off guard. 'What did you get up to?'

Polly hesitated before replying. Should she tell him about the flat? The strange connection with Maxine? Both things? Neither?

'Fine,' she said in the end. 'Nothing special.'

'Really?' said Lucas. 'Because you look like you've been run over. Why don't you tell me what really happened today. Where did you go this morning? When I got up you'd already gone out.'

'What do you mean?' asked Polly.

'Mum,' said Lucas, leaning over the table towards her, 'I'm your son, I can read your face like a Snapchat post. I've had nearly twenty years to learn when I can ask for an extra biscuit or when it's better to leave it, and what I'm reading on your face at this moment is some kind of stress situation. I would not be asking you for a Garibaldi right now. The biscuit tin is closed.'

Polly said nothing, although she couldn't help smiling. Apart from Lucas's general adorability, the mention of Garibaldis had made her think of Chum.

'Tell me, Mum,' said Lucas. 'I know it's going to be something about Dad and I can take it. I'm not going to freak out. I'm here to support you, so spill.'

'I know where your father is living,' said Polly, feeling her happy mood dissolve.

'So do I,' said Lucas, raising his beer bottle to her, before taking a large swig. 'He's living in a block of flats near Holborn Tube station.'

'How on earth do you know that?' asked Polly.

'I followed him,' said Lucas. 'That day you went to see your friend last week I seized my opportunity. I rang Maureen and asked her what time he would leave the office on that particular day and then I waited outside King's where he couldn't see me but I could see him, and then I followed him back to Holborn. It was quite fun, in a super-weird way. I felt like a spy in a film.'

Polly's head was working overtime.

'So that was over a week ago?' she said. 'I went to see … my friend … last Wednesday.'

Lucas nodded.

'Yeah, it worked out perfectly that you didn't come home until late that night and Clemmie was out too. Gave me time to compose myself afterwards. I watched four Harry Potter films and ate a whole tub of maple pecan ice cream. And quite a lot of double chocolate chip.'

He grinned. The little boy again for a moment. Polly's heart clenched.

'But why didn't you tell me the next day?' asked Polly.

'It had to be the right moment,' said Lucas, 'and you seemed so happy last week, with Clemmie and me at home, and Shirlee and Guy being hilarious, and that really fun lunch we all had with Granny and your uppy-downy friend Edward and his dad. I didn't want to burst your bubble. I made a decision I'd tell you just before I went back to Brighton, so here we are.'

'Does Clemmie know?' asked Polly

'No, I had to tell you first,' said Lucas, he took a pull on his beer. 'How did you find out?'

'It was a hunch,' said Polly. 'When Maureen said he was living at a WC1 address I had a good idea where it would be, and it turned out I was right.'

'But he wasn't there, was he?' said Lucas.

'No,' said Polly. 'And how do you know that, Eagle Eye junior spy?'

'Because he's gone away.' He paused, slumping back in his chair and looking more serious. 'I made him talk to me.'

'He was there?' said Polly.

Lucas nodded.

'Didn't he try to run away again?' said Polly.

'Yeah,' said Lucas, 'but I made sure he couldn't ...'

He sat up again and pushed his plate to one side, the steak unfinished, and put his arms on the table, folded.

'We can take that home for Digger ... I followed him to the building, and just before he went inside, I grabbed him and pinned him to the wall. Made him talk to me.'

He paused for a moment and screwed his eyes up really tight. Polly could see he was trying not to cry and put her hand on his arm.

'Sweetheart ...' she said.

'I'm stronger than him, Mum,' he said, in a small, tight voice. 'It's so odd, but he's got quite puny. He tried to fight me off, but then he just went limp. It was horrible. And I think after what happened at King's that time, he might be a little bit scared of me.'

'You're amazing, Lucas,' she said. 'Amazing for having the courage to do this.'

He drained his beer and signalled to a passing waiter for another.

'Don't worry, Mum,' he said. 'I'm not going to take to drink again, but I could do with one more to get through telling you this – do you want some more wine?'

She nodded. 'In the circs, yes – and go on with what you were telling me. So what did you say to him?"

Lucas sighed sadly.

'I told him I wanted answers. I said the way he's treated you – and me and Clemmie, but you particularly – is unforgivable, and that we need an explanation and to know what his plans are. Has he left us or what?'

Polly's mouth was dry. Digger was going to have a feast later; she couldn't eat another bite either.

'And what did he say?' she asked, very quietly.

Lucas looked at her for a moment, rubbing his chin.

'That was the weirdest thing,' said Lucas, 'and why I had to find the right time to tell you about this. He said you could ask your friend Maxine. He said she knows everything and he was going to give her permission to tell you. Do you think she's his girlfriend?'

'No,' said Polly, shaking her head slowly, taking it all in. 'She's not his girlfriend, she's his therapist. I found her card on his desk today and her name all over his calendar. He's been seeing her every week, for ages. Every Thursday morning.'

'Bloody hell,' said Lucas. 'Do you think she knew you were his wife when she started coming to your yoga classes?'

'I don't know,' said Polly, 'and wondering about that has been making me feel crazy all day. But the great thing is that – thanks to you, my wonderful brave boy – now I can ask her.'

She smiled across the table at him, tears springing into her eyes – tears of relief, that some of the gaping holes in her life were finally going to be sewn up.

For a moment she just sat and enjoyed that feeling. She'd ring Maxine's practice in the morning and make an appointment, that was the best way to do it. Keep it professional.

Lucas ordered chocolate ice cream for pudding – saying he thought he could probably find space for that – and Polly asked for another glass of wine. It wasn't like her to have three, but this was no ordinary evening, she told herself, and they were walking home.

They chatted more generally for a while, until other questions started to intrude into Polly's thinking, too urgent to ignore.

'I've got to ask you something else about your father,' she said.

'Fire away,' said Lucas.

'Did he give you any indication of whether he's planning to come back home ever? It's only two weeks until Lori and Rich are coming over and I'm going to have to tell them something.'

'No,' said Lucas. 'He just said Maxine will explain everything you need to know and we'll have to make do with that. But he did say Rich has been in touch with him about the visit and he's told him he'll be away on a research trip, so they already know he's not going to be here.'

'So has he really gone this time?' said Polly. 'Or is he hiding somewhere else in plain sight?'

'He's gone,' said Lucas. 'I've had it confirmed by the all-knowing entity. Maureen has confirmed that he's gone to Turkey. For a month. She booked the tickets for him.'

Polly sipped her wine, processing it all. She was beginning to feel like she needed an external hard drive to store some of the data. It was too much for one human brain.

Then it occurred to her what would make it all easier to deal with: seeing Chum. She didn't need to tell him about it, just being with him would make her feel better.

So when Lucas nipped off to the loo she sent Chum a text asking if he felt like a walk and had an almost immediate reply: Tomorrow?

Friday, 1 April

Polly's heart was beating so fast she thought it might be visible through her clothes as she stood just inside the sliding glass doors of Rockham Park, waiting for the chugging sound of Chum's diesel engine.

She'd arrived early to have lunch with Daphne to be sure she'd be able to leave her in time to meet Chum at 3 p.m. Although it was Friday, he hadn't been able to make it over for his usual lunch date with Bill, but he was coming to collect her.

She was already feeling a bit woozy from sleep deprivation, after spending the night obsessing over whether she should have had the meeting with Maxine before she made arrangements to meet up with Chum again. But in the end she'd decided she had to see him first. She couldn't work out what was morally correct any more. It was all too bewildering. And she needed the boost of some Chum company to get her through it.

She fidgeted from foot to foot, feeling as though time was stretching as she waited, but a glance at the clock on the wall behind her confirmed that it was only five-past-three. You couldn't really call it late yet, but why wasn't he here? She wanted to drum her feet like a frustrated toddler.

She stepped forward so the automatic doors slid open and put her head out into the fresh air, as though that would somehow speed him up. Then, as she stepped back again, she finally heard the tick of the Land Rover's engine.

At exactly that moment she felt a hand on her shoulder and heard her mother's voice.

'Polly darling?' she said. 'You're still here. I thought you'd left right after lunch.'

Polly spun round to look at her, gaping like a fish.

'I was just going to have a rest,' Daphne was saying, 'but then I thought it was such a nice afternoon I'd come down again and sit on the terrace outside for a little while, and then I saw you were still here.'

'I, um, well ...' Polly was saying, when she heard the glass doors swish open again, and the smile that broke across her mother's face said it all.

Polly swung round to see Chum, just as he stepped over the threshold and took in the scenario.

'Hello, both of you,' he said, collecting himself brilliantly. 'How are you, Daphne?'

He stepped forward and kissed her on both cheeks.

'Hello, Edward,' she said. 'Have you come to see Bill? He's out on the terrace, doing the crossword. I was just about to join him.'

Polly was still mute.

'Hi, Hippolyta,' said Chum, kissing her cheeks and giving her left hand – the side Daphne couldn't see – a reassuring squeeze. Polly's innards danced.

'Yes, great,' he said, 'we can all have a cup of tea together and then Hippolyta and I are going for a walk, aren't we?'

'Yes,' said Polly, her voice restored. 'With the dogs.'

'Oh, how nice,' said Daphne. 'It's just the day for it.'

'Yes,' said Polly, 'that's what I thought. That's why I just texted Edward to see ...'

He nudged her, as he walked over towards Daphne.

'Don't overexplain,' he whispered as he passed, then stopped next to Daphne and crooked his left arm for her to take.

Then he looked back to Polly and stuck out his right elbow, so he had one of them on each side as they walked through to the coffee room towards the French windows that led onto the terrace.

'Look what I've got, Bill,' said Chum, as they stepped outside, 'two beauties.'

'Oh, I say,' said Bill, standing up. 'I think that's a bit greedy. Are you all coming to join me? How delightful.'

Chum pulled out one of the cane chairs for Daphne, and Polly hovered, not knowing what to do with herself.

'Right,' said Chum. 'Polly and I will get the tea. I think we know who takes what between us.'

She practically ran inside and he came in after her, grinning, and wrapped his arms round her, backing her into the sideboard and pressing his body against hers.

'Chum!' she said, squealing. 'They'll see us.'

'Oh, who cares?' he said, nuzzling her neck in a way that made her feel quite faint. 'But they won't, anyway. Not looking from the bright sunshine into the dark room, and with the glass door carefully closed by *moi*. Bill's half-blind anyway.'

Polly giggled. 'And Daphne's too vain to wear specs,' she said.

Then she couldn't say anything else, because Chum was kissing her.

'Just relax, it's all fine,' he said, letting go of her and starting to put cups on saucers, teabags in cups. 'Act normally. They know we're friends, they know the dogs are mad about each other, and if they do figure out there might be a little frisson between us as well ...' He wiggled his eyebrows suggestively. '... I think they'll be delighted.'

Polly couldn't help laughing. But she was still nervous, and could feel her face creasing into some kind of rictus spasm.

Chum looked at her, his own expression more serious. He took hold of both her hands. 'What are you so worried about, my sweet pea?' he said.

Polly couldn't say it, she just sighed heavily.

'The husband aspect?' he asked.

She nodded.

'Bill doesn't have the foggiest idea about your marital situation,' said Chum. 'And as your mother hasn't seen or heard of your husband for the past three months, I imagine she might have an inkling that things are a little ... shifted, in that area? Have you talked to her about it?'

'I have, actually,' said Polly.

'What did she say?' asked Chum.

Polly couldn't help laughing. She felt like she was on an emotional see-saw.

'She said she never liked him,' Polly said.

'Great!' said Chum. 'I love Daphne more every time I see her. Right, let's get this tea out to them. Your mum takes hers black, doesn't she? You bring the biscuits, I'll follow on with the hot beverages.'

Now Chum had calmed her down, Polly started to enjoy herself. Bill was always good company and Daphne was at her sparkling best, enjoying the presence of two gallant chaps to reflect her glamour back to her.

Polly was just happy to be with Chum, watching him interact with the others. Apart from the Easter lunch and the odd chat with the olds over coffee, she hadn't spent that much time with him when other people were there, and seeing him teasing Bill and being interested in what Daphne had to say – even when she was going on a bit too long about a shoot on

Tobago with Parkie – made her like him even more. He had a very appealing, confident ease, not at all arrogant, just an air of feeling comfortable with himself and others.

Polly couldn't help thinking that David would have been so different in the same situation. Not rude, just not very happy to be there, and even though he would try to fit in, Polly had always been aware that people picked up on his unease.

Had he been sitting with some terrible secret the whole time? Was that what she was going to find out from Maxine? From what he'd told Lucas, it seemed so.

Polly pushed the thought away, irritated that anything to do with David had come into her mind at all in that happy moment. She'd be seeing Maxine soon enough. She was allowed to put it to the back of her mind until then; she had given herself that permission.

'So, Hippolyta,' she heard Chum saying, realising she'd tuned out for a moment.

'Yes?' she said, shaking her head a little as she came to.

'Shall we go and have that walk, then?' he said, the edges of his mouth tweaked up in his naughtiest grin. 'The dogs will be getting very restless.'

'Yes, that would be super,' said Polly, then tried not to laugh at herself. 'Super'? Where had that come from? Super-duper.

'Good plan,' said Bill, 'make the most of this lovely afternoon.'

Chum stood up and raised his eyebrows meaningfully at Polly, who stumbled to her feet, nearly landing face down on the coffee table. She could see he was trying not to laugh.

'Bye, Bill,' said Polly, leaning down to peck him on the cheek.

Then, as she leaned down to kiss her mother, Daphne took hold of her upper arm in a tight grip.

'Well done, darling,' she said. 'Go get him.'

Polly was so surprised she forgot the kiss and stood up, blinking at her mother in amazement. Daphne smiled broadly and closed both eyes at her, like a contented cat.

Chum was laughing as they bowled along the country lane outside Rockham Park at his usual reckless speed, the two dogs lying happily together behind the metal guard in the back.

'You are so funny,' he was saying. 'You could do slapstick. Is that the result of all your years of yoga? Expressing everything you're feeling through physical movement?'

Without warning he suddenly wrenched the vehicle over into a small layby and stopped, pulling the handbrake up violently.

'Actually,' he said, 'I think I need to express my own feelings through physical movement right now.'

In what seemed like one action, he unclipped his seat belt and Polly's, and pulled her into his arms, kissing her.

'Mmmmm,' he whispered. 'How I've been longing to do that again.'

He pulled back to shrug his jacket off and then looked at her with his head on one side.

'Shall we put the seat back down?' he said.

Polly giggled and felt down the side of the seat to find the lever. The back of it flopped flat and Chum half-climbed over to her side of the car, kissing her and running his hands over her body.

Then he pulled her jumper up and started kissing her tummy, from her navel down a little and then up again, brushing his lips over her skin, biting it very gently, then kissing it again. Polly heard herself start to pant as wave of desire swept through her.

Then his face was up by hers, kissing her, then pulling back, looking into her eyes, before kissing her again.

'Bloody hell,' he said, 'you turn me into a madman.'

Then he glanced away for a moment and Polly saw his face crease into a grin.

'Look,' he said, gesturing to the back of the car with his head.

Polly turned her head and saw Digger and Artemis standing with their noses pressed to the metal grid, watching them keenly, tails wagging. Digger saw her and barked his quick friendly greeting.

'I think they approve,' said Chum, leaning on his elbow and gazing down at Polly. He traced the lines of her face with his left forefinger, then kissed the end of her nose.

'This is lovely,' he said, 'but I think I'd like to be somewhere more comfortable with you … and less public.'

Polly smiled in agreement. He kissed her quickly on the lips and clambered back into his seat. She flipped hers up and they set off again.

'Would you like to come to my place?' said Chum, sounding uncharacteristically shy. 'Not Hanley Hall, sadly, but where I really live. It's rather more modest, but it's cosy.'

'I'd love to,' said Polly, with no hesitation, thinking she would have quite happily gone to a tent in a desert with him.

They drove on in silence, Chum holding Polly's hand tightly on his knee, only letting go of it to change gear. It made his driving even more terrifying, but Polly didn't care, feeling as though she were floating along on a magic carpet. Nothing seemed quite real, but everything was wonderful.

'Not far now,' said Chum, turning quickly to smile at her, as he veered left and they drove through a small, pretty village.

Chum raised his hand in greeting to a couple of people they passed.

'That's my local,' he said as they drove past a thatched pub. 'I might take you in there later. Show you off.'

Polly smiled, assuming he was joking.

A couple of miles along the lane on the other side of the village, they came to a cluster of farm buildings.

'Here we are,' said Chum, coming to a stop in front of a crossbar gate.

Polly jumped out to open it, then followed the Land Rover up a short track to where Chum had stopped just outside a large gateway set into a lovely old red-brick building.

She caught up as Chum was letting the dogs out of the back. Digger pushed his nose against her hand for reassurance and she patted him, letting him know it was fine for him to go with his doggy friend. The two of them raced off and Chum came and put his arm round Polly's waist.

'This is where I live and work,' he said, walking her through the gate into a quadrangle, which she realised had stables on three sides. 'It's a livery yard. A sort of equine boarding house.'

Horses heads appeared over the half-doors, looking out to see who was there.

'They can smell me,' said Chum. 'I'll just see who's here from my team; they're probably in the tack room. You can introduce yourself to the horses – their names are on the stalls.'

Chum strode off and Polly went over to the nearest horse, quite a small black pony. It shook its mane when it saw her coming and pushed its head towards her. Polly stroked its head, breathing in deeply, relishing the warm horse smell, mixed with grassy notes from the hay in its feed basket and a tang of ammonia from the straw on the floor.

'Hello, Freddie,' she said, looking at the name over the door. 'You're lovely, aren't you? I'm sorry I haven't got anything for you.'

She scratched him behind his ears for a bit then moved on to the next stall, working her way along the row. Most of the horses were inquisitive and happy to be stroked and talked to, except for one grey, which flinched away from her touch and skittered against the floor with its hooves.

There was a loud whinny from the far left stall and Polly could see a beautiful bay, tossing its black mane and seeming to demand attention. She went over and saw the name 'Sorrel' on the plate.

'So you're Sorrel,' said Polly, bringing her hand up slowly so the horse could smell it. Then Sorrel pushed her nose against Polly and she stroked it very gently, loving the velvety feeling under her hand. The horse stepped back suddenly, tossing her splendid mane and whinnying, her metal shoes striking the brick floor, then she came back and pressed her head against Polly's hand again.

'You are beautiful,' said Polly, 'and absolutely huge. Look at you. No wonder he loves you.'

Polly hadn't heard Chum come up behind her until he spoke.

'That's a very lovely picture,' he said. 'She likes you, Hippolyta. She doesn't let many people stroke her like that, especially when she hasn't been formally introduced. Let me do that now: Polly, this is Sorrel. Sorrel, this is Polly.'

'Hello, Sorrel,' said Polly, stroking down the horse's long shiny neck. 'You are very fine and very big. What is she? Sixteen hands something?'

'Very good,' he said. 'I'm impressed. She's sixteen hands three. So you do know something about horses.'

'Like I told you, I had riding lessons when I was a kid. I loved it, but my mum wasn't keen for me to take it seriously. She said it was bad for my skin being out in all weathers, and I might get a big bum.'

Chum laughed and the horse's head appeared over the door again.

'Hello, lovely one,' he said, kissing its cheek. 'Don't get jealous, Polly, but I do love my horse.'

'She's stunning,' said Polly. 'I don't blame you.'

'I can't promise she won't get jealous of you, though.'

He fished around in his inside pocket and produced an apple.

'Give her this, it'll help.'

Polly took it and saw Chum's eyes crease in approval as she put it on her hand and held it out, fingers flat. She felt the tickle of the horse's dry lips on her palm and stroked behind Sorrel's ears with her other hand. The horse nudged her gently with her head.

'She wants another one,' said Chum, 'but bribes aside, she definitely likes you. This makes me happy.'

'And my children liked you, which makes me happy,' said Polly.

Chum put his arm around her waist, kissing the top of her head. She heard a commotion behind them and turned round to see two young women in jodphurs and boots filling buckets with water from a hose. Polly could see they were pink from giggling and were sneaking looks at her and Edward. One of them dropped a bucket and the water splashed everywhere, making them both laugh more.

'They're my stable girls,' said, Edward, smiling indulgently. 'Sophie and Lottie. They're good eggs. I've just arranged for them to stay late tonight and lock up for me after the last riders have gone.'

'They seem very amused by something,' said Polly.

Chum laughed. 'Seeing me with a female who doesn't have four legs, probably,' he said. 'Right, I've given myself the afternoon and evening off, so let's make the most of it.'

He gave Sorrel one last pat.

'Goodbye, beautiful, see you in the morning,' he said, then he turned to Polly, pulling her closer to him. 'Hello, also beautiful.'

With his arm still round Polly's waist, he turned back towards the girls, who were now lugging the buckets of water over to the far row of stalls, but with their attention still glued to Edward and Polly.

'See you tomorrow, girls,' he called out.

'Bye, Edward,' replied the blonde one. 'Have a good night.'

The two of them turned away, clearly helpless with laughter.

'What are they like?' said Chum, shaking his head fondly.

'Young?' suggested Polly. 'I can remember feeling like that.'

'You make me feel like that again,' said Chum, and taking her hand he led her towards a small gate on the far side of the yard, whistling for the dogs as he went.

Chum's house turned out to be a small red-brick cottage with white-painted windows, a hundred metres or so on the other side of the gate.

'This used to be the head gardener's gaff,' he said, pushing open the door, which wasn't locked. 'When it was still part of a working estate. Now it's Chez Chum.'

The dogs raced in first and Artemis stood by a closed door looking intently at Chum, willing him to open it. He did, and the lurcher ran through, keenly followed by Digger.

'It's like she's showing him round,' said Chum, laughing. '"Here's my water bowl, this is where I sleep, these are my toys ..."'

He hung their coats on hooks in the narrow hallway then took her through to a small sitting room. It felt quite damp, and everything looked a bit shabby – without any 'chic' aspect. The furniture was a random mix of bits and pieces, and none of it looked personal.

'I'll get the fire going,' said Chum, kneeling at the hearth and starting to roll up pieces of newspaper. 'Would you like some more tea? Actually, I think I've had enough of that for today; it's only four o'clock, but shall we have a drink? It is Friday.'

'I'll get them,' said Polly, spotting a shelf with bottles on it. 'Gin?'

Chum gave her a thumbs-up.

'The kitchen's through that door there,' he said, pointing behind her. 'There's tonic in the fridge.'

Polly walked into the kitchen and stood for a moment looking round, wondering where the glasses would be. It was pretty grim, and didn't look as though it had been redecorated since the 1980s. The cupboard doors were an ugly oatmeal brown, the finish peeling off at the corners. The tap was dripping into a stainless-steel sink and there was one cereal bowl, one spoon and one mug in the drainer.

It was the sad kitchen of someone who ate breakfast alone every day – and came back later to find it all exactly as they'd left it in the morning. Just what hers had been like before Shirlee had made it into a bustling hub of fun and friendship.

She remembered how cosy Granny's parlour had been at Hanley Hall. And that dining room with seating for forty people. Poor Chum indeed.

She'd just found some dismal tumblers, which looked as though they'd been free from a service station, when Chum walked in. He stopped in the doorway holding a half-made paper spill in one hand.

'This isn't working, is it, beauty?' he said, chucking the piece of newspaper onto the countertop.

Polly shook her head slowly, not wanting to hurt his feelings. He came over and put his arms round her.

'You know it's not my place,' he said. 'I had a lovely house on the estate at Hanley Hall, but my sister-in-law changed the locks. All my stuff's still in there; that's just one of the battles I'm fighting against her. My friend who owns the stables here very kindly offered this cottage with the job and I haven't bothered getting anywhere better because I'm still hoping to get my own place back. It's the second son's official res ... supposed to be mine to live in until I drop off my perch, but Flavia doesn't seem to think laws apply to her.'

He pulled her closer, resting his head against hers, and they stood for a few moments saying nothing, the silence broken only by the tap dripping into the sink.

'I've had an idea,' said Chum suddenly, pulling back and looking Polly up and down, nodding. 'Yeah, this will work. Just give me one minute.'

He headed out of the kitchen at speed and Polly heard his feet clatter up the staircase, while she sat on the arm of the sofa watching Digger and Artemis pulling on two ends of a rubber pheasant.

'Do you think that's your pheasant, Digger?' she said. 'Yours is at home, that's Artie's toy and you'll just have to share it.'

She was about to intervene in the canine squabble, when Chum appeared in the doorway. He'd changed into a pair of black jodhpurs, with riding boots and gaiters up to his knees. Polly felt her eyes snap open wide.

He took her jacket down from the peg, holding it out for her to put on.

'Come on,' he said. 'We're going for a ride.'

~

Polly closed her eyes and thought of nothing but the sound of Sorrel's hooves drumming across the ground, the fresh air on her face and Chum's arms around her, holding the reins.

Riding with someone so completely confident on a horse was like experiencing it for the first time. She opened her eyes again, feeling exhilarated by the speed, the beautiful countryside and the wonderfully bracing air. It seemed purer at the height of a horse's back somehow, enhanced by Sorrel's warm smell, the green note of grass as it was crushed beneath the cantering hooves, and a faint trace of Equipage from Chum.

'You all right?' said Chum, into her ear. 'Not finding bareback too uncomfortable? How do you like Sorrel?'

'I'm fine, and she's magnificent,' Polly said, leaning back into him and loving the feel of his body behind her, his thighs gripping hers.

He steered to the right, up a gentle slope, and as they crested the rise Polly gasped with surprise, looking down onto a wooded valley with a lake stretching away from them.

Chum reined Sorrel to a halt and let her graze while they took in the view.

Polly turned round to look at him.

'It's so beautiful,' she said. 'Where are we?'

He pointed with his finger, resting his chin on her shoulder.

'If you look just to the right of that big copse down there, you can see Hanley Hall in the distance,' he said. 'Capability Brown put this lake in.'

'Is it the one we could see from Granny's parlour? In the moonlight?' asked Polly.

'That's it,' said Chum. 'We're looking at it from the other side here.'

He pulled Sorrel's head up and clicked his teeth for her to walk on, and they made their way down the slope towards the lake. As they got closer, Polly could see a white building through the trees.

'Is that where we're going?' she asked.

'Yep,' said Chum. 'It's one of the Hanley follies. This one is called the Temple of the Four Winds. It's my favourite.'

When they arrived at the building, he jumped off and helped Polly down, then tucked the reins in at the horse's neck and left her under the trees.

'Will she be all right just loose like that?' asked Polly.

Chum nodded. 'As long as she's got grass and knows I'm near, she'll be perfectly content.'

He led the way round to the front of the building, stopping by the door to lift up a rock, which revealed a large old key. He grinned at Polly, holding it up.

'This key has been under that rock as long as I can remember,' he said. 'Probably since they finished building this thing in 1756, actually.'

'I wonder how many generations of your family have known where to find it,' said Polly.

'All the naughty ones,' said Chum, turning the key in the lock and opening the double doors.

Polly walked in to find a circular room with a domed ceiling painted dark blue, with a compass carved into it.

Alternating with domed windows, there were niches in the walls containing classical style statues. A low stone bench ran round the perimeter of the room.

Chum opened double doors to the left and pulled out some rugs.

'We can sit on one of these,' he said, 'and wrap ourselves up in the others, if they're not too stinky, and look at the lake.'

'So you always keep a stash of bedding in there, do you?' said Polly.

'There's all sorts in here, have a look.'

Polly went over and saw that the small room, illuminated by windows to the rear, was full of old garden furniture, barbecues and beach mats.

'There's an inflatable dinghy in the room on the other side,' said Chum. 'Fishing rods, kayaks. My brother and I spent many happy days here in our youth. Pretty funny, when you think of the house we lived in, but we loved it down here. One summer holiday we camped here like savages, just going home to steal more supplies. We'd paddle across the lake in our kayaks and try to get in and out of the house without anyone seeing us. I wonder if parents would let their kids do that now? We had our horses down here with us too. Good times. The house was open to the public then, but not this part of the grounds.'

He went over to the door and gazed out over the lake, looking wistful.

'I miss Charlie so much,' he said. 'He was my best friend, and this place makes me feel connected to him, remembering the boys we were. Watching the sun go down over the water here is pretty special. It was a spur-of-the-moment idea tonight, so it's not set up, but we'll do it properly some time.'

If the oligarch doesn't get here first, thought Polly, and put hot tubs in.

Chum made a little nest with the blankets on the steps of the building and sat down, smiling at Polly.

'Come and get cosy,' he said.

She sat down, too, and he arranged a blanket around her shoulders, then started rummaging around inside his Barbour.

'I think that game pocket of yours is like Mary Poppins's carpet bag,' said Polly. 'What's in there now? A standard lamp? An aspidistra?'

Chum smiled and held up a hip flask.

'Brandy,' he said. 'Want some?'

She took a sip and he had a deep swig, wiping his mouth on the back of his hand. Then he turned to her, and taking her face in his hands, started to kiss her.

As his tongue slid into her mouth, Polly felt everything melt away, until she was just in that moment, in that place with him.

And, as always, when Chum's mouth touched hers, that spark ignited inside her, so that very quickly, the kissing escalated into something much wilder, like they were trying to consume each other. Fully clothed, on a very hard surface, in damp evening air ...

They broke apart and looked at each other, swallowing hard, chests heaving. Chum started laughing.

'What happens?' he said. 'I kiss you and turn into a raging beast.'

'I don't know,' said Polly. 'But I like it.'

'I like it a lot,' said Chum.

He pulled her close and they sat, Polly resting her head on his shoulder, just gazing out over the tranquil water, with birds flitting in and out of the trees and moorhens paddling past. Polly closed her eyes and concentrated on the smell scape. The rich damp wood from the ancient trees was almost spicy. The smooth sweetness of a large body of fresh water.

Sorrel's lovely scent on both of them. And the tang of the brandy.

Then Chum started to laugh. Polly lifted her head and looked at him.

'What's funny?' she asked.

'I've just remembered one night when we were about eleven and nine, Charlie and I camped here with some friends – four other boys. We sat round a fire – you see that circle of stones down there? That was our fire spot. Anyway, we sat round it swapping stories and toasting marshmallows and all that and we made a solemn vow ... that we'd never bring any girls here. So I guess I've broken that.

'Sorry, Charlie,' he said to the sky. 'Mind you, I bet he brought loads of hot babes here. Charlie was a player. And then some.'

'And you weren't?' said Polly.

'Not like him – he was much better looking than me and you know, the Earl thing, some girls really go for that.'

'There were a lot of girls at St Andrews who seemed quite happy with your status of one remove from Earl,' said Polly.

'Well, I'd like to think it was my magnetic personality they were attracted to,' he said.

Polly chuckled.

'I do admit I had a good time up there,' continued Chum, opening the hip flask again and passing it to Polly. 'You'd be mad not to – and you weren't short of dance partners yourself, Miss Hippolyta Masterson-Mackay. I can remember one party, I spent the whole night trying to find a moment when I could get you to dance with me. It was my goal for the evening, like a mantra, but every time I saw my opening some other git got there first. Usually one of those annoying handsome actor types.'

Polly laughed. There had been a number of those.

'And they were all such bloody good dancers,' said Chum. 'I'm a terrible dancer.'

'No, you're not. I'm sure I boogied next to you loads of times.'

'Maybe next to me, but never with me,' said Chum.

'Well, every time I saw you at a party,' she said, 'and believe me, I did look – you had some breathtakingly pretty willowy blonde on your arm. Those girls with ankles so impossibly tiny you wondered how they didn't snap.'

Now Chum laughed.

'I did have a bit of a type – but was that before or after that night on the beach?' he asked, smiling at her so sweetly Polly took his face between her hands and kissed him, very, very slowly.

'Mmmmm,' said Chum, growling slightly and holding her tight in his arms. 'That's exactly why I wanted to kiss you again so much after that night. Exactly that.'

'So why didn't you?' asked Polly.

'I tried. Like I said, I stalked you around the cafes and pubs of St Andrews and once in the library ...'

'I remember that!' said Polly. 'I was in the stacks and you suddenly appeared.'

'It wasn't accidental,' said Chum. 'Took me ages to find you. And I didn't really know my way around the library. Wasn't in there much.'

Polly laughed.

'And I thought you were mortified to have bumped into me,' she said. 'Some ghastly common girl you'd kissed while under the influence and now couldn't get away from. I was so embarrassed, I legged it.'

'I do remember,' said Chum. 'I stood there like a wally, after you'd gone, smelling my breath, trying to work out what I'd done wrong.'

'What would you have said, if I hadn't run off?' asked Polly.

'I was going to suggest we had coffee,' he said, doing his tight-lipped, sad smile.

'Oh,' she said, clasping his hands. 'That's so sweet. Why was I such an idiot? I would have liked to have had coffee with you more than anything. And I just thought you hated me.'

'Star crossed lovers, eh?' said Chum. 'What an opportunity we missed.'

He paused, looking back at the lake and then at her.

'We'll have to start back soon,' he said. 'The light's going and I really need to put Sorrel away, but let's not let this one go by, Hippolyta. Having another chance with you is the best thing that's happened to me for years and I don't want to lose you again.'

Polly put her arm round him and squeezed him tight.

'Will you stay with me tonight?' he asked, very quietly. 'It won't seem so grim at the cottage with low lighting. I'll get a good fire going and make some dinner. It'll be lovely – just to be together. Finally.'

Polly hesitated before replying. She wanted to stay with him, so much. More than she could ever say – and not just because of her overwhelming physical desire for him. Her feelings already went much deeper than that, but she knew she still couldn't take it any further than the advanced-snogging level.

Chum was looking at her with his head on one side, waiting for her answer, an expression of uncertainty coming into his eyes.

'It's fine, if you feel you have to go.' he said. 'Your kids ...'

'It's not that,' said Polly quickly. 'They've gone back to uni. I'd love to stay, it's just ... I can't take things any further with you, Chum. Not yet. Not until I've found out what's going on with David.'

She paused, looking down at her hands, gathering her thoughts. She had to get this right.

'I want to be with you Chum, but as my full self – not with part of my head wondering about what might have been going on with my husband. As you said, we've been given this amazing second chance and I don't want to mess it up with unfinished business elsewhere. Does that make any sense?'

'Absolutely,' said Chum, nodding. 'You're in a very strange situation, Hippolyta, and it's bound to affect everything. I thought my life was complicated, with all the legal stuff, but at least I know exactly what I'm up against. It must be so difficult not knowing what's actually happening.'

'Well, that's the thing,' said Polly. 'I've got the means now to find out what it's all been about. Lucas went to see his father yesterday—'

'I thought you didn't know where he is.'

'We didn't,' said Polly, 'but my brave son followed him from work, to the flat where's he living ...' She made a decision not to complicate things by telling Chum all the other stuff about that. 'And he made him talk.'

'He's a good man, that Lucas,' said Chum. 'But that must have been very hard for him. His dad ...'

Polly nodded.

'Yeah, Lucas has grown up a lot this year. He's had to. So my husband – David – told Lucas that I had his permission to ask his shrink to tell me what it's all about.'

'His shrink?'

'Yes,' said Polly. 'It seems he's been seeing someone for over a year, at least – and the really nuts thing is I know his therapist. She comes to my yoga class – or used to.'

'Gosh,' said Chum. Didn't she know her patient is your husband?'

'I don't know,' said Polly. 'That's one of the things I'm going to ask her. I'm dreading that conversation, but I have to do it. I can't carry on living in limbo like this.'

'I don't think I can either,' said Chum, 'just to be selfish. But seriously, it must be awful for all of you, and at least you'll know why. When are you going to do it?'

'As soon as possible,' said Polly. 'I want to get it over with.'

'Promise me one thing,' he said. 'When you make that appointment, you'll tell me? I want to be there for you, in case you need someone afterwards.'

'Thank you, Chum,' she said. 'That means a lot. I've felt more alone at times than I thought was possible since this all started, and knowing you are there for me now is just … well, it's wonderful.'

He pulled her close and she climbed onto his lap, looking out over the lake into the deepening twilight, relishing the peace.

Chum broke the silence first.

'There's one more thing I have to tell you, Hippolyta Masterson-Mackay,' he said, lifting her chin up with his finger, so he was looking into her eyes.

'Whatever it turns out is going on with David, you need to know this. If he decides after all is revealed that he wants to come home to you again, it's not a done deal any more. He's going to have to fight me for you.'

Monday, 4 April

It was Monday morning and Polly was sitting at her desk feeling numb.

She'd called Maxine's office half an hour ago, and the earliest appointment they could offer her had been in six weeks' time. Then the receptionist had rung back to say they'd been able to find an unexpected 'emergency slot' for her and she could come in at 1 p.m today.

She'd been going to ask Clemmie and Lucas to come with her, but now she had no choice: it was going to be her, solo. Remembering what Chum had said about telling him when the meeting was happening, she sent him a quick text. He replied immediately:

> Be strong, my beauty. It will be difficult – but it's always better to know what beast you are fighting xxx

Polly's brain felt scrambled. It was all happening too fast. She'd only gone to David's flat and found Maxine's card four days before; she needed more time to process it all. But then again, she reminded herself, she'd had over three months to get used to the idea that something had gone very peculiar with her husband. Chum was right: she needed to know what.

She slumped onto the desk, putting her head in her hands. Then she sat up again and clicked on the world clocks on her computer. It was 10.30 a.m. in London, 8.30 p.m. in Sydney. The perfect time to ring Lori, to tell her what was going on and why she'd been avoiding her calls.

Polly hit FaceTime on Lori's contact and Lori answered immediately.

'Hello, darls,' she said. 'So you've finally remembered I'm alive. I've tried you so many times.'

'Sorry, Loz,' said Polly.

She hesitated for a moment, then took a deep breath in.

'Things have been a little difficult,' she said. 'I've wanted to tell you, but—'

'All this shit with David?' said Lori, the picture of her on the phone showing her raising a large glass of white wine to Polly. 'Cheers. I'm surprised you haven't got one of these on the go yourself, after what you've been going through – even though it is ten in the morning or something over there.'

'You know?' said Polly. 'How? What?'

'David rang Rich last week,' said Lori.

'What did he say?' asked Polly. Lucas had told her David had rung Rich, but she'd assumed it was to fob him off with some lie about being away on a research trip while they were over.

'He said you two were having a trial separation,' said Lori. 'So he wouldn't be at your place when we come next week.'

'He said what?' said Polly, springing to her feet she was so outraged.

'That you'd decided to have some time out. Now the kids are gone, there's no glue between you any more and all that, he needed some space – the usual male mid-life crisis shit. What's your take on it?'

Polly sat down again, too stunned to say anything. Was this what Maxine was going to tell her? That David felt they should have a trial separation now the kids had left home? Surely he could have told her that himself?

She laughed bitterly.

'That's almost hilarious,' she said. 'It's a long story and I'm really looking forward to telling you in person when you get here next week – with bottles of wine involved, if not crates – but I can't stand to go into it all now.'

And I need to decide what I'm going to leave out first. Like Chum, for instance.

'But suffice to say,' she continued, 'that's absolutely not the story as I see it. We never discussed having a "trial" separation, he just told me he was going and left. He hasn't spoken to me – well, not willingly, or normally – or the kids, since 20 December. He's living in the apartment he had when I met him. Turns out he's kept it on all these years, without telling me.'

Lori looked uncharacteristically fazed for a moment.

'Are you frigging kidding me?' she said eventually. 'That's seriously messed up. Poor Polls. What a sneaky bastard. He hasn't had another woman in there the whole time has he? Or a bloke?'

'That would be the obvious explanation,' said Polly, 'but I can't see any evidence of it. I went to the flat when he was out – I still had the bloody keys, which I'd kept all these years for sentimental reasons, like the dope I am – and it was very much the sad, overly tidy apartment of an anally retentive bachelor.'

'So do you reckon he's just gone, you know, kookalooka?' said Lori.

'Yes,' said Polly, laughing. 'I'd say that was the appropriate clinical term. He's gone kookalooka, and I'm going to see his shrink this afternoon, so she can tell me all about it.'

Lori shook her head and took another sip of wine.

'Sure you don't want to get a glass?' she said, with her head on her side and her eyes screwed up, one of the characteristic expressions that Polly had always loved.

'When you're here, I'll be happy to drink white wine from the moment we wake up,' said Polly, 'but today I've got to keep my head on straight, to hear what his therapist has to say.'

'Are the kids going with you?' asked Lori.

Polly shook her head.

'It's all very last-minute, so I'll have to go on my own, there isn't time for them to get here. But it will be fine.'

'Are you sure?' asked Lori. 'Couldn't you put it off until someone can go with you?'

'I'll be OK,' said Polly. 'I just want to get it over with. I'll ring them straight afterwards and tell them about it.'

And Chum, she thought. I'll ring Chum too.

They talked a bit longer and Polly rang off feeling much stronger, and very happy that she was going to be seeing her best pal in just a few days.

All she needed to do was to get through that afternoon.

'I'm sorry.'

Those were the first words Maxine said when Polly sat down in her office.

'Sorry for what?' asked Polly.

'Sorry that I couldn't tell you what was going on with your husband,' said Maxine.

'But when did you know he was my husband?' said Polly. 'That's what's been driving me nuts. Well, one of the things.

Have you been sitting in my kitchen all this time, knowing what's going on with David and not telling me?'

'No,' said Maxine. 'I only made the connection a couple of weeks ago, when we were having that breakfast with your kids and Guy and it all came out. That's why I haven't been back to yoga since then. I didn't know what to do, it's so awkward.'

Polly mulled it over for a moment, taking a sip from the glass of water Maxine's PA had given her.

'But I still don't understand how you didn't realise I was your client's wife right away – surely there aren't many yoga teachers in North London called Polly,' she said, trying to keep her voice steady. 'Married to a historian called David, with kids called Clemmie and Lucas? I would have thought that would have narrowed it down from the very first time you came to yoga.'

Maxine sighed very deeply.

'That's one of the distressing things,' she said. 'He's never talked about Polly, Clemmie and Lucas.'

'What?' said Polly, wondering if she would ever find her way out of this maze of complications. 'He's pretended he's not married for however long he's been seeing you?'

'It's over two years now,' said Maxine. 'And your GP referred him to me, if you're wondering how he came to be my patient. She sends a lot of people to this clinic And he didn't pretend he wasn't married, but he always referred to you as Jane, and the children as Susan and John. I did think they were unusual names for modern kids.'

Polly sat for a moment trying to take it in. Susan and John? Jane? It was almost funny. Almost.

'And I didn't even have the clue of your being a yoga teacher,' Maxine continued. 'He said you were an aromatherapist.'

'What?' said Polly. She felt a sudden flash of anger and had to restrain herself to avoid taking it out on Maxine. It was David who had denied her very identity, Maxine was just the dupe.

'Once again, I can only say I'm sorry,' said Maxine.

'It's not your fault,' said Polly, 'and maybe there is a tiny crumb of comfort for me in this, because it means it's not just me he's lied to, he's lied systematically to the therapist he was paying to see. Is this something people do when they see a psychotherapist – lie about every aspect of themselves? Doesn't that defeat the purpose?'

'It's never happened to me before, as far as I know,' said Maxine, 'but it's not unheard of, particularly with conditions like David's. When there's a lot of shame, they try to block out everything that matters most to them by not talking about it. Giving you and his children false names would have allowed him a sense of separation between you three and what he came to me for help with. But I should have picked up on it, and I'm very disappointed in myself that I didn't trust my instinct that those names sounded odd.'

Polly licked her lips. Her mouth had gone dry and the glass of water wasn't helping. The false names had really brought it home to her.

'Is he very ill?' she asked quietly.

Maxine sighed.

'He's not great, Polly,' she said. 'What I have to tell you is difficult – but I know that what you've been living with since he left like that has been very hard too.'

'It has been a testing time,' said Polly, feeling the tears prickling.

Not again, she thought. I'm turning into a human fountain. Who haven't I cried on recently?

Maxine pushed a box of tissues towards her.

'I've been doing a lot of this,' she said, pulling one out.

'I'm not surprised,' said Maxine.

'I should have come to see you when you offered that time, to talk about my mum. We might have found out this connection a lot sooner.'

Maxine smiled sadly.

'I don't think we would have,' she said. 'David is a very smart man, as you know, and he covered his tracks impeccably. He didn't slip up on those names once. I've checked all my notes.'

They sat there for a moment. Polly felt she could hear the the blood rushing in her veins. It was her last moment of not knowing, and she felt as though she were standing on the edge of a cliff about to jump off.

'So what is it, Maxine?' she said. 'I need to know now – what is the big deal?'

'He suffers from intrusive thoughts,' said Maxine slowly. 'It's a clinical term for a form of obsessive–compulsive disorder in which the patient can't control unwelcome thoughts that come repeatedly into their head.'

Polly said nothing, trying to take it in.

'You know when you get an ear worm from a catchy song?' Maxine continued.

Polly nodded.

'Well, intrusive thoughts are like that,' said Maxine, 'and just as you don't want to keep hearing that wretched song in your head, you don't want to think the thoughts. But they keep coming back and back and back until you can't think about anything else. The more you try not to think them, the more they occupy your mind.'

Polly thought for a moment.

'Like when you're a teenager and you can't stop thinking about a boy?' she asked.

Or a grown woman, for that matter, thinking about a man.

'A bit like that,' Maxine replied, 'but these are very disturbing, unsettling thoughts. Ideas that the person who has them doesn't want to share, or impulses to do things they really don't want to do, but they can't stop thinking them.'

'What kinds of things?' asked Polly, starting to feel more uneasy.

Maxine shifted in her seat now, looking really uncomfortable.

'Sometimes it's very offensive racist thoughts. Or another example might be for a woman who has been triggered by post-natal depression to have uncontrollable intrusive thoughts of wanting to harm her child.'

'Oh, my God,' said Polly, her hand flying up to her mouth.

Maxine patted her knee in a gesture of reassurance.

'She doesn't really want to harm the child, and she won't harm it,' she said. 'She loves the child as any mother does, but she still can't stop the intrusive thoughts. That's what's so awful about it for the patient. These thoughts are completely disconnected from their true feelings. It's a very distressing condition.'

'Are those the kinds of thoughts David's been having?' asked Polly. 'That he wants to harm our kids?'

'No,' said Maxine. 'It's nothing to do with you or the family, but his line of intrusive thinking is particularly difficult and it's made him very unhappy. He went to live on his own in an attempt to get over it, and because he doesn't want it to affect you.'

Polly shook her head.

'And he didn't think going away under mysterious circumstances would affect me?'

'He's not thinking straight about anything, Polly,' said Maxine, 'that's the whole thing in a nutshell.'

Polly sat and thought for a moment before speaking again. She needed to digest it all.

'So he's having these awful thoughts,' she said eventually, 'whatever they are, but he's not going to act them out, so he's not actually a psycho, he just thinks like one. I think I'm glad he went away.'

Maxine topped up their water glasses from a jug on her desk.

'Would you like a cup of tea, Polly?' she asked.

Polly shook her head. She felt nauseous from it all.

'Did you know that flat he's run away to is where we lived when we first met? It turns out he's held on to it secretly for twenty years. Did he tell you that bit?'

Maxine nodded. 'He said he'd lived there with Jane.'

'So has he had this problem all that time?' said Polly. 'The whole of our marriage?'

'I'm afraid so,' said Maxine, 'but not so badly, it's got much worse recently. He had a very bad episode when he was younger – before he met you – and knowing what that was like, he kept the flat on in case he ever needed somewhere to escape to. He has used it from time to time over the years, whenever he's had a relapse.'

Polly put her hands on her head and shook it from side to side.

'So all those times he was supposed to be at conferences, or on a research trip, he was probably just hiding out in Holborn?'

'Some of them, yes,' said Maxine. 'It's been his way of dealing with it. Isolating and burying himself in work until he could control it again.'

'Did he do anything else?' asked Polly, finding it increasingly strange to talk about her husband as a third party. 'Drink and drugs, the usual escape stuff?'

'No,' said Maxine. 'Although that is a very common response in people with this condition. There's also a tendency to be obsessed with rituals, routines and order, the more classic OCD symptoms, being very tidy—'

Polly's head snapped up. Tidy? It was practically David's middle name, and while she wasn't aware of any 'rituals', he did do things like lay out all his clothes the night before in the order he'd put them on and he always left the house at exactly the same time every morning. She'd always thought of that as just part of who he was – being professional about his job.

'They will also go out of their way to avoid triggers for the thoughts they have,' Maxine was saying. 'Subjects who are tormented by thoughts of sexually abusing or hurting children ...'

She saw Polly's horrified face and stopped.

'It doesn't mean they want to do it, or they will do it, Polly – in fact, it's been shown that people with OCD intrusive thoughts are actually the least likely to act on them – but they will go out of their way to avoid situations that trigger the thoughts. They won't go to parks, or to a family event where there will be young children. Some sufferers seek relief by finding other things to obsess over, such as overworking, over-exercising, over-hobbying. Collecting things, building stuff. One method I've heard of is playing music all the time.'

Polly's mouth fell open.

'David does that,' she said. 'He had this really expensive system put in that plays music through the whole house. I used to love it, I thought it was his charming little eccentricity, and it's one of the things that's been weird about his absence, not having music playing all day long. And it turns out it was really because ...'

Suddenly she found herself feeling quite faint.

'Are you all right, Polly?' asked Maxine, leaning forward and putting her hand gently on Polly's arm.

'I think I will have that cup of tea, after all,' she said.

She needed a moment alone to sit with it all more than anything. Her brain had gone into overdrive – doing a mental inventory of their entire relationship, looking for signs, symptoms and causes – and it was freaking her out how many of them there were.

His recent lack of interest in going to friends' parties, or hosting them. The only parties he'd been to for months were the ones that were really essential for work.

And then she remembered something else that had changed in the previous couple of years. He hadn't wanted to go on beach holidays any more. He'd insisted they went walking in Romania, or on a cultural visit to Berlin. Polly had been mystified when it first happened; now, she feared it pointed to one thing: his intrusive thoughts were about children.

Parties with family friends and beach holidays were full of kids. And not wanting to go and see his own sister when she had young children. That made sense now. She felt sick.

Then there was the park thing. Maxine had specifically mentioned that avoiding parks was one of the measures taken by sufferers with intrusive inappropriate thoughts about children. David didn't ever take Digger to the nearby park. It was Hampstead Heath or a street walk.

He'd made some waffly excuse when she'd asked him about it, saying it was either a proper walk off the lead, or a perfunctory one on it, and that anything in between was insulting to Digger. She'd thought it was a load of nonsense at the time, but now it turned out to be something much worse.

Maxine came back with the tea and Polly knew she had to come out and ask her.

'Are David's intrusive thoughts about children?' she said.

Maxine paused, then nodded.

'I'm afraid so,' she said. 'As I said, he would never act on them, but the more anxious he gets about having such unwelcome thoughts, the more of them he has – it's a very cruel condition.'

'So he's been living in a hell like this for years,' said Polly, thinking out loud. 'Unable to stop obsessing about doing something he finds totally abhorrent ...'

Maxine nodded, but said nothing.

'And he was so ashamed he couldn't tell me ... and he left us to go and live in that flat on his own to try to get on top of it, because he hates himself so much he doesn't think he deserves us. Is that it?'

She paused for a moment, before continuing.

'So he didn't leave because he's bored with me and there's "no glue between us" now the kids have left home – which is what he told our best friends last week. He left because he loves us too much and thinks he's not worthy.'

'That's pretty much it,' said Maxine. 'Yes.'

'Poor David,' said Polly, shaking her head slowly, her eyes filling with tears again. 'Poor, poor David. My poor husband.'

Polly walked out of Maxine's office in a daze. She finally knew what was behind David's mysterious disappearance and it was so far outside her experience she still didn't quite know what to do with the information. She'd never heard of intrusive thoughts as a medical condition before. Obviously she knew what OCD was, but she'd had no idea it could manifest itself in this form. It was so hard to take in.

But there was one thing she did understand: she could no longer allow herself to feel angry with David for leaving. How could she? Through no fault of his own, he suffered from a really horrible debilitating illness that affected his whole life in an appalling way.

Polly tried to imagine what it might be like to see an adorable little child playing in the park and immediately have thoughts that you wanted to hurt them, or molest them, to the point where you were terrified you were actually going to do it. Even though you knew you didn't want to ...

She shuddered even thinking about it, and as she pushed the horrible thought out of her head, she had an insight into what it would be like not to be able to do that. You'd be living in a torture chamber of your own mind – with no escape. How appalling.

OK, his way of dealing with it had been hard on her and the kids, but she could see why, faced with what he had to live with, he would have made bad choices. You wouldn't be angry with someone for getting cancer, or multiple sclerosis, she told herself. You'd make allowances for anyone in that situation, you'd expect them to behave differently – so why was this any different just because the illness was in his mind, rather than in his body?

Polly stopped on a half landing on the stairs leading down from Maxine's office and looked out of a side window.

A cherry tree was coming into bloom, shooting out a froth of sugar-pink blossoms. She could see from its size and the gnarled branches that it was a mature tree, yet still capable of putting on such a wonderful show.

A new beginning every spring, even from an old tree. That was what she was going to have to do. Find a way to bring their gnarled old marriage into blossom again.

David was her children's father and he deserved to be supported through this crisis. Her life had been cruelly affected by his illness – just as it would have been if he'd developed a serious physical condition – but that didn't give her the right to go and do whatever she liked, just because it was nicer for her.

Even as she thought that, an image of Chum leading Sorrel out of the stable came into her head. Chum's long legs climbing out of his stinky Land Rover. Chum opening the champagne in Hanley Hall. Chum laughing. The way Chum looked at her just before he lowered his head to kiss her.

Polly screwed up her eyes and pushed it all away. Unlike poor David, she could do that. She could stop herself thinking about inappropriate things she'd like to do and the ones she'd already done.

She could stop herself from thinking about them – and she could stop herself from doing them. David was her husband, he was a very sick man and what he needed was not reproach and rejection, but acceptance and support. And love. Unconditional love. For better or for worse, she reminded herself. In sickness and in health.

Sitting down on the stairs, she pulled her phone out of her bag and sent Maxine an email. She wanted to get on with it immediately, while what she had to do next was all clear and fresh in her head.

Dear Maxine,

Thank you for putting me out of my misery. I'm deeply shocked about David's condition, I had no idea that people suffered like that, but it's so much better to know why he's behaved the way he has. He's not cruel and uncaring - he's ill.

Now I know what the problem is I have to support him the best way I can, which is to bring him home to be looked after by the people who know him best and love him most. I'm absolutely certain the children will feel the same way.

So please can you ask him to agree to see me as soon as possible? I need to talk to him, to tell him I don't blame him or hold his actions - or his illness - against him. I just want to help him get better. I'm happy to see him with you, or on his own, whatever suits him.

One other thing - please come back to yoga! It's not the same without you.

Polly xxxxxxx

She tapped 'Send' and stood up, feeling much better. She had a plan now and a new sense of purpose. The first thing to do was to get home and call the kids, to tell them what she knew and to arrange for them to come home to see their father.

She rushed towards the door, then as she stepped out of the building she noticed a tall figure stand up from a bench across the road. She thought no more of it, and had turned to head back to her car when she heard someone call her name.

Her head snapped round and she saw Chum running across the street towards her, dodging the traffic.

He made it to the kerb just before a bus went past and put his arms round her, pulling her close.

'Hippolyta, my beauty,' he said. 'Are you OK?'

Polly looked at him stupidly and said nothing. It was so strange to see him unexpectedly in this context that she almost couldn't place him.

'What are you doing here?' she asked, realising as it came out that it sounded a lot brisker than she'd intended.

He dropped his arms and stepped back, clearly sensing her discomfort.

'I just came to make sure you're all right,' he said. 'After seeing Maxine ...'

'But how did you know?' she asked, still nonplussed. She'd told him when the appointment was, but not where it was.

'You texted me about the appointment,' he said, a frown line appearing between his eyebrows.

'Yes,' said Polly, 'but ...'

'Why don't we go and get some coffee?' he said. 'You can tell me what happened. I'm sure you know all the good places round here. Where shall we go?'

Polly didn't want to go for coffee – not in Belsize Park, not anywhere. She wanted to go home and ring her children and make a plan together about how they were going to help their father.

Yet Chum had come all this way; she couldn't just walk off.

'OK,' she said, and led the way to the nearest café.

Chum ordered a latte and a sickly-looking cinnamon whirl, while Polly asked for hot water. She couldn't stomach a milky coffee, she still felt too churned up from the meeting with Maxine.

'Are you sure this is all you want?' he asked, putting the tray on the table in front of her.

Polly nodded, as he slid into the chair opposite.

'So how did it go?' he asked, taking a big bite out of his sugary pastry.

Polly still couldn't speak. She remembered Chum had said he'd be there for her, if she needed support after seeing Maxine, but she hadn't expected him to show up and sit around eating cake, like they were having a jolly catch-up.

'How did you find out where I'd be?' she said finally, still in too much shock to bother with social pleasantries.

'I rang Shirlee and asked her,' said Chum, licking his lips and pushing in a stray crumb with his finger.

'Shirlee?' said Polly. 'How did you get her number?'

'When we all had lunch at Easter, she gave it to me.'

Polly's eyebrows shot up.

Chum laughed. 'She wasn't hitting on me – that's what she said as she did it – "I'm not hitting on you, Fauntleroy." God, she's funny isn't she? She said she wanted me to have her number in case there was ever a problem between us, and she could "oil the wheels". Those were her words, and I was very glad to have her number today because I wanted to be here to support you, after the meeting. So what did Maxine tell you?'

Polly thought for a moment, taking a sip of her hot water. Maybe she should have had that coffee; she needed an energy kick to take all this new information on board. Her brain was already struggling to process what Maxine had told her. She really didn't need this complication.

She knew Shirlee was an interfering busybody and mostly she found it funny – and very helpful with regard to running the yoga classes for her – but offering to act as a go-between for her and Chum was way too much.

And something else was bothering her.

'Did Shirlee know I was seeing Maxine today about David?' said Polly. 'I haven't told her anything about it. Only you and my friend Lori. I haven't even told my kids yet.'

Chum looked blank.

'I'm afraid I don't know the answer to that, Hipp,' he said. 'I just rang Shirlee and asked if by any chance she knew where you were seeing this person Maxine today, and she knew right off where that would be. Maxine's a friend of hers, she said.'

Polly felt a crackle of irritation run through her. Did she have no privacy? Was everyone in her life happily discussing all the developments in the Polly soap opera behind her back?

'Anyway,' said Chum, reaching over to take Polly's hand, 'I'm sure she'll explain, and none of that's important really, is it? I just wanted to be here to support you, so you wouldn't feel alone at such a difficult time. Shirlee offered to come along as well, actually, but I asked her not to. So tell me, what did Maxine say? Do you know what's going on with your husband now?'

Hearing Chum say the words 'your husband' seemed to have some kind of electric effect on Polly. Her husband indeed. Her husband of twenty-four years' standing, currently going through a desperately difficult time of a devastatingly private nature, which Polly had no intention of discussing with someone who didn't know him. Even someone she'd done a lot of snogging with like some kind of superannuated oversexed teenager.

The irritation was followed by a wave of shame. While David had been imprisoned in the torment of his own head, she'd been carrying on like a floozy, like he'd ceased to exist.

She felt disgusted with herself. Her marriage had been tested – and she'd failed. Horribly.

'I'm sorry, Chum,' she said, gently pulling her hand away from his. 'It was incredibly kind of you to come here today, I really do appreciate it, but it's not something I feel able to talk about yet. I've got an awful lot to process after that meeting with Maxine and I need to go home now and just sit with it all for a while. On my own. I hope you can understand.'

She was about to add that she'd left Digger on his own there and she needed to get back to him, but stopped herself just in time. Thinking of Digger made her remember the day she'd first seen Chum again, and then of all the happy times their two dogs had spent together, and she just couldn't allow herself to go there.

She stood up and collected her things.

'Bye, Chum,' she said, kissing him lightly on the cheek and walking out of the café quickly.

She didn't look back. She felt mean leaving him like that, with his childish pastry and milky coffee, but she had to get away. It was very sweet of him to come and wait for her and offer his support, but there was something else that nagged at her.

It felt a lot like pressure.

~

Polly's phone pinged to let her know she had a message before she'd even got to her car. She fished it out of her bag, strongly hoping it wasn't from Chum. On top of how she was feeling about David, she really didn't need any more guilt.

But it wasn't from Chum, it was from Shirlee. Wanting to know how the meeting with Maxine had gone. And was she still with Chum or could Shirlee come over to the house to hear all about it? Or maybe she could come over even if Polly still was with Chum and they could all 'talk it through' together.

Polly was so furious she had to restrain herself from throwing her phone into the skip she was walking past.

This was intrusive even by Shirlee's standards. Polly deleted the message, hoping Shirlee wouldn't just turn up at the house and let herself in. Polly would have to deadlock the door from the inside and leave the key in it, but then Shirlee would only shout through the letterbox.

The phone pinged three more times before Polly got back to the house. She pulled up outside and read the messages sitting in the car.

There was another one from Shirlee asking if she'd got the first one and saying she was going to come right over, because she'd just rung Chum and he'd told her Polly was on her way home. Polly deleted it in a white-hot fury.

The other two were from Lucas and Clemmie, both saying something along the lines of just hearing that Shirlee hadn't been able to get hold of Polly since the meeting with Maxine and wanting to check she was OK, as well being desperate to know what Maxine had told her about their dad ...

That was it. Shirlee had officially gone too far. She had no right to speak to Polly's children about the meeting with Maxine before Polly had been able to talk to them herself. Polly hadn't even talked to Shirlee about the Maxine connection – had Maxine told her? Or had she just put it together after Chum's indiscreet phone call?

And Shirlee had no business contacting Chum either. Even if she wasn't hitting on him, that was a no-go area. You didn't go around giving your phone number to other people's – Polly's thoughts stopped dead. Other people's what? Boyfriends?

She slumped forward, resting her forehead on the steering wheel.

Oh, what kind of a mess had she got herself into? In a state of extreme confusion and vulnerability, she'd let a psychotically pushy and interfering person into the very heart of her life, and been recklessly indiscreet with another man, who was already pretty damaged himself, which made her feel even worse about everything.

In her vulnerable state after David had left, she'd been swept away on a wave of nostalgia and the Yah glamour that still adhered to Chum. Anyone would have been seduced by a champagne picnic in a private stately home, she told herself, but still she should have known better. Especially with a man as handsome and charming as him.

The only thing she could cling on to was that she hadn't gone any further with him that night, or the other time at his cottage. That was the one shred of dignity she had left.

Her phone pinged again and a glance told her it was from Shirlee – yet again – asking what 'flavor' of doughnut she wanted, because it was a 'Krispy Kreme emergency moment' and she was stopping off on her way. The doughnut shop was just around the corner from the house.

Polly jumped out of the car and dashed into the house, calling for Digger and grabbing his lead off the hook. He came running into the hallway and she ushered him straight out the front door and into the car, gunning the engine and racing off.

Waiting to turn onto the main road at the bottom of her street, she glanced in her mirror and saw Shirlee's yellow car pulling up outside her house.

That was close. Too close. Polly just hoped Shirlee wouldn't look down the street and recognise her car. A gap appeared in the traffic and she turned into it with relief.

She'd got as far as the big Archway junction when she wondered where the hell she was actually going. Her normal response to a situation like this would have been to head north to her mum, but that no longer felt like a safe haven. What if Chum decided to do the same and visit Bill?

And after what Daphne had said the last time Polly had seen her – 'Well done, darling. Go get him' – she'd want to know all about how things were progressing with Chum. She certainly wouldn't want to hear about David's mental illness and how Polly was going to bring him home and look after him. Daphne had revealed her true feelings about David and it was going to be difficult to come back from that.

The lights changed, and as she was in the lane to turn right, down Holloway Road, that's what she did. Her phone went off yet again: no doubt Shirlee wanting to know how she'd like her tea. She felt like throwing the damn thing out of the car window, but what she wanted to do more than anything was to ring the kids. They needed to know what Maxine had told her.

She turned off into the next side street and pulled over. The last call had been from Clemmie. Polly didn't bother to listen to the voice mail, just hit 'Dial', and Clemmie answered immediately.

'Oh Mum, thank God,' she said. 'Are you all right? Where are you? Shirlee says you've gone missing. Are you going up to Granny's? That's what I thought you'd be doing—'

'Forget about Shirlee,' said Polly, with a cold calmness that surprised her. 'This is nothing to do with her, and the reason I'm not at home is that she's there and I need to talk to you and Lucas privately about what Maxine's told me. I don't need a nosy parker poking around in our family business. If Shirlee rings you again, please don't talk to her.'

'OK, sure,' said Clemmie. 'But please just tell me about Dad.'

'Well, to cut to the chase,' said Polly. 'He's got a severe form of OCD with extreme intrusive thoughts.'

'Oh no,' said Clemmie, sounding truly shocked. 'I know

what that is. We covered OCD last year. That's an awful condition. What are his main triggers, did she tell you?'

Polly took a deep breath, but she couldn't bear to say it.

'Is it to do with children?' asked Clemmie quietly.

'Yes,' said Polly.

'Poor Dad,' said Clemmie, her voice breaking. 'What a living hell.'

'I know,' said Polly. 'But why couldn't he tell us, Clemmie? He didn't need to suffer alone like this.'

She wanted to say he'd been seeing Maxine for over a year at least, but then she'd have to explain why she didn't make the connection – and she couldn't bear to tell Clemmie the thing about how David had called his children Susan and John. Not yet. That would be too hurtful.

'It's all part of the condition, Mummy,' said Clemmie. 'The shame they have to live with is almost worse than the thoughts.'

'That's what Maxine said.'

'I'm going to come home, Mummy,' said Clemmie. 'I need to be with you. Have you rung Lucas yet?'

'No, I'm going to ring him now, but I can't go home today, Clems. I can't deal with Shirlee butting in – and I don't want to be reminded of your dad's suffering everywhere I look.'

'I understand,' said Clemmie. 'Do you know where you're going to go?'

'I'm not sure yet,' said Polly, 'but I'll ring you when I'm settled somewhere.

'OK, you do that, and I'll get straight on the train to London and find you when I get there.'

Polly rang off and let out a deep sigh. One down, one to go. She tapped Lucas's number.

'Muuuuuum,' he said, answering after half a ring. 'Tell me ...'

'Hi, Lukie,' said Polly. 'Well, it's good news and bad news.'

'Tell me the good first and that will give me strength to take the bad,' said Lucas.

'The good news,' said Polly, 'is that it's not about us – it's about him. The bad news is he's got a really horrible mental illness, which makes him have constant intrusive thoughts – urges to do things he really doesn't want to do and would never do in a million years, but his brain keeps making him think them.'

Lucas said nothing.

'It's like when you get an ear worm after listening to a rubbish song,' added Polly.

'What kind of things does his brain think?' asked Lucas quietly, with a frightened tone in his voice.

'Oh, sweetheart,' said Polly. 'I don't want to talk about it on the phone. Can you come up? Clemmie's going to.'

'Of course – but how bad are we talking?'

'Horrible enough to make him do what he's done – run away from us,' said Polly. She'd said it to Clemmie, but she just couldn't bear to tell Lucas over the phone. 'He's really trying to run away from himself.'

'I'll get the train right away,' said Lucas.

'Give me a couple of hours, and don't come to the house,' said Polly. 'I can't stand being there today, so I'm going somewhere neutral, I'm not sure where yet – I'll text you as soon as I've found somewhere to be. And one other thing: if Shirlee calls you, please ignore it. She's being a royal pain in the arse.'

After she rang off, Polly sat for a moment looking at the residential London street, not that different from the one where she lived. What secrets and strange situations were lurking in all these houses? she wondered.

She wished she could just walk into one of them, get into a strange bed and pull the covers over her head. And possibly never get up again, it was all too hard. But she couldn't do that, so where was she going to go? A hotel?

She flipped down the sun shade to check her reflection in the mirror, to see if she looked as bad as she felt.

As she put her hand up to smooth her hair, she caught a trace of the perfume she'd sprayed on her wrists that morning. She'd chosen PM for strength. And then it struck her who she could ask to give her sanctuary on this strangest of days, who wouldn't judge, or offer intrusive advice ...

Guy.

~

There were three customers in the Great Eastern Fragrance Company when Polly opened the door – the most she'd ever seen in there at once – and judging by their clothes, hair and handbags, they weren't the usual Shoreditch shoppers. Guy was in full charismatic mode, fussing around them with glasses of mint tea – Polly wondered if they were getting the Iranian grandmother story – and looking very sleek in a charcoal-grey raw-silk suit and a crisp dark-green shirt.

He smiled when he saw Polly in the doorway, but it was more guarded than his usual greeting. That was a relief, as she'd been worried for a moment that he might launch into a big introduction of her as a perfume blogger. Instead he raised his forefinger to indicate he'd be with her in a moment.

Polly stepped back outside and waited by the door, not sure if Guy would mind having Digger in the shop. She leaned back against the wall and closed her eyes, getting lost in identifying the delicious smells she could pick up through the door.

The overpowering oriental oud that had first led her there was tempered now by a much more varied and subtle fragrance palette. She could pick up strong threads of the most classic florals, rose, lily of the valley, magnolia, which Guy would have turned his nose up at before, alongside the more Mediterranean jasmine and neroli, with the warm notes of sandalwood and tonka, balanced by the bite of citrus.

She was snapped back to reality by Guy's voice.

'Hey, Pollster,' he was saying. 'Why are you standing out here?'

Polly opened her eyes to see him looking at her round the edge of the door with a concerned expression, and pointed down at Digger, who stood up and wagged his tail in greeting.

'Ah, I see,' said Guy. 'Thoughtful of you. But tell me, honeybun, are you OK?

'Did Shirlee ring you, by any chance?' said Polly.

Guy nodded. 'She wanted to know if I knew where you were. I didn't then. She said you needed help. What's happening?'

'Please don't tell her if she rings again,' said Polly, putting her hand on his arm. 'I need a break from Shirlee.'

'I hear you,' said Guy, then looked over his shoulder as one of the customers asked him a question in an American accent.

'I'll be right there,' he said to her, then turned back to Polly.

'Look, Poll,' he said, 'I need to look after these ladies, but can I help you with whatever's going on?'

'I need a place to be for the afternoon,' she said. 'I can't go home, Shirlee's staking it out. I've had a horrible shock.'

She could feel tears rising up and tried to hold them back.

'Hey, sweetie,' said Guy, very tenderly, putting his arms round her. 'Don't cry and don't worry.'

He paused for a moment, seeming to consider his options.

'You can stay here as long as you need to. Why don't you and Digger go upstairs and chill out? Make yourself some tea – or a drink, whatever you need. I'll come up as soon as I can.'

She hugged him quickly, pecking him on the cheek, and followed him into the shop, then kept walking through the bead curtain and up the stairs.

She headed immediately to one of two big inviting sofas, kicked off her shoes and threw herself down, allowing a long breath to stream out out as she looked around. It felt so good to be somewhere completely detached from the rest of her life. Especially as it was so elegant, humming with discreet luxury.

The whole first floor of the building had been knocked through – which she wasn't sure could be legal in a house that old – to create one big space, with two marble fireplaces, and a kitchen area off to one side. The rest of the room was furnished with great sophistication, featuring low tables and cabinets of highly polished wood, beautiful lamps and big vases of flowers. The floor was parquet, with large rugs in strategic places, and there was a magnificent 1960s brass chandelier overhead.

But what really jumped out at Polly were the framed vintage fashion photographs covering most of the walls, many of which she recognised as iconic images from the 1950s and early '60s. She scanned the nearest ones to see if she could spot Daphne and, sure enough, alongside Barbara Goalen and Dovima, were all the most iconic shots of her mother, most of them by Mark Shaw, with some John French and a couple of Cecil Beatons.

Lying back down again, she checked the time, desperately wanting to message Clemmie and Lucas to tell them come and meet her there, but didn't feel she could until she'd asked Guy. She wished he'd hurry up.

Feeling a bit chilly, she unfolded a cashmere throw that was over the back of the sofa and arranged it over herself. Then, despite all the jangling thoughts, her eyes closed and she allowed herself to float away for some blessed respite from the clamour in her head.

She was woken – she had no idea how much later – by a great commotion.

'Polly! Polly! Polly! Polly!' Guy was shouting, as he ran up the stairs and into the living space. He'd taken his suit jacket off and was twirling it round his head like a flag. 'Polly! Polly! Such news—'

He came to an abrupt halt when he saw her tucked up on the sofa, and laughed.

'Who's been sleeping on my sofa?' he said. 'Wake up, sleepy head, we have to celebrate.'

Polly blinked at him, still coming to. She'd never felt less like celebrating in her life, but Guy's enthusiasm was as infectious as ever and she sat up.

'What's happened?'

Guy put out his hand to help her to her feet, then clasped her in a ballroom hold and waltzed her over to the kitchen. Polly stumbled along as best she could and Digger ran alongside, barking enthusiastically.

'We must have champagne,' said Guy, letting go of her and throwing open one of the kitchen cabinets to reveal a fridge full of wine.

'Now, which one?' he said, peering in and rubbing his hands together, before pulling out a bottle.

He popped the cork, filled two flutes and handed one to Polly. She took it, hoping her lack of enthusiasm wasn't too obvious. It was early afternoon; the sun was nowhere near the yardarm. Just that morning she'd had a terrible shock, followed by the realisation that she had to end the teen fantasy romance she'd been indulging in, which had forced her to be horrible to someone who really didn't deserve it ... and she still had to talk it through properly with her children. She really wasn't in a party mood.

Despite all that, Polly did her best to put on an appreciative expression and held her glass up for a toast. She'd take a few sips and hope Guy didn't notice if she only pretended to drink the rest of it.

'To the Great Eastern Fragrance Company,' he said, 'which will soon be stocked exclusively in the USA by Bergdorf Goodman, New York!'

'Wow,' said Polly, understanding why he was so excited now. 'Is that who those women were?'

Guy nodded and took a deep drink from his glass. Polly pretended to do the same, sipping as little as she could.

'Yep,' said Guy. 'They're in London on a buying trip and came to the shop after a tip-off from one of their scouts – who'd read about it on your blog and came for a look incognito. So I owe you and your FragrantCloud big-time, Miss Poll.'

'Gosh,' said Polly. 'How lovely. But I'm sure they would have found out about you eventually. You're too good to go unnoticed, Guy.'

'Well, thank you,' he said, picking up the bottle and heading towards the sofas. 'Let's go and get comfortable. How do you like my little place?'

'It's beautiful,' said Polly, taking the opportunity to tip half her champagne down the sink while his back was turned, then catching up with him.

'Let us lounge,' he said, settling on a sofa.

'What about the shop?' asked Polly, sitting down, with her feet tucked underneath her, reclaiming her sofa as he suggested.

'I've declared a national holiday,' said Guy. 'I need to take a moment to celebrate this great leap forward for my little business – and I also want to pay some attention to you. From what Shirlee told me, things have come to something of a head for you today.'

'What exactly did she tell you?' asked Polly.

'She said you'd been to see Maxine to find out what's been going on with your husband all this time, and that she hadn't been able to get hold of you since. And that she'd spoken to your friend Edward and he's really worried about you too. Also that the kids don't know where you are ...'

'God, she's the limit,' said Polly, reaching down and grabbing her phone out of her bag. 'I'm just going to check the BBC website, because presumably everything about my personal life will be on there by now. She's probably instructing some skywriters as we speak.'

Guy roared with laughter.

'Oh, Poll doll,' he said. 'I can see why you feel invaded, but it's only because she cares about you so much.'

'I appreciate her caring – Shirlee is a wonderful friend – but she needs to understand boundaries,' said Polly. 'She doesn't have a right to meddle in my private life to this degree, especially with the kids.'

And with Chum, she thought.

'She rang them before I could, Guy, that's just wrong and the thing is I really need to see them today, to talk it all through, but I can't bear to go back to the house, because she has keys and I saw her car pull up outside it. She's probably still there, waiting to interrogate me.'

'Bring them here,' said Guy.

'Can I?' said Polly.

'Of course,' said Guy. 'And you'll have the place to yourselves, because I'm going out tonight – all night ...'

Polly was so happy she jumped up and gave him a hug, then picked up her phone to text Clemmie and Lucas.

'Thank you so much,' she said, the messages sent. 'You're a true friend.'

'But there's something I should probably warn you about, before you go upstairs,' he said, a twinkle in his eye, Polly hadn't seen before.

'What's that?'

'There's some quite, shall we say, "interesting" art in my bedrooms,' he said.

Polly put her head on one side, inquiringly.

'It pertains to the great mysterious riddle of my sexuality,' said Guy, toasting her with his glass and draining it. 'The thing Shirlee is always trying to find out about me.'

'So what are you?' said Polly.

'Well, you could call me bisexual,' said Guy, refilling his glass. 'I'm not going to offer you any more champers, I can see you're not drinking it.'

'So you like men and women?' asked Polly.

'Yes,' said Guy, sitting back down again. 'But at the same time. Together. That's my bag. I don't talk about it to people, because it doesn't fit into a box that they can slap a name on, but I only really enjoy sex if I have it with a man and a woman at the same time – or a man and two women, five men and three women, any combination as long as it's mixed and multiple. That's my thing, it works for me and I don't need to tell anyone about it. People are always trying to find out if I'm gay or straight – sometimes they decide I'm "asexual", but I'm not. I'm multisexual.'

'Sounds like fun,' said Polly, feeling calmer than she had all day. It was so nice to be looking at someone else's life under the microscope for a change. 'Nice work if you can get it, and all that.'

'Oh, I get it,' said Guy, smiling broadly. 'I get it plenty. There are people out there for every sexual persuasion. You just have to know where to look and how to ask for it.'

'I won't tell Shirlee,' said Polly. 'I'm going to relish knowing something she so wants to know and doesn't. It will give me a small sense of revenge.'

Guy laughed.

'So what about you, Polly?' he said. 'What floats your kinky boat? You know I had ambitions to introduce you to the very exquisite pleasures of my bed – really, you don't know what you're missing as a girl until you've had a threesome with two men – but I realised early on you were too straight for it. But your husband's been gone a long time. Are you getting some? Are you at it with your friend Edward?'

'No, I'm not,' said Polly. 'I'm still a married woman, Guy. I'm very fond of ...'

She felt odd calling him Edward, but she couldn't bear to say 'Chum'. It felt like a stab in her guts even to think it.

'I've known him since I was young and he's been a great friend to me during this strange time, but I'm not ready to go off sleeping with other people. I can't deny that my marriage is going through a very difficult patch, but it's not over, and I'm going to do my very best to save it. David needs me and I'm going to be there for him.'

'Really?' said Guy, opening his eyes wide in surprise. 'After all he's put you through, I thought you were ready to cut and run and I really didn't blame you. Was it something Maxine told you this morning that has turned you back into the good wife?'

'It's all connected,' she said. 'But I have never stopped being David's wife.'

'Are you absolutely sure about that, Polly?' said Guy, leaning towards her, putting his elbows on his knees and looking at her in great concern. 'I was watching you and Edward together when we had lunch at your mum's place that time and I could see he's really into you. And from the way you were with him, I couldn't help thinking it was mutual. It was quite nauseating, really, how at ease you looked with him. Of course, I've never met your husband, but you and Edward just look so right together.'

'If only it were that simple, Guy,' said Polly.

He looked thoughtful, but didn't say anything else. They sat in silence for a bit, Guy sipping his champagne and gazing into space.

'You know what, Guy?' said Polly. 'As I don't have to drive anywhere, I think I will have some more of that bubbly after all.'

'Good girl,' said Guy, sitting up and filling her glass.

Polly raised it to her nose, relishing the sharp apple tang and the tickle of the bubbles before taking a deep drink from it.

'This really is a beautiful room,' she said, 'and it's lovely to see the pictures of Mum. They look like photographers' prints, like the ones she has.'

'They are,' said Guy. 'I only buy those.'

'That chandelier is spectacular too,' said Polly.

'It's an Angelo Lelli,' said Guy. 'I'm glad you like it. Took me a while to find the one I wanted.'

'I'm sure,' said Polly, thinking Sotheby's must have been delighted to help him. 'And these sofas are divine, so comfortable ...'

'George Smith,' he said, smiling as though it were the most natural thing in the world to have a pair of £7,000 hand-made sofas.

'You have exquisite taste,' she said.

Guy smiled.

'Very expensive taste,' she continued.

Guy threw his head back and laughed.

'I get it,' he said. 'Oh, you backed me nicely down that alley way didn't you? You want to know where the money comes from, yes?'

'Yes,' said Polly.

'I'll show you,' said Guy and he stood up and walked over to the bookshelves that covered the back wall, then returned holding something in his hand.

He passed it to Polly and she looked down at a piece of black metal in an interesting shape, a bit like a shell.

'That's where it comes from,' he said, walking back to the bookshelves and picking up a small photograph in a black frame, which he also handed to Polly. 'And here.'

It was a black-and-white photograph of a forbidding building. A factory, as far as she could tell, judging by the tall chimneys at one end, with copious smoke coming out of them.

'That's a widget you're holding,' he called over his shoulder, on his way to the kitchen. 'That's where my money comes from. My clever great-grandfather invented a widget, which helped to make factory conveyor belts run more reliably and luckily for me, he patented it. That's one of the prototypes. Webber Industries. You can google it.'

He came back and put a bowl of olives on the large coffee table between the sofas, then topped up her glass.

'We still have factories on that very spot,' he added,

pointing at the photograph, which Polly had put on the table. 'In Walsall. I grew up in the Black Country.'

He said it in that area's unique accent, like Birmingham, tinged with a slight Northern flatness, then tossed an olive in the air, catching it in his mouth. 'Orroight, our Polls?'

'That's amazing,' said Polly. 'But why are you so paranoid and secretive about it. Aren't you proud of your family business?'

'Yes,' said Guy, 'but I don't like to go around bragging about it – and in all honesty, I don't think it's much of a fit with the perfume world, so I like to keep it quiet. Can you imagine your friend sleazy Lechêne if he'd known I come from a family of factory owners? He would have stuck his nose up so high he'd have done a back flip.'

Polly laughed.

'I don't agree,' she said. 'I think your amazing industrial pedigree is a great story. Rather than doing overblown orientals based on a fake heritage, you could do something amazing based on your real one.'

'Engine oil and smoke stacks?' said Guy sarcastically. '*Charmant.*'

'I'm serious,' she said. 'Authenticity – that's what it's all about these days.'

'Hmm,' said Guy, tossing a couple more olives into his mouth. 'Maybe you're onto something. I'll think about it. Maybe you'd like to be my marketing advisor? I could put you on the pay roll, with Shirlee. I could do with some help on that side of things.'

Polly didn't say anything. She didn't know if he was serious or not.

'I mean it,' he said. 'We'll talk about it another time, but I do need help with the advertising campaign. I know what I want visually – Daphne – but beyond that, I'm a bit clueless.

Ponder it. Now, do you have any other questions, because I'm getting bored with myself.'

'Yes,' said Polly. 'Two. Number one – who runs Webber Industries now? Is it still in the family?'

'My clever big sister,' he said. 'She's a whiz kid. Next.'

'If you're not half-Iranian, where does your wonderful colouring come from, that jet black hair ...'

'My mother's black Irish,' said Guy. 'You know the ones who are supposed to be descended from shipwrecked Spanish sailors? From that.'

'Well, there you are, another interesting bit of background to work with. You don't need to make anything up, Guy Webber, you're the full package for real.'

She was going to say more, but his phone started to ring and at the same time someone began pressing the buzzer on the door downstairs – and holding it. Digger started barking.

'Shoosh, Digger,' said Polly. There was only one person that it could be, and Polly was really hoping she hadn't heard Digger's bark.

'That would be Shirlee, then,' said Guy, glancing at his phone, then holding it up to his ear and walking over to the window.

'Get off the goddamn buzzer, Shirlee,' he said. 'I can hear you. In fact I can see you. Yoohoo!'

He looked down, waving.

'Stay there,' he said. 'I'll be right down.'

Polly had her head in her hands. There was no escape.

'Don't worry,' said Guy. 'I've got a plan. I'll make sure she can't get up here, I'll deny all knowledge of your whereabouts and I'll send her off on some mission that will take up the rest of the afternoon, so you and Digger and the kids will be safe here.'

'Thank you, Guy,' said Polly, getting up to hug him again.

Guy pulled her close and pushed his nose into her hair.

'Mmmm, you smell good,' he said. 'I'm glad I bottled you.'

He lifted his head again and looked at her face closely with his head to one side.

'Are you sure you don't want to have a little interlude with me and a very beautiful Swedish dancer friend of mine? He has the most exquisite backside you've ever seen and a simply huge ...'

Polly shook her head, smiling.

'I'm happy for you,' she said, 'but it's not my thing.'

'Well, if you won't have sex with this old pervert, I really think you should reconsider Edward. He's hot, Poll. I'd do him in a heartbeat, with you, in the stables—'

'Guy!'

'I'm teasing,' he said, 'although I would like to see him in his tight riding trews.'

An image of Chum in his black jodhpurs, leading Sorrel, came into Polly's mind and it took a great effort to push it away.

'Enough,' she said, putting a finger on Guy's lips. He opened his mouth and bit it lightly, then began teasing the end of it with his tongue.

'Stop it!' she exclaimed, pulling it out and wiping it on his shirt. 'You are the limit, Guy Webber, do you know that? Now, please go and deal with Shirlee so I can relax.'

And before she had even finished the sentence the buzzer started again.

Tuesday, 5 April

Polly woke up feeling disorientated. She didn't know where she was until the very distinctive pictures on the walls of Guy's spare room brought it all back. They were all drawings, etchings and prints of people disporting themselves with great sexual abandonment – at least three of them in every composition, far more in some.

There were many styles, including Indian paintings depicting scenes of complicated group couplings, colourful Japanese prints of geishas up to all sorts, eighteenth-century French engravings featuring frock coats and billowing bloomers, and one that looked like an Egon Schiele ink drawing. It was quite something.

Clemmie was no longer next to her in the bed – and noises from downstairs told her she and Lucas were already up. She could hear Guy's coffee grinder working. A happy bark from Digger indicated he was enjoying herself.

As she took it all in, the events of the previous day rushed through her mind. The shock of what Maxine had told her followed by Shirlee's outrageous intrusions had just about flattened her – but the evening with the kids, who both got a big kick out of Guy's luxurious living quarters, had been very comforting.

They'd talked it through for hours, generously availing themselves of Guy's wine store, as he'd urged them to do before he'd disappeared for his assignation, and had all agreed they had to stand by David.

She got out of bed and pulled on the silk dressing gown that was hanging on a hook, checking her texts as she headed for the door. There were several more from Shirlee, the last one saying she'd heard from Guy that Polly had gone to stay with a friend and she'd messaged all the regulars to cancel that morning's yoga class.

It made Polly feel a very small stab of guilt. That was the good side of Shirlee – and it was very good. She was so helpful and supportive. If only she knew when to stop.

Polly felt a much sharper pang when she saw there was also a text from Chum, and read it with a sense of trepidation.

> Just checking in. I'm so sorry I sprung myself on you like that. It was very intrusive, but I just wanted you to know I was there if you needed me. I still am. C x

Polly bit her lip, feeling bad all over again that she'd made him question himself like that. Chum always seemed so relaxed and loose-limbed the way he went about life; even with all his own issues, he never seemed to overthink things, and it didn't sit right with him to have to analyse his actions and motives like that.

She'd done that to him. How self-indulgent she'd been, how casual with his feelings. She was going to have to tell him the truth, it wasn't fair to keep stringing him along, thinking that whatever there'd been between them – and what was it really, beyond some fairly basic snogging? – was going to develop any further.

It wasn't. It couldn't. She was married. To a man who, it turned out, was very ill and needed his family.

Lost in her thoughts, she got to the bottom of the stairs and nearly fell over Digger.

'Morning, lovely Mummy,' said Clemmie, coming over to give her a kiss. 'I hope you had a good sleep. You needed it.'

'Morning all,' said Polly, so happy to have them both with her. 'How did you two sleep?'

'Once I could stop myself from looking at the absolutely filthy photographs on the walls in Guy's bedroom, I slept very well, thank you,' said Lucas, clearly enjoying playing with the state-of-the-art espresso maker. 'I think Guy might be in some of those pictures.'

'I'm not going to have a close look,' said Polly.

'I wouldn't,' said Lucas. 'You'll never eat sausages again.'

'I thought we could go out for brekkie,' said Polly, sitting at the table and accepting the mug of tea Clemmie handed her. 'There are so many great places round here. Have you found something for Digger to eat?'

'Yes,' said Clemmie. 'I took him out for a wee and got him some dog food.'

She pointed to the kitchen counter, where there was an open tin with a bright yellow label. Pedigree Chum. Polly didn't know whether to laugh or cry.

Clemmie and Lucas joined her at the table.

'I can't stick around, I'm afraid,' said Clemmie. 'I've got a big practical this afternoon. I've got to get back for it.'

'Me too,' said Lucas. 'I've got band practice. We've got a gig tomorrow at the pub that every band that gets to play in the Students' Union plays at first. It's our stepping-stone gig.'

'That's great, Lucas, said Polly, 'and I totally understand about your thing, Clemmie. I'm so proud of you both for having such great things that you need to go and do. And thank you both so much for coming yesterday. I really needed you after that bombshell.'

'Nothing would have kept me away,' said Lucas. 'I'm still taking it all on board, but I'm really glad we know why he's being a psycho ... which is because he basically is a psycho.'

'Please don't use that pejorative term,' said Clemmie. 'He has a borderline psychotic illness, Lucas. The word "psycho" is not acceptable.'

'Well, pardon me, Dr Dog,' said Lucas. 'Sorry I've forgotten to be politically correct the morning after finding out my father is an actual nut job.'

'Oh, do fuck off, Lucas,' said Clemmie. 'Go and play your xylophone.'

'Pack it in, both of you!' said Polly sharply. 'I know it's a lot to digest, but it won't help if we squabble with each other. We should be bloody grateful we have a medical expert in the family, Lucas. We're going to need her, and we must stick together through this. And don't be snarky with your brother, Clemmie. I didn't have any siblings, you're very lucky to have each other.'

'Sorry, Mum,' said Clemmie. 'Sorry, Lucas.'

'I'm sorry, both of you,' said Lucas. 'I know it's not his fault, but I can't help feeling cross with him for being like this. It makes me feel itchy in my skin.'

'I know,' said Polly. 'I feel like that sometimes too. I'm very relieved we finally know why he's behaved so strangely, but I'm not under any illusions that it's going to be easy to help him through it. We must be stick together, though, or we won't be able to cope.'

~

They all left Guy's place together and said their goodbyes on the corner of Cheshire Street and Brick Lane. Polly found the car in the multi-storey where she'd left it, then sat behind the wheel, wondering where to go.

She still didn't feel like going home. She didn't think Shirlee would bug her there any more, after Guy had told her she'd gone away, but she didn't feel ready to be in the house again.

She felt so strangely detached from her life it didn't seem like somewhere she belonged any more. But then again, if she was going to bring David home and support him through this crisis, she was going to have to get over that pretty quickly. How could she make it a safe haven for him if it didn't feel like one to her?

That reminded her to check her emails, to see if Maxine had replied.

Polly felt her heart rate quicken when she saw Maxine's name on a message in the inbox, and she closed her eyes and took a couple of slow breaths before opening it.

Dear Polly,

I've now heard back from David and I'm afraid he says he still doesn't feel able to see you.

He asked me to give you this message – I've copied it over from his email:

Please tell Polly I'm glad she knows what's going on with me now and I appreciate her generous reaction to it, but I still can't see her or the children. It's not fair and they all deserve better, but this is the way it has to be.

I'm really sorry it's not the response you were hoping for, and I'm sure you will understand that in my professional situation, I couldn't try to 'persuade' him to do anything else, whatever I might believe would be best for him – let alone what would be best for you. I can only make measured comments within my clinical role.

I've told David that in the circumstances I can't treat him any more, and have suggested some other psychotherapists I think he would be able to work with when he comes back from his current trip away.

Once again, I'm devastated by this turn of events, which was beyond the control of any of us, just a result of us all living in the same London 'village'. I'm very grateful for the way you've taken it, and if you would like me to suggest some therapists for you to see to help you through this difficult time, I would be very happy to do so.

With love and thanks,
Maxine xxx

P.S. And yes, I'd love to come back to yoga. Thank you! x

Polly read it through twice, before she could quite believe it. What an unsatisfying outcome. Unsatisfying and hurtful. David had rejected her offer with no discussion, and without allowing her any sense of – what was it they called it? Closure, that was it. Twenty-five years together and he just wanted to fob her off with a second-hand email?

It was all still so open-ended. While he wouldn't take her help, or even talk to her about it, they were still married. How could she move on in any way, if he wouldn't even discuss it with her?

Then she had an idea. Perhaps her polite inquiry via Maxine had been too restrained and a more concerted effort was required from her. She turned the ignition and headed for Holborn.

Polly felt nervous going up the stairs to the flat, even though she knew David wasn't going to be there. It had been confirmed by Maureen – and Maxine – that he really had gone away this time, but she still felt anxious.

She let herself into the silent flat, wondering if she should call his name just in case, but she could tell there was no one there. In fact it was hard to believe that anyone had been there since her last visit; everything was exactly the same, perfectly neat and tidy. And it smelled the same, too.

Glancing into each room as she went, she noticed there were no towels on the rail in the bathroom now, which confirmed someone had actually been there, presumably David.

She went into the kitchen and put two packs of his favourite liquorice, old-fashioned Pontefract cakes on the counter. Then she went through to the sitting room and sat at the desk, picking up the yellow HB pencil that was sitting in perfect alignment with the A4 lined pad. All set out exactly as his desk at home was.

Then she gazed into space, wondering how to start.

She'd got as far as 'Dear David' when her phone bleeped to announce a text. Glad of the distraction, she pulled it out of her bag.

Shirlee. This time she looked at it.

> Sorry Poll, I've been a pain. Guy has told me to back off. You know it's only because I love ya, but I promise I'll stop bugging you out until you get in touch with me. It might kill me but for you I'll do it. S xxx

Polly couldn't help smiling as she read it, hearing it all clearly in Shirlee's voice. She looked down at the phone for a minute and then tapped on the message. Time to give Shirlee a call, and move on from this silly stand-off.

Her phone had rung a couple of times when Polly heard something that made her jump up from the chair. It was the unmistakable sound of a key in the lock.

Who the hell could it be? Should she try to hide under the desk and then sneak out when they went into the loo or something?

But she didn't have time to do anything before she saw David's so familiar frame in the doorway.

She dropped the phone in shock, just as Shirlee answered it. She could hear her voice saying 'Pollster! Hey! What gives? Speak to me ... what the fuck?' and she fumbled around on the floor to pick it up and end the call.

David was still standing there. He'd said nothing. Then they spoke at the same time, as Polly came out from behind the desk and went towards him.

'David!' she said, feeling tears spring into her eyes.

'What are you doing here?' he said. His voice was tense and cold. He did not sound pleased to see her.

Polly stopped halfway across the room. She'd been going to throw her arms round him. Seeing him again, looking just as he'd always looked, ruggedly handsome in jeans, brown lace-up boots and his pea coat, she just wanted to hug him, to feel his body against hers again.

'I just needed to ...'

She started walking towards him again and he stepped back, away from her.

'David?' she said, bewildered. 'We thought you were in Turkey. I just came to leave you a note. Please don't run away from me again. We have to talk. I want to help you. Come home with me, let me and the kids look after you. You don't have to suffer this alone. We love you.'

Tears started running down her cheeks, but when she took another step forward he turned away, going into the kitchen. Taking it as a positive sign that he hadn't just bolted for the front door, Polly followed him in there. He was standing facing the wall, his arms stiff, holding onto the edge of the counter, his head down.

'How dare you come here,' he said, without looking round at her. 'I suppose it was you who told Lucas where I was.'

'No, it wasn't,' said Polly. 'He followed you here from work. That's how desperate he was to see his father, to find out why you have rejected us all like this.'

'Well, you know now, don't you?' he said turning round to face her, seeming more angry than Polly had ever seen him look. 'Maxine has told you about my issues, so now you know, can you please do as I ask – as I asked her to tell you – and leave me alone? Did she not give you that message?'

'She did,' said Polly uncertainly. 'But I just want to help you and so do the kids. We love you and we want to help you get through this.'

David laughed, a cruel, mocking sound.

'Well, sorry, Mother Teresa, but there's nothing you can do for me. I'm a sick fuck and I just want to be left alone to get on with it. I don't need your do-gooder help. No number of Sun Salutations or pretty smells are going to cure me, Polly, so I would ask you to respect my wishes and leave me alone. Go and do some chanting and get over it.'

Polly stood and stared at him for a moment. He looked the same as the man she'd been married to all these years, but he was so different. He wasn't the same person. Her David could be tricky at times, with his strange little ways, but he was never nasty like this.

Her tears dried up and she felt she ought to say something, but she couldn't think what. She wasn't even sure what she was feeling. He was being so horrible it was hurtful and shocking – but she didn't feel angry. She remembered too clearly what Maxine had told her, that he was in the grip of a devastating illness. He couldn't help it. It wasn't him who was being like this, it was the illness. He was like a puppet in its grasp. She had to be strong.

'David,' she said, 'do you think I could have a glass of water?'

He poured her one and she sat down at the kitchen table with it, playing for time, trying to think what to do.

'Please sit down and talk to me, just for a moment,' she said, after taking a long drink and putting the glass on the table. 'Then I'll go. But there are some things I have to say to you first.'

He sat opposite her, stony-faced.

'We thought you were in Turkey,' she said, trying to break the ice in any way she could.

'I came back,' he said.

Polly decided to launch in.

'I'm so sorry that you have this horrible condition,' she said, speaking slowly and quietly, the way she spoke to Digger when she wanted to reassure him. 'From what Maxine told me, it sounds like a living hell. Like having a Hieronymus Bosch painting in your head. I was also desperately sad to learn that you've lived with this torture throughout our marriage and haven't felt you could tell me, but I understand that it's nothing to do with me and I'm not going to take it personally. It is what it is.'

She paused, taking another slow drink of water, while she gathered her thoughts again. David looked at her blankly.

'I still love you, David,' she continued. 'How can I not? You are the father of my children and I have loved you for more than half my life, I can't just turn it off like a tap. But the last few months have been very difficult for me, as I'm sure you understand, not knowing where you were, or what was wrong.'

David nodded, closing his eyes.

'I'm sorry,' he said.

'It's OK,' said Polly, reaching over and touching his hand. He snatched it away.

Polly paused to take a breath, shocked by his reaction.

'So the thing is,' she said. 'I have to say this to you one last time. The kids and I want you to come home, so we can support you through this. Or maybe you need to go to a residential unit for a while – Maxine mentioned that – and then come home. Or perhaps you want to stay living here for a while, but be in regular touch with us and come home for visits, with the aim that one day you will move back permanently and we will be a family again. Whatever it takes, we'll be there for you.'

David started to say something, but she raised her hand to ask him to wait.

'That offer is still there,' she said, 'but I can't go on in this limbo, so I'm going to have to give you an ultimatum. I know you're ill, I know you're not in control of your thoughts, let alone your emotions, but you have to make this one decision. You don't have to give me an answer right now – take some time to think about it. Twenty-four hours? A week? Two? It's your call, but we have to reach an agreed conclusion. I can't go on in this half-life.'

As she said it, she was surprised how clearly and calmly it came out, because she hadn't known exactly what she was going to say until she heard herself saying it.

David was still eyeballing her with that steady, cold gaze, so different from the way he used to look at her.

'I don't need twenty-four hours,' he said. 'I've already made my decision. It's very sweet of you to say you still love me – if rather childish, because how can you love someone you don't even know any more? But no, thank you, I won't be coming home. I don't want to live with you, or the kids, or anyone, I just want to be left alone to get on with my work. It's the only way I can live.'

'Are you sure?' said Polly.

'Well, I was hoping not to have to say this to you,' he said, standing up and looking down at her, 'but as you've insisted on ignoring my request to be left in peace, you've forced me into it. The thing is, I don't love you any more, Polly. I haven't for quite a while now. You had an innocent dizzy charm I adored when we were young – and you were beautiful-looking then, of course, so I was in lust as well as in love with you – but I don't love you now. It was great while it lasted, but the kids are grown up, so what's the point of playing pretend happy families? You're old and faded and I'm bored with you. The end.'

Polly looked at him in puzzled astonishment, hardly able to process what he was saying. It was so cruel.

'I think you need to leave now,' said David, starting to pull the back of her chair away from the table.

Polly got to her feet, feeling something new that it took her a moment to recognise.

That detached way he was looking at her, the horrible things he was saying. She was afraid of him.

She stumbled out of the kitchen and David went into the sitting room and brought her coat and bag out to the hall, handing them to her without meeting her eye, and going straight over to the door.

'One thing before you go,' he said, as she came over. 'I want those keys. I had no idea you still had them or I would have had the locks changed.'

Not quite sure what she was doing, Polly took them out of her pocket and handed them to him.

'What shall I tell the kids?' she whispered hoarsely.

David looked down with an exasperated expression, as though the question was an inconvenience.

'I'll write to them,' he said, 'and explain I want a divorce. Of course I'll see them if they want to see me, as long as it's not too often. I have to protect myself. And if you're wondering about all the property stuff, you can keep the house. I don't want anything. Just not to be bothered by any of you.'

Polly stared at him, feeling almost dizzy with shock.

She was just about to walk out of the door on some kind of autopilot when something occurred to her, something she really wanted to know the answer to.

'That time you came to the house,' she said, 'while I was having lunch with Clemmie. You burned something in the wood burner. What was it?'

David thought for a moment and then a smile passed over his face. Not a nice one. A cruel smirk.

'It was several drafts of a letter to you,' he said, 'saying all this, but I thought better of it. At that point I couldn't be bothered with all the bullshit mentioning divorce would bring with it, so I burned it. So now you know. My solicitor will write to you.'

Polly walked through the doorway and turned round to say one last goodbye to him, but he already had shut the door.

FragrantCloud.net

The scent of … an ending

Sometimes things that seem like they're at the very centre of your life come to an abrupt end. It's an inevitable part of life. As the ancient Greek philosopher Heraclitus once said, 'The only constant in life is change.'

So you'd think we'd all be better at dealing with it!

In the worst cases it comes as a horrible sudden shock that can take a long time to recover from, but in others it takes a reality check to make you see that the change in question has been coming along for a while and you just hadn't realised it. Or wanted to.

I've just experienced a big change like that in my life. It was quite a trauma when the reality of it was suddenly forced upon me, but very quickly I understood that deep down inside I'd known it was going to happen for a long time and just hadn't wanted to face up to it.

The way I explain it to myself is by picturing it as something I knew was happening just on the other side of a curtain, but I couldn't summon up the courage to pull that curtain back and actually look at what was behind it.

In the end someone did that for me, wrenching it open – and while it felt like an almost physical blow to be confronted with it so brutally, in a funny way, the harshness of the revelation has made it easier for me to come to terms with it. There's no 'perhaps' or 'maybe' in the picture.

Boom.

Of course, like all big changes, it will lead to a lot of unavoidable smaller changes – the pond-ripple effect – but I'm not allowing myself to think about them at all. Every time one of them pops up as a 'But what will I do about the ...?' anxiety, I bat it away. Each new challenge, big and small, will come along in its own time and I'll deal with it then.

So that's how I'm living right now, moment to moment, and embracing this big change, rather than lamenting it. Acknowledging feelings of loss and sadness when they come over me, but not dwelling on them.

Above all, seeing it not as an ending, but as a new beginning. And if that sounds like a dopey affirmation, so be it. It works for me!

So, you might be wondering: how can an emotional shift like this have a smell? Well, all I can say is that in my world everything has a smell, even the intangibles. It's how I navigate my way through life, and analysing the aromas I associate with this big life event is really helping me through it.

My smells for this change first acknowledge what I'm leaving behind: the naphtha of boot polish, the petroleum reek of coal tar soap, the fresh wood of just-sharpened pencils, strong black coffee, lanolin, and the very particular sweet aniseed of liquorice.

Then there is my current reality, the smells that are constants in my life: lemon slices and fresh ginger, the sharp tannin and milky contrast of builder's tea, and the slightly sickly green scent of freshly cut flower stems. And not forgetting the classic ingredients of the chypre base of so many of my favourite perfumes – bergamot, oakmoss, patchouli and labdanum (rock rose) – which I'm finding so reassuring in this time of transition.

Other comforts are my dog, yoga and my children – not necessarily in that order, ha ha – which can be summed up in the olfactory shorthand of wet grass, honeysuckle, sweat, sticking plasters, cheap biscuits, new wool and roasting nuts.

Quite a mixture, all that, but complicated feelings inspire a complex scent-scape.

My scents for change are (and there's a lot of them, because there's a lot going on for me at the moment!):

Pour Homme by Yamamoto
On the Road by Timothy Han
Santal Blanc by Serge Lutens
Oud Wood by Tom Ford
Dear Polly by Vilhelm
La Flâneuse by Lucien Lechêne
PM by the Great Eastern Fragrance Company
Je t'aime Jane by Bella Freud
No. 9 Benjoin by Prada
Shalimar by Guerlain
Original by Eight & Bob

COMMENTS

LuxuryGal: This post is such a coincidence! We've had a big change too. We've had a new kitchen put in. It's really beautiful.

AgathaF: Change can be good, but it can also be unsettling. Good luck.

LeichhardtLori: Hang on in there, gf xxxxxxx

PerfumedWorld: This is great. I love Bella Freud's perfumes too.

Ros: This is beautiful. Thank you.

JayneAgain: This brought a tear to my eye.

WhirlyShirlee: You go girl. We've got your back.

ClemmieMedic: 💘 💔 💕 💖 ❤️ 💘 💚 💙 💜 💛 💝

EastLondonNostrils: You know I always have champagne at the ready for you, darling xxx

Saturday, 9 April

Polly was in her bedroom with Shirlee, packing David's clothes into two large suitcases.

'I don't know why you don't just stuff it all in bin bags,' said Shirlee, rolling up T-shirts while Polly carefully folded. 'That way we'll get it all in, with no rolling or folding, and it'll send him a message too. "Here's your junk, shithead. Enjoy!"'

Polly couldn't help laughing.

'I've told you already, Shirlee,' she said, 'I'm not getting into any of that stuff. I just want to move on with my new life as smoothly as I can. You know what Maxine told me: he's very ill and it affects his judgment in ways I can hardly imagine. And I've got enough to deal with – supporting the kids through it, for one thing – without stirring up any extra aggro. I'm just trying to let him go with a loving spirit.'

'I'd let him go with a punch in the guts,' said Shirlee. 'You're a much better person than I am.'

'I'm not,' said Polly. 'You're a very good person for helping me do this, because if you weren't here I'd probably be sobbing over every sock.'

'Try this one,' said Shirlee, lobbing a rolled-up pair of thick winter socks at Polly's head. She caught them, then turned and chucked them into the waste-paper bin, where they landed with a satisfying thud.

'Goal!' she said, and they both laughed.

'Did that feel a little bit good?' said Shirlee.

Polly nodded, but at the same time she remembered buying that particular pair of socks. She knew every pair personally; she'd washed and dried and put them all away so many times when David had still lived here and things had been normal – or at least when she'd thought they were normal. She felt the energy drain out of her as she glanced back at the wardrobe with all his jackets and shoes still to do.

'You know what, Shirlee?' she said. 'You're right. I don't think I can be bothered to pack up any more of his crap. Why don't we just put it all in his study and he can have it taken away when he gets all his books?'

'Plan!' said Shirlee. 'Why don't we just dump it all on the floor in there?'

'You're right,' said Polly. 'I don't need to pack it for him. I'm not going to be deliberately antagonistic, but there is a limit.'

She grabbed all David's jackets from the wardrobe, carried them through to his study and dropped them on the floor. It felt good. Shirlee was right behind her with a pile of jumpers.

'Howzat?' she said, throwing them down on top of the jackets. 'What's next?'

Very quickly they cleared everything out of the wardrobes and drawers and threw it all into the study. Polly closed the door on the mountain of belongings, making a mental note not to glance through the hole she'd kicked in it, so she wouldn't accidentally see any of it again until he took it all away. And the next time she spoke to her solicitor, she was going to ask her to fix an official date for that to happen. She'd had enough of not knowing what was going on in her own life. From now on it was going to run according to a schedule that she set.

'So we've done that,' said Shirlee, following Polly down the stairs and into the kitchen. 'Is there anything else we can do to make you feel less edgy in the house? Or shall we go out and do something? I don't think you should spend too much time sitting around here on your own.'

'I never sit around,' said Polly. 'There's always stuff to do for the blog, and—'

'OK, I know you don't watch daytime TV, but what I'm saying is, I think that right now, you shouldn't be home alone too much.'

'You're probably right,' said Polly. 'Digger needs a walk. We could take him up to the Heath together if you like, and have a nice long ramble.'

From the moment they set out from the house Polly wished she'd thought of any other excursion. Every step they took towards the gate onto the Heath reminded her of doing the same walk with Chum and Artemis; she could see his smile and hear his laugh.

It churned her up, but not so much with longing for him as guilt. She still hadn't spoken to him since that awkward meeting outside Maxine's office. She'd replied to the text he'd sent her the next morning, apologising if she'd been abrupt, but saying she'd had a big shock and lot to deal with subsequently, and just needed some time to process it all.

He'd replied immediately, wishing her well and saying that he was always there if she needed him. He hadn't been in touch since, which was four days now.

Polly was grateful he was giving her some space, because she couldn't help feeling strangely disconnected from him. The whole episode from the moment they'd met again in the dining room at Rockham Park – how long ago had it been? three months? – had taken on a detached, dreamlike quality, like something that had happened to someone else.

He kept popping into her head so clearly, triggered by the memory of doing that walk on the Heath with him, yet at the same time, none of it seemed real. Apart from those two occasions at Rockham Park, when she'd had her family, Shirlee or Guy with her, he'd always occupied a separate space outside her real life, and somehow she couldn't reconcile the two.

And, she increasingly realised, she didn't want to. It was the otherness of her time with Chum that had been so appealing. An escape.

All that horsey stuff and the stately home were very beguiling, but they didn't really have anything to do with her. The two of them were from such different worlds. They'd been thrown together at university and then again via Rockham Park, and there was certainly a powerful physical attraction between them, but beyond that, what did they really have in common? Dogs?

Once she and Shirlee got onto the Heath, she deliberately took a different path from the one she'd taken with Chum that day, and immediately felt better for it. With all she had to process about David, she just couldn't manage thinking about Chum as well.

The track she'd chosen went steadily uphill, and after about ten minutes of the climb, Shirlee had grown uncharacteristically quiet. When they came to a bench, with views looking out across the landscape, Shirlee sat down on it and Polly assumed she was puffed out.

'Are you OK?' asked Polly, sitting next to her and turning to look at her friend.

'Not really,' said Shirlee.

'What's the matter?' said Polly, feeling alarmed. Had the hill been too much for her?

'The thing is, Poll,' she said, spreading her left arm along the top of the bench and looking intently at her, 'we're in this beautiful big open space, but I can hardly breathe.'

'I'm sorry it was such a steep path ...' Polly started.

Shirlee raised her hand and shook her head.

'It's nothing to do with the path,' she said. 'What's suffocating me is the great big elephant that's here on the Heath with us. He's filling the whole damn space and I can't stand it any longer. I'm calling out on the elephant.'

'An elephant?' said Polly, not getting it. Was Shirlee hallucinating?

'Not a real elephant, you idiot,' she said, slapping Polly on the top of her arm with the back of her hand. 'It's the elephant in the room ... you know, the thing we're not talking about?'

'Oh,' said Polly, getting the point. '*That* elephant.'

'Yeah,' said Shirlee, 'the elephant called Edward.'

Polly's head snapped round to stare at her.

'What do you mean?' she said.

Shirlee laughed, rolling her eyes.

'What do I mean? What I mean is, what the hell are you doing here with me? Why aren't you with him, Mr Yum Chum? You're free now, your husband has released you with his nasty insults. I've been thinking about what he said to you and it was so unbelievably mean I think he did it on purpose, so you'd properly let go. Because if you're set free, so is he – and that seems to be what he needs to survive. So take the gift he's given you, Polly. God knows you've earned it.'

Polly felt a flash of anger – how many hours had it taken for Shirlee to start meddling in her life again? – but just as fast, she was overtaken by confusion.

'I can't just go running off to him,' she spluttered.

'Why not?'

Polly paused for a moment, conflicting thoughts racing into her head.

'I'm not one those ping-pong-ball women. I don't ricochet straight from one man to another. It would be ... unseemly.'

'Oh, apologies, Miss Brontë, I'd forgotten it was 1847.'

'Well, maybe I need some time to get used to the fact that I'm getting a divorce? It's quite a big adjustment to make,' said Polly, starting to feel got at.

'Haven't you already had several months to do that?' said Shirlee. 'And if you needed some decompression between guys – how come you cosied up with Edward the way you did, before you knew you were really off the hook with hubby?'

'I don't know,' said Polly, her head dropping forward. She felt completely deflated. 'I wasn't thinking straight. I shouldn't have done it.'

She turned and looked at Shirlee, tears smarting in her eyes.

'I think I used him,' she said.

Shirlee looked at her very sadly, then shuffled along the bench and put her arm round her.

'Come here to your Aunt Shirlee,' she said. 'And stop beating yourself up. He was clearly very happy to be used, if that was what you were doing, but when we were at the lunch at your mom's place, from where I was sitting – and you know that's always as close to the action as possible – you were looking pretty loved up yourself.'

'Oh, I don't know,' said Polly, standing up quickly. She couldn't let herself wallow around in this conjecture. 'I just got caught up in it all. I was in a very messed-up place in my life and I did things I never would have done normally.'

She called for Digger. She wanted to get going. She'd had enough D & Ms for the day. For a lifetime.

'That's because what you thought was "normal",' said Shirlee, making quote marks with her fingers, 'was that you were a married woman with a husband at home. You behaved differently with Chum because you weren't that person any more, because even if it wasn't official then, David had gone. And you know what, Poll? I think he'd actually left long before that. From what you've told me, even though he was still physically in the house, it sounds like he checked out emotionally a long time ago. He kept that flat on all that time.'

'Well, I really don't want to think about all that right now,' said Polly, beginning to feel exasperated. 'I've got enough on just coping with today.'

'OK,' said Shirlee, getting to her feet. 'But bear in mind, please, you had a very sweet thing going with Edward, and while it might seem too soon, I'd hate to see you regretting that in the future – and Poll, he's just such a *lovely* guy.'

Polly put her hands up in surrender.

'I do know that,' she said, 'it's why I'm feeling so bad about all this, but I can't take it on now. So I have to ask you to promise me one thing, Shirlee.'

'What?'

'You must promise that you won't stage one of your interventions to try to get Ch ... Edward and me together. Don't turn up with him at the house or anything like that. In fact, promise you won't contact him again. It was really wrong that you ever did.'

'Sorry, Mama,' said Shirlee in a baby voice.

'I'm serious,' said Polly. 'I won't let him be hurt. I've done enough damage already. Do you promise?'

'I do solemnly swear,' said Shirlee, with her right hand on her heart and her left hand up, 'that I won't intervene to try to stop my beloved friend Polly from throwing away her chance of happiness with a smokin' hot straight-up guy who was clearly put on this earth to complete her. OK?'

'And you won't keep bringing him up in conversation? Especially when other people are around? Or talk to other people – for example, people called Guy – about what might have happened, or not?'

'I do swear, by the almighty Goddess ...'

'Thank you, Miss Katz,' said Polly, 'I accept your oaths, now let's finish this walk and not talk about anything to do with men for the rest of it. OK?'

Monday, 18 April

Polly was taking Lori on a tour of her perfume-blogging life. They'd done a couple of PR open days in the morning, been to a lunchtime launch, and now she'd drafted Lori in as an assistant at one of her own events in the afternoon.

'Is this a normal day for you now?' asked Lori, as they watched the well-dressed and expensively coiffed women – and a few just as smartly groomed men – filling up the tables of ten in a function room at the Berkeley Hotel.

'Not every day,' said Polly. 'But this is what my blog life can be like.'

'Wow,' said Lori. 'And to think I used to tease you about smelling everything. Remember that time we took the kids to the Botanic Gardens and you were trying to analyse the smell of the fruit bats and one of them crapped on your head?'

'Not something I'll forget easily,' said Polly, laughing. 'I had to wash my hair five times to get that stink out.'

She pulled the end of her hair up and sniffed it. 'I think I can still smell it, now you've reminded me,' she said. 'Fermented rotten fruit.'

The theme of the talk was one of Polly's most popular – 'The Scent of the 1950s' – and Lori had got into the spirit, buying a vintage little black dress and a cocktail hat specially, and doing a great job of handing out the blotters and keeping the bottles of scent circulating round the room.

'This actual bottle of Diorissimo was given to my mother by Christian Dior himself, in 1956,' said Polly, holding it up before handing it to Lori to show to the audience. 'She modelled extensively for him and they were good friends. This jacket I'm wearing is one of her Dior couture pieces from that era. I just can't quite do it up – I don't have her eighteen-inch waist.'

There was a bit of hubbub when she said this – which she was used to, she'd done this event so many times now, although this was the first time at a five-star hotel for a handsome fee.

Glancing round the luxurious space, she remembered the scruffy rooms over pubs where she'd done her early presentations, back when the idea of a perfume history event was a novelty in itself. She'd come a long way – and so had her audiences. She'd noticed some very serious handbags come in.

'Mum was the model for one of René Gruau's famous illustrations for the Diorissimo advertising campaign,' she continued, tapping her laptop so the wonderful painting of Daphne in black opera gloves, her hair growing into roses, was projected onto the wall. 'And this is her modelling in one of the fashion shows, in a photograph that appeared on the cover of *Time* magazine ...'

Judging by the enthusiastic question-and-answer session, followed by a long queue of women wanting personal perfume advice, and the smile on the hotel PR's face, the event was a success.

'Bloody oath, Poll,' said Lori, 'you're a superstar.'

One of the last women in the queue held back a bit until the others had finished asking questions, then she walked up and handed Polly her business card. Polly glanced down at it and saw the words 'Literary Agent'.

'Call me,' said the woman. 'I'll take you for lunch. You could do a great book and I can see you doing television as well.'

Polly was too amazed to answer.

'That would be great,' said Lori, beaming at the woman. 'She'll call you. I'll make sure she does.'

'Thanks,' said Polly, finding her voice again. 'I will. Thank you. Yes. Thank you for coming today.'

The woman smiled and left, and Lori gave Polly a hug.

'Result!' she said. 'The audience loved you and your talk was fascinating – I had no idea perfume was so interesting. There's so much more to it than smells.'

Polly laughed and recited the list from one of her other events, 'The Perfume University': 'history, chemistry, art, sociology, popular culture, economics, neuroscience, business, psychology, botany, marketing, fashion, and not forgetting sex, before you get anywhere near your nose. That's what I love about it.'

'Well, it's given you a new life,' said Lori, 'and now you're going to do a book. You can send a copy to Dreary Dave.'

Polly smiled but it gave her a pang. It had been wonderful to finally be able to tell Lori what had happened with David – someone who really knew him, who had known them together when they were still a happy family unit – but she wished she could be a little more tactful about him.

'It's not his fault, Lori,' she said, as they packed up. 'He's got a horrible medical condition.'

'I know,' said Lori, 'it's a bastard, but you've got to admit, Polly, he's always had his tricky side.'

'It seems likely he's always been fighting these intrusive thoughts,' said Polly. 'It does explain a lot of things I had to tell myself were his "little ways".'

Lori nodded. 'Reckon you're right about that,' she said. 'Rich has thought for years there was something a little bit crook about David. He says that's why he's always been passed over for the big jobs. No one could put their finger on it, but there was something not quite right about him.'

Polly said nothing. She was remembering all the times David had said Rich was 'very ambitious' – and hadn't meant it as a compliment – but she wasn't going to say that to Lori. Ugh, she was glad to be out of all that academic position-jockeying. She'd seen it with her father and then again with David. It could be vicious.

This was clearly what David had meant when he'd asked her – well, told her – not to let the university know that he was away from home for any other reason than a research trip. She understood that now. He hadn't wanted any of his rivals to know he was vulnerable.

So he'd been more worried about saving his professional reputation than how his absence would affect her and the kids. Thinking about that, Polly felt betrayed all over again. It might be caused by an illness but that didn't stop it from hurting.

'So what's next?' said Lori, after they'd said goodbye to the hotel PR and were heading out to the lobby.

'I've got just the thing,' said Polly, linking her arm through her best friend's as they walked out onto the street.

The doorman asked them if they'd like a taxi as he opened the door for them. Polly nodded.

'Claridges, please,' she said to the cab driver as they got in, then turned to Lori.

'They're doing a menu of perfumed cocktails in the bar,' said Polly, 'which I consulted on. So I get complimentary drinks there at the moment and I think we should go and have a couple.'

'We most definitely should,' said Lori. 'And I'll raise a toast to academic research, because I wouldn't be having nearly so good a time if Rich was here with me. This way we're both happy. He's got his war graves and I've got my best girlfriend and a scented cocktail or two. Or three.'

'I'll drink to that,' said Polly.

It was a quarter-to-midnight, and Lori and Guy were arm-wrestling on Polly's kitchen table – over lit candles. Lori was winning.

'Owwww!' Guy started yelling.

'Some don't like it hot, eh, perfume boy?' Lori was saying.

'Please stop!' said Polly. 'I can smell burning hair.'

'That is gross,' said Shirlee, who was the referee, 'but don't let it stop ya. This is too much fun.'

With a grunt of effort, Guy managed to raise his arm a little and started to slowly push Lori's down towards the other candle.

'Don't burn my friend,' squealed Polly. 'I've only had her back a week, I need her unsinged!'

But Polly knew Lori was going to be fine when she saw her chest expand as she took a super-slow deep breath, then, as she released it noisily out of her nostrils, she came back, firmly pushing Guy's hand back down again.

'Yow!' he said, jumping up and running to the sink. 'You win, you freak.'

He ran cold water over the back of his hand.

'You're very strong, for such a slender person,' he said.

'She's a yoga bitch, like me,' said Polly.

Lori smiled graciously.

'Strength is in the head, not in the arm, grasshopper,' she said. 'Your muscles are just fashion accessories. Shot me up, Shirl.'

Shirlee grinned and filled a set of shot glasses from the set Lori had brought as a gift for Polly – along with a bottle of tequila. They were more than halfway down it. She passed one to Lori.

'I think the runner-up gets a shot as well, doesn't he?' said Guy, sitting down again and rubbing an ice cube on his hand. 'Damages.'

Shirlee filled another glass, then supplied them both with a salt dose. Guy and Lori raised their glasses, licked their thumbs, slugged and bit their lime slice, without ever losing eye contact, then slammed their glasses on the kitchen table.

'*Ariba!*' they both shouted.

Polly shook her head.

'This is the kind of thing Lucas used to get up to,' she said, 'until he grew out of it recently – something it seems you two still haven't done.'

'Wanna shot?' asked Shirlee, grinning.

'No thanks,' said Polly, who'd already had three, on top of the scented cocktails earlier, and felt quite dizzy enough.

'Polly! Polly! Polly!' Lori started chorusing and the other two joined in, getting louder and faster, until they were all drumming their feet on the floor and their fists on the table.

'The neighbours!' said Polly. 'They'll call the police if you carry on. They've done it before. I think it was the last time you were here, Lori.'

'We'll give them a few shots,' said Lori, who seemed to be high on the tequila rather than drunk. She had an ox's constitution and never got messy with alcohol, just more energetic.

'What's happened to the music?' said Guy.

'Oh, it must be the end of the playlist," said Polly, getting up from the table and heading for the hifi system. As she stood up she felt a wave of vertigo – and a little nauseous. She'd definitely drunk too much. She fumbled about and managed to get one of Lucas's party mixes going and then headed out of the kitchen.

'You can run but you can't hide,' Guy called after her, before he started a chorus of Shirlee's name.

Polly walked to the front door and went outside, pushing it to, but not shutting it. She needed some fresh air – and as she heard another chorus of SHOT! SHOT! SHOT! from the kitchen, she realised she also needed a break from her friends.

She loved the way they all got on so well. The fact that Lori adored Shirlee and Guy, and they felt the same about her, made Polly feel reassured about her choice of new friends.

Sometimes she wondered why she gathered such high-octane characters around her, but seeing the three of them together she'd understood that – particularly in the difficult times she'd been going through – she needed their energy to feed off.

From the moment she walked back into the kitchen a few minutes later, Polly felt a palpable shift in the atmosphere. They were all quite pissed – they seemed to have got noticeably drunker in that short absence – but it wasn't just that. Shirlee was looking uncharacteristically uncomfortable.

'Here she is,' said Lori, 'the world's best friend and best yoga teacher, who also annoyingly has the best legs. Where've you been, Pollski?'

'Oh I was just having a breather, I can't keep up with you party animals.'

'She always was a bit of a grog wimp,' said Lori, grinning at her. 'Come and sit by me, Poll doll, I'm going miss you soooo much when I leave.'

Polly sat next to her, putting her head on Lori's shoulder and closing her eyes. Lori kissed her hair.

'You came back at just the right moment,' Lori said.

Polly opened her eyes again. Guy was clearly hammered. Shirlee looked even more uneasy than she had a minute before.

'Who wants another shot?' she asked, reaching for the bottle.

'I'm holding,' said Lori, 'and I reckon perfume boy's going to pass out if he has another one now. Besides, we've got important things to discuss. I declare this meeting of Polly's Best Mates open. We have quorum and top of the agenda is: how we're going to get you laid. And soon.'

Polly sat up and looked over at Shirlee, who opened her eyes wide in an expression that seemed to convey she'd had nothing to do with the direction the conversation was taking.

'Well, I did offer,' slurred Guy, 'and it would change her life to fly Air Guy, but she's not into my scene, more fool her.'

'Yeah, well, the group thing's fine when you're young,' said Lori, 'but at our age, it's a bit more delicate. Specially as this will be the first bloke apart from her hubby that Polly's rooted since she was about nineteen. How old were you when you met Dreary Dave?'

'Twenty-two,' said Polly, wondering how soon she could go to bed. She really wished Lori wouldn't call David that.

'I think I might make us some early breakfast,' said Shirlee, starting to get up from her seat.

'Sit down, Shirl,' said Lori, 'or we won't be quorate. So, you guys know the field in London. Who's Polly going to get with?'

'I don't know what you're worrying about,' said Guy. 'She's already got horsey boy on the go. If she hasn't climbed onto that saddle yet, it's only a matter of time. And he is h-h-h-h-h-hot. I've already told her I'd do him in a heartbeat. With or without his riding boots ...'

Lori had turned to look at Polly with her mouth open.

'You've got a bloke on the go and you haven't told me?' she said, looking appalled.

'No,' said Polly. 'Guy's got it all wrong.'

'Well, you know gaydar?' said Guy. 'There's also something called "laydar", which is when you just instinctively know two people have been wildly at it – or are very soon going to be – and my laydar went off in a major way when I saw you two together, so there. Proof.'

'But who is he?' said Lori. 'Spill it, Poll! This is too much. I think I'm going to need another shot, after all. Set 'em up, Shirl.'

Polly summoned all her self-control to avoid running out of the room screaming. She hadn't told Lori about Chum, because she was trying not to think about him. It made her feel bad and sad.

And there was something else. She didn't want to tell anyone what had happened between them because she was worried it would spoil it.

Although she wondered now if she'd been slightly deranged, her time with Chum had been so magical she wanted to keep those memories untarnished, and just for herself. Telling someone else about them would make them sound tawdry.

'He's talking about someone I ran into where my mum lives,' she said, trying to sound casual. 'Someone I went to uni with and I haven't seen since, but his stepdad lives there and so we met up, in the dining room. That's it.'

'That's it?' said Guy. 'And I'll have another shot too, Shirlster. I need my strength to face this outrageous torrent of denial. I've seen you two together. There's an electromagnetic field between you and horsey boy that could pull a satellite back to earth, and I've seen all the little looks over the biscuits and the "Let's take the doggies for a walk". It's quite emetic really.'

'Why do you call him horsey boy?' said Lori.

'He's a classic type,' said Guy. 'All long legs and razor cheekbones and a narrow head. Just like all the upper-class twits I went to school with. You know those posh fox-hunting types? Tally-ho!'

'He doesn't hunt,' said Polly, the words out before could stop herself, and the three others exploded with laughter, even Shirlee.

Lori shoved her shoulder.

'Polly Masterson-Mackay, you dog!' she said. 'You are *so* doing him!'

'I am not,' said Polly.

'"He doesn't hunt … he's much too nice for that … he's strong, but he's gentle",' said Lori in a high-pitched imitation of Polly's accent. 'You are seriously into this guy. You gave it all away there in three little words, so you better tell all, girlfriend. We want details. How often, how big, any tongue action …'

Guy roared with laughter.

'Does he use his riding crop on you?' he asked.

'Very funny,' said Polly, summoning all her self-control. 'I knew him at uni, I bumped into him at my mum's place, we've been for a few dog walks, but I have never shagged Edward Cliddington-Hanley-Maugham.'

They were all silent for a moment, just looking at her incredulously, then they burst out laughing together.

'Is that seriously his name?' said Lori. 'Edward Clitlicking-Manley-Horn?'

Polly rolled her eyes.

'Yes, that's his name. His dad was an earl, they have a big stately home. Loads of my friends at uni were like that – that's why I didn't stay in touch with him all these years. He's a very nice guy, but he's not part of my world.'

She looked over at Shirlee and smiled. She was so grateful to her for not joining in with the others, when it must have been so tempting. She'd only laughed. She hadn't chipped in, she'd kept her oath.

Shirlee smiled back, with her lips pressed tightly together, making the point.

'You know what, Shirlee?' Polly said. 'I'd love some of that early breakfast. I'll help you.'

Monday, 2 May

As she watched everyone in her Monday-morning yoga class sink into a deep meditative state, Polly took a moment to think about her own concerns. Now Lori had gone home, she was doing her best to get her life back to some kind of normal – or at least the new kind of normal it had settled into since David had left.

She was doing her classes, blogging, going to as many perfume events as possible, and hanging out a lot with Shirlee and Guy. Mostly it was fine. Sometimes it was great. She still had pangs of guilt about Chum and still more now about Lori, because she never did open up to her about him, although Lori had teased her endlessly, in her usual way.

It hadn't been a lie, Polly told herself as she picked up her temple chimes. She hadn't shagged him. So not a lie, just an omission of the full truth.

There was one thing to be cheerful about that morning, though: Maxine was back in the class and was staying for breakfast with Shirlee and her afterwards. Polly had been surprised how much she'd missed her steady, quiet presence, balancing out Shirlee's frenetic tempo, and was delighted she was back.

Polly gave her a big hug when she came back into the kitchen after seeing the last of the other yoga students out.

'Maxiiiii,' she said, 'it's so good to see you! My soon-to-be-ex-husband's ex-shrink.'

Maxine glanced over at Shirlee, who was already manning her frying pans, a spatula in each hand.

'It's fine,' said Polly. 'I've told her everything, we can talk freely – well, as freely as you can with professional discretion.'

'That's great,' said Maxine, 'and I'm glad to see you looking well. How are you doing?'

'Oh,' said Polly, 'you know, a bit this and that. I had my best friend over from Oz for a couple of weeks, which was great.'

'Now, she is one fun girl,' said Shirlee. 'Such a shame she doesn't live here all the time. We loved Lori.'

'That must have been very comforting, having her to stay,' said Maxine, using what Polly now recognised as her professional tone.

'Yes, it was,' said Polly.

It would have been more so if I could have been honest with her, she thought, but I seem to have forgotten how to do that with anybody. Especially myself.

'So has David found a new psych, then?' she asked Maxine. She didn't know why she was pushing it, but she wanted to know for some reason.

'I don't know,' said Maxine. 'It was quite, er, tricky convincing him that he needed to.'

'Did he get angry with you?' asked Polly.

Maxine said nothing for a moment, then seemed to make a decision.

'Yes, he did,' she said. 'In fact he was physically aggressive to me. I had to press my panic button.'

'What the fuck?' said Shirlee, turning round from the stove, holding both spatulas in the air.

'You don't look surprised,' said Maxine, observing Polly keenly.

'No,' said Polly. 'The last time I saw him, there was something about him I found very disturbing. He didn't attack me, but I felt quite afraid of him.'

'You never told me that,' said Shirlee.

'I don't tell you absolutely everything,' said Polly.

'Oh,' said Shirlee, like a disappointed child.

'Is this something that can happen with his condition?' Polly asked Maxine.

'It's controversial,' said Maxine. 'I've never seen it before. Some psychiatrists do diagnose psychosis in OCD patients with very poor insight – that means they don't recognise that their OCD symptoms are irrational – but I don't support that position. I think David has another condition, alongside what I was treating him for, and I don't feel qualified to deal with it. He needs a psychiatrist, not a psychotherapist. He possibly needs antipsychotics that I can't prescribe.'

'Oh, poor David,' said Polly. 'Is there nothing we can do?'

'I'm afraid I don't think there is,' said Maxine. 'Your children might be able to, he might listen to them – and if he gets worse, they could have him committed. I know that sounds appalling, but better that than having him attack someone.'

Polly put her hand on her forehead. She felt as though it were physically throbbing as she tried to take this new information on board. Poor, poor David.

'Clemmie really wants to come and see you,' she said, 'to talk about it all, and with her medical training, she'll understand this new stuff.'

'I'll see Clemmie any time,' said Maxine.

Shirlee put a mug of tea down on the table in front of Polly and squeezed her shoulder.

'It's a tough ride, baby girl,' she said. 'But you got friends.'

'I'm so grateful for that,' said Polly.

For the rest of the breakfast, Shirlee valiantly steered the conversation towards jollity. They kept to light topics and even had a laugh. By the time Shirlee and Maxine got up to go, Polly was feeling much better.

'Are you sure you're going to be all right here on your own?' asked Shirlee as she opened the front door. 'I promised Guy I'd help him shift some stuff and I can't let him down, but you could come too. It'll be fun hauling boxes around if we do it together.'

'I'll be OK,' said Polly. 'I've got lots of stuff to sort out for some events I'm doing, and if I do feel low, I'll call you and come over to Guy's.'

'And I'm so glad you're back,' said Polly to Maxine. 'I really missed you.'

'I missed you too,' said Maxine 'and your Pigeon Pose. My back's been playing up since I've been skipping your classes.'

They stood silently for a moment.

'I'm sorry to have been the bearer of more bad news about David,' she said. 'But I decided you had to know. And your kids need to know.'

'I'm more grateful than I can possibly tell you,' said Polly.

She kissed Maxine's cheek and gave her shoulders a squeeze.

'One other thing,' said Maxine. 'Cut yourself a lot of slack, Polly. You might feel that you're over the worst of it, but you've had some very big shocks – and I've just given you another one. You'll get through it on a kind of extended adrenaline rush, but one day that will stop and then it may hit you like a truck. And even before that, you can feel very disorientated and confused and uncertain about things you used to be absolutely sure of.

'So don't be surprised if you're a bit muddle-headed and make decisions about things and then don't understand why you made those choices. You'll be better than most people would be, because of your yoga and meditation practice, but don't underestimate the trauma you've been through, OK?'

Polly nodded. Speechless. It was like Maxine had been in her head the past couple of weeks.

'And if you need to, call me any time, night or day,' Maxine added. 'I'm here for you, as a friend with professional benefits.'

After they'd had gone, Polly tried to settle down to work, but couldn't stop thinking about what Maxine had said to her. She tried to remember her exact words, but couldn't quite pin them down.

She opened a document on the computer and made notes, trying to draw the words down from her memory, a technique she'd used for revision in her uni days, but she could only come up with fragments. 'Muddle-headed' was one and 'making decisions you won't understand later' was another. They definitely applied to her – but weren't all busy middle-aged people a bit foggy-brained like that?

So how could she cleanse her head and start to see things more clearly? Surely now she knew exactly what had happened with David – he was very ill – and what was going to happen between them – they were getting divorced – she should be able to. But even trying to think it through was giving her a headache.

As Maxine had said, her daily meditation usually helped Polly think more clearly, but, although she still practised it every morning, it didn't seem to be working its usual magic. She looked out of the window wondering what else she could do. Spring-clean the house? It certainly needed it, but that would just make her think of David, who'd be horrified if he could see how grubby she'd let it get. Go for a walk with Digger enjoying the wild flowers? No, that would just make her think of Chum.

In the end she decided to do some work and take her mind off it all.

She opened a new document, ready to write a blog post – but about what? She was sure she'd had an idea for something the day before, but couldn't remember what it was now. It had got tangled up with all the unfinished business in her head.

Polly groaned and typed the heading 'FragrantCloud', to get herself in the zone, as she always did. Perhaps if she just kept on writing she'd remember what the idea was. 'The scent of ...' she wrote. But the scent of what?

She chewed her finger for a moment and then typed 'being hopelessly brain boggled'. She laughed and was about to delete it when she suddenly had an idea. Maybe that was the answer. What was the scent of being brain boggled? She'd smell her way out of it.

She ran upstairs, grabbed a tote bag and put every box of perfume she had in her cupboard into it, then all the ones next to the bed and the one she had carelessly left on her dressing table that morning – which was PM, as it so often was these days.

Carrying the bag downstairs, she tipped them all out on the floor of the study and then opened up the bigger perfume cupboard in there. She got down the loose-leaf folder where she kept a printout of the text of each blog post, a throwback to university days she just couldn't stop herself doing. Sometimes she just needed to read things on paper.

She started at the first blog post she'd written after David left, 'The scent of yoga', and scanned down the list of perfumes she'd chosen for it. Just reading the names – Madagascan Jasmine, Exhale, Black Lapsang – she could summon up the smells in her head, as she imagined composers could hear their music as they wrote it.

Then she worked her way through every post she'd written since then and pulled out the ones that felt like they marked turning points – not the general posts about new launches, shops, events and stuff, but the ones that were really about her life.

From each of them she chose one, or two, perfumes that seemed most to sum up that particular moment in her journey since David had left, and lined them up in a row along her desk.

Then she took out a packet of sampling blotters and got to work. For 'The scent of yoga' she chose Black Lapsang because its smoky opening always made her think of incense and sacred spaces – which is what she tried to create in her former dining room, but without using joss sticks because she didn't think they went well with deep breathing.

She closed her eyes as the perfume developed to reveal its Assam-tea middle note, which made her think immediately of that first yoga breakfast with Shirlee and Maxine and the yogi bears.

What a landmark that had turned out to be and how important those friendships had become, a lifeline to get her through such a bewildering time. She couldn't imagine life without Shirlee's party-popper energy now. However maddening Shirlee could be, Polly had come to love her.

And, Polly reflected, she'd had no idea then, at that first breakfast, when she was as vulnerable as a newly-hatched turtle trying to find its way to the sea, what a role Maxine would end up playing in her life.

The next blog post was 'The scent of the elders' and there was only one possible perfume choice for that: Mitsouko. Polly hesitated before bringing the blotter to her nose. She knew that perfume – which scent connoisseurs considered 'the greatest chypre' – so well, she wanted to play it through in her mind first, from the sparkling peach top note to the spicy vetiver base, because she didn't have time to let all the stages of it develop.

When she did smell it, even just from that opening hit, she felt catapaulted back to Rockham Park, meeting Bill at her talk and then seeing Chum again at that lunch with the dogs. She could remember the exact moment she'd seen his face for the first time for well over twenty years, and had suddenly realised who this smiling, handsome middle-aged man was.

And then she could see him again, as a young man, by the light of the bonfire on the beach, surprising her in the library ... She moved on quicky to the next blog post: 'a daughter'.

Darling, earnest, brainy, loving Clemmie. Although now she was wearing lots of different scents – all made by Guy, because he was giving her commission on any sales she generated among her well-heeled student pals – it would always be Cristalle, for its clear, bright, citrus purity, which Polly would associate with her daughter.

What a rock Clemmie had been through it all – even despite that awful day when David had used her to get into the house undisturbed, and splitting up with her own boyfriend in the middle of it. And how helpful it had been to have her steady, rational, medical mind to keep her and Lucas grounded through the most difficult moments.

Polly bit her lip when she looked at her list for the next blog post: 'university days'. There would be no surprise what Yardley's Lily of the Valley would make her think of. She had almost certainly been wearing it that night on the beach, which had been an impromptu event, because if she'd known she was going to a party, she would have sprayed on one of the birthday-present perfumes she used to keep for best, before she knew better.

Calvin Klein's Obsession had been just that for her, and she'd treasured that bottle so much she hardly ever used it, so the memory connection with that wouldn't be nearly as strong as it was with the cheap eau de toilette she bought herself in the chemist.

Polly felt a great sense of affection for her young self, when she inhaled that pure and pretty Lily of the Valley. How innocent it was. Just as she had been, but not a goodie goodie – what was it Chum had said? You'd have been mad not to have had a good time up there, and Polly was glad she'd made the most of the dashing actor types Chum had been so funny about.

Then, suddenly she remembered him by the lake at Hanley Hall. Not in the past, up in Scotland, but as he was now, in her current life – or what had been her current life, until she'd walked away from it.

She moved on quickly, hoping for distraction from that line of thought, but finding none because it was 'The scent of a dog'. Dear, adorable, badly behaved, farty Digger. What a comfort and companion he'd become. Life without him was unimaginable now and she couldn't believe she'd been angry with David for dumping him on her. Well, he wasn't having the dog back. Digger was hers now.

She called for him and he came running through from the kitchen, tail wagging, head raised in eager anticipation, no doubt expecting a walk. Polly fell to her knees and hugged his furry neck, covering his head in kisses, before rummaging in her handbag to find him a handful of treats.

'Good boy,' she said, as he snaffled them up.

Polly sprayed a blotter with the scent she'd pulled out from Digger's post – Barbour For Him – wishing she'd had one of the others, like Dirt, by The Library of Fragrance, to use instead.

She knew what the Barbour aftershave would make her think of, and of course it did with its forest violets and cinnamon bark. Walks with Chum. Both of them wearing their Barbours. His green and ancient – it was probably the same one he'd had at St Andrews; hers black and only a year old, bought when they'd become fashionable in London.

She closed her eyes, remembering that first walk they'd taken. It hadn't been anything special in terms of landscape, but what a surprise how much she'd enjoyed it. Being in the proper country, air so fresh it was silky – and Chum's company. The ease she felt with him right from the start and the fun of walking Digger with someone else and another dog. It was such a wonderful change from her 'real' life, in the family home, constantly reminded of the strangeness of David not being there.

She was relieved to see the next post was 'The scent of a son'. Her heart contracted just at the thought of her baby boy, which is what he would always be to her, even though the last few months had made him grow up so much. It seemd corny even to think it, but the stress of it had turned Lucas from a boy to a man. His courage in standing up to David, forcing him to talk, and not letting her and Clemmie sink into despondent inaction – he'd pulled them all through it.

Which was even more impressive after his first reaction to the situation – alternating beers and shots with his old friends, until oblivion took his mind off it all.

Polly laughed to think how outraged Lucas would be that she'd chosen one of Britney Spears's perfumes to represent him, but the name – Rocker Femme – and the sweet gourmand mix was just perfect for him. It opened with blackberry liqueur and coconut cream, which made her think of one of his horrible biscuits ... Aaagh, up popped Chum again.

Onwards, thought Polly. What was next? Easter. No escape there. It had to be Thierry Mugler's notorious Angel for its sweet chocolate caramel mix.

It wasn't a perfume Polly liked, but you had to admire it. Just smelling it made you feel like you were on a scary ride at a fun fair – and it brought to Polly's mind very strongly the fun of rolling Bill's wooden Easter eggs, and Lucas and Chum's competitive gorging of the huge chocolate egg Shirlee had brought.

What a fun day that had been. Probably the best she'd had in all the months since that shock on 20 December. Next ...

There was one more blog to go – appropriately enough, 'The scent of an ending', which meant it had to be Atelier Cologne's Oolong Infini', with it's gauiac wood notes that reminded her of David's coal-tar soap.

Not a smell she ever thought she'd have happy associations with, but over their years together, she'd found it had become very comforting as a reminder of him. Her strong, reliable husband, who had always made her feel so safe and protected.

How could she have been so deluded? Because, she reminded herself, he was a very clever man and brilliant at hiding what was really going on. And because he did – he had – in his own way really loved her. The last few months had made her doubt everything, but in her deepest heart, she was sure of that.

For a moment, she felt intensely sad, as though the end of their relationship had somehow wiped out all that had been wonderful about it, at the beginning and through the joyous family years.

But they had been happy, she had been loved, Polly knew that in the core of her being, and she wasn't going to allow the bitter way it had ended spoil it. She was going to separate the two things. Be proud of one and put the other down to experience.

So where did that leave her now, she wondered, putting the stopper back on the last perfume bottle and packing it up in its box. What came next? Well, the obvious thing after 'The scent of an ending' would be 'The scent of a beginning', but what would that be?

She let her eyes run over the pile of perfume boxes on her office floor. There was nothing there that seemed right. She stood up and went over to her cupboard, scanning the shelves for inspiration.

Then her eye fell upon a very simple cream-coloured box and as she reached for it, she knew exactly where it would take her. Hermès Equipage could only make her think of one thing, of one person.

She didn't bother with a blotter, but sprayed it onto her arms, round her neck, behind her ears and down the front of her shirt. Then as the smell settled on her skin, releasing its refreshing bergamot, mixed with lily of the valley – one of her own signature notes, she realised – blended with the more subtle outdoor smell of pine, it was almost like Chum had been conjured up in front of her.

The way he smiled with his lips tightly together, his eyebrows up, eyes wide, but mischievous; those deep creases in his cheeks. The feeling of his strong arms around her. His surprisingly youthful laugh. The very smell of him.

And then finally she remembered the other thing Maxine had said that morning, which had resonated so strongly with her: 'you will be confused about things you used to be sure about'.

Suddenly, all confusion was gone. She was sure again and she knew exactly what she had to do.

~

An hour and three-quarters later, after many wrong turnings and frustrations with her phone's map satellite not working in the no-signal country lanes, she finally pulled up in front of the entrance to the stable block.

Digger jumped over her and was out of the car door before she'd even got a foot on the ground. He could smell Artie – that was the only explanation – but was it just the dog's lingering scent, or were she and her owner actually there?

Polly had the answer seconds later, when Digger appeared again running out of the stable entrance and then back in again, in hot – and hopeless – pursuit of his favourite lady dog. And where Artemis was, Chum was likely to be too.

Polly heard him before she saw him.

'Digger!' his distinctive voice exclaimed. 'Is that really you, old boy? Come here, you rascal – and is your human with you, by any wonderful chance?'

Polly had just closed the car door behind her when she saw Chum's long-legged figure framed in the gateway, silhouetted by the early-afternoon sun behind him.

'And there she is,' he said gently, walking towards her. 'Returned from her long journey.'

He came up to her, standing very close, but not touching her. Even over the powerful residue of the Equipage on her own skin, she could smell him. She could smell Sorrel too.

'How are you, Hippolyta?' he said very quietly.

For a moment Polly felt shy and stupid and looked down at her feet in confusion, wondering if she'd been mad to spring herself on him like this. She should have texted first, he might not want to see her ... but then Chum put his finger under her chin, in that way he did, and very gently lifted her head up to look at him.

'Hey,' he said, almost whispering.

'Oh Chum!' she said, overwhelmed, and threw her arms around him. 'I'm so sorry. I've been so rude and so stupid, I've just been completely confused, I haven't known, well, anything ... but I've missed you so much.'

He held her tight, rocking her back and forth, kissing the top of her head.

'You don't have to say sorry to me,' he said. 'You're here now and that's all that matters, and – if you don't mind – I'm not going to let you out of my sight again for a long time.'

Then he kissed her and, as Digger and Artemis ran over to see what was going on, tails frantic with wagging approval, Polly knew there would be no more wasted chances.

FragrantCloud.net

The scent of ... a wedding

My wedding was in the chapel of a stately home.

It was my second wedding, but that didn't take any of the shine off it. My first was in a grim London registry office, so it meant even more to me to hold this one somewhere special.

And it wasn't hired for the occasion. It was the family chapel of my husband Edward's (eek! it still amazes me to type those words!) ancestral home.

I should probably say here that I call him Chum. It was his nickname from childhood and how I was first introduced to him, so I can't think of him as anything else.

Chum grew up at Hanley Hall, but the family doesn't live there full-time now. The house is owned by a family trust that has recently negotiated a contract whereby the National Trust will run it, opening it to the public for a certain number of days a year, with parts of the house and grounds still private for the family to use.

It was so special to have our wedding in the chapel where Chum had been christened, with a reception in the garden, followed by a brilliant party in one of the estate's follies, down by the lake. We danced until dawn, when we served breakfast.

My mother had a lovely time being whisked around the dance floor by Edward's stepfather, Bill. He's not too steady walking, but he's still a great dancer. He says it's easier when you're moving faster.

And she looked absolutely beautiful in several changes of outfit, including a fuchsia-pink raw-silk Givenchy suit and hat she's had since the early 1960s, then a full-length dress from the current Givenchy collection for the dancing.

She lent me her own Christian Dior couture wedding dress to wear. It had to be taken out quite a lot – as she kept telling everyone(!) – but it was thrilling to wear it.

My daughter wore a beautiful contemporary dress lent to us by Gucci, because we had agreed to have a photographer from *Vogue* come and take pictures for the magazine. Mummy is doing a blog for them these days; she's become very famous again after doing the ad campaign for my friend Guy Webber's wonderful perfume brand, the Great Eastern Fragrance Company.

Chum and I spent our wedding night in the house – but not in one of the state beds, which look terrifyingly hard and damp, with old drapes that are probably dripping with spiders. Instead, we were very cosy in the suite of rooms where his grandmother used to live: a little corner of the huge house that is very special to him, and also now to me.

Although the house is ridiculously grand, there was nothing stuffy about the wedding. Chum's dog Artemis was our ring bearer, although just with one for me because Chum refuses to wear a wedding ring (due to a complication with the family signet ring he wears on his left little finger). I wasn't going to have my dog left out, so Digger was a page. Not the most well-behaved one, but he had to be there. Chum's nephew was the other page.

My son Lucas gave me away and my daughter Clemmie was my bridesmaid. My friends Shirlee and Lori were my joint best women and they gave a hilarious two-hander speech, which had everyone roaring with laughter.

Chum had an old friend from school as his best man, which was lovely, because I knew him from university too – which was where I first met Chum. We had a piper to accompany us from the chapel to the wedding breakfast. Chum wanted us to ride his horse but I put my foot down. (Too Sting and Trudie.)

All in all, it was the most amazing day – although I have to say that every single day with Chum is a joy, whether we are in our house on the estate, where he runs a farm-shop business, or at the flat in London I bought after selling my house.

My smells of a wedding are roses and lavender, which were both blooming all round the marquee in the formal garden, and were used to decorate the chapel. All the flowers for the wedding were grown on the estate.

Then there are the wilder outdoor smells of wet grass and mud, which are so entwined with my falling in love with Chum. He would no doubt add cow poo in there, because we did walk through a lot of fields in the early days of our romance.

I'd also have to include the autumn tinge of apples, because he always seemed to have them in his pocket. The waxy smell of his Barbour jacket has to be in there too.

In with all that I have to include the vanillic chocolate of bourbons and all the other cheap biscuits my husband (my husband!) so adores, and the beautiful clean floral that is mimosa.

Then there are the leathery smells I associate with horses, which always linger around Chum, but as it was my wedding too, I'm throwing in my mum's smells, my daughter's, my son's, my dog's and my best friend's. They all played their part.

Which leaves just two things to add: rosemary for remembrance of Chum's parents and his older brother, who sadly died young. And the heathery peat of single-malt whisky for my darling departed dad.

So those are all my wedding smells, but there could only be two possible scents for it: the bespoke fragrances that my friend

Guy Webber blended for me and Edward as his wedding present to us, following a tradition invented by Jacques Guerlain in 1907.

Edward's is wonderfully leathery cologne with a hint of animalic sweat and a top note of vanilla, to reflect his equestrian and biscuit interests. For me, Guy brilliantly combined echoes of those elements into my favourite chypre, PM, which is his best-selling perfume.

So my scents for a wedding (as named by Guy) are:

Horsey Boy by the Great Eastern Fragrance Company
Thanks, Digger by the Great Eastern Fragrance Company

Acknowledgments

First of all my most devoted thanks to my best friend Josephine Fairley and my new friend Lorna McKay, the founders of the amazing Perfume Society, who allowed me to go and hang around in their London offices for several heavenly scented weeks. (Also heavily scented because I was spraying myself with everything in there that wasn't nailed down.)

The winner of multiple Jasmine Awards, Josephine is a world authority on perfume and her knowledge of the subject is astonishing and inspiring. It was through her I came to understand just how rich and fascinating the world of perfume is.

Thanks also to the fabulous Perfume Society team – Carson Fairley, Penny Sheard and the extraordinarily talented perfume writer Suzy Nightingale.

It was Suzy who told me I wasn't allowed to have one 'signature scent' to wear all the time or to 'save for best', but must gaily spritz whatever takes my fancy on any particular day. Also that I must keep all my scents in their boxes and out of sunlight in a cupboard, however beautiful the bottles.

I have been opening and closing complicated boxes every morning since. And a different one in the evening.

It was Lorna MacKay who warned me off the wrist banging

thing. You must spray each one individually – spritz, swap, spritz – or you will *bruise* the fragrance. Who knew? Lorna, that's who.

Have a look at their splendid work on perfumesociety.com, and I heartily recommend their magazine *The Scented Letter.*

I named my lead character Polly after my new absolutely very favourite perfume which I discovered while I was there: *Dear Polly* by Villhelm. I'm obsessed with it.

Also on the research side, massive respect and honours to the gorgeous Lizzie Ostrom for her superb book *Perfume, A Century of Scents*, which is entertaining, fascinating and scholarly in equal measure, and her wonderful Odette Toilette events, which are so inspiring.

Other books I have found invaluable:

Perfume Legends: French Feminine Fragrances by Michael Edwards

The Perfume Bible by Josephine Fairley and Lorna Mackay

The New Perfume Handbook by Nigel Groom

The Book of Perfumes by John Oakes

Perfumes, The A-Z Guide by Luca Turin and Tania Sanchez

On the publishing side of things, massive thanks to the wonderful (and *very* patient) team at HarperCollins. My publisher Anna Valdinger deserves a medal. Her colleague Mary Rennie and editor Emma Dowden were also brilliantly helpful. And big thanks to the legendary Shona Martyn.

I am also madly grateful to the brilliant HarperCollins design duo Lisa White and Hazel Lam, who have delivered another cover that made me squeal with delight when I first saw it. I can practically smell it.

Big thanks as always to my agents Fiona Inglis and Tara Wynne at Curtis Brown, who are there for me in a snap whenever I'm having a neurotic-writer moment (frequent).

I must also thank Josephine Fairley again here, for reading the manuscript on loose sheets of paper to check I hadn't made any perfume bloopers. That was a big ask. Mwah mwah.

Thanks to my lovely friends Emily and Richard Ault (and not forgetting Dudley the labradoodle) for making me so welcome at their lovely house, while I studied at the Perfume Society. Also to my friend and teacher, Hilary Totah, for telling me how a real yoga guru starts her day.

And to the shining lights of my life, Pop and Peggy, for supporting me so tirelessly through the ups and downs – and all nighters – of the writing process and making me laugh (and cups of tea) all the way.

PS. If you want to read more of Polly's blog posts, check out fragrantcloud.net

Maggie Alderson is the author of nine novels and four collections of her columns from *Good Weekend* magazine. Her children's book *Evangeline, the Wish Keeper's Helper* was shortlisted for the Prime Minister's Literary Award. Before becoming a full-time author she worked as a journalist and columnist in the UK and Australia, editing several magazines, including British *ELLE*. She writes for the *Sunday Age* and at maggiealderson.com. She is married and has one daughter.

Follow Maggie on Twitter @MaggieA
and Instagram @maggiealderson